Romance in a Rough Chemise.
Viv Protheroe

Prologue

.

This must be the cusp of the sixties from some of the comments our working class hero makes. About the time of "you've never had it so good," a quotation, which retrospectively has a greater ring of truth about it than it did, to our protagonist at the time.

And what sort of time was it? It was a time of kitchen cabinets, black and white televisions with jam jar screens, modern fireplaces, red double-deckers, full employment, hire purchase, east of Suez, the last remnants of empire, anti-communism, cold war, sputniks, the H bomb, Castro and Guevara, spies, and a general feeling, despite the comparative affluence, that Britain (by which most people really meant England) was complacently basking in the fading afterglow of empire.

A portent of imminent disintegration seemed to linger on the horizon and to young men like John Davies the stench of political corruption was indicative that the rotten corpse was ripe for its overdue burial. The Suez debacle had been the example par excellence of this decadence.

Some say that Merthyr Tydfil is a queen, The Queen of the Valleys , Frenhiness y Cwnau; others maintain she is a whore, Hŵr y Cwnau, the Whore of the Valleys. The truth I suppose is that she is both; a tattered Queen fallen upon hard times, though one who even in her magisterial prime always had a touch of the wanton in her.

She was born sometime in the Dark Ages when Wales was a hostile Principality where Christian princes such as Brychan, the Martyr's father, ruled over a territory where the old Cymru were essentially pagan and the land was subject to the rapacious raids of the wild Picts. In such a raid was Brychan and a number of his family including Tydfil slain, allegedly while at prayer. The spot where Tydfil died gave rise to a commemorative church and the hamlet was henceforth known simply as Merthyr (Martyr) Tydfil.

It is generally accepted that Tydfil was the victim of rape, and rape has been a major feature in the history of the town which bears her name; for Merthyr , born out of rape was to suffer the rapacious greed of the Victorian industrialists in the nineteenth century. The contrast between Daniel Defoe's description of the hamlet in 1723 and that of George Borrow at the height of the industrial revolution is revealing.

Defoe describes ".... a most agreeable vale opening to the south, and a pleasant river running through it called the Taaffe."   While Borrow sees...... "an edifice at the foot of a mountain halfway up the side of which is a blasted forest and on the top an enormous crag. What edifice can that be of such strange mad details. A truly wonderful edifice it is, such as Bosch would have imagined had he wished to paint the palace of Satan."

From the Guests of Dowlais in the north of the borough to the Homfrays and Crawshays in the centre and the Hills of the southern fringe the violence of that repeated rape is still evident in the scarred and battered landscape.

And rape by the great ironmasters allowed to go unpunished, indeed rewarded, encouraged further rape by every little landowner with a plot wide enough to sink a shaft or simply dig into the hillside where the seams of rich black coal break through the steep valley sides. An eruption of filthy pustules like a virulent plague pocked the once verdant hills and great mountains of bile from the valley bottom shafts simply dumped to hover threatening, angels of death , ready to reap a dreadful harvest on the innocents of the future.

Even now the tears and tatters in her green chemise reveal the old whore for what she always was, the victim of a bestial ignorance which still persists.

CHAPTER 1

The hands of the broken faced old clock hovered at the stroke of seven, a sadistic mechanism bent on arousing its unwilling owner from his soft warm bed and his hard hot dreams, to face a cold grey day. But John Davies had developed a temporal sense, for which the ticking tyrant was no match. At precisely five seconds to seven, even as the inanimate fiend arched and prepared to broadcast its shrill alarm, a pair of bluegrey eyes blinked open, drugged with sleep and stared for a moment into the cracked angry face. A hairy arm slid out of the sea of rumpled bedclothes and struck it dumb. It shuddered with pent up frustration.

"Wake up," it yelled inaudibly.

"Time to get up," he mimicked, turning over onto his face and falling instantly back to sleep.... where she still stood, an innocent coquette in the far away corner of a long room, hands behind her back swaying and giggling childishly. As he neared, her face sweetly innocent and smiling suddenly assumed an adult look and her slender figure like a ripening fruit grew round and full.

He led her out of the room proud as a bridegroom, away up the steep high hill, the moon bright and brittle as a plate of ice thin frosted glass. Its iridescent light imbued her with a magic and mysterious glow. The lovely initiation upon which they were ineluctably embarked took on a heightened sensuality. She smiled, and he held her naked, nerve to nerve. Her lovely mouth devoured him. His flesh and bone existed only as a vehicle for this force, which was his true essence, which fused and integrated with hers - two as one - blessed duality.

The sudden shock.

The purple faced, bulging eyed figure of her father as he hung and swayed grotesquely from the stairwell. An image simultaneous with his own voluntary involuntary emission. He awoke with a start.

"Come on its quarter past bloody seven," his father's voice called impatiently from the foot of the stairs. His lean hairy leg dangled from the side of the bed, momentarily detached, the only living portion of the drugged mass of muscle and sinew from which it suspended. At last the rest slowly stirred to life and tumbled beside it onto the cold oilclothed floor. It knelt facing the ancient varnished dressing table, a simple box of rosewood drawers with a spotted mirror perched on top. The posture might have been mistaken for one of prayer.

He rose painfully and examined himself in the glass through puffed half open eyes. "Oh God," he exclaimed, genuinely appalled and still shaken from his wet nightmare. "You hedonistic fool," he reproached, fingering his swollen eyes. "Allright, allright, I'm bloody coming," he responded to further entreaties from the foot of the stairs. He walked across to the faded rose coloured curtains and tugged them back on the bare spiral wires from which

5

they hung. He looked out over the grey slate roofs of the adjacent houses. A wet mist hung low over the chimney pots and the dirty black gas holder, which dominated the landscape, peered ominously through the gloom at him. It did not hold out the prospect of a new day dawning.

" 'You are then," his father pushed the plate across the breakfast table, "don't blame me if they're dried up they wouldn't be dried up if you came when you were called iss alf past bloody seven late again as usual won't do you any good late for work all the bloody time now will it well don't just stand there in a bloody dream mopin' jump over your bloody 'ead at your age I would jump over your bloody 'ead now come to that..." He switched the torrent off, a learned technique like anticipating the alarm clock, he'd heard this particular tirade so often before.

The plate contained two pieces of brittle toast covered with baked beans as hard as processed peas from being reheated under the grill. His father had been up since six when he had seen the elder son off with his lunch box under his arm. When John left it would be the girls to get off to school while his wife took care of the nipper's needs. John greedily devoured the beans, which had been fried with a little lard. They were the best beans he was ever to taste in a lifetime of bean feasts. The table was a riot of food and dishes. Its red and white squared cloth spotted with the stains of last night's supper when the brothers had raided the larder late after football training and a few pints. That quiet time when the rest of the family was abed was his favourite time. They listened to radio Luxembourg turned down low and ate plates of roasted cheese. Their lazily abandoned dishes now added to the table's turmoil. Sliced bread spilling from its half open wrapper, a half empty milk bottle, a half full one, butter with a knife in it and bread crumbs, a box of corn flakes, a packet of sugar with a wet spoon, a box of chocolate biscuits, a steaming teapot, a bottle of brown sauce with a congealed top, salt, pepper and a bottle of vinegar testament to their late night profligacy. This too would feature in the unheard sermon.

John pushed the plate away from him, spotlessly swabbed with a piece of bread, and sipped dreamily at the tea. He heard his father's voice nag in angry protest as if from a long way off. "Why the 'ell don't you answer when I'm talkin' to you. Are you bloody deaf or what?"

"What?"

" 'Ave you made your mind up yet?"

"About what?"

"About what I've jest been sayin'. Am I talkin' to myself or something? This scholarship, are you goin' to take it?"

"I told you dad, passing the exams doesn't guarantee anything," he replied evasively.

"But you said that ICI would sponsor you."

"Aye, well I've got to apply formally."

"You got nothing to worry about on that score though. It's just a matter of course, your big union mate told me. But you don't 'elp yourself if you keep clockin' in late. How many quarters you lost already this week. If you'd only get up when you're called. I was never late for work in my life. Wish we'd 'ad 'alf your chances. You youngsters never 'ad it so good. Macmillan's right about that at least. Down the bloody mines at fourteen it was for us. Three-foot bloody seams. Crawlin' on our bellies for a bloody pittance 'til I got this lot." He went into one of his awful morning coughing spasms as if the very memory of it was sufficient to cripple him with its wracking pain. The veins stood out in his neck and on his bald blue scarred head until he finally retched a mouthful of black bile into the back of the hearth. He gasped for breath and continued the tirade where he left off. "Then your mother sick and you lot to bring up on the dole. Don't know you're born you don't. Don't want to see any of you..." He broke off coughing again until the tears streamed down his cheeks.

John hated it. He turned away to avoid the sight. It was true and terrible and it made him feel awful. More than that it made him feel guilty because he had neither the intention nor the ambition to live up to what was now expected of him. How could he tell that to this prematurely aged man - that his sacrifice had not been great enough, could never have been great enough because their aspirations were so much at variance.

All the old man wanted was for the son to escalate, through scholarship, a few rungs up the ladder to salaried respectability. But poverty had left scars on John's soul, which no salve would heal. He had been obsessed with and oppressed by it. Grammar school, which he somehow understood was to be a watershed, held few pleasant memories for him. A blank sheet relieved only by the faces, clean and shiny, of an elite to which he did not belong. Theoretically egalitarian, it did not take him long to work out that it operated principally on behalf of such a clique. In retrospect it was horrifying how, in the name of educational egalitarianism, that it should have been so, particularly here in South Wales where it was the product and the very essence of collectivism.

His precocious abhorrence of the terrible bourgeoisie was nurtured from the rough naive socialism of early adolescence to the sophisticated dialectical materialism of early adulthood. As a night-school student he was testament to Marx's axiom that you cannot be a genius in the tool-room and an imbecile outside the factory gate. He attended classes at the local branch of the WEA. He was exposed there to the literature and philosophy which were not part of the grammar school curriculum. He shared Shaw's abhorrence of the poor but not his Fabian optimism. He became drunk on Engels, Marx and Trotski; then Lenin, Marcuse, Camus and Sartre.

The 'new middle class' represented the very worst human product of a bourgeois economy. They had ascended for the most part from a lower stratum, which they despised, and emulated a higher stratum, which they envied and was well beyond their means. They had nothing of their own except money, and the value of that was ever changing. They were to inherit the kingdom with the advent of that most bourgeois of all Prime Ministers, the awful awesome Mrs Thatcher. But not even his worst nightmares could conjure up such dreadful images as were to be realised by that political and moral nadir.

The parental disdain was an ambivalence, which troubled him. He fully appreciated that they were a product of the unequal society, which had deformed them. And it was for them that he had embarked upon the study of electrical engineering and all but completed an apprenticeship with the great Imperial Chemical Industries Limited. He had hated every second of it, rebelling against becoming one of the new technocrats, intelligent only in a very narrow way, like robots programmed to react predictably to recurring situations.

How could he tell his father that the industrial process sickened him, that he was no engineer but a poet, that he lived and breathed to propagate something of which his job was the absolute antithesis? How could he begin to explain this to a man who had crawled in the blind black bowels of the earth, scratching at the coal until it almost killed him, to keep his wife and kids from hunger. And had choked on the remnants of his shattered pride to beg from the Assistance Board to cover their nakedness.

No he must keep up the pretence for their sakes. How could he pour it all down the drain before their eyes, they were so proud of what they perceived to be his advancement. They were old and careworn in their mid forties through hard work and the constant struggle against poverty. He hated the system that they were a product of, but by his acquiescence wasn't he too becoming a product of it; wasn't he being subjected to the selfsame dehumanising forces, which had made them what they were.

It was hard to imagine them now, young and in love and full of hope and aspiration as they surely must once have been, as they were indeed depicted in carefully posed faded sepia studio shots which lay in the dresser drawer. Their eyes had held a sparkle, their lips a smile, their feet the possibility of dance and an air of hope, she attractive, he handsome. In vague corners of his memory he still cherished recollections of a lovely woman smothering him with soft milky breasts in a great warm oven of a bed, and of a virile man hoisting him strongly onto proud blue-scarred shoulders.

He looked across the breakfast table at the tired man again. 'Grammar school did nothing for me,' he wanted to shout. 'Awoke nothing in me. It was only the start of my dehumanising. The steamrollering of my soul. Amoamasamatamamoamatisamant, jaituiilleellenousvousilleselles, yrwyfiyrydwytiyrydimniyrydichchwi, the capital of Mongolia, the square on the hypotenuse, sinAcosBoversecAcotB equals jayomegaalpha, drink to me barbra allen. The pious early morning hypocrisy, the daily dose of public sadism, the worn down shoes, the cut down corduroys with the low slung arse. The black gowned bat like masters and mistresses aping an alien system.'

"Where's my lunch dad?" is what he actually said, quietly, apologetically. It was on the first shelf of the food cupboard carefully wrapped in yesterday's bread-wrapper, where it always was. Tomorrow, or tomorrow, or tomorrow he was going to have to hurt the old man, badly. He sighed, took the bundle off the shelf and tucked it under his arm. "I'm off then."

"So long."

"So long." He raced out through the door down the short path and onto the road where his ancient battered Norton stood propped against the curb. He glanced across at the bedroom window across the narrow street where his voyeuristic amour smiled at him. He leapt flamboyantly onto the saddle and kicked the machine as it rolled off its stand. The engine spluttered and died - ignominy. The chuckling face disappeared behind the curtain and he cursed again. Today was going to be a bad day. Heydock, the Personnel Manager was after his guts and now he would be late again. He'd been giving Heydock ulcers over the past few weeks. He kicked the machine again angrily for deliberately making a fool of him. It coughed into life. He let the clutch in too fiercely and screeched up the street in a cloud of blue choking smoke.

CHAPTER 2

He scrambled through the gap between two high pressure pipes. A hiss of steam from a safety valve almost blasted him off balance and down into the deep dark oily pit where a turbine pump roared its incessant primeval hundred and thirty decibel scream. "Fuck this for a game of soldiers ," he complained to an unlistening God, precariously balancing on a valve box from which the asbestos lagging flaked a storm of Klondike confetti, a mesotheliomia maelstrom on the heads of a gang of fitters on a scaffold platform below.

"What the fuck you doin' up there?" a gruff angry voice boomed.

"Sorry boys, can't get at this bastard transmitter any other way. I reported the fucker to the safety committee but you know how long these things take." An ammonia leak brought the tears to his eyes and took his breath away. The already cold mist froze solid to the leaking pipe and formed a two inch thick ice pack. One more hazard to be avoided. "Fuck this for a game of soldiers," he repeated loudly this time for the benefit of the fitters below. "I know what's fucking wrong anyway," he continued sotto voce to himself. I'll tweak the receiver on the control panel. I'm not paid enough to risk life and limb crawling about up here." Another waft of ammonia temporarily blinded him and his foot slipped scattering more asbestos flakes into the swirling mist. "Allright, allright," he anticipated the chorus of complaints. "I'm getting out of here."

"How about a nice 'ot cup of tea then John bach?"

"Lovely," John replied slumping into the hard utilitarian chair. His oversized black oilskins dripped onto the rubberised concrete floor of the control room. He removed the greasy over-trousers and turned up his nose with exaggerated disdain. "This thing's humming," he complained. "We've been negotiating for our own personal issue of wet weather gear for the best part of a year now. They wouldn't put up with these conditions in the Brum plant that's for sure. We ought to refuse to work in the bloody rain, I bet they'd soon come across with it then. Phwoo I think Black Matt must have been wearing this before me."

The operator smiled and poured out the tea into a chipped enamel mug. Black Matt, as his name suggests was as black as the ace of spades, but the colour was not due to his ethnic origin, he was as Welsh as wet Sundays, it was rather a lifetime accumulation of ingrained dirt. The blackheads on his jowls were like stubble, so close together that John had christened him the black Seurat. "Management my arse," he continued with his grumble. "I reckon I deserve this Dai."

He picked up the enamel mug and swigged a good mouthful of the hot sweet brew. "Oh, this is the stuff Dai boy, the stuff that dreams are made on." He laid the mug down on the console and took off the yellow jacket, which he deposited in a heap with the trousers on the floor. "You haven't lost your touch." He savoured another mouthful and nodded his head like a connoisseur savouring a rare wine. "Had any good winners lately," he stopped his grumbling and changed the subject, in better humour as the hot sweet drug took its effect.

"Good winners? Don't bloody talk man," Dai sighed with exaggerated exasperation. "I 'ad a stormer last week, Golden Lady. 'Andlin 'er for a friend I was. Made a bit on 'er in the Smoke 'e did. 'Eld 'er back for best part of nigh on a month I did didn't I, til the odds were right for a killin'. Put next months rent on 'er I did." He thumped one of the gauges on the instrument panel. John winced as the reading shot up and Dai recorded it on his record sheet. "That'll give old Hawksworth heart failure when he reads it," he chuckled. "Anyway onto a fortune I was as I was sayin'. Pen'darren park; had a big one on with every bookie in the ground, from Offie Davies to Dai Dee. Out of the trap she went like a flash of bloody lightnin', down the straight like a bloody jet. All wrapped up it was, all over bar the shoutin'. On my way to pick up my winnins when there was a commotion. Never seen anythin' like it John. A bloody grey'ound with a sheepdog's bloody brains. Jumped off the track over the bloody rail she did, right across the football pitch and waited til the bloody 'are came round and bloody pounced on it and tore it to bloody bits." He shook his head sadly but with the air of resignation of one accustomed to such tragedy.

John laughed. "I'll make you and your shaggy dog stories famous one of these days Dai," he promised. "But above all else you'll be immortalised for your superlative tea." He held out the empty mug for a refill. "What's the secret Dai, is it column bottoms?"

"It's an art John bach, just like your writin', 'cept it takes a lot more skill." John flung a wet souwester at him as he dodged behind the instrument panel where the tea making paraphernalia was kept. Just as he returned with two fresh mugs the door burst open and Big Jack the gargantuan foreman burst in like a melodramatic Victorian villain entering stage left.

"Ho," he boomed. "I might have guessed as much." John swung round on the swivel chair careful not to spill his precious tea.

"Just in time for tea Jack," he offered with a conspiratorial wink at Dai.

"Tea, you cheeky bugger," roared Jack. "What about gettin' the bloody job done?" The door flapped in the wind as the self-closing mechanism struggled against the wild Welsh elements. His clothes ballooned around him. The wet weather gear issued by the company did nothing to improve his gawky awkwardness. Clothes did not become Big Jack, not even his Sunday best. He stood clumsily, a huge semi-deflated wet oilskin dirigible. "Skivin' in here drinkin' tea," he bellowed without humour. "Tea break's not 'til half past nine." He removed his huge souwester and a shaggy mane of sandy hair flopped down across his eyes. He flung it back with a characteristic nod of his massive head. "Righto, come on then, lets be avin' you, get out and get that system fixed."

"Come off it Jack it's pissing down out there, and you know what Dai's tea is like when the winter wind blows from Dowlais Top." He smiled another conspiracy at Dai, his eye indicating the row of handover certificates which were clipped together in columns relative to the various locations in the plant to which they applied.

Dai took his cue and as Jack turned to vent further spleen on John he deftly appended his signature to the relevant document.

"Come on Davies, don't fuck about, you heard what I said. You got until..." he paused to consult the watch which he hauled from an inner pocket of the swathe of clothes...." about half past eleven to finish that job - if you want to make any bonus on it that is."

"Good, then there's plenty of time to finish my tea," John responded with a calculated insolence. "If you'd like to check the handovers, which is what you ought to have done before charging in like a mad rhinoceros, you'd find that the job has been done, the fault rectified, the inspection completed and the handover certificate signed off - finito." He swung the swivel chair around with a flourish. "So my sardine catcher's gear is thrown down to dry," he indicated the crumpled dripping pile, "and I'm enjoying a well deserved early tea break."

Big Jack stood there awkwardly feeling foolish. His humour, already bad on arrival at work that morning, had steadily deteriorated. His young wife was having it off with his smarmy landlord, and not bothering to be discreet about it. His compulsive gambling was getting worse, his debts were mounting, and the heavy mob was closing in on him. He had only had a few hours sleep and had tramped around for hours in the cold misty rain. Water was running down inside the neck of his ill-fitting oilskins. He was soaked, angry, miserable and depressed, and now this jumped up little runt of an apprentice, still wet behind the ears was making a cunt of him in front of the process operator. He had suspected for a long time now that he was the object of scorn and gossip in the works. The laughter of John and Dai aggravated his growing paranoia. He shook with anger. "I don't believe it," he croaked.

"Well go out and check it then," John invited. "I don't do shoddy work Jack you know that. I was lucky. The nozzle on the receiver was blocked. Removed, cleaned. Simple job. All realigned. Working perfect. Go and check."

Jack reeled as if punched in the solar plexus, his fists clenched with rage. If he had stayed he would have punched the little bastard. It was as if John Davies, idiotic writer of poems, a boy with the women if the canteen stories were to be believed, the sort that would screw another man's wife, was the direct cause of all his problems. Why was his life so fraught with unbearable frustration? That morning he had been taunted with his impotence - the bitch, it was her infidelity that caused it. He didn't bother to check whether the job had been done, that was no longer the issue. He had put up with as much as he could take. Heydock the Personnel Manager was gunning for the little bastard. This time he wasn't going to get away with it. He stormed out into the driving rain heaving the heavy metal door behind him. Even that was a futile gesture as the hydraulic mechanism eased it gently to its closed position.

John looked at Dai. Dai looked back at John and shrugged. "They tell me he's got domestic problems," John explained. "Better sign that handover certificate Dai. The mood he's in he's likely to make an issue out of this, and that bastard Heydock only wants half a chance to do for me."

"Don't worry John bach," Dai smiled. "Signed while the bugger's back was turned." He indicated the certificate which signified the satisfactory completion of the job.

"Ah, young Davies," Heydock said patronisingly. "Sit down," he gestured with a mock politeness. He and John were old antagonists. He had been assigned by Head Office to "sell" the productivity scheme to the Merthyr plant. The previous personnel officer had singularly failed to break the opposition of the unions at Merthyr and had paid the penalty. The active opposition of John and his friends had continued to frustrate Heydock's best efforts so far. John, although still in his final year as an apprentice was a shop steward for his section, the youngest in the plant. He had even been encouraged to run for the Convenor's post but wouldn't so long as old Dai Thomas was still prepared to do the job. Although he was getting a bit long in the tooth and was not as sharp as he used to be, Dai had served the union well and deserved to go out of his own volition as far as John was concerned. He was due for retirement before too long anyway.

John deliberately took another chair than the one offered. "Well my lad, what have you got to say for yourself this time?"

"Say for myself? In relation to what may one ask?" he aped Heydock's cultivated RP.

"Don't play the innocent with me lad."

John sat for several minutes in dumb insolence staring into Heydock's tired face. It reminded him of his cracked clock. Heydock was forced to concede the psychological advantage by breaking the long silence. "You're guilty of a serious breach of discipline." He watched in vain for a reaction, flicking over the pages of a file on the desk before him. "I see from your file," he continued, looking up with a smile of satisfaction, "that you already have two recorded warnings for bad time keeping. A third recorded warning means automatic suspension without pay. You'll find it in the Disciplinary Agreement and a reference in the Company Rule Book." He pushed a copy of the rulebook across the desk to John. John immediately pushed it back to him.

"I don't need to look at that. I was one of the team that negotiated the Disciplinary Agreement with your predecessor. If there is any question of disciplinary action other than a warning being considered in respect of a bona fide union representative, which I hardly need to remind you I am, then the District Officer must be brought in, that's in the agreement too. You haven't even bothered to put the complaint to me."

"You're suspended Davies," Heydock said abruptly. "Bring in your Convenor if you must and I'll simply repeat it for his benefit." He held up a hand to stop John's interjection. "No doubt you'll wish to appeal but in the meantime the suspension will stand. If you win the appeal you'll get your pay. Now I have some urgent work to attend to. I'll meet with you and your representative in half an hour." His face was wreathed with smug satisfaction as he rose to indicate that the short interview was over.

"You must be cracking up if you think you can get away with this," John fumed. "Is this the way you conducted industrial relations in the Northeast. No bloody wonder you had them out on strike last year.

By three o'clock the Joint Shop Stewards emergency meeting with the Management Team had got nowhere. The meeting had been in session for two hours and had re-convened after a short recess. Heydock looked a little grey. Had he miscalculated? Was the whole issue snowballing out of hand? Old Tom Williamson the Maintenance Manager banged his fist on the table and called for order. His face was tired and he looked as if he would rather have had no part of this. But here he was caught up in Heydock's machinations and he didn't like it. Just two more years to his retirement and he'd be well out of it. Management just wasn't the same these days. He had been a tough nut as far as the unions were concerned, but he prided himself that he had always been fair. He was one of the older breed who had risen through the ranks from the shop floor. This Heydock didn't know his arse from his elbow. He looked at John and half smiled as if to say, "And what do you make of all this lad?" Davies was a bit wild, but who wasn't a bit wild at that age. He liked a lad with spirit. He had been pleased to nominate him for the company's Apprentice of the Year Award last year and he had won it; got presented to the Company Chairman and received a youth award from the Queen at a County Hall banquet. What he actually said however was, "I thought it was necessary to call that recess because things were getting a bit heated, tempers frayed. I hope there's going to be less argybargy and name-calling now. You heard what the union reps had to say James," he addressed the grey faced Heydock. "You've had time to consider during the recess. Have you modified your position in any way?"

14

"Certainly not Chairman," Heydock retorted stubbornly. "The case is quite clear cut as far as I am concerned. Davies is guilty by his own admission of refusing to carry out the instructions of his supervisor, and further of insubordination into the bargain. The disciplinary code is unambiguous in such circumstances. The offence warrants a written warning. However in this case where there are two current warnings on file then the totting up process comes into effect and the appropriate penalty is a minimum one week suspension without pay, the actual period to be determined in accordance with the seriousness of the offence."

Big Jack nodded sanctimoniously from his seat in the corner where he had sat silently from the start, except for ratifying the statement of the case by Heydock. The first glimmerings of doubt were beginning to percolate through his thick scalp however. Heydock was making far more of this issue than it warranted. There had even been talk by the shop stewards of the possibility of a walk out, the first in the twenty-year history of the Merthyr plant.

"The foreman's request was a reasonable one," Heydock asserted. "There is evidence to support this." He patted the thick blue bound volume of the provisional productivity agreement, which lay on the table in front of him, a gesture, which provoked an angry buzz from the steward's delegation. "The only matter open to any kind of negotiation is the length of suspension. So far there has been no contrition from young Davies. Assurances in respect of future conduct might go some way..."

"Come off it." It was Dai Thomas the old convenor, who interrupted, getting to his feet, which was a signal to the others that he meant business. "Do you think you're dealing with a bunch of bloody schoolkids or something. You don't fool us with this nonsense." Heydock spluttered a protest but Tom Williamson held up a hand and gestured to Dai to continue. "No just a minute," he continued. "You've had your say and now I'm going to have mine. It's about time we stopped beating about the bush and got down to brass tacks." John smiled at the mixed metaphors.

"About bloody time too," Bill Macarthy muttered. "We've had enough bullshit from that silly bastard."

"Gentlemen," Tom pleaded. "Come on now lads, play the game."

Dai looked around and took strength from the unanimity of his support, for their part the management side seemed anything but united. It had all the appearance of a one-man show. Indeed there was a hint of muted hostility towards Heydock from the others. It was obvious however that he was calling the tune, presumably with the authority of Head Office. Local management had been superseded ever since Heydock's arrival and the introduction of the Productivity Agreement.

"Let's deal first with the question of John's alleged refusal to carry out the instruction of his supervisor. I know it's just a sprat to catch a mackerel, but let's squash the bloody sprat first before we come to the real, the." he paused searching for the word, ... "the substantial issue." He was pleased with the word he found, ignorant of his malapropism, and banged the table in front of him for belated emphasis. "We disagree with your conclusion that the instruction was a reasonable one. We insist on the right, no the duty, of our members to refuse to carry out unreasonable instructions. Now if a job has been completed satisfactorily to agreed standards then it is clearly not only unreasonable but also a waste of bloody time and money to have to do it again. The job was completed to the agreed standard, or are you claiming that the process operator signed off a handover certificate without the necessary checks having been made? His rep is present and I'm sure he's listening with interest to your response to this question since it would involve his member in serious disciplinary procedures. But of course you're not making that suggestion are you? You know that Dai Whippet is one of the most experienced operators in this plant, and holds a merit award for efficiency and safety. If you force this issue to appeal then you know you'll lose without any doubt whatsoever.

"As for insubordination. Well that's laughable, weaker than canteen tea that is. The bowler hatted gaffer is a thing of the past. If everybody who told Big Jack to fuck off were to be suspended the bloody plant would be shut down inside a fortnight. So as I said, lets deal with the real issue, which is that bloody blue book you keep referring to as if it's the bloody bible. This whole issue has been contrived to try to get the productivity deal ratified by the back door. What you couldn't achieve by honest negotiation you're trying to establish by precedent. Your whole case stands on the use of your blue book as a means of measuring individual performance, knowing full well that it was a specific factor in the provisional agreement that the work study analyses would only be used to indicate group performances. And we still hadn't reached agreement on how that was to be applied. We also had management's promise that the job analyses would never be used as the basis for any disciplinary procedure against any member. What is really disturbing is that it was you mister Heydock who gave us your personal assurance on these matters."

"I remember no such assurances," Heydock interjected. "I was not authorised to make such assurances." There was a gasp from the shop stewards at this and Tom Williamson visibly reddened. He had been a member of the management negotiating team as had Heydock's deputy Ted Morgan who buried his head in his papers. "What I said may have been misinterpreted by the trade union side. It wouldn't be the first time you heard what you wanted to hear rather than what was actually said. If you'd like me to refer to the minutes."

"Stuff your minutes you bastard," Bill shouted angrily. "There were no official minutes. That was the whole basis of our discussions. Any agreement was provisional and for a trial period only."

"And the trial period is up," John could restrain himself no longer. "That bloody book is to become the basis on which performance is measured. That was always what you wanted. It is also to be used in disciplinary matters. You expect us to crawl around this decaying old plant with a copy of that silly bloody tome tucked into our arse pockets and refer to it every time we do a job. Half of what's in there is totally impracticable. Are we to respond like programmed robots or are we to be allowed to use the skills we've developed through serving apprenticeships, attending night school or learned through years of practical experience. As far as I'm concerned you can stuff your bloody book and your bloody productivity agreement as far up your arse as it will go. You're nothing but a lying bastard Heydock, and we all know it because we all remember quite clearly what you said to sucker us into the trial period. You think that because we've enjoyed the bonus payments for the last few months that we'll swallow your crap in order for them to continue."

"I won't be spoken to in this way Mr Chairman," Heydock appealed in mock indignation.

"Aye and as soon as the agreement was ratified, how long then before bonus rates would be adjusted. Think we was born yesterday Heydock," a shop steward called. Soon the whole shop stewards delegation was shouting angrily. Heydock smiled ruefully and wiped a bead of perspiration from his brow. It had been necessary to make those promises to the negotiating committee rather than have to admit to Head Office that he had been unable to get even a provisional acceptance of the scheme. Of course he had ensured that his record of the meetings was ambiguous enough to be capable of all kinds of interpretation. Now that the trial period was coming to an end he was desperate to establish a basis for a properly drafted binding agreement. He had calculated that the generous bonus payments made during the provisional period would have been enough to ensure that carefully worded modifications would have been accepted.

John's incident with Big Jack had seemed like a heaven-sent opportunity to kill two birds with one stone. The precedent of using the Blue Book in performance measurement and disciplinary matters would be established, and he would also be settling a personal score with John. Although only an apprentice, albeit in the last months of his "improver" year, John was a strong political influence on the shop stewards committee. He was Chairman of the Merthyr Branch of the Young Socialists, and was what all personnel officers noted in their files as "left wing activist", a euphemism for what they really considered to be communists, anarchists, fifth columnists and all other kinds of loony epithets applied to anyone to the left of Randolph Churchill. John had been an active opponent of even a provisional agreement and had all but persuaded the negotiating team against its acceptance. He had scornfully resisted the usual crude attempts to buy him off with vague promises of a cushy job in the expanded Work Study Department and had responded with contempt to the threats to block his application for University sponsorship.

Other factors too made it more than just expedient to seek a showdown now. If Big Jack had not provided the incident he would have had to contrive one. He recalled D J's dictum at Head Office when he had been briefed for this Siberian assignment. "Remember James," he had said with that quietly hostile resolution for which he was renowned, "this scheme has to go. You have to make it go."

"You know what these Welsh bastards are like DJ. How bloody stubborn they can be. I had a bad enough time getting it accepted in the North East."

"Yes fifteen months if I remember rightly. Well I can't afford to let you dither about on this one James. Incidentally my maternal grandparents just happen to have been 'Welsh bastards'. You have nine months maximum James. Once we break through down there the difficult nuts will have been cracked. Midlands and the South will follow suit."

"Nine months...but.."

"But nothing James. Nine months, a suitable gestation period. I said it has to go. Believe me James if it doesn't then you will."

That was all. There was no arguing with a DJ dictum. And now the nine months was all but up. He had to go through with it now regardless of trade union militancy. He was half persuaded that the official trade union reaction would in his favour. A general election was just around the corner and much was being made in the Tory press of the whole issue of Union militancy and how the parties would be likely to deal with it. He listened carefully to what Dai now had to say.

"...we are determined," Dai was saying with new-found eloquence, waving a characteristic forefinger in the air, a mannerism plagiarised from one of Nye's famous open air meetings, "that you will not be allowed to establish this precedent on a bogus issue. We had hoped that common sense would have prevailed, that perhaps some of your colleagues might have persuaded you to take a more creditable position. As spokesman for the Joint Shop Stewards Negotiating Committee I am instructed to tell you that you leave us with no alternative but to give notice of our intention to withdraw our labour on Monday next unless the suspension of our member is rescinded. We are also as from now discontinuing our co-operation with and participation in the provisional productivity agreement pending further negotiations to establish safeguards against the kind of interpretation you have applied in this case. Unless you have an immediate positive response to this statement it is now my intention to lead my delegation from this meeting."

Heydock's face registered surprise at the militancy of the statement but shook his head in negative response to Tom Williamson's query. Bill nodded to the other shop stewards who rose as one and filed solemnly from the room.

It was quarter to four and Dai was called to the telephone for the umpteenth time since the termination of the meeting. "Something funny's up," he said to John on his return. "That's the fifth plant to ring up pledging support for our action. The only way they can have learned about it is from Heydock's counterparts up and down the country. The dirty tricks brigade is going flat out on this one John. This is a deliberate provocation to blow the whole thing up out of all proportion. It'll be press and television next. I can't get hold of Elwyn in the District Office, the bastard's lying low as usual."

"Fat lot of good that right wing bastard would do anyway," chipped in Bill Macarthy the electricians' rep on the joint shop stewards committee. "Ring your regional office man. Our full time officer is on his way from Ponty now. As luck would have it the T and G chap was with him at a meeting in Ponty. I bet that's where your bloke was. We've got to be together on this one Dai. If ICI is intent on a showdown we could have a national strike on our hands; the first in their history."

"The Tory press is going to have a field day with this one," John warned. "I can see it now. 'No control over membership. Communist infiltration. Who governs Britain?' All that crap. We're being forced into a corner. You know that London can't make this official by Monday and Regional Office will procrastinate until then. If the men are coming out then it's going to have to be unofficial Dai, and that puts you on the spot as District Sec."

Dai smiled. "I wish I could use those long words like you John bach. On the spot is it? Then that's what I shall have to be. The vote was unanimous."

CHAPTER 3

John sat replete at the kitchen table after a meal of lamb chops, boiled potatoes, fresh green peas and dark brown gravy, washed down with sweet hot tea. His father sat scowling at the dying fire. Mother sensing that a storm was brewing busied herself upstairs.

"You've had it now as far as ICI is concerned," the old man finally said. "They been good to you, sending you on courses and all. You were well thought of there." The sigh was more meaningful than any words. "This is a big blot on your copybook. Finish you as far as they're concerned this will. No university scholarship now."

"No dad."

"But perhaps you could still..." He began to beat desperately on his thighs with the flat of his hands. He started out of the chair and began to thrust angrily at the slow coals with the long tapering poker until they responded with a latent igneous burst reflecting in the moistness of his grey tear filled eyes. "Why go and throw everything away now after all these years?" He turned with the poker menacingly raised as if, for one awful moment, he would attack his son.

John knew how much this meant to the old man. "It's not like it used to be dad. The twenties and thirties have gone for good. The young un doesn't wear my hand downs or stuff cardboard in his boots. It was hard for you and mam. It isn't going to be like that again. You know what old Mac said, 'you never had it so good', well in a way he was right. It's Capitalism's last stand dad. It's a different struggle for us now. For you it was a fire in the belly, for us it's a fire in the brain, we've moved on."

"Christ boy," his father said angrily, "you think you got all the answers. Think you can change the system do you? Let me tell you something my lad - You can only change it for yourself, and the sooner you get that through your thick skull the better. Grammar school was step number one. The apprenticeship was step number two; that gave you a skill, a qualification to fall back on. Now there's the chance of university, what I always wanted for my boys."

"Oh yeah, and what about your girls," he couldn't resist. He passed his hand over his eyes and sighed loudly. It was almost incredible that the man who had nurtured his socialism, a former lodge secretary who had been falsely jailed for affray in the furtherance of the Fed, could have harboured such a paradox in his breast. Then Welsh radical fathers were renowned for harbouring bourgeois educational dreams for their male offspring. Oh how

20

green our fathers now. This illusory bubble of South Sea proportions had to be pricked quickly.

"That's wonderful isn't it. If you can't beat em join em. So that's what your philosophy boils down to. You can't cure a problem by turning your back on it. All that does is perpetuate it. Is that what you want of me? It would be a betrayal, of you, of me and everything you've taught me to stand for. The whole town, the whole valley, the whole of Wales, the whole bloody world is full of people like us, like me. I belong to them. I've grown among them, out of them; I'm part of them. To change my own predicament I have to change theirs too. You know that; you taught me."

"Aye well I taught you bloody wrong then didn't I. You don't save a drowning man by drowning yourself."

"No Dad, you save a drowning man by learning how to swim. Then by teaching him how to swim he can go on to save others in the same way. It's the same dream Dad but it's a fallacy to think that a university education teaches you to swim. University education is all about keeping yourself afloat and you know it. Isn't it enough for you that I left the CP to join the mainstream? Further right than that I cannot go lest I imperil my immortal soul." He tried to inject a note of levity into what was becoming an increasingly difficult dialogue.

"Don't try to bloody lecture me on socialist theory sonny boy. I wasn't born bloody yesterday, I heard it all before. I was brought up by my old man on the promise of a New Jerusalem. Well they haven't bloody built it yet 'ave they. I seen and heard them all, the big men with the gift of the gab, Horner, Paynter, S O when he still had something to say, Marx, Engels and Keir Hardie were the holy bloody trinity. Where are they all now though, the great socialists? ...It was an empty dream. They don't believe it any more. Who's left now apart from Nye, and he's just about worn out poor bugger. The British Labour Party has betrayed the people. There is no God and there is no justice. You might as well join them and grab what you can while the going is good." He was hurt by his own bitterness and the tears flooded his grey eyes as he fell silent and stared once more into the flickering fire.

A lump came to John's throat and choked back further argument. How hopeless and reactionary his father appeared now. Yet, occasionally there was a glimpse of the old fighter before he had been crushed flat, a hint of lost ideals and betrayed hopes. Where was that young man in the faded sepia photograph? Who was he? John didn't really know him and he wanted to so much while there was still time. He had a presentiment that time was not on his side.

John's older brother Elwyn, returning from a long day's work in the adjacent valley finally broke the long awkward silence. He breezed in brandishing a copy of the Echo, waving it aloft like a shining sword. "The sword of truth," he announced throwing it down on the table. "Who's been a naughty boy then my little revolutionary brother. Shy unassuming little

21

Shwni is the biggest threat to our way of life since Trotski, according to this rag. Careful who you drink with John, you'll be done in with an ice pick in the backroom of the Dowlo."

John picked up the evening paper apprehensively. The item had been accorded front-page prominence. "ICI Strike Threat" it proclaimed in a bold headline.

"Following almost immediately on talks between the TUC and the Labour leadership on it's much heralded 'social contract' the 'old carthorse' has once again demonstrated that it has no control over its membership. So much for promises by the Labour Party to have found a cure for the English, or in this case Welsh, disease. Any agreement with the TUC will be of little relevance to the shop floor Marxists who threaten to bring production at ICI, our most successful exporter, to a complete standstill.

A spokesman for the giant ICI stated that the strike threat had come following the suspension of John Davies, a final year engineering apprentice at their Merthyr plant.

Davies of Pant, near Merthyr, was suspended when he refused to carry out an instruction by his supervisor. A spokesman for the three unions involved issued the ultimatum at three thirty this afternoon. "Withdraw the suspension by Monday or we strike." Union officials and management representatives are attempting to arrange an urgent meeting in a last ditch attempt to avert what management are describing as a disastrous situation which could result in redundancies.

A Government spokesman said that this was a matter for the unions and management to resolve but was another indication of the powerlessness of the unions to curb the growing excesses of its left wing activists. He poured scorn on Labour Party policy dismissing it as an irrelevance and a gimmick hastily drafted in anticipation of a general election. Editorial comment page four.

John quickly turned the pages to the editorial column. "No bloody mention of productivity deals," he muttered to nobody in particular. "That's objective journalism for you. Wonder if the editor had a university education," directed this time at his father. Elwyn's eyebrows raised in query at the cryptic reference. "Ah here it is, listen to this:

'So once again a major British industry is being held to ransom by hasty and irresponsible wildcat action by the trade unions. There have in recent months been strikes against the reduction of overtime, strikes against the introduction of overtime, strikes against the implementation of new techniques and many other examples of sheer obstructionism. But this latest incident is surely the most trivial to date. That a cheeky apprentice, aided and abetted by irresponsible trade unionists should be capable of bringing the mighty ICI to its knees, at a time of severe economic difficulty, is a cause for great concern. That this should coincide with the Labour Shadow Minister for Industry announcing to the country a new social contract with the TUC is

22

a timely reminder that what we need from Government is not beer and sandwiches at number ten, which is all that Labour promises, but the firm hand of a Conservative administration curbing trade union excesses.

'With evidence of communist infiltration and deliberate attempts to sabotage our export industries of which ICI is a leader, and the TUC unwilling or unable to exercise control over its wildcats, the electorate has a right to know, prior to the forthcoming election, what action a new government is prepared to take.

'Labour we may be sure will not dare to bite the hand that feeds and will continue to trot out the same tired old clichés that we have heard over the past weeks. It is to the Conservatives we must turn and demand of them a pledge that a new government will bring in legislation which will end, once and for all, the anarchy which now pervades our industry.'

"Power, power, roll it round my tongue," he raved dramatically, throwing the paper down angrily. "Enter one wicked villain, chubby faced John Davies, dressed in black and sowing seeds of anarchy and bolshevism. In the background can be heard the screams of millions of starving children. Hohohohoho, another ten million unwilling workers on the dole, see how the dividends dwindle," he boomed in best music hall tradition.

"Bloody nutter," grumbled his brother through mouthfuls of lamb chop. Mother smiled wryly, hands on hips. Father gazed disconsolately into the fire and grunted.

An hour later he got the call from Dai Union. There was to be a meeting in Cardiff. Dai would call for him in half an hour. They'd been bounced into this strike and the politicians were making it a big pre-election issue. It was embarrassing to Labour. The Shadow Minister was involved and the General Secretary would also be there.

"What a waste of a good boozing night," John complained to Dai half an hour later. "Is this all really necessary Dai. What do I have to come for, the bigwigs will make their decisions without consulting us."

"Your personal presence has been requested by the General Secretary himself. That's all I know."

"Ha. So you vos only carrying out ze orders no." John clicked his heels and gave the straight arm salute. "Today Merthyr, tomorrow ze vorld. Lead on mein Fuhrer."

"Come on you bloody maniac we'll never get there on time."

The room at the hotel was crowded. The "big man" was the centre of attraction sitting chatting affably with a dozen sycophants hanging on his every word. "Ha - so this is the very man," he said in a loud booming voice as John was brought over to meet him. "Is this the face that launched a thousand strikes..."

"And burned the topless towers of Transport House," John added.

23

"And knows his Marlowe too," the great man commented with surprise. And he was a great man too in John's eyes - one of the giants of the labour movement - a man of great compassion and intellect. A reluctant shadow cabinet member when he had first been drafted in, but learning to love the illusion of power perhaps. He held out a bony hand and shook John's firmly. "What will you have to drink John? It is John isn't it? The South Wales Echo did get that much right I suppose."

"That and the date," John conceded with a smile. "Pint of Brains Dark please. They don't sell real beer in Merthyr so I make the most of it down here." A sycophant scurried off to the bar. The shadow minister motioned John to a seat and continued with the discussion which revolved around the mundane, nobody seemed anxious to broach the real subject of the meeting and John began to get an uneasy feeling that something Machiavellian was afoot.

An accomplished mimic, a valleys member who it turned out was the great man's PPS, related an amusing anecdote involving Churchill. The Tory hero had been dragged into the house even when in an advanced state of senility and reduced to sudden involuntary nugatory outbursts. It was typical that they had so heartlessly cashed in on his legend, after all he had been a great political statesman. He ended his days in the House just like his father, a figure of pity. The mimic was doing a passable impersonation of one of the war speeches rewritten in a way that demonstrated senile dementia. It was quite cleverly funny.

"Great man my arse," the shadow minister admonished a speaker who had ventured that opinion. "The man was a tyrant, hard as bloody nails. What was it Nye said about him? No it was a bit unkind and after all Nye often confided to me that he had a sneaking regard for the old bastard. He was the only one who could match Nye's oratory when he was at his best. In his way he was a great parliamentarian I suppose. But a great man - no. He was a warrior, right for the time but not the complete politician." The sycophants hung on his every word. A man in a pinstripe came across and slipped a note into his hand. He brushed back the mane of silver hair from his eyes. "Excuse me," he said softly. He conferred for a few moments with what were obviously an elite from Transport House, and accompanied by a few of them moved towards the door. "Duty beckons," he announced with a wave of the hand. He turned to his PPS: "Cled, see to our young friend here will you?" John felt flattered to be the centre of attention but it did nothing to allay the uneasy feeling.

"Same again," Cled offered. John nodded his assent.

"What exactly is going on?" he asked.

"Ah now that is a difficult question my boy. All will be revealed in due course. Just enjoy the drink and the chat for now eh. Have you met...." John was introduced to yet another important person. The place seemed full of important persons. He sought out Dai who was being given a ear bashing by his Regional Officer who immediately fell silent as John approached. "What the hell is going on Dai? There's a distinct smell of conspiracy in the air pal. Can you smell it?" Dai's face reddened. "Oh no. Not you as well. Come on Dai what's up?"

"Politics John bach. I think they're goin' to sell us down the bloody river. I know that bastard Williams. Regional Officers, I shit 'em. I know he's up to bloody something but he's not lettin' on."

It must have been half an hour before the Shadow Minister returned with his little entourage. He beckoned to Cled and the group conferred for a few minutes before Cled cleared out the bar staff and closed the doors.

"Righto," the Shadow Minister said. "What I have to say does not go beyond these four walls. But we're all friends here and I hardly need to counsel you on the damage, which a leak might do to our election prospects. And in case there is any doubt about it we are confident that there will be an announcement from number ten in the next few days. This business is ineluctably part of the election strategy. The Tories are playing their usual union bogey card with a vengeance." Why was it that John felt that he was being preached at personally? It was reminiscent of chapel days when the minister would single someone out, not by name as used to be the custom, but by reference to peccadilloes which identified the sinner as positively as publishing his name on a notice on the chapel door. "The press are in the lobby and there is only one version of tonight's events that I want them to receive, and that will be provided by Cled in the form of a statement. No interviews from anyone. That Welsh CBI imbecile has already been on the early news with ICI Management. He'll do enough talking for all of us. I'm happy to let him gabble on. I've declined an invitation to appear on the late news. They may well get on to you Huw," he turned to the union General Secretary who stood at his shoulder. "I think it wise if you too were to decline. No need for an explanation." The General Secretary nodded. "But let's bring everybody up to date.

"Some of you may think that the official recognition of this strike was premature and a result of a breakdown in communications between myself, the AEU, the ETU and the T&G and of course the TUC. Well nothing could be further from the truth. My recent discussions on the social contract had already resulted in the establishment of a communication hot line system, which has been well tested by today's developments. When I went public earlier this week about a new understanding between the Party and the TUC, it was not just PR, so much hot air, we do have a genuine proposal for machinery to be put in place to deal with a whole range of issues when we take office after the forthcoming election. Unfortunately the first shot in the election campaign has been fired not by us but by the Tory press fed by ICI's propaganda. An unofficial stoppage with the prospect of growing wildcat support nationally was deliberately being stoked up to undermine our position. We were faced with an unofficial strike, which

25

would rule out any involvement with the parliamentary party. This is what they were banking on. By giving official backing the unions involved have paved the way for my involvement through the TUC. If we can work out a satisfactory solution it will be an enormous boost to our electoral chances." He held up a hand to counter the murmurs of protest at the increasingly obvious impending sell-out.

"Our assessment of the current situation is that the personnel man at Merthyr has exceeded his brief and only has the tacit support of his head office. Sir David Jones is certainly no Tory and is reportedly a bit peeved with this, whatsisname, Heycock. We get the impression that he's due a tactical transfer to the Outer Hebrides when this lot blows over. They're sending a new man down to take over the negotiation and our belief is that his brief is to find a face saving compromise. So you see the possibility is that we shall be able to turn a disaster into a triumph for reason, common sense and our policy of close co-operation with both sides of industry.

"We shall prevaricate until Monday when the Leader of the Opposition will volunteer his good offices, in the person of yours truly, to bring the parties together. This in contrast with the union bashing Tory press and the Monday Club loonies who embarrass even this government. The whole episode will have demonstrated how much more effective our policy is to that of confrontation."

"There's just one snag to this cosy little strategy," Dai interjected. "What will be the terms which I will have to recommend to my members that they should return to work?"

"There's no question of you recommending anything," a functionary of the General Secretary's office intervened. "This is an official dispute now. Any recommendations will be made by our office. It is your duty as convenor to give such recommendations your full support." Before Dai could give vent to his anger the shadow minister attempted to put it more delicately.

"Well," he sighed, "there's going to have to be compromise all round in this; from ICI, from the unions and of course from young John himself."

Here comes the crunch, John thought. "And what exactly am I going to have to compromise in this deal?" he asked. "And why should I be prepared to concede anything. We all know what ICI is up to. It's the productivity agreement, or the lack of one."

"Well let's try to deal with the compromises in the order in which I stated them." The shadow minister was a polished performer. Of course he'd been well schooled in the hothouse of Midlands car industry negotiations in the early fifties. " ICI will be required to accept a reduction in the period of suspension from one week to one day." John sighed audibly, the implication was obvious. " That's a significant climb-down for them but the imposition of a suspension of any sort will allow them to save face. What it really signifies of course is a public censure on their man Heycock, Heydock whatever his name is. "

"But what about the real issue…" Dai intervened but the great man was one step ahead of him.

"Of course the substantive issue is the negotiation of the productivity agreement, the final draft of which was under active discussion immediately prior to the walk out. The removal of this man Heydock from the scene, which I am assured is what will happen, will place the negotiating team in a very favourable position. The one day suspension is simply a face saver as far as they are concerned; a small price to pay for the ultimate benefits to both the Party and the unions."

"And what would those be, precisely," John interjected, "the slight shortening of very long odds as far as the next election is concerned and status quo and further negotiations with no guarantee of the outcome for us with the productivity deal."

"Well certainly you're no worse off," the politician persisted, "and the sphere of industrial relations will be a difficult and crucial one for Labour. You've already seen how the Tory press is going to go to town on this one." John sighed and looked to Dai for some indication of moral support. Dai's head was bowed and his eyes moist with the tears of the divided loyalties which were tearing him apart. The Union had been his life. He was not naive, his hands were tainted with all the tawdry intrigues and compromises which were an inevitable consequence of the political process, but the first premise had always been, must always be the tenet of solidarity. He looked up and sought John's eyes with a shrug of resignation.

All eyes were on John now waiting for his response. He knew of course that his individual reaction wasn't really worth a tinker's cuss. What was it then which impelled him to reply as he did? Was it just selfish pride or was there a point at which the individual came before the collective, and where was the point to be, where the line to be drawn. Was this particular lie really any more heinous than the hundreds, the thousands, which punctuated any normal life? Consequences, he thought, falling back on the utilitarianism, which informed most moral judgements, and aware of the dangerous conclusions to which such philosophy can lead.

"The shortening of long odds," he mused. "But we really know, don't we, without asking Butler or Mackenzie, that this election is lost before it starts? We've all but buried clause four, reneged on disarmament, and moved so far to secure the Surbiton vote that we offer nothing more than left of centre Toryism. What imperative is there for any change? If only you had the guts to stand up and tell people honestly where you stand, instead of sitting on the fence on issues of crucial ideological significance, you might begin to get somewhere. I'm sorry Dai I can't be a willing participant in this. That the parliamentary party is corrupt has been obvious for some time. Now the corruption is contaminating close friends and people for whom I always had a respect not far short of idolatry, I feel sick to my soul, and frightened. I can't do it, I can't." Tears flooded his eyes as he took out his wallet and removed his party membership card, ceremoniously tearing it to shreds. His union card followed, the fragments scattered on the plush carpeted floor.

Dai looked at him in astonishment. This was a renunciation of apostolic dimensions, but it was surely a bit melodramatic. Bigger sacrifices had been, would continue to be made to secure progress. "One step forward two steps back John," he croaked the Lenin axiom with a lump in his throat. He felt the General Secretary's tug at his sleeve. The great man shook his head. So John was to be the sacrifice.

The shadow minister turned to the General Secretary with a shrug of the shoulders which said, 'Well here's the demise of another amateur idealist with no conception of realpolitik.' But there was sadness in the gesture too because it reminded him of a young man not too dissimilar to John who was forced to live with the painful realisation that in a lifetime of struggle society had changed him more than he had changed it.

It was the local full time district officer who now intervened. A slick valleys apparatchik who'd sold out more comrades in his short meteoric career than Stalin had sent to the gulag. "From your gesture I take it that you wish to resign from the union," he said.

"Such acute powers of observation will surely not go unrewarded Bert." John muttered cynically.

"You know the rules well enough," Bert replied. " The union does not accept resignations. You will remain a member until such time as your contributions are in default to the extent that your expulsion will become automatic. Until then you will remain a member and as such we will continue to represent your best interests."

"It's cunts like you who have turned a noble ideal into a crock of stinking shit," John spat venomously. "You and your Trumid wankers have probably been infiltrated into the movement by the CIA you bastard."

Time of course would reveal that John was not too far short of the mark in this assessment. The trade unions and the Labour Party were during this period the target of the CIA, FBI, MI5 and a whole plethora of organisations which formed the 'conspiracy' which was to elevate Thatcher, culminate with the 'end of history' and the realisation of the Blair project. But that is part of a continuing story.

The official just shrugged off the insult. It was grist to his mill. " And the best interests of the movement will be served by a tactical acceptance of an apportionment of blame," he continued.

"I wish you'd reconsider John," the shadow minister pleaded. "This is becoming increasingly distasteful. I certainly would not have lent myself to this process had I not been assured of your willing participation," with a sharp look of disapproval at the General Secretary. "Unfortunately now the die is cast, we are too far steeped in blood," he curtailed the quotation. "Now I have to consider what is best for the party and the country even if it means the sad sacrifice of someone like yourself. I beg you John with all sincerity, please reconsider."

It was a moment of high drama; the silent pause was palpable. But as the man had said, the die was cast, the blood already spilt.

"I respect your integrity," John said finally, "but I suspect you're as much of a dupe in this as I am. My willingness was never really an issue. The plan was well worked out as you have just witnessed. In fact my whole involvement in the issue I now can see was purely incidental. It had nothing to do with what happened between me and Big Jack, another poor sad dupe. The members in the Merthyr plant and those throughout the rest of the company recognise this sufficiently to be prepared to come out on a strike. Not something done at the drop of a hat, not in this company, despite what the Tory press would have people believe. But the official trade union movement, corrupt as ever, is prepared as always to sell its members down the river, 1926 and all that. As I said, I've had a gutsful, I'm off."

Nobody stood in his way. Dai stepped forward as if to follow but was once again carefully restrained. He had reached the main entrance when his local MP, a man for whom he had considerable respect, overtook him. "Hang on John I'll give you a lift. I think I've had a gutsful myself." The old man looked tired. He'd been a tireless fighter for the downtrodden, a former miner, self taught in those marvellous universities, the miners' institutes, all too few of which remained. "To think that lily livered swine Bert is after my seat. Said I have too many soviet peccadilloes. Where does an ignorant bastard get a word like that from? Been fed him from somewhere I bet. I only just got the whip back John, I've got to be careful, they only want an excuse to get shot of me."

John put a comforting arm round his shoulder. " I don't consider you in the same light as the rest of those conniving bastards S.O. you've got my vote you know that."

"Oh no I haven't," the old man chuckled, " you left it scattered all over the bloody carpet. You know how often I've done that John?" "What, torn up your membership card?"

"Dozens of times John bach. But in the end there's nothing else, nowhere else for us to go."

"Not for me S.O. You remember Germinal. Souvereine, that's me from now on."

"Don't be so daft lad. Without collective action there is nothing. Come on let's go home."

They were coming into the outskirts of Merthyr. Merthyr does not have suburbs, it has outskirts. A drunk hung characteristically with one arm hooked around an ancient green cast iron corrugated lamppost singing dolefully to the passers by. "Let me out here please S.O. I'll walk the rest of the way."

"Don't think too badly of him John," the MP said, "he's still one of the few with any real integrity. The leader handed him a poisoned chalice with this job. Only did it to alienate him from the broad left. Sadly it seems to be succeeding. I know you're an idealist who finds it hard to come to terms with the rottenness of power politics. I've had my problems with it as you know, lost the whip more times than a forgetful madam. He's had his difficulties too after so many years on the back benches as the conscience of the left. Believe me John when I tell you that to a man like him today's shenanigans will lead to sleepless nights. Sounds trite perhaps, but true nonetheless. He's not at all like the hard liners and the sycophants who inevitably surround him. He sees through those clearly enough."

John stood at the car door looking up into the cluttered hills. "Well far be it for a callow young Merthyr Rodney like me to offer political philosophy to a shadow minister of such distinction, but see that chap hanging on the lamp-post over there, he's an individual. Those people in the ramshackle houses on the hill that form society, that are the masses. In every house you'll find individuals. That's our paradox S.O. Now if he's to wear Nye's mantle he must know that, in his heart, feel it in his head, if that's not too Dylan Thomas for you. As for Bert and his lot well there's just no hope for them. In Russia they'd be commissars, in Nazi Germany Gauleiters. Tell him that on Monday ICI too will have my resignation. That should fuck his shoddy strategy up. It will hurt my old man more than he should have to bear. But I would have had to hurt him anyway. At least he can tell me he told me so. In his way he tried to warn me I suppose. Take care S.O. the bastards will have you next." With that he walked away leaving the MP looking careworn. He strode down towards the nearest pub past the man hanging like a drunken Christ on the lamppost. "I'm free, I'm free," he sang. "I'm free, I'm free, I'm free."

The drunk held out a callused collier's hand and smiled with a row of rotten teeth. "Congrashubloodylations," he mumbled and slid slowly down the lamppost to the ground.

CHAPTER 4

Saturday night in Merthyr: a night for booze and birds, for getting away from it all. But this was a special Saturday night because events had forced upon John the action he should have had the courage to take earlier of his own volition. An existential happening of possible momentous consequences, that was the way in which he now saw it. A happening following which "everything is changed, changed utterly."

His resignation was in the post and he was happy now to let them play out their little game as if it had nothing to do with him, had no connection with him. No doubt his action would be construed in ways acceptable to those concerned. Today's papers had already announced the intervention of the shadow minister and his concordat with the unions, in what was referred to as 'The Cheeky Apprentice' dispute. He chuckled at the sheer absurdity of it all, but the sounds of movement in the living room downstairs served to dampen his elation. This was the final act in this melodrama: the breaking of his parents' hearts.

I'll write slushy romances for women's magazines. I'll go to university on a mature student's grant. I'll graduate in Eng. lit and become a book reviewer for the Sunday Times. They'll like that. That will elevate me to the realms of respectability to which they aspire. But I want to be a writer and if I do that I'll never be a writer. So then I'll be a petrol pump attendant, a barman, a door to door salesman, a drifter. But that will break their hearts. Christ it's Saturday night. There's a pound in my pocket; there's beer in the bar, lovely lithe young ladies longing to be loved and destinies to be fulfilled. Fuck tonight Sunday is a better day for breaking hearts. And so his brave new world began with a coward's kiss. "Fuck tomorrow," he called loudly now, through the open window across the wet depressing rooftops to a world that wasn't listening. The faded curtains of the bedroom window of his exhibitionistic neighbour fluttered revealing glimpses of her young voluptuousness. A deific reply to his baying at the shrouded moon.

The sullen clouds had drifted from what was now a high night sky, chased away by a sharp wind. Pinpricks of light flickered through the alto strata and a thumbnail moon slid in its thin aura of luminescence like a Phoenician boat drifting slowly on a dark sea. It was cold and clear and beautiful, like the night which haunted his dreams with such significant regularity. The narrow streets of Dowlais, that "battered bucket on a broken hill", echoed and amplified his footsteps as he picked his way through the complex maze, ever downward to where the tang of spilt beer scented the air with as much allure as the perfumes of Arabia for the shipmates of the Arethusa. The grey moral sentinels of the Bethanias and Bethesdas muttered their silent remonstrances.

31

At last the friendly pool of light, warmly yellow, cast out onto the pavement from the portals of the Dowlo, grabbed and greeted him and dragged him in. He made straight away for the room at the end of the long passage labelled unpretentiously "Backroom" unlike so many of its contemporary "Lounges", which were back rooms where the beer cost an extra three pence a pint.

The room did not even boast it's own bar and it's customers had to buy their drinks from a serving hatch which accessed the main bar from the passageway. John tapped an impatient coin on the scarred dark oak counter, interrupting the tight skirted archetypal buxom barmaid from the orgy of violence which issued from the jam jar screened televisions set, the Dowlo's only concession to mid twentieth century technology.

" 'Ullo John love, usual?" she asked and answered with an expert movement which scooped a pint mug from under the counter and pulled on the long pump handle with the grace of Gilbert Parkhouse stroking the ball to the mid on boundary at Saint Helens.

"And one under the counter for my lean anaemic friend who should be along presently," he responded perkily.

She pulled again on the pump handle and the brown old fashioned ale squirted frothily into the mug, the head rising and spilling over the sides leaving a thin healthy head over the top - just right.

Three men sat in the corner playing cards, with their illegal money scattered untidily on the shelves underneath the table, two more flung exotically flighted darts at a battered board and another sat quietly sipping his beer, a faraway look in his mournful eye, the sleeve of his cardigan in a black wet pool.

It was early. Later the room would be crammed with boisterous boozy men and the occasional liberated woman and the bar would be soggy with spilt beer floating the cardboard mats like miniature Contikkies across its old oak top. The air would ring with laughter and music and the real world would become a distant thing experienced through an intoxicated haze.

"A pint for you and a transfusion under the counter for your anaemic friend," she smiled, pleased at her own humour, placing the pint on the shelf before him. He handed her a pound note. "Have one yourself Brenda," he offered. "I'm celebrating."

"Oh aye and what have you got to celebrate then," fishing among the tarnished coins for change. "I'll join you with a little G an' T if that's allright." She raised her glass and toasted him. "So what are we celebrating then."

"I don't know. Something. Everything. Everything is changed, changed utterly. A terrible beauty is born."

"Go on with you, you daft bugger, dunno what you're talking about half the bloody time. But you do have a nice way of saying it." She handed him his change and he retreated into the solitude of the backroom dolefully sipping the froth from his drink.

In a few minutes she followed him in. "Better get the fire cheered up a bit. Can't have my favourite customer suffering from the cold now can I?" She gave his pale cold cheek a playful pinch.

"You're fire enough for me Brenda," he responded to her banter putting an arm around her soft waist and pulling her down onto his lap.

"Ooh," she squealed with exaggeration. "Leave go you sexy bugger," and she jumped up smiling with delight. "You're a randy one John Davies," she laughed, brushing the sides of her rumpled skirt. "Young girls are not safe with the likes of you around."

"What about the older girls." he teased. Their eyes met and she smiled the suggestive smile of a ripe sensual forty year old with more than just an eye for younger men. He reflected regretfully that another five years would see her attractive buxomness turn to fat. The hints of ridges underneath the eyes become prominent and the already heavy breasts grow pendulant, flaccid and sag. But as she bent to pick up the black shiny coals from the scuttle in the hearth to replenish the fire's dying embers she displayed to him the ripeness of her mellow fruitfulness. He had an irresistible impulse to touch her gently, even perhaps implant a soft kiss on that sacred spot.

Was she perhaps performing some atavistic ritual to retrieve from him through contact, performed or contemplated, some seed of his youthful vigour. If he could have achieved this he willingly would. He reached out and gently brushed her buttocks with his fingertips. The banter over, she arched her back and squatted erotically as he cupped his hand under the dark valley of her skirt.

Brenda had married young to an older man no longer able to satisfy the demands of her autumnal desires. And although the temptation to assuage them with someone young and virile was great, she would never go beyond this vulgar flirtation. Her husband would be too much hurt by such infidelity now. Some years ago it might have been different when he had such self assurance. Now impotence had bred an insecurity she would not exploit. She had learned to live with it, satisfying herself with Bloom like fantasies triggered by such rare moments as this.

She stood up and turned to face him, shaking her head with mock disapprobation, tut tutting as she walked slowly out with an exaggerated rotation of her haunches. She turned at the door and gave him a smile. "In any case here comes your anaemic friend," she shrugged.

A few beers and whisky chasers later the fire had shaken off its earlier despondency and its vaporous red orange flames reached up the sootblack chimney like the tenuous fingers of a probing hand. Tonsils had eased and the topics of conversation flitted cyclically from sex to god and infinity and back again. Dave's philosophy, like John's was moulded by

Merthyr's history, the dialectic of the enlightened street and voracious reading and discussion. Both subscribed to a radical existentialism, essentially socialist, of which Sartre was of course the leading exponent and Camus the icon. They saw Stalin as an aberration and the assassination of Trotski as the death knell for Soviet communism. They reacted against the throttling of the individual which was a consequence of the industrial revolution and feared the degree to which the new technological revolution now ensuing would exacerbate that trend unless control of its development and use was wrested away from the burgeoning multi -national corporations.

John sought to give expression to his views as much through his scribbling as his political affiliations. Dave had long since abandoned overt political activism for expression through his art.

Their aesthetic development like their friendship was something which had matured steadily through their adolescence, they had been friends for as long as either of them could remember, but initially the writing and the painting had not been a mutual interest, which made its simultaneity all the more remarkable.

It had begun in both cases secretly, almost furtively and for a while even threatened a rift in their friendship. Then when each discovered the other's artistic ambitions their work for a period became a sublime dialectic. Their relationship blossomed into an intimate and beautiful thing, devoid of any physical expression for both were blatantly hetero in their sexual orientation. And yet, what they experienced emotionally was beyond normal friendship, more like the love which David expressed for Jonathan.

John began to get published in obscure unread periodicals, unpaid of course. While Dave's paintings were hung in equally obscure galleries, more often the backrooms of local pubs and working men's clubs. Recently the growing maturity of their work was receiving critical notice, and it was beginning to sell, albeit for very small beer.

This reflected strongly in their respective work which as much as anything was a reaction against Welsh, or for that matter English, or any other, bigotry and Puritanism in all its forms. John wrote a poem which Dave illustrated with a pen and ink drawing. The poem, heavily influenced by Hopkins via Thomas, was full of cynghanedd and sprung rhythm. It dealt with the seduction of a celibate young Roman Catholic priest by the beautiful atheistic wife of a crippled parishioner (shades of Lawrence) at whose sick bed he was a conscientious visitor. Dave's illustration was a nude Mary Magdalene prostrate at the feet of a crucified Christ in erection.

Gay was not a euphemism used at this time, *queer* was the term misapplied to them by their detractors.

They had continued their collaboration, which produced a slim volume of illustrated verse, settling on *causa prima* by the drawing of lots. John drew the short straw, writing the poem to inspire the ink drawing. Then, roles reversed, a further drawing inspired by the first sparked another poem and so on, each feeding from the other's creativity.

It was published in an avante garde low circulation quarterly, which was grant aided by the Academi Cymraeg, with support from the Welsh Arts Council. There followed an almighty furore in the Western Mail and on TWW on this disgraceful waste of public money. The readers" columns were filled with vituperative condemnation from chapel ministers the length and depth of Wales and the Archbishop was interviewed on the concept of heresy and its place in law.

Their notoriety made them a hot property on the burgeoning underground press beyond the strict confines of the Welsh valleys. They had dined out, or at least drunk out, on their ill repute.

They began to hold court in the Beehive, a pub notorious for its working class demi mondes who would share their beds for the price of an evening's hard drinking. They imagined downtown Merthyr as a Welsh Montmartre and themselves as Baudelaire and Lautrec hell bent on burning themselves into an early grave

They drank themselves into a semi-stupor in the company of two infamous blonde twins, Jean and Joan, who in different environs might have wooed the jetset or set alight a million silver screens. As it was some cretinous excuse for a father had conditioned them as "the buck toothed ugly sisters". The "buck teeth" in those days of the embryonic National Health Service did not qualify for corrective dentistry. So the twins grew up at the "bottom of town" a nice euphemism for the slum which was Caedraw, with their "buck teeth", stupendous mammarian appendices, and a sexual appetite of Freudian proportions. Barely literate, these unfortunates shared a filthy flat in the Dresdenesque ruins of a 'slum clearance" area.

Having vowed never to darken the ancestral portals ever again going with the "whores" was a further disavowal of everything their parents stood for, a big "fuck you" to the ignorance and bigotry of the respectable working class. The two women listened with apparent sympathy to their drunken tales of woe until stop tap, then led them off down broken side streets to the ramshackle former dosshouse which several families shared as what can best be described as a sort of commune for the socially inadequate.

They were led up dark stairs to the top floor where the twins shared two attic bedrooms and a tiny kitchen. They were absurdly prim about their sexual activities, insisting that they be conducted with due propriety, separately. Which was a relief to John, not at all as sophisticated as his bravura would suggest. Ménages a trois, let alone a quatre, had not been on his curricula.

Alone with Jean he felt it imperative to consummate this bizarre relationship or his defiance would be incomplete. She sat nude, flaccid and goosepimpled on the dirty unmade bed and even through the stupefaction of

35

his drunken haze he could not imagine her as anything other than the unpretentious unattractive whore that she had become.

Try as he might her face and form would not dissolve and resolve as a Faustian Helen. He could not will unwilling flesh to rise, or sink, to the occasion. But she too seemed possessed of some driving urge, involving all the tricks of her trade, to overcome his impotence. Manually and orally she strove, as if failure would be testimony to her incapacity, not his.

Perhaps she took a pride in her work, he thought absurdly and involuntarily began to snigger. Her efforts stepped up a gear at this affront and incredibly her diligence began to pay some dividends. But as they did the room began to sway like a trawler's wheelhouse. She took one look at his pale face and bloated cheeks and dragged him out onto the landing and down the dark stairs unashamedly naked, absurdly his erection now as stubborn to extinguish as it had been to arouse.

She bundled him unceremoniously out through a ground floor door where he was fleetingly aware of the moon and stars in a cloudless sky before being thrust through the one hinged crooked door of the communal privy. He dropped on his knees and vomited into the pan, kneeling for a while taking in great gulps of icy air before lowering his head and vomiting again.

After a prolonged pause he finally raised his head and looking up at the stars through a hole in the roof cried out, with an ecstatic expression on his face. "Oh mam, if you could only see me now." He laughed like a maniac, retched again, and passed out.

Dave helped him back up the stairs and washed him in the tiny kitchen. Still half drunk himself he constantly broke into gales of ribald laughter in which John ultimately joined. Then it was Dave's turn to slump, head down on his chest muttering absurd obscenities and John the ministering angel, with help from Jean and Joan dragging him off to his bed. On a wave of elation he assaulted the delighted Jean with a wild self destructive degrading passion.

> *Perverse insistent lips untangle the untempered drill.*
> *The blind eye blinks and sheds it's tears in a barren harbour.*
> *No soft lover's lips, intrusions wet and warm,but degradation and*
> *remorse.*

He was to pen in retrospect in the next slim volume of his self absorbed verse.

He drifted into nightmare to startle awake in a cold shaft of Damascene light which illuminated the doll like creature at his side like a cinematic projection. Morning had broken.

"Goo'mornin love," she greeted cheerfully, one of those annoying people who are smiling wide awake from the first blink. She pulled herself up in a bed so ingrained with lust a future Saatchi would have parted with a king's ransom for it. With her large breasts, dishevelled hair and sleep encrusted eyes she was a Lautrec lady incarnate. "Cor, you look a bit under the weather", she remonstrated. "Fancy a nice cuppa and an egg?"

"Boiled," he insisted quickly, his stomach revolting at the thought of anything greasy.

"Boiled it is," she smiled knowingly. "You'll be better for it." She rose and covered her nakedness with a dirty faded housecoat. Then before exiting for the kitchen she bent over and kissed him tenderly on the forehead as if this was the culmination of a romantic affair rather than the regretted encounter between a selfish young drunk and a prematurely ageing whore.

Later that day he and Dave moved some of their belongings into a broken down caravan on a tinker site in Trecatty in the mountains above Dowlais; artificial mountains of the slag and spoil of coal and iron, the flaming passion of whose fiery loins had fathered this bastard of a town.

The place was windswept and forbidding and the ghosts of Guest and Crawshay danced a mad fandango across the barren wastes. The huge old ironworks, long derelict and demolished, had left a legacy of grey molten slag in the form of a table topped Atlas which dominated the bleak landscape. "A battered bucket on a broken hill." the poet Idris Davies had described it.

In the lee of this huge tip the caravans were clustered in conditions that were primitive and appalling. Children played innocently adjacent to the black swampy sewage ditch which flanked the southern boundary of the site. Here lived the utterly dispossessed even moreso than the Hugoesque denizens of the Caedraw dosshouse.

John and Dave stood drunkenly swigging from the almost empty whisky bottle which Dave suddenly dashed angrily on the blue black igneous rocks which had been spewed out by the ancient furnaces littering the landscape like the remnants of a dormant volcano.

"This is Dante's hell," he yelled. They surveyed the ugly scene which lay before them, the dirty untidy broken streets, back to ramshackle back. The drab square boxes of chapels thrusting their horrible heads above the low mean rooftops. Beulah, Bethesda, Bethania, Zion, Zoar, Libanus. John dropped to his haunches and cried with unrestrained anger.

"Something should be done," paraphrasing the mad Windsor's reaction of an earlier decade. He stood up and unzipped his flies and taking out his ill used cock pissed into the wind which blew it back into his own face. "Piss on you God," he called. "Piss on you and all your works." Dave tearfully nodded his agreement.

"Don't you agree John?" Dave insisted.

"What? Agree what? What are you prattling on about now?"

"The world ever persecutes genius. Haven't you been listening to a word I've been saying.?"

John shuffled his legs away from the blazing fire. "Sorry, I was lost in reverie of those weeks we lived in that bloody caravan."

"Well now that happens to be a perfect illustration of my point. That was persecution if anything ever was. Don't remind me."

"A short lived gesture though," John mused.

"Long enough for me," Dave insisted, "and it did win some important concessions from our maters and paters."

"What a ramshackle shed out the back as a studio for you and a lockable trunk in which to secrete my perverted ramblings. Some concessions. But then as you claim to have been saying the world ever treated genius thus. Wait til we're dead and gone in our consumptive prime they'll make a cult of us and millions for themselves. "Ah yes ladies and gentlemen," the guide will say. "this is the shed, er studio, where the late great David Watkins ate, slept, masturbated, painted his wonderful pictures and finally expired through lack of recognition. And there, miraculously in that locked chest are the bones of one whose name was writ in beer, his lifelong friend and mentor, poet and philosopher, John Davies, who died horrifically from a terrible dose of pox contracted during one of his frequent and famous alcoholic debauches." "

"You know you're full of shit Davies. We were discussing something serious, the rise and rise of capitalism or something. I was remarking how little progress there's really been despite the blood, sweat and tears of our forefathers. We're still as enslaved as ever but more subtly so. The envisaged emancipation just hasn't materialised. But the most frightening thing is the apathy. Give em beer and chips and they're happy. Who was it said that?"

"Sillitoe," John snapped. "Beer, chips and fags I think it was. Saturday Night and Sunday Morning, a marvellous bloody book. Camus would be proud of it."

"Camus?"

"The rebel, Arthur Seaton, working class anarchist."

"Is that what it's all about. I thought it was just about getting your leg over on a Saturday night."

John lobbed a wet table mat at him. "You want to get your head out of your paint pot now and again you bourgeois bastard," he taunted. Anyway it's really all down to Darwin, the next step in the evolutionary process."

"What the fuck's it got to do with Darwin?" Bill interjected.

"Throughout the various stages of our development, so the Darwinian thesis goes," John put on his pedantic explanatory tone, "man has repeatedly cast off those physical and mental attributes which no longer contributed to his survival.

"As our dorsal bone is indicative of transition from animal to human, so this last spark of decency and conscience is indicative of our transition from human to zombie - from dignified man to the soft machine.

"The soul-less society my friends lies just around the corner and when we finally get there, someday very soon, God, who contrary to Sartre's opinion is not dead, in his infinite mercy, in final recognition of the almighty cock up he's made of us, will press the bloody button and up, or down, we'll all go.

"The trouble with us you see is that we're among the few vertebrates left, always at odds with our environment, never fitting into the allotted slots. Well my friends, the question is; what are we going to do about it for wishing will not make it so. The world is past redemption so must we simply make the best of it like Arthur Seaton. Perjure , prostitute, lie, cheat and connive and everything that we desire will come our way. But David Watkins you and I are artists and artists like philosophers should not simply seek to understand and explain the world. As the great man said." the point is to change it." I drink a toast gentlemen. To the revolution."

"Bullshit," Dave rejoined before the toast could be drunk. "Sometimes I wonder why I condescend to drink with you at all you're so full of crap. There you sit, the self proclaimed philosopher poet with unsung songs to be sung and yet you sit at your machine making parts for bikes like Arthur bloody Seaton, or worse still poisonous bloody chemicals to ruin the environment. You allow the great industrial machine to crush you flat. You dabble with Labour politics which only serves to prop the whole thing up with its tinkering at the edges of the capitalist game. Don't preach to me about greed and prostitution."

"Aha, but my good honest friend, I who was sore afflicted felt the scales fall from mine eyes and was blind no more. My resignation from ICI is in the post. My party card is torn to shreds. This is the day, this is THE day. No. No more questions. Questions can wait. There is a time and tide in the heart of man which taken at the full, and all that, and all that. Tonight just like Arthur bloody Seaton all I want is to get my leg over." He picked up the whisky chaser and threw it to the back of his tonsils where he let it lay for a precious moment before releasing it to run it's glowing path to his belly.

The little backroom was filled to overflowing now and warmer than an Avana oven. As always when semi-rational discussion gives way to inebriation talking gives way to singing and the Dowlo was no exception. Vocals ranged from the latest inane pop, and the fifties really were the pits for banal pops (*She wears red feathers and a hula hula skirt*) , to tender lyrical old favourites, and ultimately almost without exception to Boyceish Calon Lan and Cwm Rhondda complete with mispronunciation.

The Dowlais five were holding court. The leading lights of course were John and Dave with their recent success elevating them to star billing. Geraint, fair haired and fresh faced was an ardent Nationalist forever being dragged before the magistrates for defacing English language roadsigns. His heroes were Saunders Lewis and Gwynfor Evans who, although both nationalists were diametrically opposed in methodology; Gwynfor the non violent protester who through his hunger strike was later to secure the fourth channel for Welsh Language broadcasts, Saunders Lewis jailed for sabotage during the Fascist War. Geraint exemplified the schizophrenia that was the Welsh Nationalist movement of the time. He was the frequent butt of the more sophisticated politics of the rest of the group.

Bill was the veteran, a bachelor in his late thirties who felt he had much more in common with his young confederates than members of his own age group. He was a widely read autodidact steeped in the philosophies of the East. He quoted freely from Khayam and the Sufis, Hafiz, Confucius, the Buddha, Po-Chu-I and Karl Marx. He was forever extolling the virtues of Eurasian women, with one of whom he had undergone a marriage ritual and lived with until her untimely malarial death. He still succumbed to recurring attacks himself. His skin was the pallid yellow of a South East Asian and his face badly pockmarked from some tropical pox. Yet he seemed irresistibly attractive to women. He was making a moderate success in photographic journalism and had done some freelance work for Magnum which he hoped would soon free him from the toolroom; which it ultimately did with the advent of the Vietnam war which he covered to international critical acclaim.

Ted was a tall thin cynic wedded to Tolstoi and Kropotkin and whose favourite characters in literature were the mad bomb carrying professor in Conrad's Secret Agent, whose perfection of the human bomb (himself) presaged the horrors of the present 'suicide bombers" and who's plot to blow up the Greenwich Observatory as an attack on Science had a particular appeal; and Souverain in Zola's Germinal, who blew up Le Voreux, the coalmine which brooded like a decaying monster over the lives of the villagers of Montsou. In criticising Marx who he misinterprets as an "evolutionist", Souverain chillingly chides Etienne.

" Don't talk to me about evolution! Raise fires in the four corners of cities, mow people down, wipe everything out, and when nothing whatever is left of this rotten world perhaps a better one will spring up."

This summarised Ted's dangerous nihilism and it is hardly surprising that he went on to achieve infamy in the sixties when, like Conrad's Stevie, though lacking his innocence, he succeeded in blowing himself up in a botched attempt at sabotage on the nuclear reactor at Trawsfynydd.

This then was the nucleus of the Dowlais (the Merthyr) "avant garde" for were they not synonymous. Held in ignorant awe by their contemporaries they were labelled Marxists, Trotskiists, Anarchists, Leninists, Diabolists, or any other "ists that a wary Welsh community could lay it's tongue to. The Dowlo was it's principal meeting place and consequently attracted to it a strange ménage of the curious, the adoring and the sinister. It had assumed, among the Merthyr, and the wider Welsh intelligentsia, the status of The Mermaid. Even Special Branch took a fleeting interest until their Super realised that the topics of conversation were somewhat over the heads of his operatives who in their reports had all and sundry listed as dangerous revolutionaries, which in Ted's case proved unwittingly to be correct.

The Dowlo was their stage and it consequently attracted all kinds of strange and interesting people to its backroom. It was not unusual to walk in and find some self confessed genius on his feet passionately espousing his philosophy or reciting his poetry before retiring once more to his retreat in the bleak Welsh hills or dark brooding valleys. What the Dowlo's regular denizens made of all this is unrepeatable and poets and preachers were often sent on their way with friendly advice to , "Stop talking crap and fuck off back to where you came from."

Tonight a small group of undergrads were the only strangers sardined, standing room only, adjacent to the serving hatch. Attracted by the reputation of the place they sat uneasily sipping their drinks alertly waiting for the big event. Bill brushed past them with a trayful of drinks. John in serious mode had just explained the strike situation and cautioned them with threat of violence not to raise the subject again that evening. Sunday was the day for politics, he opined. Sunday, Welsh and respectable, ideal for insurrection and rebellion.

Young Paddy Macarthy was trying to sing some lullaby of old Ireland to his white haired mother in the corner, but was barely audible above the general din. The Macarthys were Irish as poteen and porter and the tears shone in her old green Irish eyes as he sang in a fine lilting tenor, "I'll take you home again Caithlin to where the hills are fresh and green." It was a Jungian memory as far as they were concerned as the closest they had been to Galway Bay was Swansea, since their ancestors swopped the famine of peasant Ireland for the impoverished slum of "China", the immigrant area of metropolitan industrial Merthyr.

Bill's own one quarter Irish ancestry had him joining in and soon the five added their own accompaniment signalling that intellectual discourse was over and the maudlin gamut of backroom vocalising about to begin. Soon the whole pub, front room and back were in tune and by some indefinable process the songs slid seamlessly from Irish to Scottish to Welsh until the Gaelic oeuvre had been exhausted, and it was assumed, patriotic fervour assuaged.

Suddenly a dark slender member of the collegiate was on her feet and vainly trying to get general attention. John's attention she already had. There was something indescribably sensual about her. But it was an understated sensuality owing everything to a kind of languid poise. Hers was not the brash attraction which generates wolf whistles in the street but soft silent sighs in the hearts of the cognoscenti. In one of those windows of silence which inexplicably occur in the middle of a cacophonous hubbub she was heard clearly to proclaim. "What about the English?".

Before the inevitable barrage of catcalls which would otherwise have automatically ensued John, the shining knight, leapt to her rescue. "Now

41

then," he called, commanding immediate attention. "Fair is fair. And this young rose of England is certainly fair, though dark. Welshmen have always sung the praises of the English rose. After all you can't blame a rose for the ground in which it nourishes it's roots. Of course it took a Welshman to compose the song equal to the loveliness of this rose." He addressed her with the drunken confidence of an aficionado of too many romantic crooners of the silver screen and broke into a sugary sweet rendition of Novello's "We'll gather lilacs in the spring again." The catcalls soon subsided into equally inebriated accompaniment. He winked at her. She winked back and he was lost.

"Oh very sick," muttered Ted after the strains had died. "Poor Geraint has turned green, and it's not the beer."

Geraint scowled from behind his pint. "What sort of Welshman writes a song about walking down English lanes. What sort of name is Novello anyway? Sounds like a bloody spick to me."

"There we have it," retorted John, "the irrationalist nationalist racist mind."

"Fuck you and your alliteration," Geraint spat back. Dave thought it prudent to inject a little levity.

"Perhaps it was an English lane of some special significance to Ivor," he suggested. "Might he have lost his virginity there?"

"More likely his knickers," Geraint snapped scornfully.

"Tell you what, let's rewrite it to give it a Welsh significance if it will make you happy."

"Why is everybody suddenly talking such utter crap," Bill complained. "And as for you and your obnoxious charm," he turned to John. "It's enough to make a saint throw up."

"Well what it wasn't was the idiom of the people was it," John persisted. "I'm sure the combined talents of so much creative genius can make an improvement on it. Now let's see. Yes.. *My English rose is driving me insane*

when we go walking down the Goetre lane
she brings her knee up gives me such a pain
that's why I love her so...

and on and on he went in this vein composing verses increasingly more bawdy culminating in a great cheer from the rapt audience and a gale of laughter.

"Surely the work of a major poet," Bill applauded sarcastically.

"So delightfully sick," Geraint growled.

"So excitingly anarchic," Ted added.

"Will rank with Eskimo Nell as one of the great ballads of our time," Dave announced.

Oh you bawdy Baudelaire and a bit, you ribald Rabelais, you randy Rimbaud he thought to his inebriate self. You are a one and doesn't this lithe lovely think so.

He clambered onto his chair, a little unsteadily, to the groans of those who recognised an imminent peroration. He held up his hands as he imagined Christ about to impart wisdom to the multitudes. "She will always be remembered as "the dark lady of the ballads"," he said, "but who was she in reality? This is the mystery that future literary historians will grapple with. Was she the seemingly shy Jenny Prendergast Pring? Did she sport a pair of black leather panties beneath all that organdie and lace? Or was it dedicated to that mysterious English rose, the black rose of Trecatty? Did she conceal a thorny stem behind her flowery facade? Oh antic love why hast thou played me false? Some have it that she was an old woman with a padded bra and that the original phrase from the first folio contained in the Black Book of Pengarnddu was...oh antique love why hast thou played me false? .. Has the time now come to tear open the tomb of the Bard of Taff Fechan. What terrible secrets lie hidden in that musty coffin? What catastrophic disaster is implied in that cryptic warning on that cracked and faded headstone. "Leave well alone you Dowlais vandals, lest you unearth some dirty scandals." "

"He's off," Dave chuckled to Bill. "Found a bird to impress. Wont shut the bugger up all night now."

He half stumbled from his rostrum and like the consummate performer he was transformed his error into a grand running exit, sweeping past her and not stopping til he found himself outside in the cold sobering air gulping in icy draughts. He sat on a crumbling low stone wall slowly recovering a measure of composure and sobriety. Soon she followed sitting alongside him with a quizzical expression on her austerely beautiful face. "I'm Josephine," she introduced herself holding out her hand palm down like a courtly Guenivere expecting him to brush the back of it with his lips. So he did.

"John Davies my lady," he responded. "Where are your friends?" Her shrug was coldly careless.

"Jolly Roger and co," she answered. "He's taken Jean and Sam to see some local architectural masterpiece carved out of solid coal by the gnarled hands of the miners to welcome their King. Edward the Abdicator I believe it was. Now there's a paradox, the Merthyr miners, socialist to the core, throwing their hats in the air for a fascist numbskull."

"Not the miners exactly," John corrected. "Oh they carved the Coal Arch allright. Hardly a masterpiece though just a good example of the mason's craft. A curio which stands appropriately outside the dole office. You know the place the unwashed go to get a job, and where they used to go to beg for assistance at the time of His Majesty's visit. The people petitioned and pleaded more than they cheered. The poor dimwit was apparently quite moved. Something must be done, he said, but very little was."

"Actually something was," she contradicted, if a little wistfully. "Not by or because of the royal dimwit but strangely enough by the little moustachioed corporal he admired. The exodus of Jews from Germany and Poland in the thirties brought my late father to unlikely places like Merthyr to set up business with a little direction from central government."

"And what business was that?"

"Knickers," she laughed.

"What?"

"Knickers, well and other associated underwear." She waved her hand vaguely in the direction of a tip top (literally in that it was situated on the top of a tip) plateau lit by red argon, in the middle distance. "Mason's Fashions, Poliakoffs that was", she explained. "That's our factory - mine and Mum's. Not that I take the remotest interest in it, mum's the business brain. Changed it's name and its fortune long before dad's death. Modernised, new chic, sexy undies for the masses, that sort of thing. With dad they were still making boned corsets."

"My God," he reacted. "A fully fledged bloated capitalist-you Masons."

"I'm afraid so. So not English at all you see. A little dark eyed Welsh Jewess. So what are you going to sing me now?"

"I'm sure I'll come up with something, but what was all that for in there then." He gestured to the door through which the strains of an Irish lament had again began to filter through.

"That," she said, "all that Celtic yearning, all that Hiraeth, all that bloody crap."

He looked at her seriously for a moment. "There's nothing wrong with us Welsh," he insisted, "we're emotional, tactile," he reached across and touched her hand. It was a manoeuvre straight out of the handbook "one upmanship" a popular fifties phenomenon. Pull her hand away she was remote and prim, leave it there and it was an invitation.

He burst out laughing and she momentarily wrong footed joined in. "Come on then," he invited, " I'll show you the true monuments of this "battered bucket on a broken hill", not involving the great coal arch."

"I don't know," she feigned hesitation, "Roger warned me about you."

"Roger, what does Roger know about me?"

"You were at grammar school together. Roger Cavendish."

"Oh that Roger, thought I recognised him from somewhere. Father's managing director of the toy factory. God you capitalists stick together don't you. What is it, an arranged marriage, a merging of empires."

"Come on," she said taking his arm, "don't be so bloody preposterous and prejudiced."

"Don't get alliterative with me babe," he snarled in his best Bogart. "You out slumming, let's go slumming."

44

"I'll just get my coat," she said beginning to shiver in the cold Dowlais night.

When they re-entered the Dowlo the knowing glances were almost accusatory. John remembered the smarmy Roger from his grammar school days, the privileged son of one of Merthyr's most prominent businessmen. Always chosen to represent the school in all kinds of activities, none of which he was particularly accomplished at. Got a scholarship to Cambridge .It would be a pleasure to steal away with something of his. Even a spoiled little bitch, if that's what she was, albeit a very attractive one. His experience of spoiled bitches had, in any event, been generally very rewarding on the purely physical plane. So he gave his confederates the thumbs up as he grabbed his coat and escorted her out into the chilly night.

"What the hell do they see in him," Bill complained with a chuckle.

"It's the gift of the gab," Dave opined. "Beats being six foot six with a ten inch dong any day of the week."

"I wouldn't know from either perspective," Ted rejoined sullenly.

Outside John looked up at the sky. The weather was holding. "You wont want that symbol of your *opulence,* he said as she made to open the door of her elegant sporty Volvo, midnight blue, so out of place in the dingy Dowlais street. "My God you are a rich little bitch aren't you?" he mocked. "Come on its the proletarian mode for our purpose. Perambulation I believe your class call it - shank's pony to us." He led her along Balaclava Road, the smell from the rubbish tip adjacent to it wafting up despite the cold and began the ascent of Regent Street, steep as an Alpine ski slope. The window sills of the front rooms so low to the ground because of the gradient making the tiny interiors visible behind the aspidistras and potted geraniums, sharing their intimacy with all and sundry. But front rooms were seldom used and most activity was confined to the middle room and the back kitchen. Front rooms were preserved for weddings and funerals and visits from posh aunts from Muswell Hill. In some of the houses a flickering blue light advertised the ownership of a new fangled jamjar screened Bush television. What was the point of possessing such a status symbol if it's light was to be hidden under the bushel of the middle room.

"Do you know," he said with the intonation of someone about to impart some words of inestimable wisdom, "that most Dowlais prols live in kitchens which are triangular, and have developed feet which subtend an angle of fortyfive degrees with the ankle."

She laughed uneasily because the banter was tinged with a bitter irony. "Does this bloody street go on forever," she complained taking in great gulps of freezing air. He half dragged her to the top and they stood hands on hips panting in unison. Above them stretched another street, and above that another only marginally less steep. Dowlais had been thrown together clumsily on the steep hillside it's higgledy piggledy architecture defying Newtonian mathematics. Up they went ever higher, along Station Road, past

45

the Stables and the Market and the classically porticoed memorial hall to John Josiah Guest, the iron master without whose huge ironworks, the biggest in the world in that explosive birth of the industrial revolution, Dowlais might never have been. Onward and upward they climbed, deliberately avoiding the Coal Arch and the possibility of Roger and co, past the Ivor Works, a foundry named after John Josiah's son, and the last remnant of the great Guest empire, to Penywern and up an icy moonlit dirt track to the Top Pond. Beyond what must have been it's eastern perimeter a small cluster of tiny houses seemed to huddle together throwing tiny pin pricks of light out onto the ill made dirt track.

"That's Pengarnddu," he said. "Not much further now. Pengarnddu is the edge."

"The edge of what?"

"The world, the abyss, the known universe. Can't you feel it, see it, smell it?" He spun her round. "Look, look down there. Isn't this the edge of eternity. Imagine it," he said," as it was; whitewashed hill farms silver in the cool moonlight; bubbling streams meandering, cascading luminous ribbons into trout filled pools; free, fresh, clean green grass with roots deep in a rich tilth, waving, dancing a sensual Eastern dance in a keen breeze. And now, and now, "a battered bucket on a broken hill", the Morlais a stinking chemical sewer, not a minnow to it's name. The ghosts of Guest and Crawshay lurking in the black shadows. Oh sing a song of revolution

> "And did those feet in ancient time
> walk upon Gwalia's mountains green.
> And was the holy lamb of God
> in Merthyr's pleasant valley seen?
> And did that countenance divine
> shine forth upon our clouded hills
> and was Jerusalem builded here
> among these dark satanic mills?"

His voice clear in the cold night like a muezzin calling the faithful to prayer.

She felt small and insignificant standing there above the black abyss and her instincts warned her to run, run away now from this mad poet before he completely captivated her: but she stayed. The Phoenician boat slid out from its dark harbour and in one magic instant painted the scene in shimmering silver as if the mad magician had waved his wand. At that precise and awful moment she felt his cold lips brush the back of her swansdown neck. She turned away sharply, too sharply, as if afraid of her own reactions. It brought her face to face with the view of Dowlais and Merthyr spread out in the valley far below.

"Ugly isn't it," he muttered, "this black body with a silver shroud."

Was all this alliteration and metaphor a poetic form of seduction. It was working. She knew from the strange way she trembled. Or was that just the cold? Was confusion part of the process. She could make out the High Street from the red orange river of argon which slashed its way up from the town to the dark lop sided hillside hovels like a bleeding gash. Lesser luminaries of pale yellow patchily lit the tributaries, growing ever more sparse in the outer extremities where the little houses huddled together for company, hunched and ramshackle.

"Why should you venture out of your protective central heated closet to become a part of that : that is the question?" And it was. "Well I'll tell you. Down there in all that grime and confusion beats a heart, a broken heart, a bleeding heart, but every pulse of it is amplified and echoed in my own. There are people there, real and alive, and me I'm real and alive and burning. And isn't that what you want too - to live and burn? But to live you have to suffer pain, to love your heart must bleed a little. That cocoon of yours is a little too secure, too cosy. You're an unborn child with a glimpse of the outside world where everything is new and alive and exciting - but frightening. How much easier to sink back in and let the vaginal opening shut tight behind you.

"Below us, beneath our feet, at this very moment men are scurrying about like moles in the blind earth. And there in that red glow men still sweat in the heat of the furnace. What for? They are the real monuments my spoiled little bourgeois. Do you understand?"

His blunt insults served now only to fuel the flame. Her eyes sparkled as she saw the fire that lit his. "Just so they can hang on to the little that they have down there, because as the wise man said, they've never had it so good." He waved an arm expansively taking in the criss crossing streets drab and dirty down below them. "Untidy wives, belligerent husbands, crying kids, pubs and cinemas, bingo and television, and chapel. Fantastic isn't it that out of that mad ménage emerge real people, heroes and heroines, exciting and alive. Not the impotent observant Rogers of this world with his blazer and his scarf, but the doers and the livers. I am one of them, they are my people. I love and hate them. We live though everything around us dies."

In the awkward silence which followed she fought against her desperate desire for him. She was, despite the obvious absurdity of it, prepared to accept almost everything this wild mesmeric Welsh bard said or did. It was a complete reversal of the relationships she had previously experienced with men, with Roger for instance. She had run the gamut of witty debs escorts and was not exactly naive or without experience. But never before had she met such a phenomenon as this, who could rouse her to such passion. There was an aura of intense, almost insane genius about him which, while it signalled caution, if not fear, aroused her in a way which she did not quite understand, not just sexually but in a manner entirely new and beyond her comprehension.

"Don't worry ," he confided, "I've always suffered the love-hate syndrome. That should interest you as an erstwhile psychologist. I probably need a mother confessor, not to analyse me I've long since mastered the art of self analysis, but confession is good for the soul, and mothers are good for.....mothering?" He made a question of the statement.

His tone had changed now, she thought. He was simply being clever and having fun at her expense. She resisted his goading with silence.

"I have a problem with sex you see. I find it delicious. Do you appreciate that. A delightful activity I have no hesitation in commending to all regardless of colour, creed, religion, class or gender. Its just fabulous. Don't you agree?"

She thought silence would avoid the trap he set her. I'm the psychologist. You do the talking. But the trap he set was not the obvious one. He was too devious for her. His eyes sought hers enquiring, mocking, waiting. "There you see, you're obviously unfulfilled."

She coloured a little. "I thought we were talking about your problem," she replied.

"*We* were not talking at all as I recall it. But if you must, yes I simply seize on every opportunity for sexual conjunction. I have an insatiable desire for the humiliating act." He bit his nails neurotically. "I'm torn between beauty and ugliness, joy and pain, truth and lie, inebriation and sobriety, respectability and debauchery. I can't distinguish love from lust. Women I seduce and then abandon because their surrender disgusts me. But they all feel obliged to prove me wrong, to cure my sickness, to show that they are the one woman who can give herself to me and still retain my love and adoration. I am left unsatisfied, unsatisfiable. Is it Oedipus confessor? Is there a cure for me?"

She smiled a rather tired smile and shook her head. Why was he playing this tiresome game with her? What would be an appropriate response to his sophistry. "Such cynicism requires a simple faith," she said, knowing immediately that she had already lost this particular match. "Your inability to distinguish good from bad stems essentially from lack of faith. Not necessarily a deity, but some immutable base, an absolute truth which qualifies every action."

"Such *Kant*, he punned. "An absolute imperative. But I do believe confessor, I really do - in many things. In freedom, for those people down there, and people everywhere, political, economic, religious, racial. But those are beliefs in what should be not in what things are. I believe in man the individual and man the mass, now there's a paradox. I believe in sex as part of a wider relationship and as an end in itself. I believe in good and in bad, in pleasure and in pain. I believe in God and the Devil. I believe in beauty and truth and love, components of which are necessarily ugliness, lies and hate. Nothing is simple. Nothing is absolute. Everything is relative. Yet there is good and there is evil. Life is a paradox. There so much for your psychology.

Anyway, why bother with all this shit when all you have to do is wait for some useless Roger to honour and cherish you and keep you in the bourgeois manner to which you are accustomed."

The tears started now. "If you brought me here simply to humiliate me you've had your success," she mumbled. "Please take me back."

"On the contrary. I brought you here to further your education. You see you've become the latest episode of my love hate syndrome." With which he took her in his arms and she complied and sighed like a love hungry child. They kissed, not passionately but tenderly, and he brushed away her tears with the back of his hand.

"Perhaps you're right," she said. "I am rich and spoiled and useless. I only study at mummy's insistence. She thinks I should do something useful with my time until I come into my inheritance."

"Inheritance," he queried. "Now that is the language of the bourgeoisie. You mean you really are a rich bitch. I mean *rich* rich."

"I thought you already knew. Mummy holds it all in trust but in due course it comes to me - all of it. You mean to say you didn't know. I thought everybody in Merthyr knew. So you don't want me for my money after all." Teasing now.

"Good God," he feigned shock and horror. "You're not just petit bourgeois, you're one of the captains of industry, a bloody live and kicking industrial tycoon. I shouldn't even be seen talking to the likes of you it will destroy my credibility as a socialist."

"Why? A socialist with such impeccable credentials would surely have no interest in money."

"Money, achyfi," he spat, a wide grin spreading across his face. It's not your money I want baby, it's your body," pulling her close to him. Now here was a woman to be wooed not taunted. Had the fates conspired after all that tonight of all nights this Faustian Helen should appear, to damn his soul for all eternity. He reached out a cold white finger and stroked her marble cheek. Midas waiting for the metamorphosis. "Come on I want you to meet someone."

The little house was typical of the hundreds of precariously erected little boxes of which the majority of Dowlais streets were then comprised. Soon to be swept away in a plague of urban renewal to create the soul-less deserts of Gellideg and Gurnos. John knocked and opened the door beckoning her in with the familiarity of one about to enter his own home. The entrance to the tiny room was only sheltered from the draft of the winter chill by a heavy red baize on a bamboo runner which acted as a draft excluder. Inside a fire blazed a hearty welcome in the small hearth. It was a typical old miners cottage and Josephine was enchanted with it. A dresser stood against the wall with rows of cups on hooks lining the shelves. Their matching saucers and plates lending a splash of "gaudy Welsh" colour to the room. The other wall was completely taken up with a big ugly Victorian sideboard on which stood rows of framed photographs from sepia to tinted, of smiling newly weds and cherubic babies, a photographic genealogical tree. The limestone slabbed floor was scrubbed to an almost white grey and partially covered with corded matting. The hearth and oven were black leaded and gleaming. The fender and other brasserie adorning the mantel reflected ruddy orange in the fire's glow. Thank the NUM for widow's coal. A grey haired old woman, her shapeless body shrouded in a flowery pinafore peered from behind rimless NHS glasses from a heavily cushioned corner armchair in which she sat reading the Echo.

"Oh John bech," she smiled. "Now what is it you've been up to?" brandishing the Echo and its lurid headline. "Causin" strikes now is what it says here. Too much of your dadgu in you, and your dada too. Nearly went to Cardiff jail he did for picketing the scabs in Bedwas. Who's that with you, not Maggie May's gel is it? Oh no you're too pretty for Maggie May's gel," she chuckled peering more closely. "Far too pretty to be bothering with the likes of you John Davies that's for sure.

"Don't you let him talk you into things you didn't ought to my girl. Gift of the bloody gab like his dadgu always getting him into trouble. Oooo", she hooted. "Didn't mean it to come out like that gel."

"This is Josephine Mamgu, she's very rich, very posh, so mind your p's and q's."

"Oh is she now. Still drinks tea like the rest of us I suppose," she said of her, to her.

"Yes please," Josephine responded.

"How's Lyndy.?" Mamgu shook her head non committal.

"See for yourself. You promised her you'd call last week." She waddled off to the foot of the stairwell in the corner of the room and called up, "Lindy, John's here."

The girl who ran excitedly down the stairs must have been about John's age. A very attractive girl but with features marked with a deep pain. "Hullo Lindy love," John laughed, but as always the laughter masked the dreadful ache of sadness he always felt whenever he saw her. He held his hand out to her and she took it with the awkward shyness of a young pubescent child with a jealous eye on Josephine. "How are you then?"

She looked down at her feet averting eyes. "You promised you'd come and read to me again. When will you? Will you now?" looking again at Josephine. "He always used to come and read to me." With just the hint of accusation.

"It's not Josephine's fault Lindy, we've only just met. Id like you to be friends. I'll come soon I promise."

"Are you a nice girl?" she offered Josephine her hand who struggled not to let a tear fall as she took it.

The recurring dream of the innocent coquette, the child with the ravishing body, haunted him again as Mamgu came back with the steaming tea.

Out in the untidy Dowlais streets the damp wind gusted dark scurrying clouds across the sky. He walked her quickly down to the yellow lamplit corner. They paused for a moment and he shielded her from the icy blast with his body. He felt the spray of her loose dark hair in his face and caught the tang of her expensive perfume in his nostrils. For the first time he really studied her face, peculiarly illuminated by the weak yellow lamplight which the gusty wind caused to flicker like a wan flame. A general description of her features he supposed would be that they displayed a haughty sensuality. The haughtiness attributable to a somewhat aloof expression in the eyes emphasised by a head tilted slightly back on a slender neck, the sensuality almost entirely due to the full pouting Jewish lips, fellatial lips he thought them. The cheekbones were high and the cheeks hollow, the look of inbred quality, and yet paradoxically there was a certain animalism too. Not just the loose flowing hair, it was more than that. A glint in the eye, a resolution of the chin, no sign of weakening there, definitely a proletarian chin. A stubborn-ness, a wilfulness which he might have to come to terms with.

It was the bardic mysticism which attracted her, he told himself, and so he must woo her with the popular clichéd conception of it, shock and shatter her gentility with a rousing Rabelaisian exhibition. The angry young man levelling everything with his axe of truth until all was reduced to a basic level of honest reality.

The descension was certainly quicker than the long haul up to the summit and they were soon welcomed back to the suffocatingly warm backroom of the Dowlo with knowing nods and winks in John's direction. Roger and co had departed in high dudgeon on their return from the coal arch expedition to the absence of Josephine. Which pleased John no end. They were quickly supplied with drinks by Dave and all around people were babbling heartily, but for old mother Macarthy who cried silently in the corner as she did every Saturday night for as long as anybody could remember. Nobody knew why she cried except perhaps her Cymro Irish son who sang softly to her of the "old country".

Betty the buxom barmaid came in with a cheerful smile to collect the empty glasses and gave John a mock remonstrative scowl. "Come on," Dave called, "drink up or we'll be too late for the dance."

"You are coming to the dance," John instructed Josephine.

"Dance. What dance?"

"What dance? What dance? The dance to end all dances of course : the danse macabre." No Saturday night could be complete for any self respecting hedonist without a visit to the Dowlais Catholic Hall dance.

51

The insanity of the crowded dance was over. Geraint had been sick all over his suede shoes. Bill had latched onto a big blousy redheaded divorcee and sloped off to his Market Street bachelor pad. Dave and Ted had picked up two snub nosed cousins from a deserted hamlet high up on the black hill, one of several which had formerly served the myriad drift mines with which the mountains south of the farewell rock were littered. Josephine had laddered her silk stockings from thigh to toe. And several yobbos had been ejected by Father O'Halloran for fighting in the middle of the crowded floor for the prize of escorting Pretty Polly, the well loved nymphomaniac, to her tiny tidy hovel in Brynseion Close. Father O'Halloran enjoyed these regular skirmishes almost as much as he relished Polly's confessions. But the cacophony had now subsided, the mirrored globe which had cast it's magic reflections into every dark corner had ceased revolving and the place had emptied as if someone had pulled a plug in the middle of the chalky floor. John had sweated himself sober and now the fine wind blown cold rain was fresh and refreshing on his face.

"Danse macabre it certainly was," she confirmed with a hint of bemused ire. A bedraggled throng, plastic macs flung over dance dresses and suits struggled to board the fleet of overcrowded double decked buses. "Well," she paused awkwardly, waiting for him to make the essential move.

"I suppose I should do the decent thing and offer to take you home." It didn't sound as gallant as he intended.

"Don't know that I should accept," she teased. "Mum's away on business. You might try to take advantage of the situation."

Be bold, be brave, be bawdy, he thought. They reached the place were her sporty Volvo was parked so obtrusively in the dingy back street. "So long as I can get inside your lovely vulva, er Volvo, that's what Id really like." It was a clumsy double entendre and she let it pass without comment.

Soon the streets of Dowlais were left behind and the mist hung low over the common as they sped through the drab deserted main street of Brynmawr down through Gilwern and across to Crickhowell. Now he was on her territory. Up a narrow road onto a long parkland drive to the stepped portal to what could only be described as a country mansion. At the entrance to the drive an archway with the title Carnford Manor, was this whimsy or megalomania. Were these the new Guests. Did she really see herself as a new Lady Charlotte, pillar of high society, friends in high places, a litterateur and philanthropist? If so it was as Marx had stated, history repeating itself as farce. Now *he* felt an even deeper resentment. This was not just the domicile of the well off, this was the manse of someone seriously rich. John knew of course of the existence of such places and often wondered what kind of lives their inhabitants lived. He had some outdated notion of the old landed gentry quietly eking out their dwindling fortunes in a kind of genteel poverty, but this old pile belonged to the nouveau riche. Electronically operated garage doors of a "coach house" adjacent to the elegant Georgian facade welcomed them into its heart without getting their hair wet.

The door from the back of the garage opened into the hallway of the house. A magnificent curving stairway swept grandly to the upper floors . The hallway floor itself was of highly polished grey and white Italian marble, elegant and exotic, a far cry from the scrubbed limestone slabs of Mamgu's tiny "hallway". He was awestruck but tried manfully not to show it. "The rates must set you back a bit," he said weakly. "I bet mummy has to do some part time work to make ends meet."

The door off the hallway opened into a magnificently elegant lounge. A huge Adam fireplace dominated one wall and the flick of a switch saw its hearth burst into a realistic flame. He'd thought such effects were only to be found in Hollywood. He'd seen dangerous femme fatales reduce square jawed hard guys to jelly in such settings.

Antique but comfortable furniture filled the room and the oak floor was almost covered with an ankle deep cream rug. The lighting was concealed and soft and a hi-fi unit and TV were housed in the opposite wall to the Adam, tastefully hidden behind limed oak facades. A small alcove in the lateral wall provided an amply provisioned bar, the glistening rows advertising every conceivable agent of alcoholic delirium. The other wall was lined from floor to ceiling with shelves crammed with books of every shape and size.

"Job lot was it?" he commented dryly.

"You don't know mum," she retorted. "A genuine bibliophile. I'm sure she enjoys some kind of perverted sexual pleasure simply browsing in second hand bookshops...and she reads them too."

He glanced at the poetry selection, all neatly arranged in alphabetical order. "I'm impressed ," he said. "Owen, Sassoon, Auden, Eliot; Thomas, Keats, Shakespeare and Idris Davies; Watkins, Milton, Yeats; Hopkins, Larkin, Yeats, but none of mine. Perhaps we ought to be introduced, your mother and I, poetically speaking."

"No way," she warned, "poetically or otherwise."

"Why ever not?"

She eased herself into the seat before the fire and stretched her nylon clad toes out towards it wriggling them with the satisfied expression of one scratching an itch. "Because poor mum would be a pushover for a brash young genius like you. But more to the point, a brash young genius like you would be a pushover for a beautiful sophisticate like her."

"But she must be...." he started but she interrupted with a flourish of her arm.

"Mother," she announced. He looked back to where she pointed wondering how Mother had made such a silent entrance. For a moment he was nonplussed by her absence, then his eye was drawn to the large whitewood framed portrait a la Gaugin which for some extraordinary inexplicable, probably Freudian, reason had not registered initially. A magnificent beautiful nude woman reclined on a white rug strewn with scarlet roses, one of which she pressed seductively to the nipple of her left breast. Close inspection revealed a tiny worm " i 'the bud". The figure itself was perfection in every detail. Her every supple curve and turn masterfully rendered on the canvass. The hair was raven black, eyes dark and brooding, the pose feline yet nymphlike and virginal. Hers were the pouting fellatial lips of the daughter with a hint of sensual promise in the smile that was still somehow innocent. It was a portrait of stunning perfection executed by an artist of superb talent who had clearly *known* and loved his model. He was self consciously aware of the awed expression which registered on his face.

"She must have been a lovely young woman," he deliberately understated the disturbing effect that the portrait had on him.

"Is," she corrected. "Is a lovely woman. Dad commissioned it for her fortieth birthday when he knew he was dying, by that Italian buffoon, very effeminate, very expensive, and it must be admitted, very good. He makes a fortune painting the bright young wives of the rich and famous. They all think he's safe, but I very much doubt it. That look on her face celebrates something more than an artists intuition. So you see I would certainly not be happy to let her loose on you. At least not until I've had my wicked way and done with you." The inflexion was playful but tinged with something more bitter. He was not entirely at ease with her frankness. Rich sophisticated bitches unencumbered with respectably middle class sexual morality was an idyllic concept. But now that the dinner was set steaming on the plate before him he felt like a peasant presented with haute cuisine , unsure of the correct basis on which to proceed according to the strict rules of etiquette.

"And exactly which page of Debretts did she step from?" he asked.

"The Dowlais Jones's actually," she replied. "True proletarian stock. She started as a fifteen year old on the shop floor. I've a photograph of her in her turban and overalls. My father must have reacted to her in exactly the way you just responded to her portrait, though it was a more primitive beauty in those days. They were married within six months, much to the extreme annoyance of my grandfather, which continued up to and beyond my father's death.

"There was a protracted legal battle over the will. To cut it short she made an out of court settlement which the Masons considered to be an offer they couldn't refuse. Out of sheer obstinacy she used the Mason's name to set up her new company while they held on to Poliakoffs. Her's was the small underwear offshoot which she had persuaded my father to establish. The Poliakoffs got the then thriving cotton business. In the five years since then she's become the biggest nylon lingerie producer in the country. Twelve flourishing branches, the headquarters of which she has always insisted, with an obstinacy that runs counter to her otherwise impeccable business acumen, on maintaining here in Dowlais." The tone was strange mixture of jealous resentment and idolatrous admiration.

"All that and beauty too," was all he could think of in response.

"So you can see why I don't want you within a hundred miles of her, so let's forget about her. How about finding something nice to say about me?"

He slipped into the role of the great seducer again, rising and striding nonchalantly to the cocktail bar pouring out a large Glenfiddick and a G and T with a dash of Angostura. He placed them casually on the mosaic table in front of the sofa and sat beside her, taking her hand. "You're very beautiful," he said, "I want to make love to you very much," and drew her to him and kissed her softly on those full pouting fellatial lips. Her reaction was one of almost withdrawn total surrender. There was no rebuttal when his hand stole to her breast, but no gasp of sexual pleasure either, just a slight barely discernible reciprocation of pressure, the smallest intake of breath inflating almost imperceptibly her beautifully formed bosom.

Here was a girl who clearly always wanted to be in full control. There was no complaint when his hand slid down the contours of her lithe body, around her hip and thigh and cautiously up her skirt until he cupped it comfortably over her soft mons veneris. He stroked her gently for a little while, opening her with his middle finger, and still the only evidence of her arousal was the moist secretion seeping slowly through the sheen of her chic underwear.

It was strange, so long as she retained her self control he found that he could too, whereas at this stage of the ritual proceedings he would have been half delirious with uncontrolled sexual passion. Suddenly she restrained his probing hand.

"Put something romantic on the hi-fi," she said calmly, and he responded like an automaton. The "hi-fi" was, at that, the ultimate in stereophonic technology, a Bang and Oluffsen system housed in an art deco cabinet. He pulled a sleeve at random from the vertically stacked LP's and dropped it on the precision balanced turntable. He returned to her with the sound of soothing strings pouring through the room like oversweet honey. He benefited from the short intermission, no longer overawed by the situation. The facility to shock returned. She was after all just another valleys girl, richer certainly and perhaps a little more sophisticated, but her psychology revolved around her genital orifice just like all the rest. If his conventional unconventionality was the key to its unlocking then his whole vocabulary of hackneyed clichés was at her disposal.

He stripped off slowly and calmly, non erectus, and the balance of power was immediately tilted in his direction. Her eyes drank in his unaroused condition. Her cheeks flushed and her nipples swelled. Her expression betrayed her incomprehension. He kneeled and placed his head between her thighs.

"The deed is higher than the word, as Trotski once said," he told her, pulling down her black damp pants and drinking deeply of her succulence. Her immediate reaction was to grab his hair and push him away. Instead she fell back drawing him to her, opening her thighs and thrusting her hips hard up into his face. He continued sucking until her gyrations became uncontrolled and spasmodic and she began to make long low moaning noises like an animal in pain. He greedily devoured the copious flow of her shuddering orgasm before rising and easily entering her.

"Oh no, please no," she sobbed, but soon he had brought her to the heights of a new sensual experience. It was pleasure which bordered on the threshold of pain. His own orgasm was as nothing compared with hers. He held her on the peak so long that the tears rolled down her cheeks and she began to scream. He held his hand over her mouth to stifle the cries and she bit him savagely.

"Bitch," he cursed, "bitch, bitch, bitch, bi-ii-tch," thrusting and quickening until he spent his seed in her. His bitten fingers hurt like hell and blood dripped onto the expensive upholstery, but every time he made to withdraw from her she clung to him like a frightened child. Her ecstasy had been agony. She had so completely lost control. It was a new experience for her and it frightened her.

Her previous lovers ,of which Roger Cavendish was an example, had been shallow and inconsequential, and she had derived the greatest sexual pleasure from those she could most easily dominate. Best of all had been obtained by skilful masturbation with digital and index finger in that pre-vibrator age, coupled with fantasies of submission. Manifestation of the dominatrix were however well concealed. She was the kind of young woman who could make a man feel that he was having his way by utilising all the attributes of demure feminine charm secure in the knowledge that she was in total control and clinically having hers.

This time had been different. She had been completely overwhelmed and it had terrified her. She could not rest now until he had prostrated himself at her feet and licked her shoes, if not actually then metaphorically. Then she would give herself coldly, wide eyed, while he destroyed himself inch by inch and a slow prolonged paroxysm until she devoured him. Until then she would submit herself helplessly fulfilling his every whim and desire.

He took her to her sumptuous bed and she fell asleep almost instantly like a sated child. He looked at her and there was something about her even in sleep which lacked innocence. He lay awake with her head in the crook of his arm trying desperately not to think of the timeliness of fate and the possibilities which the exploitation of this relationship might offer. Would it not be a kind of revenge on the ghosts of Guest and Crawshay?

The rain drove in gusts against the window, swirling down from the hills where the Chartists had fashioned their failed revolution, making marvellous swelling sea noises in the leaves of the oaks swaying like demented demons in the stormy night. The voices of the restless spirits remonstrating with him for his callousness and wept for his long lost innocence. He lay back, looked at the expression of sweet repose on her face, closed his eyes and allowed the distorted remembrance of the long fall from grace to disturb his consciousness.

The images drifted like a silver fog into the room and the ceiling became a flickering screen displaying the heroic exploits of the Hollywood heroes of his adolescence. The musical accompaniment dantarantanned with the rhythm of restless drums as it always did. He was sixteen, sweet and innocent and looked around at the white halflit faces with eyes transfixed on the silver screen with the avaricious apprehension of an adolescent desperate to rid himself of the embarrassing epithet of *virgin* .

Maggie O'Leary sat opportunely at the end of the row with her little sister Kate and returned his look of desperation with a smile less enigmatic than the Mona Lisa. Maggie had been smiling at him like that for the last three programme changes in the Victoria Cinema, the Vic, even during the Curse of the Werewolf which had been last Saturday's main feature. He knew Maggie through her brother Skinny. Maggie wasn't skinny, she was pleasantly ripe and rounded. He had watched her bathing through the cracked front room door at Skinny's invitation. She shared her bath with an older sister Merle who was a goddess as far beyond his wildest dreams as the screen sirens he adored. These were the days long before the terraces of Dowlais grew a rash of grant aided bathroom extensions and most bathnights, traditionally Friday night, took place in the 'front room', in a zinc bath.

Later that summer he'd had to masturbate madly in the balcony toilet of the open air baths in Pant after she had shamelessly teased him by stroking herself in her tight fitting one piece until her gusset was soaking wet - and alongside her Merle simply lounged dismissively with whisps of stray black curls carelessly escaping hers.

Suddenly as his focus of attention shifted to the mammarian marvel, Jane Russell, as she gave her all to sweat away the fever of the wounded Billy the Kid, (who wouldn't get wounded for that kind of medical treatment) a small hand tugged at his sleeve. "Maggie said she'll meet you at the top of the White Road," the little girl said tersely, with the quizzical expression of appraisal of a child with a knowledge far beyond her tender years. "She said to gimme thruppence for chips. Dad will give 'er a beltin' if he finds out."

His hand felt behind the grubby handkerchief in the pocket without a hole in it for a loose threepenny bit which he handed over like an automaton, wondering if the angelic creature might be better bought off with a sixpence. The child took it with the sly smile of a shared act of wrongdoing and he knew in that moment that his soul was lost.

Half an hour later he stood in the corrugated bus shelter at the top of the White Road, stamping his feet and rubbing his hands. He didn't want to hear complaints about cold hands when he finally caressed those orbs which had been the subject of his erotic dreams since last summer. He hadn't envisaged it happening suddenly like this, though he had lived every day in constant hope since leaving school on his fifteenth birthday and becoming a man of the world. Now with the advent ticking down to its realisation he felt completely unprepared for it.

An eternal quarter of an hour and the gnawing doubts began to torment his fevered mind. She hadn't actually stipulated any particular time now that he considered it. She hadn't even positively indicated tonight. But the thruppence for chips surely meant that. Could it be another hour, another night, next week. Why hadn't he been more authoritative with the little brat. Perhaps Maggie had nothing at all to do with it, it was all a threepenny scam. Then just as he abandoned hope she appeared striding imperiously down the hill past the Carnegie library dressed in the fashionable translucent red rubber mac carelessly belted at the waist with a pixie hood pulled up against the drizzle obscuring her lovely untidy Irishly auburn hair.

"Me big bad wolf, you little Red Riding Hood," he joked with mock confidence.

"Me big bad Red Riding Hood, you little cub," she corrected knowingly. "Sorry I'm late. I had to wait til dad went off to work - he's on nights, and send Katie for some chips to keep her quiet. Mary Morris, big Mary next door is keeping an eye on her. " She hooked her arm under his. "Come on," she said," can't leave her for long Skinny'll be home soon and I don't want him knowing about this or everybody in Mason's will know about it. That's where we work."

"Yeah," he said. "Skinny told me. Allright there is it."

"Allright? Bloody white slave market innit. Told me you got an apprenticeship. ICI Chemicals. Posh. Come on I know a good place." She led him down the White Road past the Army and Air Cadets huts and up the steps of the huge high dressed limestone wall where the furnaces of Dowlais Ironworks had once lit up the developing world of railways and steam.

"Where are we going?"

"Caeharris sidings. Have you ever ridden first class?"

Her double entendre was scaringly exciting. Why wasn't he prepared, he thought, as he had been taught by the scouts, the earlier taunt still fresh in his mind. Why hadn't he the nonchalance to say : "and a packet of three Bryn", like the older apprentices who strolled with adult ease into Bryn the Barber's little shop without even the pretext of 'just a quick trim' in the hope that he would enquire 'and something for the weekend sir'.

"I know all about you," she interrupted his foreboding, and he wondered which of his many foibles she had magically divined. "My friend Polly told me all about you, Polly Prosser, you know." He knew. Rolly Polly worked in Mason's too of course. Well half the girls in Dowlais did. What could Polly have said to intrigue Maggie, the furthest he had ever got with her was sticky fingers, which was above par for his track record to date. "She told me you talk like a preacher but you got hands like the restless wind that yearns to wander." She paraphrased the popular Frankie Laine song. There was more to Maggie than met the eye, at least she knew the value of a simile which was more than could be said for the majority of the Mason's girls.

"Well yes it's true that I am very religious," he replied sternly. "But hands that yearn to wander, I don't know about that." Sliding a hand down her rubbery back until he could feel the wobbulations of her mysterious mechanism as she walked. She led him over the old cinder tip around what was now the Ifor Foundry football pitch, the foundry was the surviving tiny rump of the once huge ironworks; past the magnificent derelict engine house, Guest housed his machinery in a palace which contrasted starkly with the hovels of his workers, and finally to their destination the Caeharris railway halt sidings. Although this was pre-Beeching the halt was almost derelict and long abandoned relics of the steam age rusted and rotted in the bleak railway graveyard. "Is it safe," he asked realising her intention. "Isn't there a guard or something?"

"More people ride in this train every night than the August bank holiday special to Barry Island," she replied opening a carriage door and shutting it again immediately to grunts and curses from the occupants. "Ah well," she sighed. "It won't be First Class tonight, that's the only First in the place, that's my favourite." So it was that they ended up in Third. It had the musty smell unique to neglected railway carriages of the steam age, a mixture of damp and smoke and cigarettes.

The initiation could not be said to be sublime. It was over almost as soon as it had started. Instead of mocking his lack of performance as he expected she held him close and smiling told him it would be better next time as she wiped away the semen from her red mac with his grubby handkerchief. So worldly and yet hardly a year older than he was. No better than she should be but so tender and understanding. Next time, she had said, next time, the words were like a song repeating in his heart as he skipped home. Now he had a real sexual experience to relate to the locker room fraternity, suitably embellished of course, a young widow, a ravishing divorcee. Oh Maggie, Maggie, Maggie.

Over the following months he was diligent apprentice to a skilful mistress.

> *I knew a woman lovely in her bones*
> *When small birds sighed she would sigh back at them;*
> *Ah, when she moved she moved more ways than one*
> *The shapes a bright container can contain!*
> *Of her choice virtues only gods should speak,*
> *Or English poets who grew up on Greek*
> *(I'd have them sing in chorus, cheek to cheek).*

59

How well her wishes went! She stroked my chin,
She taught me Turn and Counterturn and Stand;
She taught me Touch, that undulant white skin;
I nibbled meekly from her proffered hand;
She was the sickle; I, poor I, the rake,
Coming behind her for her pretty sake
(But what prodigious mowing we did make).

*1

They ran the whole gamut of sexual experience - then his attentions turned to Lynda. He was eager to exploit his newly acquired sexual expertise in effecting a *real* conquest. He and Maggie never really terminated their relationship, they simply began to oscillate on a diminished frequency. Maggie's natural promiscuity could never limit her to the constraints of monogamy. When random chance brought them together that was fine, they enjoyed the moment avidly.

The Lynda of childhood kisses had blossomed into a lovely virginal seventeen year old. Since her mother's untimely death she spent more and more time at Mamgu's. Coincidentally John's own visits increased as the plan for the great seduction took form.

Brimming now with self confidence, satisfied that he was equipped with both the knowledge and the expertise for the seduction of such an innocent, Davies the Deacon's daughter was surely easy meat for a man with such savoir faire, he waited the appropriate moment like a predatory cat stalking a delicate bird. It presented itself on that ice cold night which now so regularly chilled his dreams.

At the moment of truth he had lost what he had thought to be his sophisticated urbanity. It had been different and wonderful beyond his wildest expectations. At the crucial moment love had entered into it. "You do love me, say you do."

"Yes, yes, yes." And although in retrospect it was probably true, it was not out of truth that he said it. He did not know the substance of love then. Saying it had been the point of no return, the point when all that mattered to him was the satisfaction of his physical desire.

After the surmounting of that initial most difficult hurdle, the surrender of her virginity, her moral tractability proved to be a revelation. They became the complete cosmopolitan lovers and it wasn't long before initiate was showing the tutor a thing or two. They were obsessed with their new religion. Nothing was too course or vulgar between them in their passion. They had discovered a new sensual universe in which only they existed.

---

[1]From "I knew a Woman" by Theodore Roethke.

Her enthusiastic conversion to the new non-conformity was largely a reaction against the strict Puritanism of her father, the deacon, against all the repression and restriction of childhood and early adolescence, the gnarled hand and the cuffed ears. Davies the deacon's views on sex would have made a Victorian moralist seem like an enlightened Romantic liberal. Sooner or later the confrontation was inevitable and her blatant actions appeared to invite it.

All the lights had been blazing in the house when he called for her. Another flouting of the deacon's frugality, he thought, anticipating an hour of debauchery under that very roof, the deacon on the afternoon shift at Hoover's. There was no reply to his happy ratatat, so he walked boldly in calling her name. Turning towards the stairway, was she waiting for him in her room, he froze. Nothing in all his nightmares could have prepared him for this. He looked away and retched. A grey shapeless mass of flesh dangled in the stairwell, suspended by the neck from a piece of white plaited packing cord. The protruding eyeballs and the wide open mouth with gorged tongue a horrible indication of the botch up which Davies the deacon had made of his suicide. He fought back the urge to retch again and called her name in a panic. Had the bastard found out about them and killed her in his mad puritanical wrath. He heard a murmur from upstairs and rushed with eyes half closed past the hideous mound of cold flesh, going clammy all over as he felt it sway and groan as he brushed it with his shoulder.

As he burst into the bedroom she looked up and smiled. "Hullo love," she said calmly. "He was human after all." And she started to laugh, a strange chuckle at first, gradually giving way to a shrill hysteria as she screamed, and screamed, and screamed and screamed.

Then stopped and smiled again, looking over his shoulder towards the doorway. There was Davies the deacon nude, erect, a wild expression in his eyes, the cord dangling from a horrible wound in his neck. She seized John's hand pulling him with irresistible strength towards her. "Love me, love me," she demanded, her open mouthed kisses soaking his face. Torn between repulsion and surrender he finally gave way in complete abandonment despite the wild eyed monster in the doorway. Alternating with spasms of sheer ecstasy he was aware of the kneeling praying ghost his voice booming, resonating loudly through the house.

"Oh God why makest thou me the instrument of thy wrath," it wailed. "O Absolum my son Absolum," it cried passionately. Then Lynda's voice crying out even as he entered her.

"Enter ye into his gates with praise. Come into his halls with thanksgiving."

"Cleanse our sins oh lord with the blood of the holy lamb. " The shade responded. "Wash us til we're clean as driven snow."

"Tell it not in Gath, publish it not in the streets of Askalon, lest the daughters of the Philistines rejoice."

"O Lord send forth thy vengeful angel. Bless me with thy holy power."

"Lay your sleeping head my father, human on my faithless arm."

The grey figure transmogriphied into a knight in shining golden armour with a huge erect penis. John rolled into the corner cowering. "This is the sword of righteousness, the rod and staff of Moses."

"Father I have sinned. Plunge the sword into my wicked heart and cleanse my soul."

"Cleansed in the blood of the lamb." And with the first thrust of his sword a lightning flash which illuminated the whole world. A tearing open of the thighs, laying bare the secrets of the soul. A scream, a laugh, a cry, a sigh - and silence.

And ever since the Ophelian madness, which is not a madness but a weird game, a mad charade. Readings from Auden and Goethe and the queries, probing, rational and sane. Then the regression to childish innocence, fantasy and fairyland.

Awake, sweat and sticky astride his latest conquest.

"My insatiable pet," she mumbled. "Last thing at night, first thing in the morning. Are you staying for lunch?"

He stared at her uncomprehending for a moment, wondering who she was and where he was.

CHAPTER 5

The ten o'clock bus up to the sprawling council estate where Dave lived was surprisingly full. Early Sunday morning worshippers with a piety strong enough to drag them out of warm beds. They sat sullenly silently staring straight ahead as if Armageddon lay just around the next bend. A prim spectacled woman with a smug Pekinese dog perched insolently on the seat beside her gave him a look which would have frozen a Dowlais furnace. She purchased a ticket for the dog and began to talk to him in endearing terms about the day ahead. John noted a striking resemblance between her and her pampered pet and mused on such a manifestation of narcissism, unless of course she was simply growing daily more like the object of her obsession. She fuelled his speculation with absurd cooing noises to which the animal responded and for one awful moment he envisaged its wet nose burrowing up her skirt while she wailed and coo-ed with canine rapture.

Such thoughts on the Sabbath, he remonstrated with himself and transferred his attention to the admirable gent opposite, poring diligently over his book, no doubt a scriptural tome, or even a philosophical treatise on morality by Kant or Berkeley. The gent furrowed his brow, scratched his nose and closed the book. A paperback with a lurid cover of a blonde lying in a pool of blood with a skirt halfway up her thighs. "Dames Die Young by Mickey Spillane" in bold yellow cursive script.

The p on a notice which was undoubtedly a Kantian imperative. "No Spitting" had been predictably altered to an h. Like everything else in the age of 'never had it so good' Sundays in Merthyr were changing.

The bus swung onto the estate stopping at frequent intervals until it was almost empty. The square featureless red brick buildings which passed for the shopping centre, the artificial heart of this New Jerusalem, one of many spawned by the post war Atlee housing boom and continued enthusiastically by Macmillan (the Tories were essentially of the paternalistic, patronising one nation, 'we know what's best for you' faction in those days) was reminiscent of those Western frontier towns depicted in those cinematic sagas starring Buck Jones, Rod Cameron, Tim Holt and the young John Wayne. All front and no interior they were utilitarian in the most denigratory sense of the word. They didn't even possess the dubiously saving grace of representing a triumph of function over form, because they failed miserably even in the functional element.

Run down communities, which at least had a vibrant heart, were being replaced by the soul-less slums of the near future. The new 'homes fit for heroes' did have the advantages of better sanitary facilities, four square yards of cultivable rectangles at the rear and open plan frontages, ideal repositories for dog turds and free grazing for mangy Merthyr sheep, unlike any other sheep in God's green Welsh acres, with wool like rusty wire, the colour of the coal tips which they grazed to a bare dirty brown.

But worst of all was the monstrous regimentation, like a desert waste, each drab grain identical with its ugly neighbour. It had no soul, no heart, no pulse only the prayer of the faithful, or rather the hopeful with a faraway look in the eye, that by some miracle a spurious grain might spit some life into it's fellow. The bus pulled into it's terminus and John dropped off the platform with one hand clutching the vertical rail while it was still in motion, the impetus propelling him forward until he almost collided with a battered dolls high pram pushed by a demure angel with a dirty face.

"Careful mister," she scolded with a gap toothed smile, "it took me ages to get the naughty little bugger to sleep. If she wakes up now she's goin' to get a good smacked arse cos she's gettin' on my bloody nerves she is." He apologised and as she passed looked under the hood. Instead of the expected grubby china headed rag doll, the age of plastics had not yet come into it's ubiquitous own, there lay an empty beer flagon with a dirty hanky for a bonnet tied carefully around it's neck.

"What a sweet little baby," he congratulated the child who smiled capriciously and passed on her way calling back.

"Trouble is I'm bloody pregnant again an' I 'aven't got this little bugger off the breast yet." Perhaps there was hope for the new generation after all, perhaps the drab grains were already starting to spit life into one another.

The Watkins' were up and about, except for Dave who was enjoying his customary Sunday morning lie in, recuperating from the excesses of the night before. John sat by a stoked up fire while Mrs Watkins went to the foot of the stairs calling Dave with a high pitched nasal shriek which would have roused Lazarus. A few minutes later Dave literally stumbled down the stairs and into the stuffy overheated room, stubble chinned and red eyed. "Good God," he exclaimed looking queryingly from John to the clock, "it's not even lunchtime yet." He acknowledged John with a curt nod, poured himself a cuppa from the ever brewing pot on the fireside hob and grabbed a piece of cold toast from the messy uncleared breakfast table. "Let's go down the studio," he said through a half chewed mouthful, articulating the vowels of *studio* a la a BBC newscaster, no regional cadences in those days. So they made their way out to the ramshackle shed at the bottom of the uncultivated 'garden'.

Dave carried his tea and toast with him wearing a thin vest and faded blue denims, the flies of which were precariously unzipped, were in fact unzippable. The dark haired wife of the dangerously aggressive next door neighbour observed with smiling admiration as she irreverently hung her, what were at this time considered to be shamelessly exotic underwear on the Sunday line, taking advantage of a rare break in the dismal weather. She had the dark raven haired beauty of a Romany. Of tinker antecedents she had lived previously in the Bogey Road settlement of ramshackle caravans in the wasteland dunes of the old Dowlais ironworks.

"Hullo Ann my love," Dave greeted. "Haven't seen those black lacy ones on you before."

"Nor off me - yet," she responded with a coy smile. " 'Ullo John love. Don't see much of my little sister these days then? She misses you. Dunno why you bother with the likes of 'im though," indicating Dave with her thumb. She turned her back on them and continued to hang her washing on the line. As she stretched she emphasised her lissom figure, a figure that John knew well from Dave's sketches and paintings.

Her husband was doing a six month stretch at Swansea for stealing the lead off the roof of Cyfarthfa Church and sundry other holy buildings, and she was far too vibrant a woman to be chaste for long. She had never taken those silly vows anyway. Despite three young children she had the figure of one of those long legged dancers of the Hollywood musicals, Cyd Charisse, which haunted the dreams of the adolescents of their generation.

Little sister Eileen, Ann with puppy fat, had been a shortlived passion for John. Sister had obviously confided in sister and now Ann seemed to hold him in some kind of esteem. This baffled John for Eileen had remained stoically virginal despite a month of persistent wooing. It was she who finally dumped him for a fellow apprentice at ICI with a reputation for conquests about which he was happy to embellish with intimate detail. One such detail imparted quite candidly to John was her disappointment that he, John, seemed unable to determine when "No" really meant "Yes".

Some of Dave's best work to date were the studies of Ann which he had completed in recent months. This had led to long and serious discourse on the effect of such a relationship on an artists creativity. The artist could certainly not attain that degree of dispassionate interest in the subject which Collingwood demanded as a pre-requisite for a 'work of art'. The upshot of which was a general agreement with Lawrence's contempt for that whole aesthetic movement epitomised by the Bloomsburies in his description of Duncan Bell and his accolytes as "dung beetles". The matter, like most argument and discussion at the Dowlo got lost and laid aside with the onset of serious drinking to be picked up again at some future conference on aesthetics when the participants had gained some further practical insights on the issue. Praxis was their Marxist watchword.

Dave blew her a kiss over the broken fence then stuck the stale toast between his teeth while he fished for the key to the studio, now carefully secured against the prying eyes of puritanical parents. Inside the place was strewn with all the paraphernalia of the developing artist; oils, rags, canvases, brushes, pots of poster paint and a myriad other bits and pieces. A high powered bulb hung nakedly from a frayed flex. The windows on either side were shuttered against the world, secured with large black bolts accessible only from inside. On the easel a canvass awash with an orgy of vivid energetically applied colour, on first consideration abstract and yet it had substance, a vaguely familiar form.

"This ," Dave explained, "is the reason for my dissipated appearance." Unlike you I was not frolicking in anyone's bed last night, and the lovely Ann had no direct part to play in it I'm sorry to say. Last night my art was my mistress." He stroked his stubbled chin. "Four o'clock this morning I finished it," he mused ruefully, stepping back to make a fresh appraisal.

"What the fuck is it supposed to symbolise you untidy untalented dauber."

"Symbolise. Who said anything about symbolism?"

"Well you're always on to me about obscurity in modern poetry. Why don't you practice what you preach? I've never seen anything more obscure in all your years as a Royal Academician."

"Christ all bloody mighty man, it's as plain as the nipples on lovely Ann's tits." He pulled out a recently completed canvas from a pile of frames on which Ann was depicted as Aphrodite rising from a sea of rumpled bedclothes. He held it aloft to catch the light and waved at Ann in the flesh squinting in at them only a matter of yards away in the adjacent garden. She chuckled and shook her head from side to side in mock remonstration.

The breasts John complained were excessively exaggerated, indicative of Dave's neurotic obsession. Though he had to admit to himself that this was not really true as he watched Ann stretch the thin fabric of her dress taut across her full form as she reached deliberately for the high line, smiling teasingly at his rapt attention. He looked away returning her smile, one felt no embarrassment with Ann he mused. "Eureka I have it," he shouted, looking at the canvas again. "It's rock and roll at the Catholic Hall."

Dave struck a rickety table with his fist in triumph and gave a little bow cocking his head to one side. "There you see," he crowed delightedly," how much more objective it is than all that obscure unmetrical unrhymed nonsense which passes for poetry with you lot."

"I was being facetious," John roared with outrage. "How typical to take a derogatory remark and turn it to your own advantage. Unprincipled bastards like you make capital out of everything - particularly other people's talent or misfortune. You're destined to go far Dai Watkins. Your kind inherit the earth and piss on the meek.

"You'd have smirked with self satisfaction if I'd said that the bloody thing looked like nothing if not Dowlais Lucania shit house, which on mature reflection it certainly does. Green baize, multicoloured balls, a cue or perhaps a thin syphilitic prick and all that drab brown dirty shit. In fact your whole working environment, this crummy stuffy shed full of detritus which you euphemistically call your 'study', is very reminiscent of the Lucania shit house - graffiti splashed on canvas and called art.

"Come on Dai bach with your muffler and scarf, let's get out into the fresh free mountain air. I'll recall memorable words of some great forgotten men, including my own, men whose names were not writ in water but on the wind. I'll sing them to you and inspire you to real art. Forget all this, this pornography," he indicated the pile of canvases with derision. " This is nothing but sophisticated masturbation. You might just as well come all over them with that big ugly dick of yours. Without that prick you'd be an intellectual cripple, all your grey matter is contained inside it's great dome. Between those floppy ears there is nothing but a lake of sterile semen."

Dave smiled to himself with satisfaction in the knowledge that John was at his most derisive when he was most impressed. "Glad you like it. I'll pull some decent pants on for the sake of Sunday Welsh respectability," he said, "and we'll climb the hill and sit behind Bethania and listen to sad souls pleading with a cruel God."

Bethania was a monument to Welsh architecture. It stood solemn and square among its slanting moss covered gravestones in a large open field high on the mountainside. It was miles from nowhere and yet its pews were as packed for Sunday service as the Dowlo on a Saturday night. It was the centre of traditional non-conformist culture in Merthyr. Its choir competed successfully in eisteddfodau and its minister made verses like the Reverend Eli Jenkins, in Welsh. The sermons these days alternated weekly between Gods own language and English reflecting the political divisions in the ranks of the deacons between the Nats and Labour.

The charismatic Caradog Prys had been responsible for its erection in the days of the roaring ironworks. He had built it away from the sinful contamination of the cosmopolitan town, wrought by the hands of his fanatical followers from the drab grey rock quarried from the nearby limestone belt, which had been worked from time immemorial in these bleak hills. The quarries, supplying the insatiable appetites of Dowlais, Cyfarthfa, Penydarren and Plymouth, which together constituted the greatest iron producing complex in the world, ringed the town like the towers of a great fortress.

At the opening service Prys had dedicated the ugly monument to the purification of the scarred Welsh soul. With eloquent rhetorical hwyl, which bordered on the edge of heresy, he was scathing in his condemnation of a system which flourished on the exploitation of man by man, and prophetically predicted that it would stand as a symbol of their aspirations long after the furnace fires were snuffed out in the basin down below. Now it stood, gaunt and impressive in its ugliness, staring down on the even uglier ruin and dereliction of the great ironworks. The scarred soul as yet unpurified.

On the hill above the chapel overlooking the ramshackle town the friends sat listening to the plaintive old Welsh hymns drifting up to them. They would have loved to discover parallels with the Negro spirituals but sadly there were none. The links between chapel and protest were there, Prys was testament to that, Chartism had been preached from the pulpit. But there was little or no expression of protest let alone revolution in the hymns, and the popular music which grew from the hymnal as exemplified in Joseph Parry was essentially romantic.

Further north and higher up over the brow of Galon Uchaf the bleak brown hills of Dowlais with its own wasteland and its gigantic greywhite Atlas, table topped slag slab jutted out and hovered over the untidy cluster of humble dwellings that was Penyard, grown like a cancerous scab from the molten wastes of the Goat Mill furnaces.

Down below lay Merthyr Tydfil, the dirty Taf winding its way through the overgrown spoilheaps and ruins of the old works and the narrow streets of tiny hovels that had been thrown up haphazardly cheek by jowl with the furnaces, brooded over by the absurd gothic folly of Cyfarthfa Castle. It was set among pinewoods and flower gardens fronted by a lake fed constantly with clean fresh water diverted from the Taf Fechan through a limestone feeder a mile upstream above the filth and squalor responsible for the plague of Cholera which ravaged the denizens of the dirty hovels. John's eyes flashed angrily at the scene and all it symbolised.

A squall of seagulls suddenly swooped and squabbled for some titbit in the shallow waters of the bilious Taf bringing to mind the words of Idris Davies from 'The Angry Summer' and 'Tonypandy'

> *Those few smooth gulls from the Severn*
> *Floating and crying below the clouds*
> *Complaining and floating above the valleysides*
> *Do the sea birds awaken our sorrows at dusk*
> *There at the corner of Pandy Square*
> *As they circle and sigh above the slag heaps*
> *And the narrow brown river trickling*
> *Between the crooked streets and the colliery sidings?*
> *Are they as poems from the Severn Sea*
> *Sad little lyrics born on the dusk wind*
> *Over the coastal plains and over the valleys*
> *Up to the mountains and mists of Glamorgan*
> *Haunting the twilight, haunting the heart?*

"So bloody ugly - yet so bloody beautiful," he muttered to nobody in particular. The wind drifted wistfully up from Bethania carrying the plaintive cry of a people in chains, '*I bob un sy'n ffyddlon* ', to a long absent God to whom their tenacious faith incomprehensibly adhered.

The friends remained staring silently at the ruined town, a scab on the lovely hills which lay beyond, unravaged. No words were needed.

"What about this bloody strike then," Dave said at last, breaking the long silence. The hymns had stopped and the worshippers retreated down the lane back to the estate and back to the buses.

"Fuck the bloody strike," John muttered. "I'm no longer involved in it am I?"

"Come on John you can't be really serious about that." Dave chided. "Christ you've only got a month to go to complete your apprenticeship."

"Another month would be a month too late," John replied. "It's been working up to this Dave - you know that."

"Yes but, well it isn't just you is it. You can't let the bastards get away with it again. And your workmates - they struck for you. What about the struggle, you always advocated struggle."

"I dunno' Dave. We always seem to be struggling in the wrong place at the wrong time for the wrong things. They always seem to set the agenda. We fight at their time, at their place, on their terms and what do we get out of it - bugger all. If we strike for eight percent and win it's only reflected by a ten percent increase in prices and we end up worse off than we started.

"Reduced profit is not an option for the investor, the graph has to go forever up, another step in the giddy inflationary process. It's always heads they win, tails we lose every time. The real struggle just isn't taking place - the struggle for control. It still lies firmly in the hands of an elite clique. They've got the whole country by the balls and all they have to do is give a little squeeze and we're all begging for mercy.

"And what does our Party, the glorious Labour Party offer as an alternative - a socialism so watered down as to be insipid. On the other hand 'enlightened' Conservatives give us Toryism with the rough edges sanded off sufficient to satisfy the demands of a drugged and stupid lumpenproletariat for fags and beer and baked beans. Neither prospect seems to me to bear the promise of a social revolution does it?"

Dave rubbed his chin ruefully. "I don't think sleeping with the enemy has done much for your political analysis boyo. Faced with two alternatives the only choice is for the least worse. Getting the Labour Party elected would be at least a start - something on which to build. It's a slow Fabian process John, we always knew that. There's no such thing as instant socialism, that was always a pipe dream.

"As artists we can have a unique part to play in accelerating things. We've discussed this into the early hours. We can protest and prognosticate freely with no party whip to restrain us. Our influences can transcend all the usual boundaries, even narrow class bigotries. It's no accident that among the very first groups to be proscribed in totalitarian regimes are always the artists. We can transform the lumpen by speaking to them, for them. It's our role to shape, or at least modulate the future. The true poets, painters, novelists and philosophers that we envisaged as the vanguard of the revolution have sharp axes. Uncluttered by the pragmatics and downright lies of the professional politicians ours is the closest it is possible to get to an unviolated and pure ideology."

John stared at him in open mouthed amazement. "That's so much crap Dave," he challenged. "Pure Platonic crap. Fuck the dictatorship of the proletariat, replace it with the dictatorship of the best - who happen to be people like us - artists.

"It's been tried before man. Bone up on your history of ancient Greece.

"I can't wait comrade. I can't wait for the Fabian process to work itself through. It will take for bloody ever. The Webbs and Shaw have been dead a long time. I listened to the old man coughing his lungs up the other morning. I saw a faded photo of him with me on his shoulders. He was young, really young you know. I never knew him like that. He must have grown old overnight.

"He was a disciple of Cook and Horner and the rest, he campaigned for S O and Nye, and he waited - waited for the process to work its way through, education, slow but sure social reform, all that marvellous Labour Party stuff, the soft soap, the soft pedal. He's still waiting. He was misled and now we're in danger of falling for it too. Gaitskell, Crossland, Wilson, Jenkins, Callaghan and all, is theirs the road to the New Jerusalem for fuck sake. Yet theirs is still the predominant philosophy in the Party.

"As for the artists role, it's surely not enough merely to prognosticate. When society is in crisis the only truth is to be found in action. The artist must identify fully with the progressive element in such a society. As a Marxist that can only mean the exploited class, the workers, even the lumpen. Not by telling what they must do but going out and doing it."

"Oh. And going out and doing it means opting out of trade unionism because you've come to the sudden illuminating conclusion that the issue is just too trivial. Balls to all those poor misguided sods you used to be so concerned about, you hypocritical bastard."

John laughed and lay back on the flat grey limestone rock. The breeze blew chill now across the valley. "I'm not opting out brother," he chuckled. "As comrade Trotski was more than once to exclaim , 'infiltrate'. But not the Labour Party, where's the sense in that. No my friend the door to the temple of the priests of High Toryism has been left ajar and I intend to slip inside."

"You mean that daft bloody deb?" Dave reacted with alarm, his eyes flashing angrily. "You really intend to sell out?"

John held up his hands in mock horror and laughed again. "Now friend, comrade, brother Watkins, remember the basic principles of infiltration. First get inside and then...." Dave's angry expression melted, a smile lit his dark eyes, a grin spread across his face and he began to chuckle. John's chuckle joined and augmented his until it swelled to outrageous laughter. They laughed helplessly until the tears poured down their cheeks.

"I always knew the revolution would start in the genitals of the grande bourgeoisie," Dave managed at last.

"The trouble with you, as I've already stated earlier, is that all your grey matter is......"

"Yes, yes, but it does make my intellectual exercise so much more enjoyable."

CHAPTER 6

"Late again then Ted."

"Aye. Late again John."

John and Ted converged on the gatehouse simultaneously, like two squaddies on a route march quickstepping down the dirty road, Ted stretching out his long legs in giant strides and John comically almost running to keep up.

The bike had failed to start yet again, even with the benefit of a shallow incline for a bumpstart. Now John's hands were covered in a black greasy ooze smudged across a sweaty brow with the back of an exasperated hand as he raced once more against his enemy the clock. The absurdity of it was that it didn't matter a tinker's cuss if he was late today, his last day. Yet his stomach was convulsed with the usual dread of seeing once more the red asterisk on his clocking in card which the insidious machine automatically printed indicating a deduction from his pay.

"Well that fucking strike was short and sweet wasn't it," Ted muttered. "The great man of the people intervened as you said he would, saving the country from disaster and demonstrating what a reasonable lot you Labour Party people really are. Doesn't all this shit get you down? You're not really going to apologise are you."

John shook his head breathless with the effort of keeping up. "I'm out of it Ted. My resignation's on Heydock's desk. I've got two weeks coming in lieu of notice. I've come to say goodbye, pick up a few personal bits and pieces then I'm off to dedicate my life to love and art."

"So the bastards win again," Ted said cynically. "Your resignation will be taken as an admission of guilt. I told you so often before, the only thing the bastards understand is the bomb and the bullet. It would be quite easy you know - a small device attached to number one methanol still. That would give them food for thought, teach the bastards for threatening me with suspension. That fucking Heydocks got a suspender fetish." He cackled at his poor pun as if it were a genuine bon mot.

"Ted you're fucking crackers. " John shook his head. "One of these days..." he left the prophetic unfinished sentence hanging in the stinking wind, with its stinging ammoniac vapour which brought tears to their eyes and abruptly interrupted any further attempt at conversation. He silently cursed Ted who he illogically blamed for making what should have been a leisurely amble into a mad dash for the finishing line. He recognised his folly at last and allowed Ted to draw away. "Dowlo tonight," he called breathlessly after him, but his invitation blew away in the wind. He was meeting Josephine anyway, so it would be at best a quick one - the drink that is.

He lurched into the ramshackle building which was the clocking in station and reached for his time card on the forlorn side of the clock along with the other absentees and even later comers. The clocking in corridors had the air of makeshift annexes of corrugated iron, attached to the more substantial office of the Time Clerks. Old Tom Gladstone peered over his wire rimmed spectacles through a little window at John and shook his head in remonstration.

"Fuck you," John thought. "Fuck all of you." And with a gesture of petty defiance stuck his card in the wrong slot, which would involve Gladstone in an irritating search for the wildcard. Before doing so he committed another trivially defiant act by slamming down the handle on the clocking in machine with as much venom as he had kicked his errant bike earlier, in the forlorn hope that it would inflict terminal damage on the implacable implement. It would have been a glorious finale to his last appearance at the ICI Hippodrome. But it was not to be. The machine was a tribute to old fashioned British workmanship, which according to the Mail was a thing of the past, a relic of dependability, ugly and utterly reliable.

He dawdled whistling serenely and shuffled across the road to where the new amenity block stood, reaching there as Ted came rushing out struggling into a greasy overall. The splendid block complete with showers and locker rooms and automatic cold drink dispensers was the culmination of a long campaign by John and the Joint Shop Stewards Committee. The previous facility had been thrown up on the same temporary basis as the clocking in annexe. The in all honesty John had to admit privately that ICII was a thousand miles ahead of most Merthyr employers in this regard. He swung open the door to be confronted by the miserable welcome of Creepy Caswell the 'amenities superintendent', or what the best schools referred to as a janitor.

"Morning Creepy," John greeted sardonically. Creepy was an apt nickname for the unpleasant obsequious character who crept around with his bucket and mop silently sporting a pair of battered once white daps[2] spying on all and sundry and scurrying off like a spider to his supervisor with the names of latecomers, dawdlers, those who protracted their toilet functions, lavatory librarians, regal throne hairdressers, dozers and wankers. A wizened miserable little man with grey sunken features that a smile would fracture, beady sly dark eyes and a pronounced stoop. He had the appearance that instantly attracts sympathy from the beholder, but such noble sentiments were soon dispelled by the realisation that the way he looked was a perfect mirror to his personality. He was the ultimate creep.

"Late again is it," he pronounced with the closest he could get to an expression of glee. "You know I been told to see everybody's out of here by

---

[2]Plimsolls

73

now and make a note of them what's not. You wanna be careful, they got their eye on you."

"Belt up you odious little bastard before I give in to the almost irresistible urge to ram you head first down the nearest craphole and flush you away with all the other smelly turds."

The little man scurried away to his tiny windowless hole of an office to record this damning piece of insolence. John sighed and made his way to his locker, sitting wistfully for a few minutes on the steel bench which ran the length of the bay in which it and a dozen other lockers were housed. He collected a few personal items not bothering to remove the greasy overall. He had no intention of dirtying his hands today - nor ever again if he could help it. He stuffed the items into an old canvas haversack which had served him well as a holdall for the past few years. He carefully peeled off the lovely erotic Latin American beauty who adorned the inside of his locker door. He re-stuck it on the door of locker forty-one which belonged to Dai Bowen, Alderman, Mayor Elect, Bethania Deacon, a rock of Welsh Puritanism and hypocrisy.

He made his way slowly out of the building down the road to the workshop which housed his section. In the admin block only the shadows of the office boys could be seen moving from room to room delivering the morning mail and switching on the white lights. It gave him immense satisfaction to know that in the pile finding it's way to Heydocks desk was one which bore his signature. As a former office boy who had 'made good' he was tempted to rearrange the pile so that his would be the first missive to greet Heydock's nine o'clock arrival. It was symptomatic that it was not considered necessary for office staff to punch the clock, nor start work at the same time as the 'workers', so Heydock was not due for another hour.

The atmospheric effluent blew down the dusty road causing his eyes to smart again. The road lights suddenly went out and everything was shrouded in the grey autumn halflight of the cloudy morning. The weak lights of the gaunt structures seemed almost snuffed by the grimy haze. The sky threatened rain. Thank god he was soon to be free of all this, from the stink and noise, the mechanisation and efficiency, the ten minute tea break, the Methodism, the strangulation of intellect and invention. But how was he to live, how tell his parents. He still hadn't faced up to the question though it's inevitability was imminent.

He preferred instead to daydream with images of Josephine as a latter day Lady Southampton. She would find the idea of supporting an out of work bard romantic, but more significantly it would give her control over a very important element of their relationship. That too was a fleeting worry instantly filed away to the back of his consciousness. He would dedicate an occasional narrative epic to her. *The Rape of Maggie O'Leary. The love I dedicate to your Ladyship is without end.* (an improbable boast) *What I have*

74

done is yours ; being part of all I have, devoted yours. It sounded better in this hetero context.

As he entered the workshop door immersed in his fantasy a huge hand clamped his shoulder and literally jerked him out of his reverie. "Late!" boomed the voice of the gargantuan Jack. "Late! I got to give you top marks for cheek. You beat Dai Union hands up for sheer..." He struggled for the word.

"Effrontery Jack, " John helped. "When the biggest and dullest meets the cheekiest it must be like the immovable mass confronted by an irresistible force. In the words of the song - *something's gotta give, something's gotta give, something's gotta give."* He sang the ditty and danced a little pirouette looking up into Jacks shaggy face . It was almost a comical threat. The face discomfited broke into an amiable grin.

"No hard feelin's kid," he said. "I never intended to get you the sack. So now that you've apologised let's call it quits." Holding out his huge gnarled hand.

John's eyes flashed with anger. He looked around the silent workshop at the pricked ears and inquiring eyes. "There never was an apology from me, and there never will be, least of all to a big daft bastard like you Jack," he said in best public meeting declamatory tones. "It was a big political stitch up between the unions and the Labour Party, desperate for the slimmest chance of political power. You've been sold down the river boys. You've got nothing out of this strike other than the removal of Heydock from the negotiations. Whoever the new man is won't be stupid enough to repeat Heydock's mistakes but you can bet he'll still drive just as hard a bargain. You're back to square one but I wont be a member of the negotiating committee this time. I've resigned, from the union, from the Labour Party and from General bloody Chemicals. I'm taking leave in lieu of notice, so today I'm doing the rounds to make my individual farewells. There'll be a proper leaving do of course and you're all invited, well most of you that is," he concluded with a chuckle.

There was a pregnant silence before the inevitable uproar and the crowd converged on Bill Union for an explanation and demands for an open meeting. By midday there was pandemonium. While the men were at a mass meeting voting unanimously for an unofficial walkout John was confronting Heydock with his resignation. He sat grey faced and silent as the double blow struck home. His gamble had failed - he was yesterday's man. John would now be vindicated in the eyes of the public. He would appear as the man of principle sandwiched between the big bosses and the big unions and the threatened walkout would inevitably lead to an airing of the underlying issues.

In the event it was one of the few occasions when Heydocks prophesies had proved to be spot on. The hyenas of the tabloid press had turned a customary somersault portraying John as the innocent victim of the

75

power game being played out between the 'Bosses' and the union 'Barons'. But the bosses had a convenient scapegoat in Heydock who had not acted in accordance with ICI's widely acknowledged personnel policy. He had been immediately shunted into the industrial executives version of Caeharris railway sidings, where he would no doubt moulder like the abandoned First Class carriage, though with less beneficial effect on the local community. From hooligan to hero in twentyfour hours. Why did it no longer appear to be extraordinary? The age of doublethink had pre-dated it's 1984 arrival, it was here and now.

Later that evening , after the dinner table had been cleared, there was one of those awkward periods of painful silence which, with a wisdom born of long experience, no one dared to break.

Father sat in the corner staring at nothing, unblinking. He had sat this way for almost half an hour now and the others sat likewise, hardly daring to breathe lest the storm should break loose. His parents' reactions had not been exactly what he expected. Mother had muttered a characteristic religious plea in Welsh, repeated in English, typically Dowlais where Wenglish, a Welsh - English patois was still commonly spoken. "Oh good Arglwydd mawrth, bendithio us all."[3] While his father had slumped like a man defeated into a morose silence.

Brothers and sisters already bemused by the sudden notoriety that John had brought upon the family had steered clear of any mention of the controversy even the young ones sensing the fragility of the familial situation. Mother since her one expletive stood intently staring into the dull coals of the fire, replenishment of which was strictly the father's prerogative.

Spent coals was an apt metaphor in John's mind. Already too much ravaged by the flames of a harsh life he was the cause of further disillusionment and pain. If only he could make them see, help them understand - but theirs was a different world. Too many bridges had been crossed and burned for them now.

At long last his father rose from his seat and everyone turned apprehensively. He picked up some coal from the scuttle in the hearth, coal which had cost him dear, and placed it delicately into the dull orange recesses of the fire from his blue-scarred hands. "No need to bloody freeze is there?" The comparative levity of his remark triggered an audible communal sigh of relief. "After givin' it some thought I suppose you're right son." He used the term 'son' only as a very rare form of endearment and a sentimental lump rose in the back of John's throat.

"I am Dad. I know I am. You would have done the same," he managed with a quiet sincerity.

---

[3] Oh good Lord bless us all.

"I don't know about that. You're lucky you can afford your pride. That shows we've made some progress I suppose."

"No Dad. It's more than just a matter of personal pride you know; though what you call it doesn't matter, it's what you understand by it that counts. If people like us don't make our stand now it will be too late. The moment will be gone forever and with it any hope for the kind of future we've dreamed about. We're at a crossroads Dad, history will recognise it. I've been convinced of it more and more and now this , this episode has brought it into clear focus. I've vacillated about what to do about it, afraid to hurt you and mam, you had such...." he paused as the word bourgeois came to mind....."ambitions for me. But you do understand.."

" No. No I don't understand, not properly any'ow. I can't see as 'ow we're at no crossroads. My life has been lived across two world wars and the depression. We're still at war with most of the bloody world and that's because the real war was never ended. There have been so many bloody crossroads that the one you say we're at now seems not to matter half so much. P'raps you see more in this than I do. It is a different world now. P'raps you're right, it is a different kind of struggle.

"All we wanted for you, for all of you, was a better life, decent jobs, good houses, good homes to bring up your own kids. No lockouts and dole queues. No parish handouts and all that indignity your mother an me 'ad to suffer. In my 'eart I always thought you might not settle for that. Your rebelliousness, your stubborn certainty, you always 'ad something in your guts from the day you were born. A little bawlin' runt you were, we didn't think you'd live. So no it's not all that much of a surprise. It's right to stand and fight for what you believe in, and I'm proud of you for that. But it's a hard road son, and a lonely one more often than not, and once you're on it there's no getting off without destroying your self respect."

There were tears now and they embraced. This was the proud man who had once hoisted him aloft. This was the man who fought for the Fed. This was the man with a simple eloquence who had addressed his fellow miners when to strike meant to beg and starve. But this was a man who would disown him if he had an inkling of what he was now about to do.

The rain had eased for a while at least, but fog had descended like a dark blanket to take its place. The red neon sign across the road glowed like the aurora borealis, its soft light hanging on the myriads of tiny water droplets which surrounded it, providing a double image of the message which it heralded as it flashed on and off spasmodically. He was reminded of a film he had seen, of many such films he had seen, and of a song sung by the divine Sassy. He tried to remember the words singing them softly to himself. "Your lips were like a red and ruby chalice dum de dum de dum de dum, your eyes were the aurora borealis la de da de da de da, your skin an alabaster palace do de do de do de do. I could see the midnight sun."

A raincoated couple welded into an inextricable shape underneath a sombre black umbrella paused and peered into the deep shop doorway which he occupied. A girl's giggle escaped from the black mass before it scurried spiderlike across the road and into the red glow of the neon announcing *The Sands* , Merthyr's response to Las Vegas. The neon, symbol of modernity, had been fixed over the still clearly visible *Palace Cinema* sign, which had been the only picture house to cater for the amorous by providing twin seats sans obstructive armrests. Alas it was no more, but Merthyr's amorous were still served by its current utility.

Soon he would join them holding Josie close and shuffling in time to a badly played oversweet reedy saxophone. She chose that moment to appear out of the gloom.

> *Ah, when she moved she moved more ways than one ;*
> *the shapes a bright container can contain.* [4]

She needed no music to dance. Her thin belted raincoat reminded him of Maggie and that first time in the Third Class railway coach in Caeharris. No more Third Class from now on; Josie was strictly a First Class kind of girl. He took her arm and smiled a silent greeting as he led her across the road and into The Sands foyer. He waited an eternity while she attended to whatever it was females attended to for such interminable periods in those mysterious closets of feminine intrigue. He paced up and down doing incredibly self conscious things like sniffing the obviously fake plastic flowers which adorned the waiting area.

When she finally emerged all anger was dissolved in her heady perfume and the tantalising paradox of her virginally erotic appearance in an exquisite high necked white dress with tiny silver leaves attached to the skirt. This was haute couture and she turned as many female heads as male as she glode with controlled undulation towards him. The dress hugged her lithe body emphasising the contours of her upwardcurving breasts. The dark hair tumbled about her shoulders like a shining waterfall. She was stunning. "I love you because you're lovely," he clichéd glibly.

The clock on the balcony was stealing up to midnight. The atmosphere was hot and hazy and they clung stickily together swaying rhythmically in the centre of the crowded floor. "Almost tomorrow," he muttered, high on coke, not the white sniffy stuff, this was a time of innocence, grass and hippies hadn't arrived yet, there wasn't even alcohol in the Sands, "let's go before the mad exodus." Outside heaven had opened her floodgates once again and the rain was torrential. It bounced like pellets on the roads and spattered to tiny fragments on its glittering surface, coalescing

---

[4]See 2 above.

78

into tributaries which streamed in all directions, eventually merging in a gutter torrent gushing down the drain with a musical gurgle. They linked arms and braved the Merthyr rain getting immediately drenched.

"Where's that bloody posh car of yours," he shouted. Her hair was beginning to straighten into long black streaks.

"The chauffeur dropped me off," she said. "So its taxi home. You are coming home?" Even bedraggled and soaked she made it sound erotic.

"The chauffeur," he exclaimed with disbelief. "You have a chauffeur. I don't believe it. I don't want to believe it. I can't be seen going out with girls what's got chauffeurs, think of my reputation. "

"Well he's not just a chauffeur. If it makes you feel any better he's a sort of general factotum. The Volvo's in for servicing and he's had to use the Daimler to take mum to some business bash in Bristol so we'll have the place to ourselves again. We inherited him from Dad, he lives in the gatehouse. So here we.."

"...*are standing in the rain, funny little fellow, frowsy little dame*," he sang to her amusement and started to dance dragging one foot in the gutter like Gene Kelly. The madness was infectious and soon she joined him. "*Singin' in the rain*." They sang in chorus, jumping and splashing until they were completely soaked. To add insult to injury a big red bus deluged them with a muddy ooze as it raced by. Frowning faces peered glumly out at them from behind dirty misted panes scarcely believing their eyes. One did a double take and tapped his temple shaking his head. "Fuck you too," John shouted waving middle and index finger in the air.

The soap lathered softly on his chest and the water beat, warmly now, on his back and shoulders as he lazed comfortably in the aquamarine marble sunken shower bath basking in a dream of ancient Rome and dark nubile concubines. To someone brought up with a cold water bosh [5] in a tiny cold scullery with a corrugated roof this was the ultimate in decadent luxury.

She called him to a wee small hours breakfast and he padded out leaving a trail of wet footprints across the rug with a thick red Turkish bath-towel draped around him. This was bourgeois splendour if you liked - and he did. In front of the flickering fire they lounged and made love and lay leisurely talking as new lovers do of inconsequential things for the sheer joy of touching and communicating. He couldn't help but think however of her approaching graduation and inheritance. She was a lovely delectable siren but wonderful as it was this was more lust than love. That awful word beyond comprehension. Soon she would want it spoken. What then?

---

[5]Colloquial for Belfast sink.

They were still basking in the near nude afterglow of lovemaking when suddenly without the slightest hint of warning her mother swept in. There was only the briefest of hesitations while she took in the situation. Poise personified she simply smiled and did a double take. "I'd better do that again," she threw over her shoulder as she left. After a decent interval which allowed at least a partial cover up they heard the front door slam as she re-entered.

"I thought she was gone for the night," Josephine explained with a nervous laugh. "Don't worry she's very modern about these things. She's often entertained in my presence I don't see why the vice shouldn't be versa'd for a change."

John looked up at the magnificent portrait again, the lines of well read books and the tasteful décor. As a manifestation of one woman's personality, and such a beautiful woman, it was all rather intimidating. He began to understand something of Josephine's desire to dominate, having lived under such a shadow all her life. His own dominance of their love making might also signify fulfilment of a paternal function which she had also been denied . It was all so Freudian. Even the rich had their hang-ups he supposed.

Josephine's mother returned after a bout of exaggerated coughing bearing a steaming tray. "Here you are ," she said. "Coffi Cymru, a wonderful recuperant."

"Diolch," John took a cup of the heavily spiked brew. Use of the odd Welsh phrase was an in thing with the upper crust. It was considered intellectually superior to the stunted vocabulary of the proletarian rabble of the valleys who it was thought knew nothing and cared less about their linguistic heritage. Crash courses in Welsh for Beginners were oversubscribed at evening classes throughout the principality.

"Oh ti'n siarad Cymraeg?" she queried his 'diolch'.

"Na," he responded, "weddol a bit, enough to struggle through Mabinogion and Llyfr Goch that's all."

She tilted her head and decided to ignore the sarcasm. "A litterateur no less. You taste's improving my dear."

"A poet," he corrected.

"My goodness," she turned to address Josephine again. "Neither a doctor, nor a lawyer, nor even an accountant, but a poet no less. Now let me see," turning back to John again, "perhaps we share some acquaintances. Do you know Delwyn Edwards. I do hope not. He's one of those Nationalist twits and writes such dreary stuff. Welsh medieval I suppose it could be called. Oh you're not a medieval nationalist I hope Mr eh.."

"Davies. John Davies. And no I'm not. Neither nationalist nor medievalist. I'm modern and I'm socialist." He warmed to the game. "And my poetry is anything but dreary."

"And is that my smart Oxford educated daughter's view too."

"Really mother I haven't a clue," she replied sweetly, "but I could compose a rare sonnet in praise of his other virtues."

"All of this in one man, why it seems hardly fair, I must get to know you better young man. I'm Marion by the way, since my daughter seems not to want to introduce us." She held out a regal hand almost as if she expected him to kiss it. He was about to take it gently when Josephine interposed and spared him the embarrassment.

"If you think I'm going to allow the slightest physical contact between you two you're very much mistaken," there was the hint of an edge on the admonition, playful with an underlying barb of warning. John began to feel distinctly uneasy. He felt as if he was being considered a tasty morsel to be served up on the plate of whichever of these divine damsels outdid the other. It was flattering to the male ego but there was something disquieting about it.

John has become something of a cause celebre," she continued. "He's the same John Davies who is the current bane of industrial potentates such as you mother, having brought the great ICI to a standstill."

"Oh *that* John Davies?"

"Yes indeed mother, *that* John Davies. Do you still congratulate me on my taste?"

"Hang on a minute you two," John felt that enough was enough. "I'm beginning to feel like some remote third person in this dialogue. This is me, flesh and blood. You can talk about me when I'm gone but in the meantime ….."

"Of course. Please forgive us John, may I call you John. My daughter and I always play this silly game with our respective men friends." She turned to Josephine. " Truce my dear. I promise to be a good little mother since this one is obviously more than just a one night stand." She couldn't resist the punch line.

"I think we'll go to bed now mother," Josephine replied with irritation taking his hand possessively. Goodnight."

John quaffed his coffi Cymraeg and raised his eyebrows in a questioning goodnight.

"Goodnight," she said. "I'll be off early in the morning dear. Company business. I'll get Joe to drive me in the Daimler so you can use the Volvo and have the run of the place. Interesting meeting you John. I hope we meet again soon, perhaps you'll show me some of your work."

"Mother!" Josephine warned. "You promised."

"An aesthetic interest I assure you. I have friends in the arts I may be able to help you get published."

"John's already been published mother. Where have you been." The coup de grace was sweet but his ears had pricked up at the offer. His publication had been obscure. Five New Welsh Poets published with assistance from Academi Cymraeg by the Bryniau Glas press. A flimsy buff

81

soft covered pamphlet which had been well received, particularly John's contribution for which he had received of course not a penny, but had hardly set the literary sphere alight.

Between the satin sheets in that strange hinterland which separates sleep from consciousness a peculiar uneasiness troubled him. Was this the antithesis of all he had appeared to be? Was this epiphany or apostasy? He contrasted the stark lifestyle and premature ageing of his parents with this lovely woman not that much younger than them. She apparently was a Dowlais girl too, not born with the proverbial silver spoon, who had hauled herself up by her bra straps. What course was he now embarked on. His befuddled mind could make no sense of it. He finally slipped into a disturbed sleep and dreamed….

…of a big house with a huge high wall around it, like a prison. It had massive doors like a medieval castle keep, securely bolted at all times. Inside the house was a huge assembly line, or rather there were two assembly lines. Off the first poured an incessant stream of consumer goods, while off the other in carefully controlled proportion rolled future consumers, the result of selective spasmodic copulations.

These products of mechanical unions were suckled on the nipples of the clanking machinery from which they had their genesis. They grew fat and docile. At puberty they were allowed to stand in the production lines and were rewarded with a percentage of the commodities which they produced. Other houses existed throughout the land and the different goods were exchanged in what was called The Market. Each had a television, a washing machine, a vacuum cleaner, refrigerator, food mixer, hi- fi stereo and even a car.

Every weekend they sat in their gleaming cars in gleaming rows with their engines ticking over, breathing in intoxicating fumes, bumper to shining bumper looking vacuously out of crystal windscreens, going nowhere. In lay-bys they polished their bonnets until they gleamed under the pale arc lights reflecting back their wan anaemic faces . It was utopia.

Among their number was an operative who's name was Legion, born of operatives whose names were Legion, suckled on the huge printing machine which he loved with a filial passion. As he grew he polished, waxed, oiled, kissed and cared for every nut, bolt, rivet, screw, rod pin and roller. Then one day it stopped. It heaved a great clanking mechanical sigh, sat back on its oily haunches and stopped.

The sun went out of his life. Oh my joy, my sweet, my love, my precious, my life, he wailed as he kissed , called, petted, probed and poked without response. Thrusting has hand at last between the blubbery vaginal rollers he sought the little microswitch, the seat of stimulation. He manipulated it skilfully up and down, up and down in a frenzy until it finally clicked. The lights flashed. The machine clanked and groaned as it stirred to life and he was slowly drawn into its interior inch by ecstatic inch into its deep darkness, rumbling a renewed vibrancy as the arc lights went out of his life forever singing…so this is the way the world ends, so this is the way the world ends. Not with a bang. Not with a whimper. With a long ecstatic moaaaan.

"Shush, shush. It's allright." Josephine was holding him, cradling his head to her breasts. He was breaking out in cold sweat. "What is it? Was it a nightmare. You were moaning and groaning." The bedroom door opened and her mother stood there eyes wide with question.

"What's wrong." She was too immaculate for a woman woken from sleep.

"It's allright," Josephine insisted harshly. " A bad dream that's all. A nightmare. I'll go down and make a drink in a minute." Again he was aware of being spoken about as if he was somehow absent.

Marion stood for a long moment observing the scene. The powerful shoulders of the young man, his head on her daughter's naked breasts. She was aroused. "Do you want me to.."

"I can manage mother thank you." Marion nodded and returned to her room and her bed. She had not been asleep she had lain awake straining for the sounds of their lovemaking, tears on her cheek, hand between her legs stroking. Now she lay listening to their subdued conversation only the odd word of which was intelligible. She cursed this demonic drive in her thighs which always had to be assuaged no matter how depraved the means of its assuaging. She heard her daughter go down into the kitchen and rose silently and stole into their bedroom.

He was sat up in bed still looking dazed and unconvinced that he was really conscious. Her bottom lip trembled with desire as she posed stroking herself to a mini climax. She gave a little cry and left as quickly as she entered. He rubbed his eyes and she was gone. In her place Josephine stood with a hot drink laced with whisky.

"My God you still look shaken," she said. "It must have been an awful nightmare. Do you have them often?"

"All the time," he admitted taking the drink and gulping at it like a wanderer in the desert. "But sometimes the dream spills over into reality and that's even more frightening."

"Do you want to tell me about it."

"Just hold me," he pleaded. The time might come when he would have to tell her but this was not it. All he wanted now was the warmth and reassurance of her flesh. Soon he was fast asleep and no dream invaded his peace

In the adjacent room Marion tossed and turned in an agony of torment and disgust in the knowledge that sooner or later she would lure her daughter's lover to her bed.

Morning dawned bright and clear with the air fresh after the heavy rain. Marion had already left and a note on the kitchen table bequeathed Josie the unfettered run of the manse for the next few days. She'd had to go to Brussels in a hurry and had left the Volvo at her disposal.

He felt and looked the epitome of opulence behind the wheel. He had dropped Josie at her hairdressers and was on his way into town, unemployed prostitute poet resplendent in his mistress' car. He reflected on Marion Mason, what a vision that had been, he was still uncertain of it's veracity. In any event, what a family, modern Borgias.

Mason senior was certainly a very attractive proposition, he'd always been drawn to the mature woman, but a bird in hand as the adage had it, and Josie was due back in Oxford soon, perhaps then…. What a bastard he was; but what a pair of bastards they were, so what the hell. His current situation left him little option but to try to cultivate both relationships without jeopardising either . In any case the interest of Mason senior could hardly be anything but transitory surely, a little bit of young rough divertissement, but then again transience had its own commendations.

Town was a heaving mass, the traffic bumper to bumper from the General Hospital clogging the narrow arteries of the town. As he crawled down through Pontmorlais people from the pavement throng stared to look at him in his posh car. Some recognised him, after all he was a minor celebrity, the subject of headlines in the Mail and the Echo and pre McLuhan he'd had his fifteen minutes of television. Some pointed and gestured. There seemed an air of frenzy in their actions. He pressed a button and his window swished open.

"Hey Jack," he called. The storeman who used frigg and friggin' as repetitive euphemisms tuned and stared open mouthed. "What's up?"

"What's up? What's up? It's friggin' you what's friggin up innit. One day friggin' strike that's what. Petition to the friggin' mayor and to S.O friggin'Davies at the Town Hall. Wildcat it is, wildcat friggin' strike."

As the traffic inched towards the Imperial Hotel he manoeuvred deftly up the narrow lane scarcely wide enough to admit the drays for which it had originally been constructed and to which the grooved brickwork was testament. He squeezed into the little yard at the rear of the Imp in a little courtyard which housed the Tiger Bar in the hotel annexe. He got out and gestured to Lindy the landlady that he was leaving the gleaming machine in her safekeeping, tapping the face of his watch and miming, "five minutes." She nodded and smiled confirming his popularity with buxom barmaids of a certain age in a town replete with buxom barmaids of a certain age.

He walked through the lane to the tramroad, the very same down which Trevithick had trundled his Iron Horse, the first ever steam locomotive to carry goods by rail, together with a horde of unofficial passengers hitching an historic ride from the Penydarren ironworks in 1804 long before Puffing Billy more famously repeated the feat.

The tramroad ran adjacent to the rear of the grand Edwardian edifice which was the Merthyr Town Hall, from which the demonstration had now moved to the neighbouring Library. Dai union was holding forth from the top of the library steps and Ted had clambered onto the plinth of a stern bronze which had been raised to, or by, one Lewis Bart. of Bwlch, one of several such 'dignitaries' who had made huge fortunes out of coal and iron in the old whoretown, but who tended, as still did the modern Masons, to reside in more salubrious parts, having ripped the heart out of this once beautiful valley.

Lewis Bart. which the young John had always presumed to be his name rather than his title, now sported a rakish battered old trilby and a red and white scarf. "What the fuck's all this about then," John called up to Ted hanging on precariously to one end of the scarf.

"You may well ask," Ted called back. "Where the fuck have you been hiding. Meeting; big speech from Dai; vote; one day strike and demo; lifting of suspension and re-negotiation of agreement or more to follow. Never heard Dai so passionate and eloquent and.....bolshie. Hark at him, thinks he's bloody Lenin at the Finland Station."

"Better late than never I suppose," Geraint had pushed through the throng to get to him. "Why weren't you at the Dowlo last night as arranged? We wanted you there to mesmerise them with your rhetoric. It was really something I tell you. As it was Dai Union was rhetorical enough for a graduate of Plato's Academy."

" Just shows you didn't need me at all. While you were fuelling the social revolution I was propagating a sexual one," he retorted glibly.

"Well while you were satisfying your lustful ego," Dave had fought his way through to join them, "we were achieving, for the first time in it's illustrious history, the total shutdown of ICI's Dowlais Works. Process workers and all, and you know how difficult it is to get those bastards to do anything. We've only got a token picket; nothing's going in, nothing coming out."

"But listen to this," Ted shouted. A minor fire on number two reactor closed the Ammonia Plant. Know what caused it? None other than your friend and mine Big Jack. They were trying to run the plant with no maintenance staff other than the foremen and the work study estimators. He switched to manual control, strictly according to the book, but panicked when the level started to fluctuate and the alarm went off. He switched straight back to Auto, again according to the book, but you and I know that the book is wrong don't we? The control valve shot wide open, the level overflowed, and POW, up she went. Luckily nobody was hurt. The volunteer firemen soon had it under control. That's what finally convinced the process men to come out. Leave's you in the clear John boy. What price their insubordination argument now."

"You spawny bastards can't go wrong can you?" John laughed. "The volunteers saved the plant although they were on strike and not being paid for it. And the cause of the fire is directly attributable to the fallibility of the Blue Book. You've got the bastards on the run. We should put in an immediate demand for average bonus payments while the new deal is properly re-negotiated."

"We?"

"Sorry comrade, slip of the tongue. I'm enjoying my new career as a prostitute. Come up to the Tiger and see the symbol of my decadence. I've sold my soul for a mess of pottage."

At that moment a young policeman pushed his way through to them. "Hey you. Get down from there." He commanded with as much authority as his youth could muster.

"Who the hell is he?" asked Dave in astonishment.

"Must be new," called down Ted seriously. "Are you new?"

"This is an illegal gathering," the policeman stuttered to a roar of laughter. "If you don't move on I'll….." but green as he was he knew it would be at best foolish to complete the threat. A good humoured resentment began to articulate itself, after all this *was* Merthyr Tydfil, the town where (working class mythology has it) socialist protest was invented. The very library where they gathered now displays a memorial plaque to one Dic Penderyn, a working class martyr hanged for his part as a leader of the Merthyr Rising in 1804, when workers took over the town for a brief revolutionary moment.

The constable was jostled, his helmet inevitably dislodged and thrown into the air, caught and claimed as a trophy, a symbol of the solidarity of united workers. "The workers united will never be defeated, the workers united……" The familiar mantra broke out.

The young policeman panicked. The son of a steelworker he had nevertheless been conditioned to believe that all workers were sheep, and trade unionists simultaneously Bolsheviks and anarchists awaiting some prearranged signal from the Russians, or the Chinese, unaware of the inherent contradictions in such stupidity. In his panic he removed his radio and called for reinforcements to quell what he described as a riot. If this was not bad enough he pulled out his silly rubber truncheon and waved it aloft.

John felt some sympathy for his plight. He was like a daft girl he had once seen on a Sunday School outing to Barry Island, trying to defend herself from the taunts of the rough boys from the Valleys. Like the girl he was finally hoisted into the air and carried shoulder high down to the bank of the coal black Taff into which he was unceremoniously dumped to a chorus of great cheers. The girl had at least been more carefully dropped clad in her modest swimwear into the equally grubby grey waves of Barry Island.

The wailing siren ululated in the distance. "Time to get the hell out of here," John announced in his best John Wayne. "Come on, up the Tiger to get the car."

The five piled into the Volvo and John drove as quickly as he dared through the rapidly clearing streets and parked outside the Lamb. A favoured spit and sawdust watering hole for the Merthyr 'chattering classes', an entirely different group than the epithet normally implies. It was just that the pub had acquired a reputation as a place where the 'long headed' gathered to discuss the issues of the day.

"Ho, here come the workers. Strikers of the world unite," taunted a fat ginger haired spotty faced youth, a lunch hour drinker from his father's estate agency office of Bradley and Bradley.

"Hullo Bradley Twice," John replied. He was known as Bradley Twice not just because of his father's partnership with his brother, but because he had been egotistical enough to lumber his son with his surname as a Christian name. Bradley Bradley was the unfortunate product of aspiring parents, never allowed the rough and tumble rigours of a normal childhood. Pampered, sheltered and privately schooled he had emerged from his adolescence still spotty, supercilious , ignorant and arrogant. He gathered around him a retinue of hangers on attracted principally by the free beer. John was in too happy a frame of mind to allow such an irrelevance as Bradley Twice to anger him so proceeded cheerfully to get the drinks in.

"ICI are employing some elderly apprentices these days," taunted Bradley loudly to the chuckles of his sycophants as the far from youthful Bill accompanied John to the bar. "No wonder they've got problems."

John continued to ignore him, and when the drinks were in began regaling his friends with the events of the previous night , not in any boastful way but with the frankness of long familiarity and friendship. "You spawny bastard," Ted retorted. "You'd fall in shit and come out smelling of roses. So you're selling out are you, you bourgeois bastard? Flogging your arse, or rather that big prick of yours to some randy capitalist bitch"

John gave him a self satisfied smile. "And I suppose you aren't flogging *your* arse to some capitalist bastard, like ICI for instance. And by God at least I'm flogging mine in a much more enjoyable way."

"Anyway," Dave argued more pragmatically, " you can't possibly hope to keep two such relationships going simultaneously, or even both at the same time."

"It's a simple question of mathematics my friend ; parallel non-convergent series; A with momma, and B with daughter, always the same comfortable distance between them. " He held up an admonishing hand to forestall interruption. "I know you maths boffins will say that ultimately series must converge, dissect and then diverge. But ultimately can be a long, long time and I the bard of Dowlais defy mathematical law. Is not science just another religion, a device invented by man to delude himself into believing that it verifies what he already insists is true; to make something tangible of his hypotheses; to develop apparent order out of what is really chaos; to rationalise his external experience.

"Calculus for example, a foundation stone of mathematical science, what is it, a device, a deception, a system based upon a lie. Find me the square root of minus one.. And how do scientific hypotheses proceed? Experience the result and then apply the hypothesis. If the one appears to lead to the other what does that prove? Does it verify the law or simply that in this particular instance , and perhaps others similar to it, the rule applies. The truth is the answer can never be stated conclusively in advance. The two things may only be found to be related in retrospect.

"Take the two halves of an apple. When rejoined they are seen to form the original whole. This does not mean, as some mathematician would insist, that the original consisted of two halves. The original was whole and one. Nothing in human experience is inevitable until after the event. This my dear friends is one of the beautiful truths of our existence. After the event the inevitable appears unquestionable. It is unquestionable *after* the event, but never *before* the event. After the first choice there is no other. Thus sprach Johannes Davies."

"What the fuck are you on you daft bugger ?" Dave snapped irritably.

"High on cuntjuice of course," Ted elucidated, " surely you recognise the signs by now. All his so called serious thinking is done with his dick."

"I know Josephine Mason," Bradley Twice interrupted, uninvited, with biblical emphasis on the *know* . "She was at Greylands same time as me. Brilliant bitch got all her A Levels with straight A's. Right little hotpants she was though. Wasn't a male in the place that didn't have it off with her, excluding the old Beak of course. He was too senile, and more interested in the boys anyway."

"Then it must have been excluding the Beak and you," John retorted.

"And what do you mean by that," Bradley demanded angrily. "I've had girls. I've had plenty of girls. I've had Dick's sister Maggie. Tell them Dick."

John's group erupted with laughter at this. This was the same Maggie with whom John had gradated in sexual practice all those years ago in Caeharris railway sidings. Part of their continuing relationship was the absolute frankness with which they could discuss each other's sexual foibles. As a semi-professional or *demimonde* as she preferred, she was a rich source of bizarre Freudian material for any budding Kraft Ebbing. He, and therefore the group were very well aware that Bradley's thing was exclusively masturbation. He paid her fifteen pounds on the first Friday of every month for her to pose for him while he mouthed obscenities and masturbated into her discarded underclothing.

88

"Bradley Bradley you're pathetic," he said. "God knows It's only Christian charity which restrains me from announcing precisely what I know about your relationship with my old friend Maggie O'Leary.

He was probably losing Maggie a regular and easy client. The wankers were the easiest she always claimed. But he excused himself in the knowledge that there was a long list of potential clients lining up for Maggie's services, for hers was a somewhat selective practise and rarely involved casual clientele. *No pimp* had been rule number one and her flat was tasteful in furnishing and décor in a better part of town. Her clients requirements were vetted , which principally meant non-violent though not precluding the less extreme forms of sm. She had no qualms about spanking fat bottoms, for contrary to the lurid stories in certain magazines, it was just a gentle flagellation that most of them required.

But who were these regular clients who were prepared to be entertained by appointment only, each on his specific day at a specific time and for a considerable fee? Butchers, bakers and candle stick makers, teachers, preachers and county court clerks. Sad, lonely and generally inadequate people or dull men married to dull women. Men for whom making money had become an end rather than a means.

The majority however clearly used her as a substitute for a compliant partner. What she provided them was what they might have established for themselves after a few evenings in pub or club or other social environment and the expenditure only of an expression of empathy for one of the growing number of unattached women who expected nothing more.

For most however this would require the disruption of the meaningless charade which was their lives. According to the shabby creed which was their only doctrine what was desired could only be achieved through purchase, like any other commodity, commodities like those by which their very essence was defined.

With John she became again the wanton nymph coupling for the animal pleasure of it. They fucked both selfishly and selflessly and both ended replete, conscious of the other's repletion, neither buying nor selling but both giving and taking simultaneously.

"Christian charity my arse," Bill countered. "If you know anything rotten or derisive about Bradley twice it's a Christian duty to broadcast it to the whole world."

"That's exactly where you're wrong Bill. The Christian philosophy tells us that we should love the bastard with all his faults and frailties."

"Which just goes to show what a stupid bloody philosophy it is," Ted interjected. "Impractical ideals have cost us dearly enough already. All that shit has to be swept away before we can really change anything. How can anybody love a cunt like Bradley Twice anyway ?"

"Spoken like a true follower of Godwin I don't think," John riposted, "or is it Kropotkin. Sounds more like Nietzsche to me."

"I'm no bloody Nazi," Ted as ever rose to the bait.

"Now, now brother," John held up a pacifying hand, " forgiveness is the essence." Smiling sweetly. That's what turning the other cheek means. Understanding and forgiveness are the very things against which the assailant has no effective weapon. It frightens him because it makes his aggression meaningless."

"You're full of crap Davies, if you can believe that rubbish. It has obvious attractions for the weak and the meek. Yeah Nietzsche was right in that. The gas chamber is where it inevitably leads..."

"Where Nietzsche inevitably leads you mean," Dave interrupted. "But you're right about the uselessness of the Christian vision. It's a lovely vision but utterly utopian and unattainable given the nature of humanity."

The Bradley ménage sat slack jawed and shuffled uneasily in their seats gulping their weak beer. High faluting stuff like this always caused unease in the bar of a pub that had once upon a long time been the locus for political philosophy in this tamed whoretown.

"Mother of Marx," John exclaimed.

"Listen up comrades, there's a sermon coming." Dave groaned.

"Where have you all been while I've been trying to educate you. Jesus was a man you clods, a man just like us, with all the faults and frailties we share. His own life fell short of the Church's highest ideals. There is a fundamental dichotomy and the showdown at Nicea meant that it was established at the very core of the Church's creed. The biggest stumbling block to a practical Christian philosophy was to anoint him with the godhead, the one and only Son of God, and the metaphysical mumbo jumbo of the Trinity.

"We are all sons of god in the metaphorical sense. We all have the godhead. We are all capable of raising ourselves up out of the slime. This is what Marx also said. Thus also sprak Karl. It was the Church, first as the State itself, and after the Reformation the State's puppet, and now as the tool of capitalism, which placed him beyond the comprehension of mere mortals, emphasising his sterile celibacy and alienating him from us.

"Had they not depicted him not just as a god but The One God, not suppressed his heterosexuality, given proper emphasis to his human frailties, and called him Man, his philosophy might be more powerful and practical and progressive.

"Since he was crucified by your Nietzschean Romans they have murdered him again and again with their lies and mysticism. Oh Jerusalem, Jerusalem, thou which killest the prophets, and stonedst them which are sent unto thee, how often would I have gathered thy children together, even as a hen gathereth her chickens under her wing, and ye would not.. That's been the cry of men of love and genius down the ages. We are All sons of god."

"Got religion now then have we," Bradley said uncertainly. "You're all bloody mad." But fell uncharacteristically silent again in the trepidation that John, mad and unpredictable, might abandon this newfound religiosity, punch him on the nose and reveal to the world his masturbatory peccadilloes. He retreated sullenly to the far corner of the bar to lord it over his cronies.

The pause which followed John's little sermon, ' The Sermon in the Lamb' as it was later referred to, according it a Blakean stature as an element in the myth of the Merthyr Five, which was itself to become an element in the already mythical status of this old whoretown as the hub of Welsh radicalism, was rudely ruptured by the dramatic entry of four of Merthyr's finest uniformed bobbies.

"Right, now then lads," the tone was all threat and menace. "Were any of you part of that rabble."

"What rabble was that serge," Bill responded cheekily.

"Was he one of them," the sergeant turned to the policeman not readily recognise as the poor sod that had been dumped in the Taff, regaled as he now was in his replacement kit.

"Well they was there," he said. "That one was up the statue when my helmet was pinched." This gave rise to a predictable risible laughter from the bar denizens.

The burly sergeant pushed his way through to the five and confronted Ted, nose to nose. "Constable Parker reckons you lot were among the yobs that assaulted him."

"We had nothing to do with that," John interposed himself between them placing a restraining hand on the fiery Ted's arm.

"What right have you got to come in here making accusations," Bill chipped in. " We're just enjoying a quiet drink."

"He was there allright," the young constable insisted. "They was all there. The tall feller I specially remember. Who's is the Volvo outside ? ", he suddenly changed tack.

"Mine," John started..

"Don't believe him," Bradley volunteered. " Bloody old Norton bike he's got. Probably still paying for that."

"That's what Christian Philosophy get you," Geraint observed.

"Do you all work for ICI," the sergeant asked.

"I don't," John insisted with all the indignation that such a truth allowed.

"Are you sure. We can soon check."

"Go ahead. Check."

"Can I see your driver's licence and insurance ?"

John opened his wallet and passed them over with some trepidation. The sergeant perused them perfunctorily. "And what's the registration number of the car?" he asked.

"Well it's not my car really. It belongs to a friend of mine."

"Oh. And who might that be ?"

"Josephine Mason. You can check that out too. You can ring her….oh Christ she's not at home, she's getting her hair done. I'm not due to meet her until two."

The sergeant was all smiles. "I think they'd better come along with us don't you George, until we can do all this checking out."

"Yes I do serge," said Parker with relish. "Now you're not going to give us any trouble are you boys," he invited. John's restraining grip on Ted's arm tightened.

"Easy Ted, don't give them the excuse."

"Bastards, they'll find an excuse once they get us over there."

"Now then sonny," the old sergeant reassured, "if you've done nothing wrong you've got nothing to worry about have you ?"

"I bet you said that to Timothy Evans," Geraint quipped. "And you hanged him."

"Timothy who ?"

"Forget it genius."

"Don't get clever with me sonny. Come on let's go."

"Oh we've got nothing to worry about," Ted said. "As innocents a mild kicking is all we'll get from these keepers of the Queen's peace."

"Oh we've got a right bunch of comedians here," the sergeant was beginning to get annoyed. It was time to assert some authority. "Allright. Come on the lot of you. We're taking you in on suspicion of car theft." He gave them the customary caution, which sounded absurd. The bar crowd began to mutter and Dave laughed nervously.

"Come on now lads I don't want any trouble in here, " the barman pleaded.

"Don't worry," Dave reassured him. "We're not going to give the Gestapo here any excuse to put the boots in. But we want you to note that we're going peacefully and none of us is suffering any personal injury. Do me a favour keep ringing this number and let my girlfriend know what's happened. He hastily scribbled a number and dropped a handful of coins on the counter.

Bradley Twice's face was wreathed in smiles as the five traipsed out to the waiting Black Maria. "Balls to Christian charity," John muttered as he observed Bradley's Cortina parked on the double yellow lines.

"Constable," he said. "the owner of that car is the fat pasty faced slob sat in the corner, name of Bradley Bradley. His father's big in the mason's. I know you won't let that stop you doing your duty."

The sergeant gritted his teeth and addressed the young constable. This lot could be trouble. "Go and book him," he instructed.

Ted inevitably 'tripped' and bumped his head as he was 'helped' into the police car. It was Geraint who restrained him this time. "That's the trouble with being seven feet bloody tall," he grumbled. "You stand out in a crowd and we all get into trouble. I bet they couldn't tell the rest of us from

Adam. Look the best ting you can do is sit very still and refuse to answer any bloody questions. Name, rank and serial number ; that's all you're required to give them under the Geneva Convention."

"We're not prisoners of bloody war," Ted snapped, rising as always to the bait.

"Then tell them you're a minor, that's M.. I ..N.. O.. R, and you want your mam here before you answer anything."

"For Christ's sake stop rambling," Bill complained. "We're not being charged with a capital offence."

"Shut up you lot." The sergeant roared.

"Hey this isn't the Third fucking Reich," Dave retorted, "we can talk as much as we…." The constable who sat in the front turned and cuffed him on the side of the head.

"Shut up sonny boy," he said with quiet menace. He was one of the old school who would brook no nonsense. John gestured for compliance. The young one, who had been dumped in the Taff still hadn't returned from the pub." Let's get these clever bastards to the station."

"Are you a member of the Communist Party," the CID man asked casually, lighting a cigarette.

"Am I now and have I ever been you mean," said the astonished John sarcastically. The five had been separated on entering the station, refused use of the telephone and as far as John could determine had not made any attempt to contact Josephine. He could only hope that Jack the Lamb would be more helpful.

He had been asked a few peremptory questions and then told that he would be interviewed by the CID officer. He had been left alone in the room for almost an hour before the detective who now blew clouds of smoke in his face came in and asked his inane question. "I'm waiting for you answer," he snapped.

"I refuse to answer on the grounds that I might incriminate myself," he teased defiantly, the sarcasm going over his head. "What's it to you anyway. Are you a member of the freemasons?"

"Now don't get cheeky with me lad," he stepped closer, prodding with his forefinger.

"Oh. I thought it was only in the filthy commie countries that police intimidated innocent citizens."

"You know I can check on your political activities lad."

"Oh I bet you can," John retorted. "I've no doubt you've got files on everybody to the left of Selsdon Man."

"Oh but you're a lad for the demos aren't you," he continued ignoring or simply not recognising the riposte as sarcasm. He was after all only the Political Officer. "Public expenditure cuts demo, Hyde Park to the House of Commons. Anti Common Market demo Sophia gardens. Lot's of

93

local stuff here in the Valleys. Principal boy in the recent ICI pantomime. Now deny you weren't leading that demo today."

"My God. You do have a dossier. I am, I was a member of the Labour Party actually. No law against that…yet. No law against demos either. As it happens I had nothing to do with today's, and as for stealing that car, which is why I'm here at all, a simple call to my girlfriend will clear that up. Or is the real reason for me being here political," he muttered his dawning suspicion aloud. "I'm not answering any more of your stupid fucking questions and I'll be making an official complaint to the Chief Constable and my MP. It's worse than Russia. At least there they make no pretence about it."

"Oh I wouldn't bother with the Chief Constable we belong to the same lodge. And as for your MP, old S O has had his day. My information is he won't even be a candidate at the next election. The local Labour Party brass have other plans." So the man was not quite the fool he appeared to be. He had his finger on the pulse. John was only dimly aware of rumours of a move to replace SO as the town's MP with one of the AEU's panjandrums. "Our inquiries reveal that the owner of the Volvo is Mrs Marion Mason of Carnford Manor near Crickhowell. I can't imagine she's likely to have loaned it to you somehow."

"Maybe not," John teased, "but her daughter Josephine might. I'm not a lawyer but I think driving a vehicle with her consent hardly constitutes theft does it?"

The detective shrugged. "That would depend on the circumstances. Does the daughter have it with the mother's consent ? Does she have the authority to extend that consent to a friend ? These things have to be investigated. It all takes time.

"At the moment we're more interested in your part in this demonstration. Have you heard of the International Socialist Party."

"The ISP, yes of course I have. What have they got to do with anything?"

The detective tapped his pen on the edge of his desk. "Well now, would you be surprised to know that several members of the ISP were present at today's scrum."

"I'd be very surprised. No I'd be bloody amazed. There are no Trots among the shop stewards of ICI. I ought to know, I know every rep there. Most of them aren't members of any political party; those that are, are members of the Labour Party by affiliation. Talk about reds under the bed. You lot are getting paranoid."

"Ah so now you do admit you know something about it."

"I've never denied I know something about it. Of course I know something about it. How could I not know something about it after all I am John Davies, *The* John Davies, the greatest threat to civilisation since Karl Marx popped his clogs. What your informants have not yet caught up with is the fact that I have resigned from ICI *and* The Labour Party. Hence I was not involved directly in today's demonstration. Of course you could still fit me up on a conspiracy charge. Always your fallback in these situations."

"Guilty before the fact then are we," the CID man shuffled and plunged suddenly into his desk drawer. "So what were you doing there today then. Just happened to be in town did you?"

"As a matter of fact yes." He could see how this would sound lame, especially to a lamebrain. "I had borrowed my girlfriends car. I was driving to town, to the library actually, when I was held up by the demo. So I parked in the yard behind the Imp and walked down the tram road to the library where the demo was in full swing. I met my pals there, it was just about breaking up, so we went to the Lamb for a drink where your colleagues, the plodders came and summarily arrested us."

"So your friends were demonstrating then?" as if this was QED.

"I didn't see them take part in any illegal activity," John retorted cautiously.

"But that's not what I asked is it ? The officer sighed and withdrew a folder from the drawer and placed it emphatically on the desk. He opened it slowly and glanced from it to John and back again several times."

"Writing my biography," he sneered sarcastically but amazed and disturbed at the size of the file.

"You're a right bloody case you are, aren't you?" The officer said contemptuously. "This country needs protecting from bastards like you."

"Oh yes. Dangerous lot we are. Urban guerrillas. You know about our plot to take the Lady Mayoress hostage."

The policeman moved around the desk menacingly and John did his best not to flinch as the butterflies came alive in his stomach. He had heard from others how they would seldom hit you on the head unless they were sure of convincing the magistrates that you had resisted arrest or had previous form for violence. But they had ways of digging you in the solar plexus which left no obvious marks. He felt his stomach muscles constrict involuntarily. The officer drew hack his hand .... And threw a photograph down with venom on the desk in front of John. "Do you know this man?" he demanded.

This abrupt change of direction threw John for a brief moment before he regained his equilibrium and lied as to the manor born. "No, never seen him before." He knew the man well. A male nurse by the name of Gerald Healey, a shop steward for COHSE or NUPE. Worked in St Tydfil's Hospital. He *was* a member of the ISP, hence Gerry the TROT.

"Was he at today's demo."

"How should I know I told you I wasn't there until it was all over. Why should he be there anyway he doesn't work for ICI I do know that much."

"Don't play the innocent with me. You know it makes no difference with them, they turn up wherever there's trouble, stirring it up."

"They, them, who?"

"The bloody Trots that's who. Your mate Ted is one of them isn't he? Funny thing is, all the demo's they were at, you and your mates were at too."

"So were thousands of others, " John replied incredulously. "These were popular demonstrations. People from all parties, well excluding the bloody Tories, would have been there. Look these questions are bloody stupid and irrelevant to the ostensible reason for me being here so I'm not answering any more without the presence of my solicitor." The fact that he hadn't yet been slapped had given him confidence. "I know my rights," he added as an afterthought.

"Huh your rights is it," the officer chuckled disdainfully. "Look you bloody commie turds I'll keep you here all bloody night if I want to. You watch too much television son."

"Oh no you won't," a bluff once initiated needs must be followed through. "My solicitor is Jenkins, Jenkins and Jenkins," he named the law firm which handled his Union's business. His *ex* Union now he realised suddenly but then remembered what the Regional Secretary had said in Cardiff. They wouldn't accept his resignation and would continue to represent him while he was still in contributory compliance. "You bend the rules of procedure in any way and it'll take more than membership of the Lodge to save you from returning to the beat."

The officer picked up the file and the photograph and returned them to his drawer. He looked at John quizzically as if assessing just how troublesome he might turn out to be. Finally he grinned his face suddenly all bonhomie and threat less as an old friend. "I'm sure you appreciate I have to ask these questions. These fellows are not peaceful demonstrators you know. They don't support the Labour Party or democracy. If they had their way it would be like Russia."

John smiled at the paradox. "The Trots are highly critical of Russia," he explained. "The Trots and the Communists are mortal enemies."

The policeman looked puzzled. "Comes down to it they're all the bloody same," he insisted.

"Oh and I suppose you've got files on the Empire Loyalists and the Nazi's.

The policeman angrily slammed shut the drawer and turned the key. John would love to have read the drivel which such a political illiterate had collated on the individuals of which he was obviously one. It was typical that having decided to create the post of *Political Officer* they should choose to fill it with a dope who wouldn't know a Maoist from cyclist.

Just at that moment the door was flung open and in came the sergeant with a hasty hostile glance at John. He took the CID man aside and whispered to him conspiratorially. They went out together and angry exchanges filtered down the corridor to him. A few minutes later the detective returned red faced. "Ok you can go," he said tersely. "Your posh tottie is waiting at the desk."

John hesitated initially suspecting some kind of trap. What had happened was so unreal that it was difficult to respond rationally. Years later a journalist friend was to inform him that what he had experienced was not untypical. That he was lucky not to have and his home ransacked and a boot in the belly for his pains. Reds were being looked for under every bed and Special Branch was busier than it had ever been in the war. In some quarters it was earnestly believed that the British Labour Party was receiving it's orders directly from the Kremlin. "What about my friends," he asked.

"You can all go, the whole fucking bolshie bastard lot of you," he shouted. "Though not if I had my way. Remember we're keeping a sharp eye on you lot."

"You're absolutely bloody bonkers," John retorted with a quiet anger he could now afford. "All we need is a Macarthy or an Adolph in this country and you goose steppers would have a field day. You haven't heard the last of this." But in his heart he k new they had, and that the Adolphs and Macarthys in other subtler guises were already stalking in the wings. As Brecht so eloquently expressed it '*the bitch was back in heat again.'*

Josephine, and who he took to be a solicitor had clearly harangued the sergeant who was saying smarmily. "I'm glad you were able to clear up the matter of the borrowed car. So no harm done then."

"Just because her name is Mason how do you know she's not a member of the Bader Meinhoffs," John shouted. "Why don't you get that political illiterate in there to give her the third degree too."

She gave him a nonplussed look and glanced at the solicitor who shook his head and took her arm. "Come on let's all get out of here," he advised as if he knew something about these situations that they clearly did not. Years later in the reaction to IRA bombings on the British mainland Ted was to pay the ultimate penalty for failing to understand what this was the precursor of.

They sat awestruck at the grandeur of Carnford as John explained and Josephine listened with increasing incredulity to his account of what had happened. "But I explained to them on the phone that you had the car with my permission," she insisted. "The landlord of some pub you were in, the Lamb was it ?, rang and gave me the gist of it. Sounded more cockup than conspiracy, but now from what you say they were more interested in your politics than the car. They wouldn't accept my statement over the phone, said I had to come in person . I got onto Blackmore, our solicitor straight away. Came up from Ponty like a scalded cat, that's why I took so long, had to wait for him, he insisted. Then they kept us waiting at the station for ages demanding proof of ownership, documents, all that lot, until Blackmore got shirty and legalistic. I'll make sure he complains to the Chief Constable about this, It's outrageous."

"Yeah," Dave added, "but apart from pushing Ted around a bit there isn't a lot we can complain about with sufficient substance to make it stick."

"It's not the pushing about a bit that got to me," Ted complained. "They really gave me the third degree. Mr Nice and Mr Nasty taking turns to implicate me in plots to blow up the water pipeline supplying Brum. We all know it's his bloody lot do silly things like that," jerking his thumb in Geraint's direction. "Me, I'm with Verloc, only it's not Greenwich now, it's Porton or even Pendine, sorry Ger, Pentywyn is it?"

"Don't worry mister anarchist I had the grilling too. They knew I was a member of the Free Wales Army. It said so in my file. Asked me if I knew the command structure, leaders' names, all that shit. I'm afraid of fucking squibs let alone explosives." Apologies to Josephine for the language.

It was Bill who brought them all back down to earth with the absurdity of it. "Us lot as revolutionaries," he laughed. "Who in his right mind would suspect that. What a farce. A real revolutionary would run rings around 'em. They were interested in my photography, not the so called porn, but 'installations'; industrial, military, coastal, strategic, you name it I was quizzed on it. Threatened me with a search warrant. What a surprise they'd have had."

"Aye and you'd have gone down for peddlin' porn." Geraint pointed an accusing finger at him.

Josephine quizzed him on the porn so John insisted that they all go to Bill's to view the latest additions to his gallery. "Perhaps you'd like to pose," he challenged. "I was always led to believe that the Crachach have no scruples about these things. Is that so, in your professional opinion Bill." But Bill was not allowed to answer and they all squeezed into the Volvo again and trekked back to Bill's Asiatically adorned flat in the heart of the old whoretown.

Bills photographs were nothing if not erotic, but pornographic they were not. Many depicted intercourse with full penetration though this was frequently anything but obvious. They had the quality of alien landscapes of sweeping hills and hollows of strange unnatural hues and shades, though the better of them in John's opinion were those in hard focus high contrast black and white, reminiscent of Picasso in a black and white period, or a Freudian inkblot which suddenly jumped into cognitive focus.

Like many seeing them for the first time Josephine was completely blown away but also uncertain how to react. Dave laughed at her unease. "You should see my Vulva," he teased, "but not tonight. There's a great film on in the Castle. After we can go for a curry in the Kenya. How about it?"

The film starred Jack Palance in a role as a failing Hollywood screenwriter which demonstrated an ability to act as something more substantial than the usual *heavy* for which he was inevitably typecast. It was of that era which boasted screenwriters of an awesome calibre such as Dashiel Hammet and even Scott Fitzgerald and others equally celebrated.

It sent John off into a daydream, or rather an evening dream in which he delivered masterpieces to RKO or Paramount and spent his days in the company of Rita Hayworth (starring) and Orson Welles (directing).

What a medium it was, larger than life, universal in appeal and minimal in its limitations. In fact its scope appeared endless although at present film noire had more attractions for him than Technicolor.

Such considerations were the basis for further discussion over curry in the Kenya, the only late night restaurant in town. A few doors down from Adeva's Spanish owned café which boasted soggy steam pies and which itself was a venue for the young cognoscenti of Penydarren and Dowlais. The Kenya was hardly haute cuisine but to these ultra sophisticates it was exotic and new. Even Josephine, accustomed to more opulent fare, tucked in with relish. She was invading their domain with a voracious intensity as though to the *manner* rather than the manor, born. She was even adopting their idiom. But it seemed to her more real than her own existence which seemed in comparison hardly to be existence at all. The paradox was that here was she trying desperately to break in while he was conniving treacherously, as he knew it to be in his heart of hearts, to break out. Both points of view were of course equally delusory. She would never make a complete break, she would drag her heavy purse around with her to the grave. For his part he would never relinquish the poetry of his poverty, it was etched on his soul.

After supper they returned again to Bill's little red pagoda and chewed over his nudes. Man Ray, Josephine decided, very Dada. The combination of whisky, wine and beer going to her head. Not quite so surreal. It took Ted to rupture the drunken arty ambience. "You're all full of shit," he slurred. "They're just a load of thinly disguised cunts." To which there was no intelligible answer.

Josephine drove slowly up the narrow terraced street looking at the numbers. John at first appeared to balk when she suggested she pick him up from home for this their last meeting before her return to college. Then he had shrugged. "Why not." She was pleased, she wanted to meet his parents. She wanted to know everything about him: the street in which he lived, the people with whom he worked, the things in which he believed. She wanted to be part of it, understand it, absorb it all. She wanted it to be part of her.

The street was exactly as she imagined it and why shouldn't it be. It was no different than so many of the other streets of Dowlais and Merthyr. It's principal feature might have been borrowed from one of those social realist films. *Love on the Dole* or some such. A huge black gasholder at the nearby ICI Works dominated the skyline. The house fronts were neat and clean with pumice scrubbed doorsteps, respectable working class, not the real slums which scarred much of the town. She was somewhat disappointed at this, it was less romantic than abject poverty. It was exciting nevertheless parking her opulent Volvo close to the kerb in stark contrast with the Ford Anglia, the only other car in the street. It was almost as if she was doing something risqué, adventuring in forbidden territory. She was amused at the twitching curtains as she tootled her two tone horn and slid lithely out of the sleek limousine.

The sound of the horn brought John to his window. He signalled her to come in and soon appeared in the doorway. His mother and father hovered in the hallway nervous and almost frightened at the prospect of the meeting. But surely this was what they had always wanted . Wasn't it really why they had such ambitions of packing him off to university, to get a decent job and bring home a nice bourgeois wife, buy a nice little property, perhaps one of those new semis, sire two shiny faced children, one of each and settle down to a trouble free life. And here she was, the answer to all their prayers, beyond all their hope and expectations, a grocer's daughter, a doctors even, but this, THIS was one of the seriously rich elite. "Better than arsehole scraping round the foreman for a few hours overtime, eh dad," he smiled the unstated words at his father. "Not so grand as your pile Madame," he said to her instead. "But they say there's no place like home," there was a definite edge to his irony. "Everybody, this is Josephine. Josephine, this is everybody. Well not quite everybody, the sprogs have been despatched to their bedroom." He gave a withering look at his sisters crouching doe eyed at the top of the stairs.

His mother stepped forward awkwardly with outstretched hand. "Pleased to meet you ," she said, and for one awful hesitant moment he thought she was about to curtsey. Josephine embraced her effusively and kissed her cheek.

"I'm so glad to meet you," she said, standing back and making a brief visual appraisal.

"I'll put the kettle on." The typical icebreaker.

"Please don't bother on my account Mrs Davies."

"Oh but I must, Whatever would you think," but she didn't extend the welcome to an invitation to the use of first names. And 'mam' would be much too precipitate a move. They talked mundanely of weather, the price of groceries, the cost of living, most of which was of course inconsequential to Josephine, though she was beginning to appreciate that such trivia loomed large in the lives of such people. Such people as John, with whom she was having this overwhelming relationship. Such people as his friends who knew and did so much more than her sophisticated associates; she no longer thought of them as her friends. Such people as that great unwashed mass who occupied the run down terraces and the new rows of council houses of Merthyr. Such people as those with which she now so much sought to identify. Such people as John's family, ground down by poverty but animated by it in spite of, or perhaps because of it.

Perhaps this was the reason for her former intellectual indolence. This was the force that had been missing from her own experience. Never anything to strive for , never anything to strive from; just an existence founded on the principle of the highest expectations. Each dawn following inexorably on from the previous night and proving a comfortable facsimile of its predecessor. No need to question the rectitude of things, the political order was fashioned for the maintenance of their status quo. And the whole realisation was subliminal rather than rational.

Now-Now that the fire had been lit in her loins and the fever flashed in her brain the word *revolution* was never far from her consciousness; and since these were the real people, the people who actually did the work from which all profit was appropriated, these and only these could forge it. The concept frightened and exhilarated her. She wanted to be part of it, at the heart of it, instrumental in it. She couldn't wait now for her return to college. She would dominate those earnest debates of the Socialist Society. The previously alien concepts of the Marxists had meant little or nothing to her, but like Saul on the Damascus Road the scales had fallen from her eyes. Like a child's puzzle the dots had suddenly been joined and everything made sense. It was not the complete picture yet but with the blind faith of the convert she was certain that soon all would be revealed.

Tea was pleasant but from John's perspective somewhat artificial and strained. There was an absurd over-emphasis on etiquette, the talk mundane and polite, even trite. She was doing her best to fit but he for one certainly didn't want her to. The last thing he really wanted was for her to become one of them, on the contrary, if he was honest, he wanted was to extract perhaps just one foot from the proletarian mud and place the other firmly on Carnford land. He didn't and wouldn't become one of them. His contempt for them was as strong as ever. All he had to do was demonstrate his utter disdain for them and everything they stood for while taking full advantage of their assimilation, rationalising such preposterous ambitions with the old adage that their stronghold was infinitely more vulnerable if attacked from within. Ted the Trot would be proud of him. To get in however he was going to have to kid people who might prove much less kiddable than himself.

Since she really seemed keen on experiencing the proletariat at play he suggested an evening at the ICI Sports and Social Club. Not as grandiose as the classical façade of the Guest library which now functioned as the Guest Keen club, the ICI Club was housed in one of the imposing buildings built for the upper echelon of the Dowlais Works management when it was the biggest producer of iron in the world The former owner, one of the many dignified crooks of the industrial revolution had, like all the others, made his pile when the going was good and cleared off for pastures greener, like the manorial heap where the Mason's now resided , monitoring their profits at a pleasant remove from the filth and squalor out of which they grew.

The club lounge was already packed with noisy boisterous people when they arrived, and the eye smarting cigarette smoke twisted up in blue spirals flattening themselves against the discoloured high ornate stuccoed ceilings. A fat woman at the corner table laughed loudly ad her enormous breasts trembled like quivering blancmanges beneath a low cut flowery dress. A jostling crowd thronged the bar at the rear of the hall with empty glasses clutched in impatient hands elbowing and shoving for prime position. Two of them argued angrily and pushed tentatively at one another with a feigned menace.

"Here John boy. Have one on me," a big blousy woman offered. He seemed to attract the big blousy types Josephine mused with a quick glance down at her own not inconsiderable cleavage. "You got em on the run now John boy," she congratulated. She was the wife of one of the bottling plant shop stewards. "Mart said they've conceded everything and old Heydock's on the next banana boat to some obscure plant in Nigeria. Serves the bastard right I say. You comin' back now then?" John shook his head negatively. "Well cant say I blame you," she smiled with a knowing look at Josephine. "I work for your mum," she said, "shop steward on the bra line. Not betraying the working class I hope brother," she teased, only half in jest.

"No," he responded a little irritably. "Josie's a new recruit to the class war. Together we are going to tear your knicker plant down."

"Ooo you randy sod, are you going to tear mine down then," and she hoisted her skirt for a quick flash. That was one good thing about the Mason's girls, they all sported the very best in chic underwear.

John refused the drink as politely as his irritation would allow, bought his own at the bar and steered Josie to an empty table at the back of the room.

"Who was that," she asked.

"Works for your mum as she said. Shop steward, runs in the family. Husband Mart's a shop steward too. Production. Represents the bottling plant at ICI. A bit raucous," he explained, "as you can see. I couldn't handle all that noisy jollity tonight."

"And what about the Dowlais Five?"

"Don't come here that often," he replied.

"I get it," she teased reproachfully, "the intellectual vanguard doesn't fraternise that easily with the proletariat. That's more Leninist than Marxist isn't it."

"Even the Syndicalists had their leaders," John said seriously. "Talk to Ted he's the Kropotkin of the group." She was lost now. She'd boned up a bit on Marxist Leninism, the Soviet version, but she was still scratching at the surface. She had a lot to learn and she was determined to learn it. She was sorry that John had eschewed the camaraderie offered to him. She would have been interested to hear what a real shop steward sounded like as opposed to the unreal John.

102

He sat moodily for a while silent, sullen, sipping at his drink and she wondered what if anything she had done to offend him. Perhaps it had not been such a good idea bringing her here, exposing her to the prols, as it had not been such a good idea inviting her to tea. Here it seemed equally stiff and artificial, not the warm jovial occasion it would have been if she was Anne Jones or Margaret Evans from Spring Street or Balaclava Road. To make matters worse there was Heydock in the middle of the floor obviously quite drunk and eyeing John clumsily making his way to their table.

" 'appy now I s'pose," he slurred. "Off to Ni- bloody-jeria me, iss the end you know, iss the fuckin' end of everything, my wife, my job everything. Iss all your fuckin' fault." He lurched spilling some of his drink on their table. "Coulda pulled it off it wasn't for you, you know that you clever bastard. Iss of to Nigeria for me," he refrained. "I gotta good mind to...." And he lunged aggressively but fell and upset the adjacent table. The two women sitting with their husbands screamed hysterically. One of the men jumped to his feet, grabbed Heydock by his thinning hair lifting his head roughly with one hand and making a cocked fist of the other. One of the wives screamed even louder and John leapt in with a restraining hand on the man's shoulder.

"Don't hit him Harry, he pleaded. It won't do any good will it. He's pissed out of his mind and, well he's probably had enough of a hammering for one day already one way or another." Harry hesitated for a moment before dropping Heydock disdainfully in a heap in the pool of spilled drinks and broken glasses.

"You're right I suppose," he muttered, "but you of all people shouldn't waste sympathy on this bastard. He wanted you sacked with no second thoughts. He lied to us about the bloody bonus scheme. Good riddance after the bastard, that's what I say." This sentiment found a ready echo from all around the hall as a couple of the committee men dragged the hapless Heydock out to a chorus of cheers.

John helped Harry and his friends to resurrect the table and the club chairman sanctioned a fresh round on drinks on the house. He returned to Josephine and shrugged, allowing himself the luxury of a hint of a smile in response to the one that played around the corners of her eyes. It had it's comic side he supposed. "I told you it was a bit of a dive," he said. "You were warned."

"Perhaps I'm the kind of girl that likes low dives," she replied. "They're so much more interesting than the high dives which I've been more used to. I take it that was the management rat who tried to do the dirty on you."

"The very same," he confirmed waving to Dai Whippet whose shaggy head appeared through the crowd.

"So the bad guy got his come uppance. What about the good guy, has he got his reward?"

103

"He hopes to get it in instalments," he quipped. "Now here comes a real character," he nodded to Dai who stood in front of them beaming. "Josephine, Dai; Dai, Josephine," he introduced. " So how did the doggies go tonight?" Dai's face was wreathed in smiles. He pulled out a wreath of fivers and pushed one into John's breast pocket. This was when fivers were really fivers, big white and rare cheques drawn on the Bank of England. He waved away John's objections with some annoyance.

"Oh no, that's yours," he insisted. "You brought me good luck with that intellectual grey'ound. I've 'ad a good night tonight John bach. Put the bitch in blinkers didn't I. She could only see straight ahead. Won by a bloody mile. I thought John bach would like that. Then I looked at Sharkey's board. On the list Saucy Lad, fifty to one no hoper. I had the Echo in my pocket. Cheeky Apprentice Strike Settled was the headline. Now I don't usually go in for omens, but I'd seen that Saucy Lad a month ago in Bermondsey. Wasn't called Saucy Lad then as I remember, and he'd won hands down. Than Dai Dee the commie bookie gave me the wink. The fix was in. Spread my bet, everything I had, not too greedy. Five ten pound bets on Saucy Lad to win. Dai was the only bookie smilin' when he came in by a gnat's dick, oh excuse me miss you're that Mason girl aren't you. So that fiver's yours by right you Saucy Lad."

"*That* Mason girl," she retorted. "I'm not *that* infamous am I ?"

"No no. It's just that I knew your mam in the old days when she was a little urchin with a snotty nose in Llywellyn Street. Lovely girl she was, lovely woman she is if the photos in the Western Mail are anything to go by."

John couldn't visualise the Marion Mason he'd visualised in his delirium as a snot nosed little waif.

"Watched her grow up didn't I. Course I'm a good bit older than Marion. Can't be that old now come to think of it, must 'ave 'ad you young Miss…"

"Josephine," she responded, "Josie. You knew my mum as a girl, fascinating. Tell me."

"Got plenty of her in you I can see that. Who'd 'ave thought, after everything that she'd end up owning Mason's."

"She never talks much about her childhood," she confessed.

"Aye well it wasn't a bed of roses for 'er I can tell you. I mean we all had it rough in those days. No work around, everybody on the dole but everybody in the same boat. But she 'ad it rougher than most poor kid."

Josephine was astonished and captivated by this revelation. Trust good old Dai Whippet to retrieve an evening that seemed to be going nowhere. "You really knew my mother as a child," her interest was really roused now. Please tell me about her."

"I'm surprised she hasn't seen fit to tell you herself." He was suddenly very sober. "I don't know if I ought to be the one."

"Oh please," she begged. "It would mean a lot to me."

104

He looked to John for sanction but there was none forthcoming, he merely shrugged having no idea what family skeleton might be let out of the cupboard. "She's a big girl now," was all he said.

"Very proper people your grandparents were," he started. "Plymouth Brethren your grandfather, very strict, very puritanical, not very popular I'm afraid. What's the word John, censorious is it, there you're not the only one with words are you? Minnie, your grandmother wouldn't say boo to a goose, a bit afraid of him by all accounts. But your mother, she was different; rebellious, full of life and a stunner, if you'll excuse me, all the boys were mad about her. Stood up to him she did. He'd rant and rave but never knew how to handle her, so he took it out on Minnie. Gave her a hard time. Don't think he beat her or anything but he was so full of all that religious stuff, overbearing he was. I think she only put up with it for the kids' sake. Your mum and her little brother."

"Brother? I never knew she had a brother. You mean I've got an uncle I don't know about?" Josie interrupted.

"Ah. Well." He looked at John. "There's the tragedy you see. Poor little Jack died. But I'm getting ahead of myself. Anyway ' though your gran seemed the timid type it seems she found someone who gave her a little bit of what she wasn't getting at home, you know attention and a bit of love," he hurriedly qualified himself for Josie's sake. Danny Dacey, bit of a wild lad when he was young but I think he was serious about Minnie. Anyway it was a bit of a scandal. You can imagine how your grandad took it. He went to pieces, started to drink, not in the pub, solitary like, the worst way. Then suddenly Minnie disappeared but not with Danny, leaving the kids. There was all kinds of talk. Danny and your Grandad were both questioned by the police but it was a mystery. There were those who said Minnie would never have left her kids, especially young Jack, your mum was in her teens working at Mason's so I suppose she could fend for herself but young Jack, well."

"What are you suggesting," Josie was horrified, surely not.."

"I'm not suggesting anything love but you know how people will always gossip, well whatever, your Grandad went from bad to worse, gave up the Chapel, couldn't stay sober long enough, lost his job and all. Your mum hung on for the sake of little Jack, little bugger he was, always up to mischief and then there was the accident."

"Jack died in an accident?"

"Your Grandad was drunk as usual, a Saturday morning, your mum had to work an extra Saturday shift, she was the only breadwinner now. Got the kid up and gave him breakfast and went off to work. When she came home no sign of Jack. The only sense she could get out of the old man was that he'd gone out to play with the gang. Come tea time still no sign of him. Called the police. They hunted high and low, by now they were looking for four kids. Eventually they found three, too terrified to come home on their own. Seems they'd been messin' about over Bolton's the knackers yard,

105

always interesting and gory things to be found there. Then they went bird nesting. A tree growing out of one of the old colliery shafts had a nest in it..."

"Oh no." Josie anticipated.

"Yes," Dai Whippet confirmed. "Little Jack was the only one daft enough to dare. When he slipped the boys were horrified, calling out his name down the deep shaft, dropping stones which didn't even appear to hit the bottom. They realised he must be dead and ran and hid in one of Bolton's old sheds. That's where they found them hours later huddled together, terrified they would be blamed. They never even recovered the body. Those old workings are all flooded. Like a rabbit warren down there. No records or anything. The rescue team went down but it seems the old roadway was like a river : impossible. 'Course they filled and capped it after, and all the others in the area, dozen's of em. Poor little Jack.

"Marion left home the following week stayed with your Auntie Maud for a bit. Wasn't long after she took up with your dad. Child bride she was. Your Grandad didn't last too long after that drunk himself to death he did. Your mother didn't even go to his funeral. You can imagine what they said. Then years later when your father died and she took over the factory. I remember thinking that's one hell of a strong woman your mother. But there you are love," he patted her arm reassuringly, " time heals everything, isn't that what they say. There was a philosopher, I expect John can put a name to him, who once said, 'Even this shall come to pass', proved true as far as Marion's concerned. A remarkable woman. Remember me to her, Dai, Dai Prosser, Llywellyn Street."

Now the tears fell. "Oh my God what a story and I never knew. Why didn't she tell me. But my grandmother John, what happened to her, do you think she's still alive?"

John shrugged. Marion must have had a good reason for keeping all this to herself he suggested. "Look I'm sorry Dai Whippet had to be the bearer of such gloom, normally he's the life and soul of the party. Anyway there's what might very loosely be called a cabaret on in the hall in ten minutes. I took the liberty of getting a couple of tickets. Come on you need cheering up."

He doubted very much whether the 'cabaret' would have such a therapeutic effect. This evening had been doomed from the outset. First the incident with Heydock then Dai Whippet so uncharacteristically maudlin. "I'd better prepare you for this he warned. There'll inevitably be a comedian who'll tell crude unsophisticated jokes; a singer who'd be ok in the backroom of a little pub, an old vaudeville routine featuring a dowdy busty basqued dancer with a tired old partner, probably dipso, and a conjurer who'll turn black wands into silk hankies. It will all be very second rate but delightfully hilarious. The audience will smoke like a blast furnace and chatter like baboons. They'll harangue the performers and cheer the singer to the hilt if he sings some sentimental slop. All in all something the upper crust should be forced to experience at least once in their lifetime. Once will probably be quite enough."

"I don't know," she articulated her reticence. "I don't quite know how to respond. To discover ," she choked on her words and almost sobbed. "....so close and not to know. I wonder if.... how can we know so little of those who are closest to us."

"That's a cross I think we all bear love," he reassured, taking her arm and guiding her into the hall, anything to avoid such introspection. "Take my own folks for example. How much more noble they are than I ever gave them credit for. Oh the faults and frailties are inevitably still there, all the minor irritations. But seen in the context of the difficulties of their lives they appear admirable. This old whoretown scarred them and scars us still Josie. It scarred your mum hideously. Perhaps some reconciliation is due don't you think. But let's forget all that for now, let's enjoy Saturday night at the Palladium."

"John," she said seriously as the steward took their tickets, " you'll always be honest with me won't you. No matter what."

If he didn't actually blush he had difficulty controlling the rush of blood to his cheeks. He laughed and promised. "Of course I will Josie love." And he hated himself.

In the main hall where the 'cabaret' was to take place there were few seats to be had. The plastic topped tables were set in long rows at right angles to the stage giving access down the aisles to the bar. 'Pack em in' was the motto and the committee had it worked out to a fine art. John and Josie managed to squeeze in opposite a thin lugubrious wages clerk and his fat jolly extrovert wife. He drank g and t while she gulped steadily from a pint of lager.

The lights dimmed and a regular standup did the intros; third rate singers accompanied by third rate instrumentalists with the resident organist contributing the occasional tired chord, a sad melancholic man who looked as if each note was wrenched from a battered heart, a third rate comedian followed by a third rate magician, the former repeating the same tired crude jokes from his previous performance, the latter pulling cigarettes out of peoples ears accompanied by a busty ageing assistant who struck absurd poses at climactic moments, all clapped, jeered, guffawed and heckled relentlessly.

John scanned the animated faces of the audience. Was this really what they had laboured all week for, the high spot. They were out to have a good time so they did, regardless of the quality of what was being dished up. It would have made little difference if the village idiot had stood up there pulling grotesque faces. John had recently attended a 'talent' contest compered by TV presenter Brian Michie at the Theatre Royal. All the local talent was there Dai Luciano the tenor from Bardi nearly burst a blood vessel.

Handel Jones did his best to outdo Max Miller in the double entendre game. Betty Williams who thought she was, and sounded like Madame Patti tried to shatter the glassware. But the winner by public acclaim measured on the 'clapometer' was none other than Johnny Donovan, a prince among the many 'village idiots' who skulked the streets of Merthyr, who dressed as a cowboy galloping around the stage with a hobby horse reciting a Gene Autry monologue about nights under the stars on the range serenading his best friend, the wooden horse. In all honesty he was a worthy winner as the best entertainer by far. And so it was with the 'cabaret'. It wasn't long before the cheers turned to jeers and the call went up for the local favourites to perform.

Volunteers were plentiful and as the mushy romantics got going on stage the audience became more rapt. Husbands held hands with tearful wives, their own and other men's. Unattached but hopeful widows and spinsters coalesced. Desertees, boyos, tarts, nymphs, virgins, swappers and swingers, the remnants of floundering and floundered relationships all grinning through bared teeth and crying into their beer, lonely and frightened and longing for an expression of honest love.

It was reflected in their searching eyes in this room full of laughter and unbearable pain. It was heard rending but repugnant to him in his sobriety. Vulturous vulgar women sauced with gin, frightened running men seeking some ephemeral solace, boozed up with weak, watery, Welsh beer. All the dolls whose names were legion, consumers gorged on the wasteful products of their labour, reduced themselves to commodities by a system in which the commodity was a fetish.

Josephine too felt the unease in him and upset as she had been by the earlier events clutched his hand. "Take me out of here quickly," she pleaded. He didn't have to ask why, she had learned her first lesson. The air outside was sweet.

"Let's cruise," he suggested unable to keep the edge of irritation from his suggestion. As he led her to the car he couldn't put his finger on exactly what it was that was irking him. A couple of weeks ago the mere prospect of bedding someone like Josephine with the further prospect of her delectable mother would have buoyed him up to the very summit of ecstatic expectation. Now he was troubled by her expectation summarised in words like *love, honesty, fidelity*. It was Lynda all over again. *Commitment.* Yes that was it. Why did it terrify him so? He shrugged with incomprehension as he opened the passenger door. "You drive, I'll navigate."

He directed her along a maze of narrow streets of broken windowed houses through the heart of Dowlais and down towards Penydarren, past broken windowed hovels and piles of rubble that had not waited for the clearance programme before surrendering to the gerrymandering of long dead tyrants and the ravages of decades of hard times. Then they were climbing again up Penyard through streets that were for all the world the Welsh equivalent of Soweto. Ramshackle dwellings in the lee of the Great

White Tip, the huge solidified slag Atlas which towered over them. The dross of more than a century of ironmaking which Sir John had left behind as his legacy. Filthy mounds of black ash delineated the margins of the huge enterprise which had been the Dowlais works. Miraculously tufts of clumpy grass and stunted shrubs clung tenaciously here and there in an environment so hostile it would baffle the minds of modern botanists. Daisies rooted in bitter ground as Idris Davies the Rhymney poet described them.

> *"And sweet it was to fancy*
> *That even the blackest mound*
> *Was proud of its single daisy*
> *Rooted in bitter ground."*

The slip road carved its way through this wilderness. Above it the hills riddled with the abandoned coal workings into which the equally invasive opencast was beginning to make its ugly incursions, below it the ruined remnants of the works and the ruined remnants of the town; and this was just Dowlais. Down in Merthyr itself Crawshay's crumbled empire had left it's scars. And between the two the forges of Homfray in Penydarren and at the southern extremity of the town Lord Plymouth had raped and ravaged with equal savagery. It was all rape and desolation. Across the Cwm the Chemical works now poured its own filth into the Nant Morlais polluting it with steaming chemical effluent as it meandered its way appropriately underground from that point until it emerged into the opaque Taff at Pontmorlais.

"Pull in," he urged and as she came to a halt in the lay-by high on the side of the black hill he slumped back and closed his eyes. It was that day again, was it one day or the remembered amalgam of several. He stood on the black hill holding the hand of his giant father looking fondly down at him. "Look daddy the sun is melting the clouds," pointing with his tiny finger to where the mist was rolling slowly down the hills which surrounded the town into a white shroud which lay like gossamer along the banks of the river. Looking up again into his fathers eyes with a quizzical expression awaiting an expecting an explanation from the one whose knowledge was infinite.

The man smiled proudly at his son and said. "Sometimes, up here, we're as close to heaven as we can get. Here there is no time. We see an hour in a second. That's how we can see the clouds melting. Sometimes on a day like this, in a place like this we can see eternity in the twinkling of an eye.

It had meant little to him then of course but the incident and the actual words came to him now as if it had been yesterday . The only spontaneous poetry he ever remembered falling from his father's lips. "Oh Josephine," he sighed. "Where are the ghosts of Marx and Heine now.

> *'But now in the winter dusk*
> *I go to Dowlais Top*

And stand on the railway bridge
Which joins the bleak brown hills,
And gaze at the streets of Dowlais
Lop sided on the steep dark slope,
A battered bucket on a broken hill,
And see the rigid phrases of Marx
Bold and black against the steel grey west,
Riveted along the sullen skies,
And as for Heine, I look on the rough
Bleak, colourless hills around,
Naked and hard as flint,
Romance in a rough chemise.'"
6

He recited the verse also from Idris Davies, the words coming to him with equal clarity. She reached across and stroked his face with tears in her eyes. "Can't we shatter it to bits and remould it nearer to the hearts desire," he paraphrased. "There surely must be a way." She pressed a finger to his lips then placed her own lips soft on his and lingered with a tenderness he had not thought her capable of.

Down far below the sussurating wind seemed to carry voices up to them, aproned wives on doorsteps scandalising each other, the scent of spilt beer wafting on the breeze from cosy pubs and the deeper sound of men's voices arguing about Marx and Heine, all knowing with their vision of the future. But there was tipsy daft talk too; how Tommy Farr had beaten Joe Louis to a frazzle, how the goal John Charles scored from the edge of his own penalty area was the best ever seen, how Cliff Morgan scored a try running from behind his own line, how Jarret kicked a penalty from his own twentyfive, how Ken Jones did an eight point five hundred yards with the ball under his arm, how Dai Evans should have had first prize as a baritone in the National but had lost to a policeman who was a Mason almost by definition. They covered all the Welsh heroes from Uther Pendragon to Ivor Allchurch and finished up with wife swapping among the crachach of Cefn Coed.

And as the clocks tocked on and the town sank deeper into the dark and the women returned to cosy kitchens and the boozy boyos tumbled out of the pubs among the tumblers old Twm Scwt who still lived in what was left of Pengarnddu, the huddled hamlet which twinkled like a cluster of dim stars on the brow of the hill above them. He meandered from side to side in John's imagining, as indeed he frequently did in reality, a consequence of the rough scrumpy which he disposed of in awesome measure. It was a very long haul

---

6 Tonypandy and Other Poems, Idris Davies, Faber and Faber

up from Dowlais to Pengarnddu, especially when like Lenin you took two steps forward and one step back. Ooops – down in the gutter, red nose up smiling at the watery moon, holding the ground tight lest he should fall up into the sky. "Ullo God mun I can see you up there laughin' at old Twm. This hill is rolling like a ship." Up, up, oops – down again. "You can laugh boy, you can bloody laugh, you made me in your image," falling fast asleep in the gutter.

Bedroom windows begin to light, ones and twos, pinks and greens, three together, two, one at a time, a dance to an anarchic rhythm, the rhythm of life. Pathos, bathos, passion all enacted there in the pin prick distance, epic drama, farce, tragedy, la comedie humaine. But all that could be seen were flickering lights like the shadows in Plato's cave. All this perceived from their Olympian perch on the black Dowlais hill.

He turned to her despairingly. The breeze blew through the open window and ruffled the white scarf which she wore closely around her dark and beautiful face. She pressed the button and closed the window . Pressed another and turned on the radio. Late night music. Sinatra in plaintive mood. Simple Arlen lyrics.

"Now a man don't care if the sky grows dim and the clouds roll over and darken him."

Just as the moon disappeared into a dark grey bank of threatening cumulus.

"As long as the Lord God's watching over him, keeping track how it all goes on."

The first large blobs of rain splash on the windscreen.

" But I've been searching through the night and the day til my head is weary and my hair turns grey, and sometimes I think maybe God's gone away...........and we're lost out here in the stars, and we're lost out here in the stars."

She turned back to him in her own sadness seeking his embrace and saw the tears coursing down his cheeks. "You're crying."

"Yes."

"Why?"

"Because Sartre's right as Harold Arlen, God's gone away, and we're lost out here in the stars." He lent across and kissed the salt tears on her lips, hers and his. Love and hate, he thought, they're both sides of the same coin.

Their lovemaking that night took on a new dimension. In place of the wild ecstasy, the lust, something warm and effusive. Not better, not worse, but different, and it somehow carried a greater commitment which was not what he had planned or wanted. His armour as well as hers was pierced. He was vulnerable now, and afraid.

111

CHAPTER 7

The morning was pale. Thin wisps of cloud curtained a turquoise sky as he drove her early to Abergavenny Station. Her mother had not been around to make her farewells and they had not seen her on their arrival last night. How deliberate was this avoidance he wondered and how deep seated the apparent coolness between mother and daughter. The events outlined by Dai Whippet must certainly have had some bearing on Mrs Mason's subsequent relations. But even if her route to the Mason's millions had more than an element of ruthless ambition attached to it he would have expected a stronger bond between mother and daughter to have been one of the outcomes. Josephine was clearly affected by the revelations and more than a little frustrated at not being able to pursue the matter with her mother immediately.

The train pulled tiredly in and the shuttered window of the little ticket office opened.

"When will you be home again?"

"Christmas, but if you want I could…"

"Let's just let things take their natural course," he interrupted.

"Yes, you're right of course. It's all been a bit hectic hasn't it. Let things settle down then shall we," she agreed with uncharacteristic aplomb. No demands of love and fidelity. But then - "You do still want to see me at Christmas though."

"Of course I do." He took her hand. "After all I'll be dreaming of that inheritance of yours. I am on the dole you know." She smiled thinly. Was it purely banter or a Freudian slip. They kissed as the whistle blew and she clambered into the carriage, and now at last the tears flowed. "I do love you ," she sobbed, "I do."

"I love you too," why did he have to say it. He bit his tongue too late as the incredulous joy suffused her face and the train pulled out. Once again he had said it and in his own way meant it. It was a simple enough statement, direct and non-committal, but it would not be taken as such − it never was. There was neither promise nor pledge in it. 'Of course I loves you darling, I fucks you don't I.' Yet it wasn't quite as crude as that either. He had tried to convince himself that it was, that lust and love were inseparable in that ephemeral moment of the act. But in his heart he knew it wasn't so. Even with Maggie there was more to it than just the coupling. And now another thought assailed him, even as the train was receding from sight. Josephine would be gone for several weeks and he had to return the car to her mother and when he closed his eyes the receding train was replaced by that other troubling image.

When he arrived back at Carnford he parked the car on the drive outside the front entrance. The Daimler was there and the factotum was polishing the chromework lovingly. "Hullo Mr Davies," he greeted with something less than the deference reserved for his employers.

"Hullo Joe. Think I could scrounge a lift over to Merthyr sometime. I've just dropped Josie at the station and…."

"Mrs Mason would like to see you," he interrupted with the implication that his request should properly be made to her.

John shrugged and smiled inwardly with some bemusement. The biggest snobs in these situations always seemed to be the hired help. John was obviously considered infra dig by the factotum. He rang the bell which was almost immediately answered by Mrs Marion Mason in an immaculate outfit. This was fifties chic. There was no concept of the power dressing enabled by the women's lib in later decades but this was Marion Mason's preconception of it. Not androgynous but suffused with a subtly understated sexuality which in this era made the statement more eloquently. Here I am, I am rich, powerful and beautiful. I am a woman and I am more than your equal. "Come in I have something of important I'd like to discuss with you."

There's something important I wouldn't mind discussing with you, he couldn't help riposting silently watching the swaying body outlined by the perfect fitting of her skirt. She led the way into the lounge, or a lounge, for the house had more than one. Perhaps in their parlance this was the morning room or some such. Anyway it was not the room with the impressive array of books and the intimidating nude portrait he was glad to discover. Because he did feel intimidated and to be confronted by that portrait and inevitably to be seen translating it's form to the chicly clothed one which confronted him in the flesh would have been, well, disconcerting to say the least. And all so shortly after his declaration of love.

She took her place sedately on an antique chaise longue; the whole room was furnished in a late Victorian, early Edwardian style, all crimson and velvet. A room he thought a high class courtesan might entertain aristocratic cads in. He made to sit beside her but received a cold rebuff. "Let's get one thing straight from the outset," she asserted. "I'm not one of your factory girl pushovers. If I want your attentions I'll invite them."

"Oh but I'm sure you've noticed, I'm into debs now," he taunted, and anyway you were a factory girl yourself once."

"Oh I've never forgotten it you may be assured," she replied, "but that was a long time ago and I didn't invite you in to talk about my past so much as your future.."

"My future. What do you mean?"

"You're unemployed," she said dryly. "There's not much future in that. I know my daughter and I know when she's got it bad; and I know an ambitious young man when I see one. You're ambitious enough to be a future son in law. I don't want my daughter to marry a bum so I'm prepared to make a decent man of you. I think I can find a place for your talents in the Mason's empire."

His angry response had more to do with her perspicacity than anything else. "I assure you I have absolutely no desire to be married to your daughter nor anyone else for that matter. Marriage and me juxtaposed is an oxymoron," he snapped. "We've got something good going – that's all."

"You can say that again ," she retorted spitefully. "I haven't seen anyone quite so cuntstruck in years." The crudity of her comment did not lie easily with her bourgeois demeanour.

"As for finding a little niche for me in your sweatshop madam, you can stuff it," he snapped. If she could be crude so could he. It was only case hardening anyway, he decided. "I've just managed to unhitch myself from one cart," he said. "I'm in no hurry to hitch myself to another which, if the information I've got from your shop stewards is anything to go by, would prove more unbearable than that from which I've just escaped."

"Allright," she conceded, "let's cut the crap. I'll make some coffee and we'll get down to the nitty gritty shall we? You can start by dropping the Mrs Mason, it's Marion, and I hope I can call you John."

"What we call each other is less significant than what the 'nitty gritty' is isn't it," he insisted. My God she'd be a bitch to deal with in trade union negotiations, he thought. "What's this all about," he insisted.

"Coffee first," she insisted, " and a little toast?"

"Well I won't say no to that," somewhat disarmed by her sudden civility. "This morning was a bit of a rush-no time for breakfast."

" I didn't get up to see her off because I thought she'd prefer to have you to herself for that little ceremony. Another misunderstanding that requires cleaning up. I always sleep au natural as you discovered. I am accustomed to being home alone at bedtime. When Josie's on vacation I am accustomed to her being alone at bedtime. Consequently we wander in and out of each other's rooms with little thought for propriety. That, I assure you, is precisely what happened the other night."

It was possible, even plausible, but he was still not sure he believed it, perhaps because he didn't want to believe it. He shrugged and managed a somewhat doubtful smile and shrugged his shoulders. "You just shattered a young man's fantasy," he smiled. "So be it."

"So be it," she repeated with a positive insistence. But still he somehow did not believe it.

"I was half convinced that I had dreamed it anyway," he laughed. "Perhaps we both had too much of that Celtic Coffee."

"Be fully convinced and forget about it," she said curtly. "Men can be so bloody boring about these things, never taking no for an answer even when the knee is brought up hard into the groin."

"No need to knee me," he insisted. "I always take no for an answer, perhaps too readily for some. Truth is I hate fartarsing about. Not that I don't enjoy the game when its played intelligently. Rape is for rapists and hunting is for the unspeakable. Its mutual or its nothing as far as I'm concerned."

"Good. I'm glad that's settled. Now for that coffee, not Celtic," she chided.

the kitchen she closed her eyes and breathed deeply. Why this charade, she asked herself. He had turned her on, she had wanted him to screw her. Now she was ashamed. It would have been the same as always – the great expectation followed by that empty anticlimax. And yet that urge was always uncontrollable and the lesson never learned, the drive and the desire always there like some insatiable drug addiction. It would not have been the first time she had seduced a pretty boy her daughter had dragged in like a cat with a tasty morsel . But this was different, this went deeper, Josie had not offered him up to be devoured. This was no callow easy boy- this was a man before his time. A special man. There was something to be feared in him. And she wanted him.

"Right," she said returning with the coffee, "Let's get down to business. I want you to come to work for us at Masons." She held up a hand anticipating his response. "Hear me out," she cautioned. "I want you to be the company's cultural officer. Your main role will be to stimulate cultural activity at the workplace." She paused to let it sink in noting the look of amazement quickly followed by scepticism which suffused his face. "Of course there's something in it for us," she replied to the question which he was about to ask. " We're about to launch a new line . I'm taking Mason's upmarket into haute couture. We've poached Marc Lafarge us as our fashion guru from the Paris house Chinelle . You'll have no direct input into that but your appointment would no doubt add something to our image. You know you and your group have a growing reputation which my contacts will exploit to our mutual benefit. We had pencilled in that Anglo-Welsh prick Steve Michaels for the job but you're both a better poet and well you're almost a member of the family aren't you. Can't you see the headlines 'Lingerie magnate subsidises art , culture comes to the factory floor.' Don't worry I don't want you to write the jingoes."

"Oh but I could manage that allright," he replied sarcastically. "Be it opera or dance there's a Mason's pants that's tailored for every occasion.

You see how easy it is, yet you pay idiots to write drivel like that more than the workers who actually produce the goods."

"The talent for writing drivel like that is actually comparatively rare, you clearly have a flare for it. We're all hewers of wood and drawers of water as somebody once said. Rare skills can demand high rewards in the free market economy."

"Are you taking the piss," he demanded.

"You'd know it if I was," she sparred with him. "But we're not talking about the jingoists. What I have in mind is a lecture programme, readings, workshops, a gallery of new modern painters, sculptors, exhibitions, readings. What more could you want. I do actually have a sincere interest in promoting the arts. You've seen my library. Before you leave I'll show you my collections."

"You are taking the piss. If not get Wesker and Littlewood I'm sure you could afford them."

"I want you."

"Ahhh."

"Be serious," she snapped irritably. "I'm making you the offer of a lifetime."

"You be serious Marion. How could this be possible, it's utterly impractical. You're going to stop the line for poetry workshops I suppose. Hang on I'll ring my old friend Bertoldt Brecht see if he can do The Woman from Sechuan next week shall I?"

"No need to stop the line. You think I'd go into this thing half cocked. Work study have been on it for a week, the schedules are possible. For years now we've had problems trying to iron out our production flow. It's been studied by every expert in the industry and the only answer they've got is to invest in new plant on such a revolutionary scale that it's completely out of the question. Groups of our workers spend periods of considerable idleness every day due to the completion of their particular component of the batch process. We've had Swedish experts in to devise a system of job rotation so that the periods of down time are spread across the whole workforce on an equal basis. A minor modification to this would allow different groups to be freed at different times during the week which would enable you to set up a rolling programme to deliver to each group."

"I'm not sure that selling someone else's art to the masses is what I want to do for the rest of my life."

"Rest of your life," she sneered. "You're unemployed," she pointed out. "Probably unemployable . I'm offering you the opportunity of a lifetime. My God there'd be plenty of time to develop your own work."

"And what about the unions," he heard his own words but could hardly believe that he was saying them. "If I were one of your reps I'd smell a rat. 'Where's the catch,' I'd be saying. 'What's in it for them. They never do anything for nothing. How does it tie in to the *productivity agreement*, or

116

whatever euphemism you have for your *incentive scheme.* 'There must be a new line, new production methods, less bonus, something. Those bastards don't give anything away.' "

"But you're not one of our reps," she reminded him smugly sipping at her coffee. "Our reps couldn't hold a candle to you and your lot. Anyway it would be your job to sell it to the reps - who better, and you could do it with a clear conscience because there is no catch. Downtime is turned into something positive for us and the great unwashed receive an education. They used to call it philanthropy. Your world is much too cynical," she smiled. "The board room is no more full of rats than the bedrooms are full of reds."

"Well the latter is certainly the case," he agreed. "All the same I don't want to be on your payroll, a salaried apparatchik. We might come to some arrangement on a contract basis though. Get your goons to look into that. I won't be answerable to your Personnel, PR or Marketing Departments he insisted. I'll be directly answerable only to the MD."

"That's me," smiling conspiratorially.

"Precisely." This was developing into a pas de deux after all but he made a mask of his expression. "I won't be used," he warned. "I'll be free to withdraw my services at any time."

She appraised him calmly. Was he really this confident. What she was doing was dangerous, but then she had always thrived on taking high risks. That was her forte. "Despite what they say my power is not absolute you know, I'll have to go back to the board with this . But before I do I'm interested in seeing how you perform under pressure. Imagine this is your first session. What sort of poetry would you use to stimulate the interest of a mainly young, or youngish, female group. Pretend I'm your audience."

"I'd have to think about that, " he replied uncomfortable at being put on the spot, "do some research." He resented being asked for an impromptu viva voce but there was something of the throwing down of the gauntlet in her challenge to which he felt compelled to respond as if somehow his manhood was being questioned.

"Select a few volumes from the study if you like," she offered. "There's a pretty comprehensive range in there. I've got a few calls to make. When I return it'll be as Maggie Jones fresh off the production line." This was fun, remembering that she once had been Maggie Jones and it had been the magnate Mason doing the 'poetry reading'.

"But what if I fail."

"Just screw your courage to the sticking place and you'll not fail," she paraphrased.

He'd walked straight into that one but rescued the moment with the quick riposte. "I think you'll find the pronoun is *we*," he corrected. "*We'll* not fail. I told you earlier if it's not mutual it's nothing." Was she just a little red faced as she swept out to make her phone call. She sat down feline before the instant fire when she returned like Caesar's wife commanding the bard to perform. So you want to be amused, he thought, allright I'll amuse you. He picked up the first of the little collection of slim volumes he'd got together from her shelves in the well stocked study.

"Allright Maggie ," he started into his role play. "Not all poetry is about dancing daffodils or the cavalry charging enemy guns some of it can be sexy.

> *"Come madam come, all rest my powers defy,*
> *Until I labour, I in labour lie.*
> *The foe oft times having the foe in sight,*
> *Is tir'd of standing though he never fight.*
> *Off with that girdle like heaven's Zone glistering*
> *But a far fairer world incompassing.*
> *Unpin that spangled breastplate that you wear,*
> *That th'eyes of busie fools may be stopt there.*
> *Unlace yourself, for that harmonious chyme,*
> *Tells me from you, that now it is bed time.*
> 7

That was part of a poem by John Donne Maggie. From the language you can tell it was written a long time ago. The end of the sixteenth century as a matter of fact the same time as Shakespeare was writing. So you can see sex has preoccupied us poets since Eve gave Adam a bite of her apple..

Marion smiled a little less comfortably now. "I get the drift," she played her part in the production. "But that old fashioned language…."

"Yes I expected you'd prefer the modern idiom. Same poem almost, twentieth century.

> *I knew a woman lovely in her bones,*
> *When small birds sighed, she would sigh back at them:*
> *Ah when she moved, she moved more ways than one;*
> *The shapes a bright container can contain!*
> *Of her choice virtues only gods should speak,*
> *Or poets who grew up on Greek.*
> *(I'd have them sing in chorus, cheek to cheek)."*

As he read Roethke's lovely poem she began to shift uneasily in her seat. He was seducing her with words, not his own but poets who'd grown up on Greek. He formed them carefully, roundly with his lips and slotted them smoothly via her intellect into her vagina, causing her to squirm uncomfortably. By the time he finished she was clearly embarrassed.

---

[7] From John Donne. Selected poems. Ed John Hayward.. Penguin 1950

"These old bones live to learn her wanton ways:
I measure time by how a body sways."
9[11]

Then before she could recover her poise or make any comment he launched straight into a verbal assault.

Why should I let the toad work
Squat on my life?
Can't I use my wit as a pitchfork
And drive the brute off?

Six days of the week it soils
With its sickening poison –
Just for paying a few bills
That's out of proportion."

He spat the words with venom hoping to provoke a hostile response. She was bemused at the sudden contrast with the seduction of Donne and Roethke.

"Ah were I courageous enough
To shout Stuff your pension!
But I knew all to well, that's the stuff
That dreams are made on."

"That bit of Larkin should prove a real hit with our fat little communist convenor." She had quickly recovered her poise. "You'll have them all eating out of your hand ."

"I would never have thought of Larkin as revolutionary," he lectured. " That's more of a salaried staff reaction don't you think, with its reference to pensions. You don't extend superannuation to the production line....yet."

Dream on comrade, she thought, then to demonstrate her awareness of the game he was playing paraphrased Orwell from 1984 "The middle classes will never revolt," she said assuredly. "Until they are conscious they will never revolt, and until they revolt they will never be conscious. The middle classes are merely agents," she threw in a little Lenin to further impress.

There was certainly something more to this particular bourgeois bitch than he had anticipated. No wonder her daughter was in awe of her. Beauty and brains, now that was a lethal combination.

---

[11]Theodore Roethke.

"Staff unions are the fastest growing sector of trade unionism," he asserted. "They recognise the need for organisation, that's a start. They know that they can run the show without you. The only thing they don't have is the capital. The first revolution is always bourgeois. The problem has always been the readiness of the working class to take it over and carry it through to completion."

"There's going to be a clause in your contract proscribing any involvement in trade union activity," she teased, but she was deadly serious with the realisation of just how dangerous this flirtation might be.

"Of course," he conceded mendaciously. "You've seen where all that's got me so far. Lenin was right about British Trade Unionism. It's an essentially conservative organisation inimical to the revolution. Anyway I'm through with all of that. I'm a poet, a lonely poet, listen…

> *There was a man whom sorrow named his friend*
> *And he of his high comrade sorrow dreaming,*
> *Went walking with slow steps along the gleaming*
> *And humming sand, where windy surges wend:*
> *And he called loudly to the stars to bend*
> *From their pale thrones to comfort him, but they*
> *Among themselves laugh on and sing always:*
> *And then the man whom sorrow named his friend*
> *Cried out, Dim sea hear my most piteous story!*
> *The sea swept on and cried her old cry still,*
> *Rolling along in dreams from hill to hill.*
> *He fled the persecution of her glory*
> *And , in a far off gentle valley stopping,*
> *Cried in all his glory to the dew drops glistening.*
> *But naught they heard, for they are always listening,*
> *The dewdrops, for the sound of their own dropping.*
> *But the sad dweller by the seaways lone*
> *Changed all he sang to inarticulate moan*
> *Among her wildering whirls forgetting him. "*
> *10*

Moved to silence by W B Yeats beautiful poem she stared at him his moist eyes pleading now rather than hectoring. "We're always baying at the moon ," he said. "William Butler Yeats," he always felt that somehow Yeats deserved the full title. "A poet Dylan Thomas very much admired. And Dylan Thomas is a poet I very much admire. Fern Hill is one of my favourites. If I could write one poem which approached that I'd feel my little

---

[10] W B Yeats Selected Poetry A Norman Jeffares. Macmillan 1965.

strut upon the stage had not been in vain and die if not happy then at least fulfilled.." He began to recite sonorously the lovely lines and soon she joined him, her lilting cadences complementing his perfectly. They sang harmoniously the exceptional poem. It was a unique experience for both of them. They sang towards a lovely climax outside the region of the white thighs, metaphysical, but with all the pain and pleasure of the flesh.

Was there after all something more to this rich dark sensual widow than money and cunning. But what the hell, so she could recite Fern Hill, was that so unusual. But there had been something in the way she sang it, some synchronicity, her tears had burned his cheeks and her heart moved in his. Then remembering what she really was, not just the class enemy but a defector, converts were always the worst. Pots and kettles registered momentarily in his befuddled head but he gave her the sermon just the same.

> *"Verily out of Gwalia*
> *Shall come a soul on fire*
> *A prophet great in anger*
> *And mighty in desire."*

A simple unexceptional poem of a simple poet. A man who expressed through his own experience the pain of his people : Idris Davies, born in the bleak black wastes of Rhymney singing a song of desperate hope for a Messiah who would point the way to the new millennium.

> *"A prophet out of Gwalia*
> *Shall rouse the heart again,*
> *Give courage to the bosom*
> *And beauty to the brain.*

Oh Idris Davies bach," he called melodramatically, "if you could come with me to Dowlais now you would weep a bowl of bitter tears. She is more a *'battered bucket on a broken hill'* than ever. The tips are all still there, the cold black monuments of shame, the broken streets and the trickling bilious river. Bingo in the Miners' Hall and boarded shuttered chapels where Gymanfa Ganu once imparted at least some vestige of a non material creed based on need rather than greed. The capitalists," he stared accusingly at her, " have gorged on their pound of flesh and left the broken corps to putrefy while we wait impotently for the Messiah."

Despite her proximity to the fire Marion felt a chill go through her bones. She felt like the bird mesmerised by the snake. Was this charismatic young man's true desire to bring about her destruction? Why was she presenting him with the means for its accomplishment? "Are you the Messiah," she asked, "come out of Gwalia with a soul of fire."

"I am a simple poet," he responded. "I have nothing but the tenderest feeling for you." He stretched out a hand to touch her but she flinched and moved away.

"I'd like you to leave now," she said. She desperately wanted him but this was neither the time nor place. "I'll set things in motion. I must go I've got a meeting at ten. I'll get Joe to run you home."

CHAPTER 8

He had heard a week ago, tersely by way of a short letter of employment in typical officialese. It contained little or no detail of the job and alarm bells were ringing as he awoke with the early dawn unusually ahead of the rest of the family. He helped himself to a light breakfast and sat huddled before the dimly glowing fire which was eternal as the Arlington flame. His father banked it up habitually with damp small before going to bed so that it always glimmered on rising in the morning. A metal 'blower' expertly fashioned from an old oil drum and dangerously covered with a copy of last night's Echo soon had it glowing cheerily. He sipped hot sweet tea ruminating, trying to get things into some sort of perspective. His parents were mollified by the employment offer, especially when he gave them some indication of the absurd salary which it commanded. The prospect of continuing with his creative work, even perhaps getting stuck into the embryonic novel he had nurtured, was exhilarating. And yet he had an uneasy feeling about the whole thing. Was he being bought, why did he feel sullied and overwhelmed by it all. It was impossible to rationalise what had happened. It was not as if he had planned all this but had simply been overtaken by the bewildering whirl of events which had engulfed him. And yet he could not accept such a fatalistic explanation. As the great man had said, man makes choices, though not always in circumstances of his own making, which was echoed of course by Sartre. So then why did he feel 'bad faith' weigh upon him like the stone of Sisyphus. He had the choice now, now this very moment simply to turn away from it all. But he did not.

His appointment was not until nine thirty but after a light breakfast he was too keyed up to wait. The sky was lighter now and more diffuse, a cold turquoise, and he felt impelled to walk to Dowlais rather than take the bus. Mason's was a major employer in the area, especially of young women such as his bedroom window teaser and he would rather avoid the inevitable crude banter to which he might have been exposed. He could no longer make out the white stars against the lightening sky as he set off. Everything was beginning to stir as the community came to life. It was that pale time of morning when the first smoke rose in steady spirals up into the dying night, just as the last stars were going out. A pale moon was still suspended there like a thin disc of melting ice sliding slowly down.

He peered into the lifeless shop windows in Victoria Street and bought a newspaper in the one shop that blazed with light and was the main focus of activity in the high street. He was suddenly caught up in a throng of bustling people making their way to one of the several factories in the area.

The Ifor foundry, The Button factory, the BSA, ICI and Masons were all situated within the few acres of Dowlais which had once been the hub of the industrial revolution.

"Are you getting' on then John?" A bus had pulled up alongside him and half a dozen women shrouded with identical three cornered headscarves were pushing past him and boarding the double decker. She held out a hand to him as it barely paused and he was hoisted on board.

"Bike not good enough now then is it? Now that you're management.." It was young Mari his neighbour from across the street.

"The working class can kiss his arse," and older colleague taunted.

"You're not due in yet though," Mari continued. "Didn't you know, management's not in til nine. Old 'abits die 'ard is it?"

"Oh hullo Mari," he greeted. "News get around quick on your grapevine," he observed. "First morning nerves and all that," he admitted. "I wanted a good mooch around before the big brass get in. Find out who brews the best tea. You know."

"Only the maintenance boys manage to get a brew goin' first thing," she said. "Bloody slaves we are on the line."

"Yeah got to hold our hands up before we can go for a piss," her companion confirmed. "I'll show you where the maintenance shop is if you like. Bloody good shop steward they got there, not like the silly cow we've got. Don't know if they'll welcome you though, bein' management and all that."

It was not going to be easy winning the confidence of this lot he mused as the bus pulled up at the factory entrance.

The two girls took an arm each, possessively, and led him off to the maintenance workshop at a brisk pace. Was he not after all some sort of local celebrity and rather good looking to boot. "This is it then John" basking in the attention they were getting from the other girls who clustered in gossiping groups around the clocking in station.

"Got to go, got to clock in," Mari said. "See you John," and they were gone .

"Thanks girls," he called to their retreating figures as he walked into the workshop which had the familiar features of most such places in his experience. There was a toolcage at the far end where the maintenance men had to sign chits for the loan of the specialist tools required for carrying out their respective jobs. It was in the 'cage' that morning tea was often brewed and here was no exception. He drummed a coin on the metal counter polished to a fine sheen by the constant passage of tools across it over the years. "Hullo," he called. "Any chance of scrounging a decent cuppa."

A bald head appeared from behind the toolbay. "And who the hell might you be," it queried in indignant tones.

"It's allright brother, I may look like a dog's dinner but I'm not a management spy."

Another equally bald head supported by a rotund truncated body swathed in an oily overall emerged slowly clasping a steaming enamelled mug in a knotty hand.

"Hey Bert," said the first, "what do you make of this then, poncin' in here callin' me brother."

Bert responded with a loud laugh. "Good god if it's not John fucking Davies," he exclaimed. "So what we heard is true then, joined the other fuckin' side is it?"

"Bert ," John greeted. "Still convenor here are you," knowing full well he was. "How are things in the Kremlin," a reference to his membership of the Communist Party.

"Better than they are up in Transport fucking House at any rate," he retorted. Bert's range of epithets was severely restricted, 'fuckin' was at the top of his list which somewhat limited his effectiveness in the higher echelons of Union negotiations, though there was no doubting his achievements at the factory floor level. He was not popular with the Labour / Union axis which dominated Merthyr politics but he had found a secret ally in John and there was a mutual respect between them. "But you tore up your card I'm told. Not really joined the other fuckin' side though 'ave you?"

"You know me better than that Bert. And before you ask I'm certainly not joining you bunch of Stalinist bastards. The only true revolutionists in Wales at the moment are the FWA and their socialism is totally negated by their nationalism."

"So where does that leave you then boyo, are you just fuckin' the boss's daughter or 'ave you joined the Trots and doin' a bit of infiltratin'".

John touched the side of his nose. He could hardly take offence. "That's for me to know Bert. Now how about a cuppa tea comrade." Yes that's how I should see myself, he rationalised, the mole within.

An hour later and he had convinced the maintenance shop stewards that he was not a turncoat brought in to implement Mason's Productivity Deal, there was always a productivity deal these days, this was the golden age of productivity deals. After all hadn't he just been successful in scuppering ICI's attempted 'agreement'. He finished his second cup, not up to Dai Whippet's standard but not a bad brew nevertheless, and walked across to the main production area. He strolled about with an air of importance and dressed as he was he knew he would be taken for a member of the upper echelon of management by the shop floor supervisors and consequently left alone. The noise of the machines was deafening and the atmosphere as hot and humid as a Carolina swamp in midsummer. Green overalled and turbaned girls sat cutting, sewing, gusseting, seaming and whatever else they were required to do in the methodical process of turning out bras, panties, girdles, nighties and all the paraphernalia of the modern love goddess. He suffocated in the dyeing sheds where the colourless nylon received its baptism as an adornment of the secret flesh. He marvelled at the ingenious machines which knitted it into sheaths for lissom limbs, attended for the most part by men, since this was the higher skilled end of the process, and this was a time when practically all the skilled jobs were reserved for men. So much for equal opportunities, he mused, it didn't always pay to have a 'modern' woman at the helm.

These girls could be extremely attractive freed from the de-sexing monotony of their hideous uniform and enhanced by the aphrodisiac products of their labour, which they could obtain from the company shop at cost price . This John knew from personal experience of the adolescent days spent almost exclusively in their hot pursuit. They were a different picture now in their sweat stained outfits beavering away to the accompaniment of the high pitched buzzing cacophony of their machines . De-feminised ; is this what the nascent libbers really wanted ; de-humanised workers who happened to be women.

Mari caught his eye excitedly from behind and machine and waved extrovertly drawing the attention of the other girls. The armpits of her tunic were soaked with sweat and her lovely hair was turbaned out of site except for some damp straggling wisps on her forehead. Was it really possible that technology would free us from all this as some of the utopians of the left were predicting; or as others warned would this turn out to be the new battleground in the struggle for ownership and control of the means of production. Surely it was the latter. This is what 'productivity agreements' were all about. It was certainly what the recent strike was all about as far as he was concerned. What would his role be now? Was he after all just selling out. The working class could kiss his arse, he'd got the foreman's job at last.

By the time he returned to the entrance foyer a smart Commissionaire had installed himself behind a glass fronted reception desk. He was given a seat in a glazed arcade, installed in the Art Nouveau style. The tables were littered with various trade journals of interest to hardly anyone, certainly not him. After what seemed an eternity a trim little secretary from Personnel came to inform him that the Staff Manager, Colonel Smythe would see him now.

Smythe was everything he promised to be; tall double breasted pinstriped with a military bearing even to the bristling moustache. "Seat," he instructed but before John could respond. "Bloody doctor first," he barked. "Bloody medical," consulting a thin file on his desk. As if by magic the secretary reappeared and motioned John to follow her down the corridor and ushered him into a room where another caricature sat slumped apparently asleep in a swivel chair behind a desk heaped with files and journals. The unmistakeable aroma of a decent quality whiskey hung in the air.

The secretary groaned before shaking the slumbering hulk awake. "Doctor Thomas," she called, half turning to John with a sympathetic smile. "Mister Davies for a medical check, employment PS1." She pushed the form underneath his nose on the cluttered desk. He looked up bleary eyed and half awake.

"You're John Davies," he managed.

"I know I am," John responded. "So you must be the doctor if Aristotelian Logic still applies in this place." The secretary giggled and left.

"Back in the Colonel's Office when you've finished. Good luck," she offered as if she felt he really needed it.

The doctor had John strip, made him cough, tapped his chest, almost made him sick pushing a stick down his throat, tapped his knees, shone a light in his eyes and ears and scratched the underside of his soles. "You'll do." He said brusquely.

"Do," John retorted. "Do. Physician heal thyself." It was going to be one of those days when his big gob would get him into trouble. He knew it. It was a perverse stubborn streak which came over him from time to time, especially when people like doctors and colonels put on airs and graces and displayed a generally boorish attitude of superiority over those they considered to be inferiors.

Smythe really did turn out to be the epitome of the personnel officer of the post war period; ex army to the tips of his toes, a proverbial woffler who couldn't quite come to terms with the fact that this young whippersnapper was being offered a senior management post. "Woffle woffle woffle old boy. Glad to have you on board. A happy ship." Limp unenthusiastic handshake. "A1," he pronounced leafing through the paperwork. "Just a few more bits of paperwork. You don't seem to have filled in the SS6. Just a formality and then there's the IQ test."

"I'm not filling that thing in," John retorted rudely. As for the IQ test you can stuff it."

"I beg your pardon."

"That's allright."

"Well I never, woffle woffle. It's just a formality you know.

"As for that SS6 as you called it. I'd have to be out of my mind to sign that. Intellectual property rights and all that crap. It would mean that you owned not only my physical but my intellectual output. You do understand the nature of the job I've been offered do you. Have you been in touch with the MD, with Mrs Mason?"

Woffler was now clearly out of his depth and waffled some more. "It's just a standard document you know. All our ad men and technical writers sign it."

"Are you deliberately trying to insult me," John interrupted him. "Ad man, technical writer. Have you signed this piece of garbage. '…all designs, inventions, copyrights and intellectual materials remain the sole property of the Company, whether conceived in part or in full, on or off the premises.' Good God man how could I be expected to sign that. That's intellectual slavery. Look my terms of reference are that I be employed as a consultant.

127

That I will also undertake to run some training courses for your shop floor workers. Now I suggest you contact your Managing Director , the Chairman of the Board, and arrange for a contract drawn up along those lines."

It was an auspicious enough beginning. It wouldn't be such a bad idea for it to become known, as it would, that he's had an up and downer with Smythe. The mole in the office, probably one of the secretaries, would inform comrade Bert by lunchtime.

The red faced Major jumped to attention and strode briskly from the room intent on securing this young upstart his immediate come-uppance in the form of his P69, only to re-emerge some five minutes later redder faced and red necked accompanied by a scowling upper echelon type in a sober grey serge. The scowl turned to charming smile as he addressed John. "Ah Mr Davies, Dewey, Director Public and Industrial Relations," his handshake firmer and more self assured. "I'm dreadfully sorry for this cock up," glaring again at Smythe. "Should have been referred to me in the first place. I have a contract drafted along the lines agreed between yourself and the Chairman (notably Dewey did not refer to her as the Chairwoman). If you'd please accompany me to my office we can dot the ies and cross the tees to your satisfaction. Smythe you'll make sure that the arrangements for Mr Davies' office accommodation are seen to won't you. And you'll find that authority has been given for the conversion of room thirty six, I think it is, to a training facility. You'll need to discuss the specific requirements with Mr Davies later."

"Yes of course Mr Dewey," Smythe positively cringed making John feel almost sorry for him, but not quite, knowing that some poor junior personnel officer would soon provide the surrogate on whom Smythe would vent his spleen. He'd known many Smythe's of old, he'd been fighting them for all his short life.

He followed Dewey down the corridor to a plush carpeted office. "Sorry about all that," he apologised, offering him a deep cushioned chair. "Sometimes you have to do everything yourself if you want things done properly." He produced a document from the drawer of his desk and handed it over. "I think you'll find everything as agreed with the Chairman, she has an incredible eye for detail. She's very enthusiastic about this project and you can be assured of every assistance from me in getting it off the ground. There were some rumblings in the boardroom when she suggested it, but those were soon dispelled. The chairman as you no doubt know is very persuasive. When she wants something she invariably has her way. In any case like everything she proposes it makes sound economic sense and in public relations terms……. but you're not really interested in that are you. It's the nuts and bolts you'll be more concerned about. Well you heard me talk about the training room to Smythe, that provision is long overdue anyway, it's been on the cards for some time now. It will provide you with the ideal facility for your proposed tutorials. I've arranged for a representative of the company who will be carrying out the work to discuss the specifications with our Technical Manager this afternoon. I suggest that you join in that discussion and let them know of your own requirements. Your own technical background should come in handy as far as that's concerned." Dewey was clearly no Smythe. He had done his homework on John. "I'm in the process of fixing up a meeting with the Production Manager to work out a system of release for workers to attend your seminars. Of course the trade unions will also be involved ," he smiled knowingly . "I'll let you know the outcome in due course. In the meantime take the contract and go over the small print, I'm sure you'll find it OK. Smythe is in the process of finding a suitable office for you. I'll see you later on for a spot of lunch." He shook hands, smiled warmly, "Welcome to Mason's," he said and buzzed for his secretary to return John to the hapless Smythe.

Friday was drawing to a close, thank God. It had been a long, hard, tiresome, frustrating week. Every kind of obstacle had been put in his way. Every department fighting to preserve its own narrow interest. He was viewed with hostility in every quarter and several times had to resort to threats to appeal to a higher order in order to get things done. The unions were suspicious that their bonus would be affected and held out for written confirmation that this was not the case. Only the Public Relations Department displayed any real sympathy and that for all the wrong and obvious reasons. Finally and grudgingly the various factions were reconciled and a timetable for the release of production line workers and maintenance staff was agreed. The size of the groups he would have to work with was undoubtedly too big, but it was a start. Now he would have to consider a curriculum. It was good to feel that he was about to embark on something interesting and worthwhile. He'd been allocated a small initial budget on the basis of which he had already contacted the local WEA Officer for the area who was keen to discuss the project with him.

As for the enigmatic Marion she had been noticeably absent, her power delegated to Dewey . Was she deliberately keeping him at arms length. Was his vision of her, after all an illusion. Was he simply one more pawn , one of many in her empire, completely in thrall to her beauty and power, another step in the Parkinsonian pyramid held squat beneath her lovely haunches with a flinty hardness which her soft exterior paradoxically denied. The telephone shook him out of his reverie. "Hullo. John Davies speaking."

"Hullo John, Marston here, PR. Look I've got this television chappie waiting for me to call him back. He's the producer for that late night arty programme, New Frontiers, had you and your mates on a few months back he says. Well he's very interested in doing a piece on our little cultural effort. I'd like to set up a meeting with him sometime next week if that's ok with you."

Well, well, things really were taking off in the right direction. His mouth had gone suddenly dry. "Yes, of course I'll meet him," John replied, emphasising the 'I'. "Give me a little time to get myself together. Suggest next Friday if that's allright with him , otherwise early the week after."

"I'll tell him you're working on the final details then shall I and get him to ring me back next week?"

John replaced the phone and smiled. Next week would be hectic. He looked forward to the weekend with his friends.

CHAPTER 9

The Dowlo had not long opened. He ordered a beer from Brenda and quietly retreated to the backroom. He sat alone and mused for a while and had half finished his pint when Dave arrived. Another half hour and the place was full of familiar laughing faces, arguments raging back and forth with the Dowlais five entrenched firmly at the heart of their domain. As usual it wasn't long before inebriation had lubricated the tonsils and Bill gave forth with tuneless interpretations of pop songs until someone heartlessly compared him with Cliff Richard which silenced him with a stiff jolt. "I'm not as bad as that callow impersonator surely," he complained. "I mean I don't flaunt my virginity as a virtue. I'm deeply humiliated by my sexual purity and pray earnestly for some good bad woman to relieve me of it."

"Well you certainly are no mewling puking boy, and after your appearance on my television programme you'll be a celebrity too. Think of all those intellectual groupies, one of them is sure to pop your cherry before you can say fellatio."

"Fuff- fuff- fuff- fellatio is a very hard word to say after a few pints. What television programme?"

John explained the situation to him. "New Frontiers, following our previous success and in response to the great clamour for more , has decided to devote a whole programme on the great cultural experiment at Mason's. I intend to insist on a specific format i.e exhibiting on the little silver screen full frontally the pornographic works of yourself and Dave in all its primitive glory, a song or two from Geraint, the ranting lunacy of Ted's political philosophy and all of us engaged in a studio discussion which will ignite the hills and vales of our hallowed land. Mason's PR machine is pulling out all the stops on this one and the production department is no doubt beavering to bring out a new line of lacy underwear labelled 'intellectual chic'. This is the moment we've been waiting for fellers - the cultural apocalypse."

"Are you serious?" Dave interrupted doubtfully. "You think we could really could pull the wool over their eyes?"

"Of course we can," asserted John with complete self assurance. "You know what a prick that presenter is."

"Arty intellectual," Dave pronounced the words as if they were a pox. "Give him something obscure that he doesn't understand and he's bound to start promoting it. You lovely man; if you weren't so horrible I'd kiss you."

"If you truly loved me you wouldn't let my looks put you off," John retorted. "Come on kiss me, kiss me quick while I'm still in the mood." He got up and chased him around the table with puckered lips.

"Get away from me you randy bugger," threatened Dave. "If you don't leave off I'll render you permanently celibate with a quick knee in the goolies. Just because your supply has been temporarily suspended you'd do anything, or anyone, even me, rather than go without."

"Nobody loves me," John complained.

"Ah but that's not true is it," Dave insisted. "Somebody love's you and we don't need to wonder who. In fact if my intelligence is correct two somebodies love you. Is that the case? And if so what sort of sordid game are you playing my little Trotskyite. Entryism takes on a whole new meaning as applied by yours truly you little shit."

"More Goethe than Trotski, I would suggest," interrupted Bill. "This flourishing is more probably the result of some dark Faustian pact with the delightful heiress to mama's fortune?"

"More Machiavelli than either, I believe," Ted added his two pennorth with more than a hint of admiration.

"None of the fore mentioned actually," John defended. "I have a genuine affection for the young woman. The four letter word has passed between us." Afraid to utter it like a luvvy in Macbeth, lest it bring the whole house of cards crashing down. "It's a modern relationship. No ties. No promises. When we're together we're together, and when we're apart.." he smiled slyly.

"You're a bastard Davies," Dave attested with less banter and more barb. "Come on bastard drink up or we'll miss the bus."

"The bus – where to."

"To town, hence the train to Ponty. The IR Society dance, remember, I got the tickets."

Quickdash through the door and over to the High Street. The red bus coming down the incline from the Bush Hotel. Sluggish Bill overtaken by the young Turks leaping onto the platform as it drifted past, dragging the panting Bill with them as he clutched the white enamel pole unable to co-ordinate his flailing feet to make the jump, finally hauled aboard by Dave and John, breathless, grey faced and wet with sweat.

As they walked down the aisle a primproper spinster woman tut tutted and shook her head with disgust at what the world had degenerated to. Dave twitched his head spasmodically in a mad saint Vitus dance as he passed sticking out his tongue. She turned away haughtily and he shuffled grotesquely to his seat. "Don't worry madam," John reassured politely, doffing an invisible hat. "We'll have him back in his cage by midnight." The conductor approached and hovered menacingly shaking his leather moneybag as if it were a loaded fortyfive.

"I'm with my dad," Ted said seriously jerking a thumb at the breathless Bill. The conductor moved towards him half convinced , hand held out expectantly.

"I'm not his dad," Bill managed, red faced gulping in the smoky air. "I'm not even married."

"That's your good luck mate. Doesn't count for much these days anyway. Come on now who's going to pay that's all I want to know.

"Allright. Five returns please. Serious Ted brandishing a pound note.

"Where to mate," expecting the obvious.

"Back here of course."

"Come on Charley Chester," patience at an end. Ted paid the man and was rewarded for his flippance with a pocketful of pennies in change.

"Hey there's a law against this," Ted complained. "Under the Collection of Fares on Public Transportation Act 1947."

"Sue me," with a chuckle. "I just love comedians", sauntering away whistling.

"Servants of the public indeed," Ted called after him in a loud middle class anglicised suburban accent. "I don't know why we pay our rates and taxes honestly. And," turning on Geraint, "if you lot had your way you'd dress them all up in some pseudo Welsh costume and have them talking that absurd Welsh gibberish all the time."

"Quite right. And we wouldn't let big mouthed anglophile yobbos like you travel on the Welsh National Transport Network that's for sure." Geraint responded. "We'd revoke your work permits and send you back to the peat bogs where you belong. Whoever heard of a County Kerry Jew anyway, apart from Poldy Bloom and he was a Dubliner."

"I'm as Welsh as you are you fake. Just because my name is Fagin Karl Marx Bernstein Baum Yom Kippur proves nothing other than that you're a gang of racist neo-nazi pigs. If I got up and started shouting 'Wales for the Jews- God gave us this land' you'd have me put down in the Ponty gas ovens. But I've got as much right to call Wales mine as you. You came over with the Barcelona snails by the look of you, Geraint don Carlos Rodrigues Thomas. Viva Franco."

"Be quiet you bloody Welsh Yid," from Bill who'd got his breath back. "Remember I'm the one with tickets for the dance. And you can shut it too Dylan bloody Davies and your friend Picarsole. I'm the only one sober enough to talk to those Ponty bouncers. So behave yourselves or else.." He let the threat hang in the air and concluded with a loud fart.

"Dirty bastard," from a tight pinched face under a Dai cap in the front seat.

"Ooooh," a shocked gasp from spinsterwoman.

"Watchewrlanguage Daicap," from a hairy chested openshirted boyo from behind. "Or I'll shove my big mit right in your gob."

"So much for the Welsh proletariat," Ted whispered to Geraint.

The Hotel Royale, the nearest thing to posh you could find in Ponty, was frequented by the best in South Welsh society, as a rule. Sometimes, as now, the hoi polloi were let in. The occasion was the Industrial Society annual dinner dance brought forward to coincide with MacMillan' s election victory during which a guest would deliver the keynote speech. Tonight's guest speaker was the President of Aims of Industry, a rabid right winger with business interests in the valleys. The dance was thrown open to the prols but limited by scarcity and exorbitant ticket prices. Bill had obtained theirs gratis from the buxom overdressed blonde who waited for them in the foyer. Her husband was something big in civil engineering. He was away for the weekend on one of his frequent 'business trips'.

They made their way into the overflowing lounge waiting to be ushered to their table. They ordered drinks and settled down. "If only my husband could see me now," she said, "surrounded by you young stallions, excepting you of course darling," to Bill . "Aren't you going to introduce me darling?" So he introduced them to Dolores. "Call me Dolores, like they do in the movies," she quoted Dylan, inflating her embonpoint in an over dramatised gesture.

Heavy velvet drapes covered the windows and the walls were hung with a rich flock wallpaper. A thick pile carpet adorned the floor, a replica of the Bayeaux tapestry. It was a complete mismatch with the oriental wallpaper and gave the place an opulent but tasteless look. Standing out in complete contrast on the walls were two large contemporary paintings. One was essentially a large red eye which Dave immediately titled 'tomorrow morning'. The other was a more interesting geometric representation of homo sapiens constructed entirely of multi coloured triangles. A large isosclese for the head, a scalene for the trunk, four acute angled for the arms, ditto for the legs with an extreme acute angled sharp and erect between them. This one John called 'the Ponty hymen stabber' which caused Dolores a little titter which sent titillating wobbles trembling along all her curves.. Dave was professionally critical of the paintings. They were not worthy of a hanging in the lounge of the Hotel Royale. On looking round he expressed second thoughts, perhaps the lounge of the Hotel Royale and they just about deserved of each other.

The tables too were contemporary. Some round, some rectangular. With coloured glass tops. The chairs were lavishly upholstered wickerwork, reminiscent of obsolete batchchairs, and once again the tasteless contrast was starkly evident. However they were spaciously comfortable and once sunk into their copious depths , with five frothy pints before them, the Merthyr Five were at peace with the world. That is until Dolores invited her three equally overdressed though paradoxically deshabille friends over to join them. They were women 'of a certain age' apparently abandoned as was Dolores to their own devices for the weekend.

John had by this time reached that state of mind which hovers on the very edge of inebriation while still retaining the essence of sagacity. He smiled happily to himself and mused how the occupants of the lounge complemented the décor, such a mixture of tastes and textures. From sixteen to sixty, painfully thin to Rubensesque, plain to lovely, and there, in the far corner most radiantly beautiful of all, amazingly Marion. Was this coincidence? He believed in coincidence and serendipity in that it had seemed to play a significant part in his short lifespan thus far.

Of course there was nothing strange in her presence here. She was no doubt high up the hierarchy of the South Wales Industrial Society. He recognised one of the group at her table as the representative, Chairman he seemed to remember, of the Welsh CBI, always on the box spouting some right wing nonsense about the inadequacies of the Welsh labour force. Fred Dewey was there too as close to her as befits a sad eyed lapdog, slick, sixty and clinging like a limpet . The rest of the group were of the same mien. Fat men with ulcers and mean faces with overdressed spouses who looked as if they couldn't wait for widowhood. Hers was the ultimate of contrasts in this room of contrasts, a butterfly surrounded by powdery moths. John stared at her with an intensity indicative of the conflicting bundle of emotions which all but overwhelmed him. She called him over with a smile but he held a finger to his nose disdainfully, a gesture which Dewey reacted to with haughty indignation. John nodded to him with a forced familiarity and he shrugged curtly in response.

Dewey had been hanging around Marion for time immemorial and had viewed the appointment of this young layabout with the resignation which categorised it as simply the latest in a long line of annoying peccadilloes. Marion's promiscuity, as he viewed it, was long something he had learned to live with. In a strange masochistic way he enjoyed the pain, but this was almost a humiliation too far. To actually secure a management post for this young gigolo was carrying her promiscuity to extremes. She had never done that in the past. A few expensive trinkets following discreet assignations in anonymous hotel rooms had been more the norm. What could he do but grin and bear it. Hadn't she always in the end put her business interests first and in any case she was Chairman with a controlling interest, she was not the type to embrace a viper to her bosom.

'I'll be around no matter how you treat me now', was the song that had been written for him. 'I'll be around when he's gone.' But his recurring nightmare was an old ugly filthy Marion, her suitors all fled, spitting calmly in his face in rejection of his magnanimous offer. On such occasions he awoke bathed in a cold sweat and staggered to the cocktail cabinet for a fresh bottle of whisky.

Dave had been watching John carefully. "My God," he whispered finally. "Who's the goddess. Can't possibly be anybody of your crass acquaintance."

"That's Marion," he answered, "magnificent Marion. My patron. Josie's lovely mum."

John responded with a low whistle. "Of course," he recalled, "the Sketch did that article on her. Dubbed her Mrs Knickers. That doesn't do her justice. Mrs Negligee perhaps, but even that demeans her. She should be preserved in aspic," he opined. "Life can only despoil something as lovely as that. Look at the crones who surround her, look what it's done to them."

"Not life you proletarian dolt, life enriches, enhances. The more you pack in the better. It's time that lingers in the shadows and coughs when we would kiss."

"Stop being so bloody morbidly Auden," Bill interrupted draining his glass. He got up from his chair and assumed a position with his arse in the air blowing raspberries like that famous vaudeville artist who lit his methane outbursts with a lighted taper. Bill didn't quite go that far but earned sustained applause from his admirers. He was such a one wasn't he Lolita insisted. Ted ever morose but never so much as when he was tight as a tic, as he was now, informed her precisely what Bill was such a one of, which brought him a hearty dig in the ribs accompanied by a squeal of girlish laughter, causing him to regurgitate a mouthful of best Brains bitter into his lap.

Needing no further urging Geraint joined Bill in pseudo song, inserting unprintable lyrics in place of the inane anodyne utterings which were standard fifties fare. Ted began making twitchy advances to the two gin and oranges at the adjacent table, simultaneously playing footsy with John and smiling suggestively at Lolita's friend, who hadn't stopped chattering from the moment she joined them. Not that anybody was paying any attention to her apart from the odd half smile from Geraint who hung onto the notion of her as a bird in hand while rather preferring either of the gin and oranges as he played out his role of half pissed Romeo. He had that 'look at me I'm irresistible' expression on his daft face. Bill and Ted sat down again having incurred the disdain of the mighty at Marion's table. Dewey scowling his hostility while Marion smiled more sweetly if with some embarrassment. Stupid beautiful bourgeois bitch John thought.

"Oh no they can't take that away from me," Bill sang loudly apropos of nothing in particular.

"As the Ponty hymen stabber said to the red eyed virgin as he deflowered her in the middle of the battle of Hastings," Ted intoned nasally, his gaze now rigidly fixed on the crotch of one of the coquettish cross legged gin and oranges. Looking more and more like the archetypal pub Don Juan he eventually rose, swayed and with exaggerated determination addressed himself to the adjacent table. "Would you charming young ladies mind awfully if I came and sat over there."

"I doubt if you could find your way all the way over here the state you're in." One of them countered and they giggled together like schoolgirls.

"D' you hear that," Ted complained loudly. "I can sit where I like lovely girl. Issa free country innit."

"Free what?" Geraint chipped in suddenly aroused. "Free what did you say?"

"Country, country, whassa marrer with you, c-u-n-t- ree country. Can't you spell or something. Cuntreeeeee. Come on you Welsh Yid less go an talk to these lovely girls." He staggered across and flopped into an empty seat. Faces frowned and voices muttered, so Dave the more sober of them suggested they all move into the dance hall in the adjacent room from where the strains of a slow foxtrot filtered sedately.

"Whaffor I like it here ," complained Geraint putting an arm around the shoulder of Lolita's friend. Bill was staring into Lolita's eyes in a world of his own. Dave shrugged and pouted from his exile and tried to start conversation with the gin and oranges.

John unilaterally decided that the nearest bog was the best sanctuary and made his way out into the corridor with some urgency. He almost bumped into Dewey who grunted and hurriedly looked the other way without comment. Allright you snotty nosed bastard he thought as he fumbled for his fly, I'll screw you. He soused his face several times with cold water, combed his hair and marched back across the lounge with a contrived nonchalance to where Dewey had rejoined the entourage. "May I have the pleasure Marion," he managed eloquently, slipping en enfolding arm around her slender waist, with a superior smile at Dewey. She nodded gracefully and moved with him towards the dancehall. Dewey's look almost calcified him.

The band was still playing a slow tempo number and he placed both arms around her and drew her to him . She resisted temporarily before yielding and moulding her sinuous body to his. He closed his eyes and they swayed, undulating in the centre of the crowded floor. The term 'dirty dancing' had not yet been coined but the rather more crude and proletarian 'dry grind' was what they engaged in. "When that marimba rhythm starts to play, dance with me, make me sway." The singer crooned and the warmth, the sensual rhythm, the booze and this beautiful woman all contrived to bring about his dreamy erection as they swayed together. She could hardly fail to be aware of it but rather than retreat a millimetre she ground her thighs closer to his and closed her own eyes. "Tonight?" he croaked hoarsely, the question sticking clumsily in his throat, realising how trite and ridiculous it must have sounded.

"Fred and I are here together," she took a small step back. "We're sharing the Daimler representing the Company."

"To hell with Fred," he wanted to insist. "To hell with everybody. Let's have it away right now, here in the ballroom of the Hotel Royale, and balls to propriety. She sensed his annoyance and obvious frustration.

"I told you," she scolded, "things are not always what they appear to be, and selfishly wishing for them will not make them so.".

"Things are always what they appear to be," he insisted, feeling reprimanded like a spoilt boy. " That's the true definition of reality." It sounded trite and ridiculous the moment he said it, and he had wanted to sound sophisticated and profound.

"That's nonsense," she laughed deflating him. "Is that how you got around Josie, I always thought her more discerning. Anyway you will have to be on top of your game next week. You have the unions and television to conquer. All your efforts should be concentrated there. You need to sublimate your excesses." She touched him on the nose with her index finger.

He had drunk too much to appreciate her teasing and responded spitefully. "Oh forgive me, the publicity, but of course, I'd forgotten. And all this time I'd envisaged you as a genuine and beautiful philanthropist, Loren and Littlewood rolled into one, bringing culture to the masses, shedding a little light on the great sea of darkness."

"Then you're a bloody fool and I was mistaken about you," she said coldly. "Certainly I love art and literature, but frankly it will be wasted on the lumpen-proletariat as you'll soon find out." She used the Marxist term self consciously. "You'll find no redemption there. I'm a businesswoman first and foremost. You think I could have sold this thing to the board if it did not make good business sense. We stand to gain substantially from this in terms of free advertising and public relations propaganda. I also have my personal reasons, not all of them altruistic I assure you," she added frankly, and this last he pondered on. "Now if you please I must rejoin my party. One way or another we are both getting unduly worked up and this is neither the time nor place."

"Thank you very much John," she said as she resumed her seat, regal and lovely as the Ice Queen.

"Entirely my pleasure," he attempted irony but ended up sounding sycophantic. He grinned at Dewey showing all his teeth. "How are you Fred." Even senior management at Mason's referred to him reverently as Mr Dewey.

"Davies," he acknowledged with the gruff disdain of a public school headmaster and John's neck bristled with indignation.

"The name's John, Fred," he insisted and Marion stepped diplomatically into the breach.

"I don't think you've been properly introduced to everyone," she smiled and proceeded to introduce him individually by his Christian name to all and sundry. She introduced him as a writer acting in a consultative role for the Company. It pleased him that she didn't dress up his role with the current Americanised jargon but simply sketched an outline of its main elements. He tactfully declined an invitation to join them and returned to his table feeling somewhat miffed. One of the women had meandered off to join another group which resolved the sexual pairing. The remaining unattached female was as buxom as her friend Lolita. Fair haired and probably in her middle thirties she wore a tight sweater and no bra giving emphasis to firm large nipples. She was a divorcee it transpired and worked in the typing pool of a local factory. The phrase containing mutton and lamb immediately sprang to mind A sure thing in his vengeful chauvinistic frame of mind. He

138

snaked an arm around her fleshy waist with a telling glance in Marion's direction.

Bill had already regaled her with an exaggerated embellishment of John's television offer, elevating him to the status of a celebrity and she tipsily fawned on him with an almost adolescent adulation.

Should they take a walk outside then. Dave having already disappeared with her friend. Yes why not. He had sufficient alcohol in him to imbue him with a seriousness of intent which any sober appraisal would have considered farcical. For her part he might have been Paul Newman. After some fumbled groping against a wall behind some bushes in the car park he realised the pointlessness of this encounter and it was only from some ridiculous sense of manly propriety that he continued.

Quietly without so much as a whispered word he pulled her sweater up underneath her armpits. The huge mounds of flesh thus unconstrained tumbled down to their natural position. She stood before him wide eyed and awkwardly smiling. There was no caress, no kiss or sigh, it was like looking at a photograph in one of those tit complex magazines, large volumes of flesh as lifeless and loveless as the flat pages on which they were reproduced. With any affection, any degree of warmth between them those breasts might have been marvellous, but there was just this cold dispassionate complete surrender, like a barbed wire barrier. After an awkward hiatus when it finally dawned on her that he was going to do no more than just look she pulled down her sweater and plumped herself up within its tight confines. "I hope you don't think I go around doing this at the drop a hat," she explained. "It's just that...."

What the hell difference did it make, he thought. But it wasn't her fault that she'd been willing, maybe too willing, after all wasn't he the big celebrity.

"How many books have you written then," she tried to make conversation and offer an explanation at one and the same time. For some reason he hadn't the heart to disabuse her.

"Oh quite a few. Novels, "he added.

"What were they called I'd like to read one."

He thrashed around for a way out and drunkenness provided him with the inspiration to answer. "Have you heard of Henry Miller?"

"Is that one of them," she shrugged. "Don't think I've heard of....."

"No that's my pen name," he added absurdly. "Tropic of Cancer, is my latest. Should be in the library now. You should enjoy that." Henry would appreciate the joke. But he felt a fraud and a complete bastard all the same.

"Shall we go back then."

"Yes , look I'm sorry I couldn't, didn't, you know."

"That's allright don't worry about it," she responded. "You don't even know my name or anything do you. I'll write it down for you." She

139

fumbled in her handbag for her diary and tore a page of it having scribbled her name and address on it. "Hang on I'll put the office telephone number on it. We're not supposed to take private calls but…." He screwed the paper up and stuffed it into his pocket where it would remain until the trouser went to the cleaners. He took her hand to lea her out of the bushes when the sound of cries and scuffles came to hem from lower down the bank.

"My God that sounds like Pam," she said with obvious concern. "She's with your friend Dave."

"Oh that's allright then," he reassured her. "He's probably just raping her." There was the sound of scuffling and angry male voices to accompany the shrill cries of Pam.

"It's her brother in law," Jenny cried fearfully, her alarm increased. "He watches he like a hawk. He'll hammer hell out of your mate." John was just drunk enough to assume the reckless attitude of a friend in need and went hurtling down the bank through the bushes, just in time to see Dave go down in a heap and lie there like a bundle of old rags. Pam was hastily pulling up her pretty pants and shrilling simultaneously. With all this distracting him and Jenny yelling "Look out John he's a boxer." He never saw the punch that hit him, just felt the sickening thud that crunched into his nose and spattered the front of his best white shirt with the epitaxic flow which followed it. This boyo could hit hard he concluded and decided that unless he followed up to put the boot in his best plan was to lie doggo and feign death. Peering up carefully through half closed eyes he recognised at once the pugilistic features of his antagonist: Jack Ponty Williams stood there swaying and sparring the air with huge fists as menacing as sledgehammers. The former Welsh middleweight champion had done six months for grievous bodily harm and only just had his licence renewed pending a forthcoming eliminator with Bargoed's Harry 'the Hammer' Hopkins for the vacant title after a two year suspension. He was a very tough nut indeed and John had no qualms about conceding.

"You fuck off home you dirty bitch," Ponty politely reproached the tearful Pam who had mercifully stopped her shrieking. "And if I ever catch you at it again you'll 'ave my brother to deal with, and you know what he'll give you. "You allright boyo," he returned his attention to John hauling him roughly to his feet. "Shouldn't 'ave come rushing in like that see. I'm in trainin' sharp like innit, reflexes see." And to demonstrate he shot out a rapid succession of bludgeons falling just short of John's bloody features. John was too stunned and scared to argue.

"Dat's my fremb ober dere," he mumbled. "He didm mow she was marrib."

"Ach the dirty bitch," Ponty responded. "She's been 'ad by 'alf of Rhondda. Just like 'er mother the old slag. But my brawd thinks the sun shines out of her arse. "Look it wasn't your mates fault nor yours. Come and

140

'ave a pint on me, no hard feelins. He'll be awright in a jiff, got him on the button see." And he jabbed again to illustrate the point.

Jenny and Pam had taken advantage of the interregnum to flee the scene and John not wishing to aggravate Ponty further reluctantly accepted the invitation. He roused the stirring Dave, helped him to his feet, and followed Ponty to an old fashioned pub on the corner as if they were old friends. Dave, as if he hadn't had enough adventure for one night soon meandered off back to the Royale in search of the gin and oranges.

"Glutton for punishment your mate," Ponty opined. "I'd go an' lie down somewhere for a bit if I was 'im."

"He'll be allright. Skull like rhinoceros. Merthyr boy." As if that was all the explanation needed. And after a cursory clean up in the outdoor toilet he spent the rest of the night listening to a punch by punch account of Ponty's every fight in his mercurial rise to the Welsh Championship. The pub was obviously exempt from the local licensing laws for long after the midnight hour two uniformed constables occupied a seat in the corner supping their free pints of watery Welsh bitter. It seemed this constabulary invasion was the signal to the locals, or else it was simply the unnerving presence of the boys in blue at any time, to finish their drinks and drift away slowly. When they eventually got out into the street Ponty was rolling drunk while John, what with the pain from his nose and the sheer boredom of Ponty's company, had drunk himself relatively sober. "Well Ponty my old son," he said. "Since you don't know who I am and we're, I sincerely hope, unlikely ever to meet again I'd just like to say what a horrible bastard I think you are." And he swung a roundhouse right with every ounce of strength that he could muster, as if his very life depended on it, which it probably did. With more luck than judgement he connected perfectly with Ponty's renowned glass jaw. Ponty with an infinitesimal look of utter astonishment went down like a ninepin flat on his already flattened nose, out cold.

Three drunken colliers shouted it out for all the world to know. "The Merthyr boy's just given Ponty the beltin' he deserves." Before he knew it he was hoisted high on blue-scarred shoulders and paraded down the high street like a returning hero in a Greek myth. This was the sight that met Marion and Dewey and the rest of her entourage as they made their way out of the Royale. The two policemen who had been in the pub came across to confront the revellers.

"Is that right," one of them asked. "You've just put Ponty Williams out of action."

"That's right," one of the colliers answered. "You shoulda seen it man. A right hook from outer space. He's still out. Look at him." He pointed back up the road to where Ponty was sitting up semi prone in the gutter. The bearers gently returned John to the pavement where he stood before the guardians of the law and shrugged, prepared to take the consequences, in deep shit now because Ponty would now know who his assailant was.

141

"Well good on you mate," one of the policemen slapped him on the back. "That'll save us a job. We can handle him now. Drunk and disorderly . Come on Bob." And the two marched up to Ponty and manhandled him off in the direction of the police station to the loud cheers of the gathering crowd.

John saw Marion and approached her with an exaggerated swagger. "Good gentle lady," he beseeched. "I have slain the wicked dragon and saved these people from a fate worse than death. Will your ladyship bestow upon me the use of your carriage so that I may quit this place in safety and return to the bosom of my family in fair Merthyr Tydfil." Marion touched his badged face with a hint of tenderness.

"What on earth….." she left the statement unfinished.

"A victim of unrequited love," he teased with a pained smile. "I did battle with the dragon to win fair lady's hand," taking hers and pressing a swollen lip to it.

"Come on you'd better get in," she offered to Dewey's snort of disgust, as the Daimler, chauffer driven pulled into the curb flagrantly disregarding the double yellow lines. He half stumbled in on Marion's arm and Dewey clambered in behind them muttering as the crowd cheered John to the rafters and waved them farewell as the salubrious saloon glided off.

"What happened," she insisted.

"Some sort of fracas obviously," muttered Dewey.

"Fracas," John chuckled, "what the fucks a fracas. You do talk funny Fred. Well it's all a bit bizarre really, not fit for repeating in mixed company."

"In that case I'm dying to hear all about it," she insisted.

"It's not you I'm worried about," with a telling look at Fred .

"Now look here I've had just about….."

"Do be quiet Fred there's a darling she commanded. John smiled and settled lower into his sea, his body pressure reciprocated sending a warm glow surging through him. The comfortable heating evaporating the vast alcoholic reservoir in his head until he was light headed drunk again and inwardly laughing .

"I was sitting on the bog," he began rudely. "Very high class bog in there you know, did you try it Fred, all marble and clean you know. And on the back of the door so much philosophy. All the complexes of a sophisticated town like Ponty writ large for all to see. If the Graig was Vesuvius then this would be Pompeii. You know the sort of thing; I like wearing my girlfriend's knickers, I like rubber macs, I like little boys, I like mummy, I like daddy, I like me, my names Cedric I like big ones. They say graffiti went into decline after the Romans but I don't know you should see the illustrations in there. Fascinating, don't you think Fred." But Fred was neither fascinated nor amused. Marion on the other hand appeared to enjoy his buffoonery. He snuggled even closer and continued. "One item particularly intrigued me. It was obviously new because it had today's date.

142

'If you want to screw my wife she's the one in the lounge with a flower in her dress. The code is *vooly voo promenade avec moi dans le park pour jiggy jig."*

"Now look here…." Dewey spluttered again but was once more hushed to silence.

"On completion of my business I duly sought and found the lady in question and put the proposition to her in my best Frelsh, er I mean Wench, oh you know what I mean. She was not at all bad in a blond and brassy sought of way and well I was desperate. You see I had been spurned by the woman of my dreams. You ever been spurned and desperate Fred, then you'll know what I mean." How long would Dewey put up with this baiting, he wondered, almost sorry for him now, but he simply stared ahead in sullen silence. "Anyway the lady gave me a Parisian affirmative so off we went to the park for some jiggy jig. I won't embarrass you with the details of what immediately followed. Suffice it to say that at the precise moment of extreme agitation which precedes the ultimate climax I was fell upon most foully by a huge brute of a fellow, her perverted husband no doubt, who inflicted this most grievous injury upon my person.

"Taken completely by surprise and physically disadvantaged as I was, I was overpowered by this perverted monster, who as I lay bleeding and half conscious on the damp ground proceeded to finish off what I had most capably started." Marion tutted and shook her head with disbelief but with the faintest twitch of a smile on her ruby lips, while the angry veins on Dewey's red neck bulged to such an extent that they were visible even in the dimness of the car's interior. "Of course my first reaction was to jump up and retaliate, but then I thought, 'Well two can pay at that game my Neanderthal friend .' So I waited until he too reached the moment of impending climax before aiming a well placed kick to the testicles which rendered him immediately impotent. Whereupon, she twice tickled with the rub of love pleaded for relief of her hypertension, to which I responded out of nothing more sinister than sincere Christian, socialist affection. Could any gentleman do less?"

"Well I hope you're going to dream up something a little more edifying for your television audience," she teased, "or you might do some real damage to our public image."

"To be perfectly honest your public image is hardly my primary consideration. I haven't given it much thought. In any case I haven't had the time, I've been too bloody busy trying to thrash out an acceptable schedule with your Production Department. Then there's the Trade Unions, but I'll handle them allright so long as those clever little bastards from Personnel keep their snotty little noses out."

She turned angrily, suddenly serious to where Dewey flinched nervously. "I said I wanted the full cooperation of Production in establishing satisfactory release schedules," she said icily. "Can't you keep your bloody

143

managers under control, its hardly rocket science is it ? Its your responsibility Fred, I wont tolerate incompetence. When I give a directive I expect it to be implemented, is that clear? And as for you," she turned her invective on John, "I want you to………"

"Don't ever talk to me like one of your hirelings," he interrupted. "We'll discuss it Monday morning."

"We'll discuss it right now," she responded coldly. "Time and a half for overtime that's what you got at ICI isn't it?"

"Overtime at ICI was negotiable," he smiled, his flash of anger dissipated. If however you wish to invite me in for a recuperative coffee I might accept. Then if you stop being such a bossy bitch I might even enter into negotiations with you and come up with some stimulating ideas."

She opened her mouth, caught her breath, paused and sighed, then smiled. "Allright," she said. "O for Christ's sake Fred stop huffing and puffing like a jealous adolescent. I said coffee and I meant coffee." John almost felt sorry for him and ashamed of himself. Fred simply grunted. She slid back the glass panel which separated the driver from the passengers. "My place first then take Fred home please."

"And the other gentleman?" With just a hint of reproach.

"Thanks for your concern but my personal chauffer will take care of Mr Davies," she said tartly making a mental note not to use the same agency again.

Inside the house they drank their coffees in silence and when they had finished she said coldly, "Go to the bathroom and get yourself cleaned up. You look like a disaster area. You know where my bedroom is."

Saturday was busily spent. She had talked to him about his role as a 'cultural ambassador' and advised him of his public image. He had pretended acquiescence rather than shatter the fragile filigree of their complicated relationship. She had not been at all as he imagined in her lovemaking. Despite her self proclaimed promiscuity she was more like an adolescent than her sophisticated daughter: a child wrapped up in a courtesan's body. She was a paradox and a frustration, she had cried like a girl in love and clung to him like a drowning orphan. Then with the day's advent had resumed her businesslike aplomb. It would be difficult to determine who was the real Marion and he wasn't certain that he wanted to go through the inevitably painful process of finding out. If he was perfectly honest with himself he had to admit that she had been something of a disappointment in bed and her awesome beauty had excited him beyond satisfaction. To love such a woman could prove to be unendurable, and yet…..

At his insistence she stopped the car at the corner of his street and for a while stared silently into his eyes, the adolescent girl again, just watching the movement of his lips and the changes of expression in his face, neither hearing nor caring what it was he said. The world outside the car was still and peaceful and even the chemical plant displayed a strange macabre beauty

144

writing sulphurous plumes against the cold turquoise sky. Tomorrow the frost would be down like a sparkling blank canvas for the paws of mysterious nocturnal animals to paint. She would hear every footfall crisp on the hard frost from the loneliness of her bed with the heightened sensibility with which she had been infused since last night. For her something magical had happened. At first she thought of it as something of a rebirth, but on reflection it wasn't, it was the initiation, she had come alive for the first time. She leaned across and gently brushed his still moving lips with hers stopping his admonition and fusing herself to him with a lingering delicate pressure. With an indefinable unease he eventually broke away, opening the car door and getting out without a word, smilingly pursing his lips and walking away without a backward glance.

This was not at all the way he planned it, if indeed there had been anything more than just a vague intention, the fortuitous realisation of erotic fantasies. However, he was in for it good and proper now. The intention for sexual exploitation, how long had that been there, with Josephine from the start, but these were things that flowed up unbidden from the darkness of his genesis. It was the very epicentre of his being. Even when he pretended it was just an act it was always something much more, something beyond rationalisation, something metaphysical if he could bring himself to believe in such a thing.

Inside, the faded faces of his parents, the TV, the kids and the pop music disturbed his reverie. He trundled up the stairs on the frayed red carpet. One day he must lay one of rich red velvet, comfort and luxury for their old age. But what sort of sop would that be now for all the scars, the tears, the anguish, bitterness and disillusionment which had been their lot in life. Their fabric was torn beyond repair, worn threadbare with the passage of the years. The bourgeoisie had surpassed the worst excesses of the aristocracy, had civilly maimed and slaughtered millions : the *beastly bourgeoisie*.

The woman in whose bed he slept last night epitomised everything they stood for, so what was this messy muddled mixed up relationship that he had begun with her. Was he bent on exploiting her, bleeding her dry and in the end destroying her.

CHAPTER 10

The first session was scheduled for two o'clock. Everything was ready. No expense had been spared since the television arrangements had been concluded. The room had rapidly been converted into a lecture theatre that any university college would have been proud of. John had kept the format of this first session a closely guarded secret much to the chagrin of Dewey and his associates who would dearly have loved to muscle in on the 'big show' which it was in danger of becoming. Marion however appeared to be taking it all in her stride. He would have preferred to think that se was sweating blood at the prospect of letting him loose in front of the watching world, but she exuded all the aplomb of the proverbial refrigerated cucumber.

There was a raised dais in the front of the room, with a rostrum perched on a teak enclosed consul with all kinds of built in electronic gadgetry. A roll down blackboard and a white screen could be activated by the push of a button, and TV, slides or films could be projected at the touch of a switch. Hi-fi tape and record systems were also incorporated into the system. The names of the workers who were to participate in this opening session were engraved in white on black traffolyte labels which had been mounted in holders on the individual desk tops. This had been the advertising departments brilliant contribution. Some managers and department heads had wrangled their way in but they were relegated by John to the back of the 'theatre'. Cameras had already been shooting as individuals began to drift in, part of the 'verite' technique of modern television he supposed.

"Testing, testing," he said into the microphone, and startled faces turned towards him. "It was my thirtieth year to heaven," he recited sonorously imitating Burton passably well, "Woke to my harbour and neighbour wood, and the mussel pooled and heron priested shore." It sounded good. Some wag applauded and he leaned forward, his elbows on the rostrum and felt the power of the hell fire non-conformist orator, from whom Dylan, consciously or not, had borrowed so much.

The last few days had been hectic to say the least. The Masons hierarchy had thrown frantic tantrums at his refusal to perform to script or even to rehearse to camera. Resignations and sackings were threatened and withdrawn. The BBC programme producer on the other hand seemed perfectly happy to film off the cuff as it were. He wanted to film over a period anyway and most of the material would no doubt be edited out to satisfy his own agenda. The unions had proved co-operative once the question of protection of earnings had been resolved. A PR manager came up and offered John some last minute advice. John looked at him coldly. "Why don't you fuck off," he invited, and was rewarded with ironic cheers from a group of production workers who had just come in and heard every word clearly booming over the amplification system.

He began to mutter into the microphone in feeble senile tones, having warmed to his immediate and future audience with the natural talent for public performance which is a curse and a blessing to the Welsh. "Ladies and gentlemen of the jury," he mimicked, "the case which you are about to hear will be a long and tedious one. I suggest therefore that you come to your verdict now before the issue is complicated by abstruse evidence and arcane argument. Capitalism is on trial and it is obviously insane and unfit to plead. I direct you therefore to return a verdict of guilty but insane and I will have the defendant painlessly put down."

There was a ripple of uneasy laughter as the lecture theatre gradually filled and the television producer temporarily asserted his authority, talking to the audience about the 'tele-verite' technique, and as he did so cameramen with hand held cameras moved about freely while the main dollies also traversed the free floor space which had been provided for that very purpose. John interestedly observed the producer at work. The medium had always fascinated and disturbed him, brought up as he was on the 'wireless' and the BBC mission to educate and inform. This he considered to be the beginning of a new era, especially with the introduction of a commercial channel, ITV which seemed to him to presage a dumbing down and the gradual replacement of *inform* with *entertain*.

Nobody epitomised the old edict better than Ray Robinson that avid, discourteous seeker after truth, whose blunt and forthright manner had cabinet ministers quaking in their shiny boots whenever they were subjected to his aggressive questioning. His was the example that the new form could serve the public good better than the old if it were not allowed to generate into the banal and the vapid. He was anything but discourteous now however having left his interviewing persona in the studio. His usual ploy was to provoke an angry initial response from whoever he had under his microscope, not caring how rude or outrageous he had to be to provoke it, and it was a consummate politician who did not rise to the bait. John was determined to prove to be such, to turn Robinson's invective back on him and fight fire with fire.

"Righto then children are you all sitting comfortably. Good, then listen carefully and Uncle John will tell you a story. Firstly I'm sure you'd all like me to thank Uncle Ray, that is Mr Robinson, for explaining the virtues of cine verite to us, verite from the French for truth of course. For Uncle Ray is a veritable seeker after truth as I'm sure you all know, for none of you will have mistaken him from his namesake Sugar who dispatches his opponents with a vicious left hook rather than the rapier like verbal assaults which our Uncle Ray launches upon his antagonists on those late night intellectual programmes which hardly anybody watches." Albert the fat commie shop steward snorted loudly to assure John and the management lackeys that he at least was to be counted among he number of those insomniacs to whom John referred. The participation of his members in what he saw as *this silly charade* had been conditional on a number of counts; one, that it was entirely voluntary; two, that all participants would receive the higher rate of productivity bonus; and three, the sessions would be *truly* educational. *Truly* was a nod and a wink in John's direction as a fellow red, though one of the *under the bed* variety with whom the political class and the media were obsessed to the point of paranoia. This was a nod and a wink which John was happy to reciprocate, though he saw himself as more of a Trotskiite mole. The question of the bonus had proved to be more of a problem with the interference of the Work Study Department until Marion's stern edict brought them scurrying into line.

The last thing John wanted was for his audience to sit there in their departmental groups simply because it was an easy way to earn their bonus and being bored out of their minds. He wanted these sessions to be more than just an escape from the tedious regimentation of the production line but actually to stimulate a response and a challenge to managerialism and all it's absurd limitations. "Feel free to move around and have a chat for five minutes," he invited. "I'm just going to play some background music which I hope will get us all to relax and forget that we're being dominated by the monotonous rhythm of endlessly reciprocating machinery." With that he pressed a button and flooded the room with the delicate vibraphonic tones of Milt Jackson in session with the Brubeck quartet. Just at the point where his audience had began to sink back in their chairs and stare at the ceiling or speak together in hushed reverential whispers the music was violently interrupted with an ear shattering shriek which brought everybody suddenly bolt upright. Before they had the chance to regain their equilibrium John struck the dais with his fist and shouted – "Why should I let the toad WORK squat on my life? Can't I use my wit as a pitchfork and drive the brute off? Six days of the week it soils with its sickening poison – just for paying a few bills! That's out of proportion...." And he continued on through Larkin's diatribe. "Ah, were I courageous enough to shout *Stuff your pension!* But I know all too well, that's the stuff that dreams are made on:..." The end of the poem was met with a hiatus of stunned silence followed by a trickle of embarrassed applause. John waited long enough for an uneasy chatter to reinstate itself. Some of the more literate of the managers engaged in a perplexed consideration of what this mad anarchist was up to. God knows it as hard enough to get the buggers to meet production targets as it was. "OK," John said at last, "what did you think of that?"

There was an awkward silence.

"Doesn't anybody have an opinion," he asked. "I knew it was a mistake to let the bloody foremen in," he quipped. "Well what do you think the poem was about?"

"Work," a sallow faced girl in the front row responded.

148

"Good. Yes, and what did the poet think about work?"

"Not a lot. But we all gotta work to earn a livin' 'aven't we?" It was one of the younger girls who spoke. He smiled a wry smile.

"Yes I suppose we do. Nobody could disagree with that I think. What do you think the poet is trying to say then. Is he denying the need to work or what."

"Well its not like real poetry is it," another girl stated.

"Hmm," John smiled, "well that depends on what you mean by 'real' poetry he replied. "It doesn't all have to rhyme you know, nor even go tum te tum te tum te tum. But we can always do 'poetry' some other time. What do you think of this." He pressed another button and a slide projector splashed an image of one of Dave's pen and ink drawings onto a huge screen.

The drawing depicted an old man chopping sticks in he backyard of a typical terraced cottage. There was the same initial uneasy silence.

"Well do you think it's good or bad," he prompted. A few people muttered different opinions. "What is it then, anybody like to describe it. Yes, you please. I'm sorry I don't know your names yet."

"It's just a man chopping sticks thassall."

"That's all ? What sort of a man is he then ?"

"An old man," somebody volunteered.

"That's better yes. An old man. Anything else?"

"A thin old man."

"Yes."

"A daft old man," from one of the inevitable wags.

"That's interesting. Why daft then?"

"Well look at 'im, 'e looks daft don't 'e. Jest a stupid old man choppin' sticks. It's nothin' much of a drawin' I don't think."

"I don't think 'e's daft," a thin girl with emaciated features said . "Not as daft as you any road," she addressed her invective at the wag. "He's very sad I think, and a bit afraid too."

"What do you think he's afraid of then, sorry what's your name."

"I'm Joan, Joan Samuels sir," she said shyly with the deference of a schoolgirl addressing a form master. "I dunnow, dying I suppose. He's very old. He must realise he hasn't got long to go. You can see it in his eyes somehow. But 'e's still got to carry on choppin' sticks for the fire cos 'e probably got nobody else to do it for him, or some old gran relyin' on him to do it for her. It's sad. He knows how 'opeless it all is. A bit like the poem really I think."

John smiled and sighed silently. Here was an alert intelligence, a perceptive heart stagnating behind a sewing machine. And how many more hearts would be like hers if it wasn't for the bloody machines. To think that at eleven the education system had labelled her a failure and pigeon-holed her to labour the rest of her days in spiritual drudgery unless some happy accident would have it otherwise..

"I still think 'es daft anyway miss clever clogs," the wag insisted. "Fancy talkin' about 'im as if 'e's real . E's only a bloody drawin' after all."

A topic for another session, John thought. "Now then let's have a look at some more photographs and drawings shall we. How about this for example ...

It wasn't long before they were leaving Merthyr behind. Marion swung the car into the forecourt of one of the multitude of filling stations that had proliferated with the inexorable growth of the 'never never' society. She asked for ten gallons and while the attendant dedicated himself to the task with sly lascivious looks in their direction she playfully pecked John's cheek extrovertly. "Nervous?" she asked.

"Only when you get this close," he responded. Oddly enough he felt no nerves at all , but he was not yet under the hot blinding studio lights which defined Glyn Protheroe's home territory. John was hoping that the old maxim that there was safety in numbers would hold good. That had been the strategy behind his insistence that the Dowlais five would appear together or not at all. He had cleverly included them all in the seminars which had been filmed as a preamble to tonight's broadcast which had left Protheroe with little alternative.

The attendant weighed up the disparity in their ages as he approached the car jingling his money bag with the same knowing smile spread across his face. He unhooked the filler and rammed it with a phallic moue into the belly of the gleaming Volvo. Some bastards have all the luck, he implied with a sly wink, to which John responded by blowing him a kiss.

They sped down the Merthyr – Cardiff valley road following the dirty Taff. Here and there little havens of unspoiled riverbank reminded him of how it must have been not so very long ago. At these points the old river seemed to roll more lazily as if enjoying the pleasant interlude. Closer to the little valley towns the black silt of the colliery tips oozed out of bilious tributaries, the banks more steeply cut, scum covered. The black beasts standing sombre against the blue sky with the ramshackle towns huddled below them around the cluttered workings of the untidy half abandoned pits already in the early stages of rapid decline. A great oak stood serene in the sludge of an altered river course. A tree which in its own lifetime must have seen stark metal thumbs sprout out of the virgin earth, iron trees with leafless branches and heard the hum of hot electrons where hitherto only the wind had sung. A tree which as a sapling lazed and languished in a pool of morning meadow mist, laughing in the afternoon sun and breathing fresh free air.

"A penny for them," she teased.

"Workers have paid an awful price for so called progress in these shabby valleys," he answered with quiet anger, "While parasites like you grew fat and rich."

"Not so much of the fat," she riposted with a smile which masked her underlying unease.

The studio lights were hot and he wriggled uncomfortably in the (deliberately?) uncomfortable interview chair. A monitor in front of them displayed a front man garrulously gabbling about some hitherto unheard of Parisian singer who the media moguls had decided would be the new Piaf. The singer's recent death from a drugs overdose had given her something of a cult status and so the deification process had begun. Her oeuvre was nothing if not derivative of Piaf's tristesse but lacking by a Common Market kilometre the emotional power of the original. The eulogy drew mercifully to a close but a performance in the irritating nasal drones of the deceased was accompanied by pseudo Parisian choreography, at least the legs were lovely. Finally the awaited moment arrived. The front man drew attention to an interesting phenomenon of the South Wales industrial heartland where the seeds of cultural revolution were being sown in the arid wasteland of the industrial kind which had preceded it. It was taking place in, of all the most unlikely places, a lingerie factory in the coal and iron town of Merthyr Tydfil famous previously as the iron capital of the world in its nineteenth century heyday, and the constituency which returned Keir Hardy to Westminster leading to the formation of the Labour Party. He went on to give a potted version of recent events culminating in the appointment of John Davies to his unique position, dwelling at some length on the political activities of himself and his 'acolytes'. "And now over to our Cardiff studio where Professor Glyn Protheroe is talking to the subject of tonight's special report, Mr John Davies."

" Mr Davies," Protheroe fired his first salvo right on cue. "How would you answer many of your critics who complain you have neither the qualifications or experience necessary to fulfil the position which you hold. A unique position it must be said, harking back perhaps to the ancient days of bardic patronage."

"Bardic patronage. I wouldn't put it quite like that. This is more like mutual back scratching I would suggest. Talk to the redoubtable Mrs Mason, the Managing Director and Chairman of the Board, there is a hard nosed lady who does nothing for nothing. The Company, I suppose I mustn't mention its name" he added coyly, "will get a million pounds worth of advertising out of this."

"Then what will you get Mr Davies?"

"That depends who 'you' are doesn't it. For me personally I get a decent salary, an interesting and rewarding job and an opportunity to develop my creative work. For the workforce perhaps at least a chance to participate in something a bit less soul destroying than eight hours a day on a production line, at best an active stimulus to their own creativity and self actualisation. Now there's a phrase straight from the amateur psychologist's guide book for you.

"But to try to answer your question I suppose there might be something in your bardic analogy and Industry could hardly do much worse than the Arts Council could they. The route to a flourishing culture is not via bursaries to cronies and cliques. The danger with a modern patronage however is that it would be neither feudal nor aristocratic but capitalist, which would ultimately be disastrous, with content driven down to the lowest common denominator."

"So where does the future lie then, let's leave that an open question for now. What about your qualifications and youth; are you really the right man for this job?"

"Well the reality is I'm the only man for this job, unique as it is. As to the critics who I'm sure are numerous I'll have to take your word for their reaction, not moving in critical circles myself. Truthfully I don't give a damn to paraphrase Rhett Butler. What is it Steiner says in one of his essays. 'Who would be a critic if he could but ague the poise of Lawrence. When a critic looks back he sees a eunuch's shadow.' Something like that I think it is. So you see I'm not overmuch concerned with what the critics have to say, save some honourable exceptions of whom Steiner is of course one. If they see me as some kind of emissary for the redundant artist that's their business, I certainly don't. All I want to do is contribute to a dialogue about art and culture and its relationship to social life, especially at working class level. If art and culture are to become progressive they have to be dragged out of the esoteric cul-de-sac and aired and debated with the man on the Merthyr bus. I take my cue from Brecht on this. If art is not given back to the people then it will deserve to die, and die it will. You can see the way in which I set out to initiate this dialogue in the short film which I think we are about to see. A tiny pebble in a huge pond but the epicentre as far as Wales is concerned is here in this awful lovely old whoretown where the Industrial Revolution began and the People's Flag was first flown. My qualifications like Bloom I have acquired in The University of Life."

"Indeed," Protheroe cut in seizing his chance, "but given your youth, how old are you " he glanced at his notes, "not yet twenty one, do you really think you have attended long enough to have graduated?" He smiled smugly.

"Surely one never graduates from the University of Life. Wasn't that Bloom's point. Your analogy with college studentship is meaningless but typical, the standard response of the sterile academic resentful of intrusion into his hallowed territory, a threat to his high priesthood. I would say that for the most part the academic's education is insular, mine was at least forged in the heat and passion of real practical struggle. I attended WEA[8] evening classes and read from Aristotle through to Zarathustra arguing Nietzsche and Sartre in the Lamb and the Dowlo. I studied engineering in Merthyr Tech, and as our old friend Marx asserted, you cannot educate a man to be a wizard in the toolroom and expect him to be a buffoon outside the factory gate. Of course the essence of the artist is artistic production, to contradict Mr Collingwood. After all 'who would be a critic if he could be a writer', our old friend Steiner again. So ultimately I will be judged on my work."

"And what is the extent of your artistic output Mr Davies?" Again the telling smile.

"About sixty poems, not all extant, a dozen short stories and a novel in the offing, half on paper half in my head, or in the air, or somewhere."

"Impressive for one so young. But how much published?"

"Not much, some poems, about a dozen in obscure scarcely read publications, ditto half a dozen short stories, but that's not really relevant. I am writing and that is what defines a writer. Good or bad are judgements other people have to make. Publication is a purely commercial issue. Often it has very little to do with any other kind of value. There are those who try to function differently to their credit but they are none of them 'patrons' in the bardic tradition which I believe is where we started."

Protheroe shuffled in his elevated interviewers chair. He was one of the new breed who contrived to be the star of their own show. It was time to get controversial. "Yes perhaps bardic is not the appropriate metaphor is it, implying as it does singing hymns of praise on behalf of your patron. On the contrary would you agree that your material and that of your friends could hardly be more inimical to the interests of your sponsor. Is it any surprise then that your work is unlikely to make commercial sense to any would be publisher?"

"That's hardly true now is it," John interrupted with a condescending tone. "Writers like Zola, London, Dickens, Lawrence, Dos Passos just to name a few, I could go on all night, all had difficulty but managed to find publishers eventually. It's a characteristic of the commercial system that it will sometimes publish material that is inimical to it simply *because* it treats it as a commodity; its controversy can contribute to its market value. one of its inbuilt contradictions you might say. It was Lenin I think who said that the capitalist will haggle over the price of the length of rope with which the revolutionary is about to hang him. The other point which you imply rather than raise directly relates to my role as an artist and my political radicalism." Protheroe hunched his shoulders with what John took to be assent. "Well I'm in pretty good company from the few I mentioned earlier. Is it the artist's role to be a propagandist you may well ask. Well to a degree it's inescapable. If a

---

[8] Workers Education Association.

writer is honest with himself then he must see himself as an informer. Why else would he or she write? Why bother to produce any kind of record of their production, why not just store it away in their heads, become a Collingwood or Bell or Fry and limit the definition of art to its ephemeral conception. Of course that kind of idealism is a dead end and to paraphrase Wittgenstein, about that which of we cannot speak we should remain silent.

"Of course that doesn't mean the artist must necessarily set out to be a propagandist. Marx himself makes this point in one of his rare essays on literature in which he extols the virtues of Balzac over Zola, who despite his admiration for the *ancien regime* lays bare the rottenness of nineteenth century society because his honesty as an artist does not allow him to do otherwise. He is despite himself as are all great artists a propagandist. But what is he a propagandist of..... the truth." Protheroe made to intervene but John had experience of holding court to tougher audiences than he. "Before you ask, 'But what is truth,' of course that is the sixty thousand dollar question isn't it? Nobody has access to the universal truth I doubt that it exists. I have never experienced the absolute in anything, nor has anyone as far as I know. I can only present my vision, one aspect of the truth perhaps. It is a grave responsibility which too many writers take too lightly and I am not talking here of the merely incompetent. Trash is trash and easily recognisable. I am talking about the thinkers, the fakirs, the litterateurs, the liars an epithet which old Plato would apply to us all."

Protheroe stammered and shuffled his papers. He had underestimated this young man, it had been a tour de force in which John Davies had seized the opportunity to present himself as a savant beyond his years. Clearly well read and articulate and with a natural skill for manipulation of the medium of television. He was clearly destined to go a long way. "Before we get sidetracked into the philosophy of literature," (he too knew what he was talking about) "and end up debating the nature of truth let us take a little time out to examine the film which was made of the first of your, what would you call them, lectures.?" This time it was John's turn to shrug and smile non commitally. "Afterwards we will return to Mr Davies and his friends who are at the heart of this remarkable renaissance in, of all places, Merthyr Tydfil."

The film turned out to be everything that John had hoped for. It cut liberally from one session to another with no respect for the original chronology. One minute he was making ribald remarks and the next reading sonorously from Dylan Thomas or Yeats. To what extent this was a truthful representation was an open question which he hoped to address in a future debate on formalism if he ever advanced that far. But the comments from the tragic face of Joan Samuels told its own story. If John had little respect for Protheroe the Presenter he had it in spades for John Thomas the Editor who he felt had captured the essence of what he had wanted to say. Then there had been the presentation of the magnificent erotica of both Bill and Dave with the background music true to the original but improved a hundred percent by the superior studio equipment. Mingus, Mulligan, Farmer, Getz, and Brubeck. Beethoven, Tchaikovsky, Bach and Vivaldi. It was a lovely cornucopia.

In the final session Ted and Geraint had appeared and the five had read sung recited and argued poetry, polemics, politics, literature, art, anarchy, pop music, nationalism, socialism, Marxism, God, Ghandi, Shakespeare, Olivier and Liz Taylor, but they never touched on darts. There was plenty of participation from the workforce in this catholic debate which culminated with the little communist shop steward standing on his chair trying to make a heated contribution only to be drowned out by his unsympathetic comrades. It was a fitting televisual climax.

Live in the studio the five were interviewed as a group. This was the moment they had been waiting for. They were first introduced individually and Protheroe gave a brief example and explanation of their individual work and their relationship to each other. "This common factor in your relationship," he addressed them collectively. "Is it political, is it Nationalism?" John burst out laughing spontaneously and Ted, ever the wit, leaned forward conspiratorially looking about him for eavesdroppers. "Actually," he confided to camera, "we form the nucleus of a very radical, subversive movement. the WZ, the Welsh Zionists, expansionist not isolationist. We intend to win back all the territory stolen from us by the so called English, really the Normans of course. God gave us that land and we want it back. The WZ will redeem the promise to our forefathers. Be warned."

"He's a nationalist," Bill pointed a thumb at Geraint, "but then he's mentally retarded and sings pseudo Welsh folk songs for the Welsh language elite, so he doesn't count." John tried to inject a note of gravity.

"You make an error common enough particularly among English commentators," he interrupted, "of elevating matters of national parochialism in matters of little importance into a grand Nationalist gesture. We may wear our Welshness on our sleeve, which is an illustration that we suffer no lack of identity. Because I assure you the face we show is quite spontaneous, except of course when we mimic the pseudo Welshness which many of the Nats display. If any group suffers an identity complex it is in fact the Nats, a reaction which finds a sympathetic response with the English middle classes and the far right who have never got over the loss of Empire and have an identity crisis of their own. If we have to be categorised I suppose we follow in the tradition of the Anglo Welsh movement, in the sense that our principal medium is the English language, which made a unique contribution to the wider field of English literature in its own very Welsh way. That stimulates us much more than the publication of some little *englyn* or *cynghanedd* which will only ever be read by some tiny elite faction. Contrast the international audience for Dylan Thomas and to a lesser extent Gwyn

Thomas with that of the founder of the Welsh Nationalist movement Saunders Lewis."

"Perhaps I should explain for the benefit of non-Welsh viewers, correct me if I'm wrong, that the forms you referred to, *englyn* and *cynghanedd*, did I pronounce that correctly, are peculiar if not unique to Welsh poetry. Perhaps it emphasises your point that I only know this through my knowledge of Gerard Manley Hopkins." Protheroe took the opportunity to demonstrate his academic kudos.

"Yes. A highly formalised structure deriving from the ancient bardic tradition and, which further emphasises the point, influenced Dylan's poetry more through his admiration of Hopkins than direct exposure to the Welsh language sources."

"So then you are aware of your cultural heritage?"

"I get so annoyed when people put that question to me. As Trotski said, we stand on the shoulders of our forefathers. I am as aware of my cultural heritage as the most xenophobic Nationalist that ever lived. But it's come to me through the medium of the English language. It would be much easier in some ways if we presented our material through the Welsh language. At least it would be published. Plays and the plastic arts would get an airing on the Welsh language broadcasting media. That's the tragedy for Welsh language artists and performers. It seems that anyone can do it. Any scribbler who can put together a few lines of doggerel is elevated to a sort of celebrity status within the introspective boundaries of a very small audience. I'm not against encouragement of the language or the provision of programmes by the BBC for minority audiences if only the standard was not so woeful…" Protheroe interrupted what he thought might become a diatribe with a question.

"Well if you aren't Nationalists, and from what you have just said John you clearly are not, we knew that already from your recent problems with the Labour Party hierarchy, but I don't want to go down that road, what exactly are you…Yes Dave."

"It's quite simple really," Dave responded as John reached across and took a sip of water, tepid under the hot studio lights, " we are all artists and the common factors which give our work a unity are fairly obvious. We are all working class, that's number one and of primary significance. We all share similar experiences of a drab and constricting environment, a harsh capitalist hangover which wont go away. We have arrived at similar concepts of political truths, and I mean political in its most catholic sense, through our common experience. As Welshmen communicating in English we have all been influenced by, non-conformity, coal tips, scenic grandeur, faith, unemployment, socialism, squalor, the list is almost endless. We also represent a rebellion against elitism, particularly in art. Intellectual isolation spells art's death knell. What we ought to share with artists internationally is repugnance for the ills and inequalities which deny the human spirit everywhere."

"So then you do admit to being political activists of some sort?"

"Of course we are political activists," John rejoined the debate. "As for definition we'll be happy to put a label on it for you later, since that seems to be what you want, but you may yet be disappointed, labels are too readily applied too often. Inasmuch as politics comprise a very large part of our shared social experience then it would be impossible not to respond politically. Of course this political truth is only a part, though a considerable part of the general truth the artist seeks to express. Sometimes he may not even be consciously aware of it, as in the comments of Marx I referred to earlier. To try to pin a Nationalist label on us is absurd. We are a strange conglomerate with debts to Marx, Kropotkin, Trotski, and oh a ragbag of others but that's a web too tangled to unweave in the time we have available and I'm sure you would want, in a programme like this, to pursue our cultural agenda. That's not to duck the issue of course, there is a real debate to be had about culture and politics. The French are having it right now but British (English) philosophy, well that's another matter. Our own Raymond Williams is a refreshing exception. To sum up since I see you twitching nervously, Brecht and Sartre. You will note that we haven't blown up a single telephone kiosk." Protheroe shifted uncomfortably in the interviewer's chair and Ted cut across him once again as he opened his mouth to counter John's rhetoric.

"Toilets are our target," he insisted with mock seriousness, determined to make the whole discussion as absurd as possible. "We demolished one in Dowlais last week because it said 'Push a penny in the slot' instead of 'pwshio un grot yn y slot'. Keep our toilets Welsh, that's our motto." Protheroe was taken out of his stride by this bit of nonsense and momentarily floundered like an actor who has fluffed his line.

"What about the recent strike in which some of you appear to have played a pivotal role, you of course John being the principal participant? Didn't this have at its heart a great deal of resentment against working conditions being imposed from outside, and then your own resignation John from the Labour Party and the Trade Unions . Do you have a problem with *outside* interference." The word was pregnant with innuendo. This time it was Bill who responded.

"Good God man that's not Nationalism, its not even parochialism. That sort of thing happens at Halewood, so what do you call it there, Liverpudlianism? Anyway what's it got to do with the price of eggs or art? Its simply industrial relations as practiced at I.C.I."

Protheroe shrugged and admitted, "Well Industrial Relations is not my bag really."

John smiled. "Any established trade union group that has successfully represented its members for many years is bound to resent what

157

it sees as unwarranted interference from outside sources whether from the Management or the Union side. That is what happened here. That was I.C.I's first ever strike at the Dowlais Plant you know. It had absolutely nothing to do with Nationalism or a small group of committed artists. To suggest otherwise is absurd. It's just Daily Mail or even Western Mail politics."

"I suppose one does take one's cue from the media," Protheroe replied, "and that's certainly what was implied – with you as the ringleader of course."

"If you think the 'ringleader' of a small disparate group of artists could persuade the hard nosed workers of Merthyr to go out on strike on some ridiculous pretext…. Well I'd suggest you know even less about Industrial Relations than you had the good sense to admit. I might well deduce that you are all in on it together, part of a great media conspiracy to re-elect the effete and rotten Tory Party."

"But there is quite a bit of English bashing in your work you wouldn't deny that," Protheroe was determined to pursue this line though it should have been clear by now that it was a dead end.

"You know this is getting a bit bloody thick," Geraint could contain himself no longer. "I'm the only one who might be considered a Nationalist, but that's because I happen to believe that socialism should begin at home. But if we do bash the English a bit it's only because you are so easy to bash (the *you* implying the mistaken view that Protheroe with his cut glass accent was an Englishman). It's simply a fact that it was the English who dominated the industrial revolution in Wales shamelessly exploiting the Welsh working class making themselves some of the richest and most powerful men in Britain and pulling up sticks and leaving us in the shit when it suited them, denying us our own language in the process. It also just so happens that it was the English who succeeded in colonising half the world and creating an Empire on which the sun never set, establishing the filthy capitalist system which is the real object of our attack. Of course the English capitalist exploited his own kind just as ruthlessly as he did the Indian and the African. Old Marx had it right when he said that capitalism ahs no country and in that sense neither has the worker. So much for our nationalism eh?"

"Then it's a nice irony I suppose, that your benefactor, if I may use that term, is a magnate of an industry that traces its roots to the cotton trade which might be said to have started it all."

"A nice irony," John agreed, seeing the interview being brought to a neat, if trite conclusion, "but not inconsistent with one of the many inherent contradictions of capitalism. We've already made reference to Lenin's little joke about the revolutionary's rope. Perhaps all we are doing now is haggling about the price."

"And that's a nice open question on which to bring this fascinating interview to a close." Protheroe babbled on for a few more minutes surprisingly beginning to heap praise on this little group of 'cultural revolutionaries' in the true Brechtian tradition.

John gave a knowing smile as the camera zoomed in on the four as the credits rolled and music the theme from The Threepenny Opera played them out.

They were in a house somewhere in Cyncoed, Kinky Cyncoed, and very nice it was too, real suburbia. It belonged to a friend of Marion, a spinster of about Marion's age John guessed. One of a circle who constantly exude an air of confidence and influence. Influence in which particular sphere was more difficult to discover. They were the kind of people who spoke with high pitched nasal accents, accents unaligned with any known geographical or ethnic location. They would speak loudly in company for the benefit of bystanders, of dinner last night with Marcello, whoever he, she or it may be, as if the very fact that they were on speaking terms with Marcello was something that elevated them to the very highest strata of society. Marion had even displayed something of it herself when she introduced her friend to John. "This is Rena Charles," as reverently as if she was the Pope's mistress.

"How do you do," Rena said, "Your television performance was absolutely fantastic. You're a natural. You knew exactly how to handle that sack of shit Protheroe, so much so you had him gushing all over you at the end."

"Yeah but everybody is so busy intellectualising that they've ignored the essence of it. What about the tits and arse. That was the real breakthrough and nobody saw it."

"What are you saying," Marion insisted. "That you perpetrated some kind of intellectual fraud, some great clever joke. Is that all it was? Are you kidding?"

"God," John chuckled cynically, "you the great litterateur, and you (turning to Rena) the grande savant, you ask *me* is it a fraud. It's you who are the fakes, the frauds : because you have to ask, because you don't know . You need the clever clichés of the those articulate intellectuals to set your standards for you, all because you lack the honesty of poor uneducated Joan Samuels . You cannot allow yourselves the luxury of a simple honest response. It was pornographic : that was it's intention. It was achieved with your sponsorship and collaboration.."

"Oh God."

"Oh God, oh God," he mimicked. "Stop being so bloody hypocritical. Why shouldn't we be free to express truth as we see it. Is it that our censors only want us to proclaim the savoury side of truth : show the best in this the best of all possible worlds. Joe Bloggs draws crude symbols on lavatory walls and wanks into the public pan. We spend our seed in more creative receptacles. Like the metaphor? The drive is identical but ours a less impotent expression : a far more erotic one. Bill has photographs of cunts

159

blown up so you could dive inside. Dave has canvasses, so lurid, of the act of fucking that they give you an immediate erection. They are masterpieces of technique and truth which is what all great art is. We showed you some of them but you only saw what you've been conditioned to see. Nudity and sex in classical or religious settings are perfectly acceptable, as a visit to even the most conservative provincial gallery will illustrate. Its justifiable too when used to titillate for purely commercial ends. Who questions half clad bimbos being paraded as anybody's for a box of chocolates or a ride in the latest sports car to hit the market. But try showing real seduction, real sexual excitement, try bringing the thing out in the open for honest discussion and appraisal and you have the Bishops and the Politicians in a frenzy of self righteousness. Publish Lawrence or Miller and end up in jail. Would you 'allow your servants to read such filth', implying of course that its allright for the upper classes to do so. And before you ask where the line between art and pornography lies, I'll tell you. People who pose that questions simply do not know what art is all about. Where do you draw the line between art and cruelty, art and politics, art and religion? The answer is that of course art cannot be separated from its context as if it exists in a vacuum as those who Lawrence once described as ' the beastly bourgeoisie' so stupidly believe. The subject of art is culled from the whole of human experience and not some metaphysical fairyland. To disqualify any subject matter from becoming art is insidious and dangerous and leads to the prescriptive and proscriptive art of the fascists and the Stalinists. The fact that the guardians of our public morality here in the free west seek just as much as the totalitarians to legislate their own perverted vision of culture into being is just as obnoxious. Read Orwell's 1984 if you want a vision of that future to haunt you. So it's the boyos and the bints we are concentrating on. Theirs will be the more honest response....we hope....God we hope."

Rena clasped her hands together joyously and threw herself around his neck. "Oh you lovely, lovely boy," she cooed. "Why didn't you tell me he was such a treasure," she remonstrated with Marion. "He's more than a 'bawdy boy and a bit'. Come on I've booked us a table in Luigi's in town. I've got a little proposition to put to you which I think you will not wish to refuse. Oh don't look so adolescently jealous," she chided Marion. "My interest is almost without venality. How could I pose a threat to you with my plain bohemianism?"

"Olé, a bottle of champers each and a knees up outside the Arcade," John enthused in anticipation of a celebratory booze up. "Come on girls what are we waiting for?"

The vino and the vongole duly consumed, it was John's first vongole and it was delicious, they repaired to the Park for coffee where they sat about in the lounge engaged in aimless chit chat where they had soon attracted a coterie as insipid as the one they had earlier abandoned. The centres of attention were a bosomy contralto from the Welsh National Opera Company,

160

an egocentric editor from the Western Mail, John himself who was the man of the moment and Rena who was once again accorded the status of a minor celebrity. Marion sat majestically aloof, her well cut skirt revealing just enough lithe thigh to distract John from the little throng. Another group of four appeared to represent the Cardiff liberal left indicated that they were off to the Arcade which was the Merthyr Five's watering hole and the pub of choice of the city's left of centre intelligentsia.

"Can't we get away from these pretentious twits," he finally pleaded with Marion. Rena her antenna bristling broke off her conversation with the contralto and rounded on him.

"Not until you've listened to my proposition," she insisted sternly. "But you're right they are an insipid bunch. Come on back to my place. Sorry darling," she brushed off the contralto, "some time soon I promise."

Out in the street the women window shopped for a while, imitating the poise of the giraffe necked mannequins. "If only we had that facility," Rena said, suddenly serious, "to stop and suspend life just long enough to examine the poses we have adopted."

"Isn't that what we are doing when we create art," John responded.

"All we do is drift," Marion added her contribution to the melancholia, "mere bits of flotsam swept along the black river. Sometimes we make the slower moving stretches near the shore, just for a few seconds, never long enough to make a landfall. The answer of course is, and this is addressed to you two, try swimming with the current instead of against it."

"And end up in the sea that much quicker," Rena replied. "No John and I are river fish that must struggle against the flow, like spawning salmon."

"Is that where you are then," John taunted Marion, "in the big wide sea with all the other sharks?"

Marion sniggered, then chuckled, Rena joined her, then John put an arm around each and laughed until he tears ran down his cheeks.

In Rena's Pontcanna palace they sat before a banked up coal fire basking in it's radiance, sipping strong tea which John had insisted on brewing and listening to Miles Davies latest LP.

"So then, what is it you do for a living Rena?" he asked during a lull. Rena and Marion looked at each other with an air of amused misbelief.

"Come on," Rena replied.

"Look if you're a high class whore or somebody big in market gardening or something please excuse my ignorance, but it might help if you assumed less and informed more."

"I do believe he's serious."

"Well darling I suppose I just took it for granted that he knew," Marion responded with a smile as Rena strode theatrically to a writing desk by the window. She picked up a manila file and handed it to John. He opened it and removed a manuscript file, one which he had submitted to the Head of BBC Drama some months ago.

"I'm the Producer of 'Saturday Night at the Theatre'," she said. "Why the hell do you think your lovely patron brought you here tonight, or should that be patroness. She's sees a golden road ahead of you and she's promoting you and cashing in on your talent, but then you're very much aware of that aren't you. She's been cajoling my boss to get me to produce this quite interesting effort of yours. It's not all bad," she condescended, "but I have other things in mind – better, bigger things. After seeing you and hearing you tonight I'm sure we can come to some mutually fruitful arrangement."

"So you two scheming bitches have been arranging things between you as if I don't exist," John snapped angrily.

"Come on John, it must be painful to be that naïve," Rena scolded. "You should be delighted to have someone pushing for you, especially someone as beautiful and powerful as Marion and as talented as me, in this business as in any other. Anyway I owe it to Marion however mixed her motives may be and more importantly I owe it to myself. This will be my swansong you see – I'm on my way out. Use your head young man, an opportunity like this may never come again."

"Well," he asked.

"Well," she replied, extracting every last ounce of drama from the situation and obviously relishing the moment. "I want you to write another play."

"Another play, another play. What sort of proposition is that. You don't like the play I wrote, what makes you think you'll like the one I haven't *wrote*."

"One difference is you'd be paid for me not liking it, though I'm sure I will like it. You see you'd be working from a synopsis: wait, before you explode it will be your play, your synopsis in collaboration with me, the synopsis I mean, the play will be entirely yours. That's the way things are done on television these days. It will go out at peak time – Saturday night. Before you respond let me promise you something. This will be the hardest hitting play ever broadcast by the Beeb, Brecht would eat his heart out. Think you can do that? I think you can. Are you up for that kind of challenge. It will make or break you, as for me I've nothing to lose and I'd like to be remembered for something more than Whitehall farces and tame melodramas. How about it?"

His mouth went dry and he felt a little light-headed. He looked to Marion who's eyes registered as much surprise by what Rena had said as he was clearly feeling. She had thought that this was just another cosy little arrangement – you scratch my back…. but what Rena had in mind might prove a little more dangerous. Never trust a lapsed Marxist, or was she just a post Hungary revisionist. God knows the Beeb was full of them.

John helped himself to a large Glenmorangie. He still experienced the light-headedness. It was all happening much quicker than he could have possibly imagined. "Allright," he croaked "We clearly need to discuss this further."

CHAPTER 11

Merthyr's Chocolate brown and cream railway station was drabber and colder than ever. December had brought rain, rain and more rain, and now in Christmas week the sleet came slithering down in cold wet sheets. His play, *the* play, was to be edited tomorrow, little snippets of film welded together to make the whole were now complete. Rena had handled the production firmly and brilliantly. The script was his and there had been some collaboration but what she did with it was her business and he was becoming mature enough not to quarrel with that. After all he knew little or next to nothing about tele-technique and his admiration for her professionalism had grown the more they worked together. She was however succumbing slowly to her illness and the bouts of fatigue increased in frequency as the production process neared it's climax.

On the phone she sounded upbeat, almost euphoric at the result, like a schoolgirl involved in some outlandish plot. The play was scheduled to go out clandestinely during the Christmas peak viewing period, replacing the play that had been originally advertised for broadcast at that time. She had plotted it with military efficiency and God knows what strings she had to pull and favours to call in to bring it about. Christmas was the ideal time because there would be few bigwigs on hand with the clout to pull the plug once it was realised what was going on. John had come to admire her enormously for what she was doing, and proud that she should have chosen him to write the script for her swan song. If it meant that this would get him blacklisted then so be it, but selfishly he calculated that this would not be the case.

So here he was, and here was Marion in the Merthyr railway station, not Isambard Kingdom's best though it had a kind of drab charm made drabber by the universal colour scheme of British Rail brown and cream. I was a reversal of the previous time here with Josie. Now he was making the journey to the great metropolis while Marion waved a tearful goodbye. Why tearful he asked himself - because she was afraid that he would re-establish his relationship with Josie? He climbed into the compartment and pulled down the window to blow away the stench of stale cigarette smoke. He immediately regretted the action as the train chugged out of Brunel's canopy and great gobs of wind, smoke and sleet blew in and smothered him. He hauled the window up on the great leather strap and fixed it to the retaining pin then plonked himself down on the big seat, glad to be underway, glad for a change of scene, even if many of the faces would be the same, off to conquer the great sinful metropolis as he had already conquered the provinces with repeats of his rousing Rabelaisian television performance.

His *patroness* in collaboration with the genius of Rena, had succeeded in promoting him as one 'helluva boy and a bit'. His recently published little book of poems had secured the Anglo Welsh Poetry Prize and the princely sum of two hundred and fifty pounds. The new Dylan, a critic had said, or so his PR machine, courtesy of Mason's Fashions, had pronounced. So the seed was sown and the myth was already beginning to take root. On his last goggle box appearance he had actually been compared with Wesker and Littlewood and the Romantics, all in the same breath, fostering a cultural revolution on the workshop floor and preaching against the '*electromechanisation*' of the human spirit. He had been quick to assert that he was no luddite and entirely in favour of the automation of the means of production, but only if it was accomplished in a way that would liberate the worker and not, as more often seemed to be the case, enslave him even further. Comparison with Shelley and Wesker were not as paradoxical as they might appear, he maintained, with no pretence at modesty. There was his youth of course and the spirit of socialism which bound them all, Shelley was after all one of Marx's favourite poets. He had quickly learned that saying such outrageous things soon got you noticed on the television. And no matter how ludicrous such outbursts were on programmes like this they were soon forgotten in the greater scheme of things. It was instant, froth, ephemeral : nobody would care in the morning what had been said the night before. So long as it was said in a self assured way, the more absurd the better. He found poets and professors of awesome repute supporting his most obscure pronouncements on late late shows. So he had a growing reputation as an intellectual controversialist too. It was all becoming too too much. He was two jumps ahead of himself most of the time, and if this had not been planned he must surely have seen the possibilities of it in the interstices of his deliberations. If he was truly a *romantic* with a small *r* he might have concluded that it was written in the stars But just what was his relationship with Josie now, and what was his relationship with Marion? Was he really such dirty shit as this?

It would be good to get away from it all for a while, away from the pretentious circle of Marion's friends, the clubs and societies, the Deweys and the double barrelled Rhys-Williams's and Prosser-Morgans and the rest of the tiresome anachronisms of the Welsh Raj. I was a slow crawl down the valley to Cardiff, and a slow rush up to London. It was always 'up' to London although it was obviously 'down' geographically. There were interminable stretches of line which now even lacked the soporific soothing ratatatah which at least used to hypnotise the weary traveller into a state of somnambulance. The overpriced beer was warm even in this cold weather and the compartments were overheated. One thing about good old British Rail it was always either too hot or too bloody cold. On the whole he was thankful it was the former today with the sleet turning to snow and dusting the surface of the fields.

The train was full, as usual, with young typists, teachers, secretaries, lawyers, all super sophisticated chic, with weekly commutations between the big city and gwlad y gan. Disguised accents were adopted immediately the train pulled out from Cardiff General, even though the speakers hailed from Rhondda, Merthyr, Ogwr and even Carmarthen where they reverted to God's own language every weekend. Oh he knew them all, haughty, with weekend bags walking past neighbours windows down to the local station. Posh it is to be London Welsh – but it's lonely too. In unlovely Paddington and dreary Earls Court bedsits the terraced cottages of Tonypandy take on a different dimension. Instead of severing those deep and sinuous roots you discover that you have merely trailed them along the track behind the Paddington Express to be wound up again next weekend when you return to the ravaged land of your fathers.

At the end of the long dash the miseries of Bute are replaced with the greater miseries of Paddington and the great girdered conch through which the lifeblood of Wales constantly seeps as through an open artery. Outside pornographic Praed Street beckons offering cheap thrills, and throngs thrustle in the damp cold of Christmas. It is a lonely London crowd, a skyful of sad stars apparently so close together as to be indistinguishable one from another, but in reality several light years adrift from its nearest neighbour. When one is extinguished in a mass like this it isn't even missed. London depressed and excited him simultaneously, it overwhelmed and overawed him.

He saw Josie wave to him from the burger caff across the road as arranged. He pretended not to notice her before finally casually making his approach. "Hullo dear," he said chirpily, "how much for a short time?"

"More than you can afford luv," she responded in exaggerated cockney dialect, quick as a flash. "All the same you bloody Welshmen. Big pricks and little boys' pocket money."

"Do you realise," he bantered, "all this energy," with an expansive sweep of the arms, "wastefully expended, if properly harnessed could solve all the energy problems of this benighted realm. Instead it's transient forces are random, rapid, multi-directional and catastrophic. Only its molecular complexity saves this mass from disintegrating in a blinding cataclysmic flash. Six quid was it. No love I'm sorry you're just not worth it."

"You're prob'ly right darlin'," she smiled. "Tellya wot buy me a java instead, must be worth that for a big spender like you."

He shrugged dubiously and followed her into the caff.

They took a window seat and ordered coffee, 'café au lait' was the thing, 'coffee made with milk' in Merthyr, which demonstrates how much less complicated the provinces were. "Well how's mother?" she asked pointedly as soon as the steaming drinks were served.

"Blooming," he replied. "Never looked better I shouldn't think or perhaps when she was your age."

166

"With a little help from her friends no doubt," the sarcasm clear but immediately ameliorated. "It's allright," she added. "I told you that's exactly what I expected. I'm not going to through a childish tantrum."

Why did that not make him feel any better. "There's nothing to throw a childish tantrum about." His lie lacked conviction. He felt mean like a schoolboy whose mother has caught masturbating. "I feel grubby," immediately attempting to recover from the Freudian slip. "It's that bloody awful train journey," wiping a hand across his brow. "Sweating like a collier," he quipped. "Can we go to your place, I could do with a nice hot shower?"

"Of course," she replied. "Want me to scrub your blue-scarred back?"

It was situated in a Chelsea mews, very chic. He had bathed, had his amorous advances graciously rejected, time of the month, eaten and phoned Rena who warned him of a party that evening which might just turn out to be one of those notorious 'swinging' sessions about which one read in The News of The World, since the guests were principally composed of new young things of the thespian persuasion.

Josie surprisingly announced that she would be going home in the morning leaving him with the keys to the flat and the freedom to indulge himself in all the licentious debauchery of his heart's desire. The odd thing was debauchery could not be further from his heart's desire. It was much more attractive when t was much less attainable.

"What's Rena really like anyway. I never really got to know her?" Josie asked.

"Oh I don't know. A bit mixed up I'd say, but at the bottom quite a warm and sincere person. She exudes a hardness to mask a real vulnerability I think. I get that feeling anyhow. I think her flirtation with lesbianism is a mask too. That's not to say that she doesn't have lesbian relationships, she obviously does, but she does flaunt them rather too extrovertly as if to cover something deeper, like fear of involvement with a man."

"You've made a close study of her problems it seems."

He shook his head. "She hardly goes out of her way to make herself physically alluring as far as men are concerned does she now. I assure you she does nothing for me in that respect. I have just grown to like her that's all."

She came over to him with tears in her eyes and pressed her lips against his forehead. "I'm sorry, there's me being childishly stupid again. Anyway I'm not jealous, I'm not the jealous type am I. Totally liberated that's me. We all have to have our moments don't we. I mean you're not going to ask me who I've been with since we last met are you?"

"No of course not," but peeved all the same. Where was all this leading to. "I'm the totally liberated type too, don't you remember?"

"Sauce for the goose," she laughed mirthlessly. "That's it isn't it?"

"Yeah allright, allright," too many question marks in this strained exchange. She kissed him again, the same affectionate sisterly kiss on his forehead. It bothered him. Passion he could handle but this passive tenderness was disturbing.

"Fidelity is so adolescent don't you think and jealousy is a just a filthy destructive beast. So selfish. The most childishly selfish of all emotions wouldn't you agree?"

"Yes, but a natural enough reaction."

"To what; reaction to what?"

"Well to….to infidelity I suppose."

"Yes." What was it she wanted from him?

"Ah I see. But it's frivolous insincere types like me you go for isn't it. You don't want some declaration of undying, everlasting eternal love, beyond all understanding, beyond the grave and all that. "

"Not at all. Not I. Not a modern sophisticated girl like me. Of course not. Come on we need to get a move on. This party will be full of modern sophisticated girls."

The pub was pretentiously unpretentious and the arty crowd which filled it was not composed of the bohemians he had envisaged. Perhaps bohemianism was a pretension that was currently out of fashion. These were obviously very 'in' people : sophisticates.

The preparation for the transmission of the play was now a fait accompli. He wouldn't see the completed programme until the scheduled broadcast on Christmas Eve. He felt a little resentment at this, remote now from the creation to which he considered he had made a major contribution. However it had never been his in the sense that his published poems and short stories were his, or the novel which was now nearing completion of the first draft. It was the beginning and possibly the end of his career as a television dramatist Rena had warned him, hinting that his talents were probably better suited to the big screen anyway and even at tentative interest in a screenplay of the tele-drama. He had considered the big screen almost dead now, all tits and bums and facile sexual escapades. The telly surely offered more to the genuine artist these days if only because of its voracious insatiable appetite for new material. The biggest stumbling block, at which the barbed arrows of his contribution so far were directed, being the sensitivity of the current guardians of decency to the protestations of the Empire Loyalists, the Women's League, the clergy, magistrates, boy scout leaders, Mary Whitehouse and a whole clutch of mentally retarded reactionaries. For Rena and co this was to be her last gasp assault on the citadels of censorship.

The discussion in the party however he found to be as pretentiously vacuous as the 'beetles' who babbled endlessly into their cocktails.

"Of course, he found himself mimicking, "Ginsberg is the only blahblahblah," and they were hanging onto his every facile word, the great oracle, the centre of their goggle eyed attention. He could talk their kind of obscurantism and they warmed to his incomprehensibility. He hammed it up magnificently : no one could quite rationalise it, except for them of course. It was like a congregation of Pentecostals listening to a sermon in Tongues. So he was one of them : a guru. All he had to do was throw in another name to start the business all afresh. A yes now Nietzsche, and of course Brecht and let's not forget Kafka and what about Proust and as for Stendahl well what more need one say. Trot out the old, old list, lard on the clichés, invent some new ones, be as absurd as can be, reel of a list of obscure never read poets, invent some who never existed, quote from them knowledgeably. What a wow this rough Welsh genius, the new Dylan without a doubt. Someone to be reckoned with. Hadn't they known it all along. Someone claimed to have discovered him in some obscure literary tract five years ago and had proclaimed his genius even then. They broke into little groups and discussed him reverently. Of course it came through in his marvellous rimbaudian vulgarity, a simple rudeness masking his complex symbolism. So he had been one of them from the start and they took him to their bosom.. the sophisticates.

Later it was all back to Rena's place drinking like fish.. A huge statuesque blonde who towered comically over him dragged seriously at a joint and made unambiguous advances. He clung to Josie like a limpet for protection and she smiled maternally, appraising the physical disparity and giving him a 'why not' shrug. Why not indeed in other circumstances but he had never been attracted to the group thing and everybody seemed intent on making it with anyone else's partner. There were a few couples who were notable exceptions, including John and Josie. Perhaps this was Josie's thing, he was aware now of how little he knew about her. Rena seemed more interested in a slime androgyne, but then that might well be a pose. Perhaps it was all a pose, it certainly bore all the characteristics of an absurd charade.

Someone knocked over a trayful of drinks and a dark eyed Spanish girl who was performing some kind of erotic dance in her bare feet, shaking out the long black tresses of her hair with lithe sensuous rhythm, lacerated her toes on a piece of broken glass and had to be rushed off to the infirmary for stitches . A loud voice shouted above the chaos ' As Margot was only telling me last week, Rudi has this most infuriating habit of removing his earwax with a used matchstick. Can you imagine that? But darling, she smiled when she saw me grimace, he does it with such divine grace, it's pure Diaghilev.

"I bet he shits divinely too," John couldn't help muttering. The statuesque blonde at his elbow giggled childishly and blew acrid essence of hashish in his face.

"You haven't met my husband have you?" she said taking his arm and dragging him away from Josie. Husband was if anything more blonde and androgynously statuesque than the wife. He took John's hand with an astonishingly limp handshake for such a muscled arm.

"I'm Mike," he introduced himself in soft not quite effeminate tones, looking from John to his wife in a way that seemed to suggest that whatever they wished to do together would receive his approval. John cringed as 'Amazonia' smothered him in a hard embrace as her husband drifted off into the crowd. She engaged him in small talk until her eyes suddenly dilated and she squeezed his arm in a vice like grip.

"Come on," she insisted, "that bedroom's empty." He had a glimpse of hubby smiling in the background and Josie's gasp of utter astonishment as he was dragged into the boudoir. Once inside she slipped the latch on the door, this was obviously not her first acquaintance with the room. She wound powerful arms around him and almost smothered him with her great orbs. Another place, another time, this would have been the nth degree of eroticism but somehow he felt overwhelmed and, yes, even slightly nauseated. Not so sophisticated after all. She was obviously turned on by something more stimulating than his charisma, groaning and grinding her amazing body against him. He lay her back on the rumpled bed and undressed her, not like a lover but like a man with something more insidious on his mind. When she finally lay writhing naked in all her Amazonian glory he walked to the door and opened it. The next couple in the small queue which had gathered obviously assumed that the real fun was about to begin beckoning eager friends to join them.

John barred the entrance, "Mike," he called loudly above the cacophony. "Mike, I think your wife needs you."

Mike followed the group into the bedroom and emerged immediately whey faced, not so much with anger or embarrassment but sheer distaste. "Oh no," he muttered his hand to his mouth. "Oh my God no," more effeminately. "Not my cup of tea at all." 'Amazonia's' magnificent body obviously did little or nothing for him.

"Come on Kiddo," John took Josie's arm and steered her towards the exit. "Let's get out of this nuthouse before the place gets busted. Goodnight Rena," he called, " simply must fly. Great party. See you in the morning."

A chorus of complaints rose at his leaving, after all he was the star of the show. What a performance a real swinger. And that trick with the queer Tarzan. A real boyo what?

Josephine laughed as they walked. "That was a cruel stunt," she admonished. He laughed. She laughed. They laughed together. A bus slid noiselessly, emptily past on its way to the depot. "You wowed them," she conceded, "you bloody nut case."

"Me a nut case, what about that bloody lot," he retorted. "What is it that makes people behave like that? Did you see them all? I mean I'm always up for a bit of fun but most of those people are…. Are…"

"Dead," she suggested.

"No not quite dead, more like neutral, no that's not strong enough. Unreal they certainly are. At least their reality is not one that I'm in contact with. They're Lawrence's Beetles. That's what he called the Bloomsbury set. The beastly bourgeoisie."

"Well whatever they are you'll have them all to yourself tomorrow. It's gwlad y gan for me. We've got our own beastlies too you know."

"Yes your mums lot, many of them at least, the Deweys and that gang. Must you go. Why not hang around for a few days. I think I need your protection."

She smiled and patted his head maternally. "Poor little lost boy from the sticks," she teased. "I think it's the Beetles who need protecting from you. You were hardly overwhelmed tonight were you. In fact you stole the show."

"That's the trouble though isn't it. Imagine becoming one of them. That's the danger and I'm halfway there already. God Josie the bastards will devour me." She linked her arm in his and snuggled up to him walking slowly in that best of all times in London. The crowds have gone and the streets are all but deserted. It is the wee small hours and the city exhibits for a brief few hours the characteristics of sanity. All those millions of people have drained from the streets, there is a light drizzle, so light it is just a dampness carried on the air and the roads glisten under the white lights. The green of the trees takes on a strange nocturnal contrast against the dull pallor of the drab architecture and a sad beauty pervades the cityscape. Later they lay quiescent in each other's arms. He loved her he supposed, but didn't he have those self same feelings about Marion too. Most deeply and most truly of all he loved Lynda and that was utterly mysterious and beyond all rational comprehension.

Josephine had departed from Paddington on the midday train. They sat in a West End pub sipping tepid tasteless beer, it was homogenous these days wherever you drank it, regional variations a thing of the past. Still the company was an improvement on last night, less pretentious. And the pub was one of those typical magnificent London edifices. A long bar of dark mahogany with polished glasses and drinks of all hues and tastes for every palate. There were worse ways of spending a Monday afternoon he supposed. He spared a thought for Dave and the others, and the boys in the chemical works at Dowlais, what wouldn't they have given to swap places with him now. Across the table from him was Rena, smartly dressed for a change. Next to John on the one side sat the archetypal dumb blonde, a bimbo accompanying Marty the equally archetypal film producer who Rena had in tow with the express purpose of cadging great wads of lucre for her next grand project, an epic of the silver screen no doubt. A charming actor and his lovely intelligent wife schooled in rep who had established a reputation on the small screen and played the leads in Rena's play, his play dammit, sat the other side of him. He had been shown snippets but still not the complete production. The recent advances in video taping were providing producers like Rena with the opportunity for new and exciting productions which had recently been subject to the limitations of live transmission.

In one of the scenes Phil and his lovely wife engaged in a very risqué clinch which was so realistic that John was almost convinced that they were really having it away. It was the obvious next step from what John had aimed for and achieved in the New Frontiers programme, but so superbly filmed and performed in a narrative context to be infinitely more effective.

Phil returning with the drinks seemed to read his thoughts. "All the snippets you've been fed may seem a bit disjointed now," he explained. "but in the final editing it will all fit together like a completed jigsaw. Rena and Max Lane her editor are the very best, you'll see. Not that it's always like that of course, sometimes it's a bloody mess as I'm sure you know. But Rena came from film and it shows. It's honestly a privilege to work with her, she's really broken new ground in television drama, and this is her masterpiece, and yours of course. We were all really knocked out with your script."

"We'll all end up doing penal servitude when it goes out of course," his wife Anne contributed. It being Christmas Eve and all the moral crusaders will have a field day and old Auntie Beeb will be outraged. Still Phil and I are off to Canada anyway. Things are beginning to happen on the box out there without the crassness of their American cousins. I don't think it will damage our reputation, far from it. Our contracts are in the bag so we had nothing to lose really. And for Rena it's only a swan song as far as the box is concerned, she's got bigger screens in mind." It was said just loud enough for her to hear, banter rather than sycophancy.

"Now, now dear. Don't scare the goose away." She smiled into Marty's admiring eyes. "Besides you'll be inflating my modest ego if you carry on."

"Darling," Phil responded, " if there was ever an ego that does not require inflating, it is surely yours."

"You were both magnificent," John joined in the mood of self congratulation. "But how did you feel about.....", for once he was hesitant in his choice of language.

"Having it off on camera. Anne's a superb actress, she has to be with my poor boudoir performance," he joked. " If I knocked her about a bit, who would even turn a hair, but the other, well that's a moral issue isn't it? But to answer your implied question – No. I felt not the slightest unease about seeing it onscreen. It was one of the most beautiful things we have ever done. Of course its bound to provoke the most hostile reactions. Joy and love and pleasure are things to which we have no right to aspire in the here and now, they are preserved for the hereafter as compensation for all the miseries inflicted on us by Popes and Archbishops and other political and religious panjandrums."

172

"Brother, you are preaching to the converted," John assured him with a chuckle. "But I'm afraid you oversimplify. There are no simple truths any more, everything carries with it undertones, overtones, innuendo, allusion, symbolism, metaphor. Ours is the age of non-communication. Nothing is capable of meaning any longer. It is all a lie. George Orwell predicted it in '1984' How do we communicate truth when communication is itself a lie. The only truth we can know is sensual, but once we intellectualise it we distort it and lose it in the process. Keats said it all didn't he "Beauty is Truth" but then he messed it up with "Truth is Beauty." What the fuck was Wittgenstein all about? Went mad didn't he. Oh I'm pissed. I'm a pain in the arse when I'm pissed."

Phil graciously ignored him and smiling refilled his glass. "In vino veritas," he toasted. "That's all ye know on earth, and all ye need to know," he added with the air of one who has shared with another the convivial experience of loose tongued nectar nonsense. "All this abstract bullshit is no use you know. Stick to materialism and you won't go far wrong, and I mean materialism in its pure Marxist and not the Capitalist sense. You'll end up a Roman Catholic if you carry on like that, and I wouldn't wish that on my worst enemy, not even the Pope. My wife was a catholic until a less than celibate priest wanted to demonstrate how the immaculate conception took place. Don't set your sights on the unattainable. Live from one modest ambition to the next. You've achieved more than most in a very short time, who knows what you might achieve. You could end up with the Olympians if you give yourself a chance. You stick with Rena, she's destined for deity. You could be Acteon to her Diana, she's more Diana than you might give her credit for. You see I'm pissed too. God I hope the ghost of that bastard Joe McCarthy doesn't make it across the lake to Canada."

Ann and the blonde who John had silently nicknamed Plumlips had concluded their conversation and were enjoying the inebriated dialogue between the two men. Plumlips not wishing to be excluded said, "I don't see anything wrong with it anyway, taking your kit off in public," taking deep breaths to emphasise her own qualifications. Her magnificent orbs overflowed a dress with a plunging neckline which paid scant heed to the winter climate.

"Are those real," John couldn't resist asking.

"Of Course," Plumlips squealed. "Feel." So he did, and they were.

He lingered languorously in the sudsy swamp of Josie's luxurious bath, big enough for two, such wasted space though he was only up to soaking with the debilitating effects of too many late nights of debauchery weighing heavily on him. The shrill tones of the telephone intruded on his soporific state from an extension perched in a tiled alcove adjacent to the bath – luxury indeed. He picked it up gingerly asking himself if he could be electrocuted if he dropped it in the bath. Of course not, the whole system ran on batteries didn't it. He recalled the visit to the brand new exchange where they'd been shown the face of the future. A technical genius like himself should surely be aware of that. The effect of the alcohol was clearly still with him. "Hullo, Renaissance man speaking," he called too loudly.

"Hi. Do you realise that Rena is at the forefront of the **Rena**issance philologically speaking," came the reply.

"Hi Rena, I'm not up to intellectual puns at the moment.

"Can you come over in half an hour."

"I'm in the bloody bath."

"So Intend to stay in there all night do you. Haven't got that mammarian freak in there with you have you?"

"All alone Rena, and happy to be."

"I've got something really important to discuss with you. No it won't do over the phone. Don't eat I've got something special on the hob for a very special occasion."

"Don't tease Rena, not trying to seduce me are you. I really wouldn't be up to it. No disrespect intended but my libido is currently very low."

"My darling boy what do you think of me, why I'm old enough to be Marion's sister," she responded cynically. "How could you have such evil thoughts about me. I'll give you an hour , you should be soaked enough by then. I won't take no for an answer." She hung up. He slid back down into the sudsy tub and allowed a further trickle of hot water until the perspiration broke out on his brow and the salt sweat stung his eyes. Steve Race was on the radio, a speaker resided behind the telephone built into the alcove, the way poor students had to live these days, Stan Getz was drifting into a Tunisian night. He dozed in the heady scents of all the perfumes of Arabia filched from the array in the glass cabinet above him. Life was hard and about to get even harder.

"What can I get you ,"she greeted.

"One large sweet mug of tea, just like Dai Whippet brews for me in the control room of the Ammonia Plant please," he demanded. In this sodomistic city a decent cup of char is a commodity rarely to be found."

"One hot sweet strong mug of tea coming up," she promised, swishing into the kitchen, her Japanese housecoat trailing untidily behind her. He made himself comfortable in the big easy chair until she returned with two huge steaming mugs. She handed him one and smiled with an air of self congratulation. He took a satisfied sip and smiled back at her.

"Cat got the cream," he suggested. "What's up?"

"Daddy Warbucks," she answered and paused for effect. "All my assiduous courting of the fat producer while you dallied with his mammarian moron, it's all paid off – he's come across with the readies John darling."

"Readies, readies for what may I be so bold..."

"Readies for the financing of our big screen debut – what else."

He swallowed hard and a mouthful of hot tea scolded his tonsils. "Did you say *our* debut?"

"I've been given carte blanche, well almost," she continued on a high euphoric note, "to produce an extravaganza for the great wide screen, backed with unlimited funds, well again almost, on the life of one Mr J C. So what, yet another biblical epic I hear you sneer, another Moses in the bulrushes - Not this time baby. This will be *my* life of Christ – *our* life of Christ."

"The truth?"

"Your truth."

"Mine."

"Your script baby, my direction. All the magic and the immortality swept away. The real Christ. A real man. A lovely man. A man of love."

He looked her in the eyes. "I don't know what to say. Why me Rena, for a project like this you could get the best."

"Because, because, because you are the very best John baby."

"Rena are you high?"

"Of course I'm high, high as a fucking kite, but unlike Wittgenstein I do know that about which I speak my young poetic prince. All I want from you is your wholehearted, undivided, exclusive devotion for six months, for which you will be amply rewarded for your endeavours. How would you respond to twenty-five thousand smackeroos worth of reward."

He almost choked again. "Rena you are high." He took another gulp of the sweet hot tea. "I think I ought to put you to bed." Now why did he say that, he knew he shouldn't have said it. She gave him a wicked smile.

"Oh but I know that you will darling," she replied. "There was more in that tea than just honey. When I worked for the British Council in Cairo we went in for quite a lot of that kind of thing."

"What kind of thing. Are you mad. You haven't poisoned me have you, I do feel a bit queer."

"Poison, of course not. A little mind expanding substance, very aphrodisiac. Won't be long now I gave you quite a dose. I've been saving it for just such an occasion."

"Rena you're nuts," he put a hand to his sweating brow. Were things really taking on a more essential shape. Was he really seeing things as they truly were. Did the silly bitch really spice his tea. Was this an epiphany. Why was he asking himself all these questions.

She put some records on the auto changer of her super hi-fi music centre. MJQ, Mulligan, Williams shouting the blues, Billie Holiday. "Rena, with or without what you may or may not have put in my tea, you're my kinda girl," he slurred, closing his eyes and listening to the best music he'd ever heard.

He closed his eyes and immersed himself in the musical feast, never had it sounded so good. Two brandies with a little something and he sank deeper into a musical syrup. Suddenly he shook his head and sat stiffly back

175

in the armchair. She was stroking his hair and smiling. The width of her smile seemed to fill the room. 'Darn that dream and bless it too without that dream I never would have you.' The rich deep tones of Joe Williams worked in his subconscious. But whose face was it which haunted his dreams. 'Just to change the mood I'm in I'd welcome a nice old nightmare.' Always the same, always her child woman's face. Now here, at least it seemed now and here Rena was moving awkwardly across him ruffling his hair, allowing the front of her housecoat to slip an indiscreet inch or two. Marblewhite softened by crimson shadow her breast was suddenly in his hands, so huge it took one span merely to circumference the brown swollen nipple. The room was filled with one soft fluid breast. It flowed into every corner and try as he might he could not squeeze it's Vesuvius into the yawning chasm of his mouth. All every each rainbow hue dancing MJQ and zipper bursting under magic load. Never such a monster, pantsoff, never so hugehardstiffred, never such widethighlipsred, teethwhite and beguiling eyes and smiles and oh oh ohhhhhh. On his knees a lance between whitethighs touching and retracting red and swollen lipsred. More tinkling syllables of MJQ dancing nymphlike colourbright grassgreen silver bayblue bubbles floating, bursting. Touch and tease, parry and thrust, turn, counterturn, stand. At last full frontal thrust and no withdrawal. Big round knobend thrust, thruuuust, aaaagh, aaaaghhh, aaaaaaghhhh. Were they dead, were they crying, were they laughing. Pleasurepain, clenched, fist-tight, virgin-tight. Quiet, gliding, vibraphonic. A cotton wool cradle, a bed of white fluffy cloud, lying thinking feeling nothing. How could nothing be so marvellous? In a lovely nightmare of dark and helpless surrender he merely wilts and knows that nothing can ever rouse him now, rescue him now. It's gone, nothing remains, emptiness. Sleep is a descending black cloud hovering above his dim and dimming consciousness. It slowly falls as thick as fog and he falls nearer to death than he will ever again experience until…….

CHAPTER 12

Christmas Eve, bright stars blinking through cracked clouds and a few flakes fluffy on the hard ground. This could be the first one to be just like the ones we used to know. Good King Wenceslas, grubby faces knocking on the doors. Kick them up the arse and send them packing. But no. Tonight is respectable carollers night. All the Beulahs, Bethesdas, Bethanias, Zions, Moriahs, Elims, Gospel Halls, Sally Anns, Saints of Illtyds, Marys, Johns, Bartholemews and Tydfils will all be carolling this happy night.

Welcome father, pastor, priest and deacon. A drop of punch or parsnip wine just to warm the cockles and suffer the little bastards and all ye who labour and are heavy laden. Peace and goodwill to all mankind except of course atheists and communists, Buddhists and Islamists and all non-Christianists, also blackmen, Jews, pimps prostitutes and homosexualists criminalists, republicanists and lesbianists

Oh what a lovely Christmas eve with a bellyful of good cheer and jingle bells ringing in the ears. Lights and holly and radios blaring the Christmas message – eat , drink and be merry and sick. And while kids abed early, scared of the red ghost with his sack of plenty, the hypnotic beast in the corner will beam out John and Rena's vision of the truth for the whole besotted world to misunderstand.

The return from London last night had been something of an ordeal. Josie and Marion had driven down to Cardiff together to meet the train. Oh yes thanks, London had been swinging, and there was this fantastic film offer brokered by Rena, and here she was wearing her conquest like a national flag draped over a returning heroine's shoulder. A drink at Rena's with awkward small talk, the drive up the valley to Merthyr with more awkward small talk. No resolution of with whom he was to spend the night finally decided after cheek pecked goodnights. Goodnight ladies and they left silently for their Crickhowell mansion. The end of an era?

Listen children, listen, through the bedroom window. Little Jesus was born this very night in the cows dung and goats fleas in a scruffy little Palestinian town which has never known peace since. And Mary the deceiver said she was a virgin o, and fooled young Yusuf the simple chippy into unholy matrimony. Born with a lie, died with a lie, lived a lovely truth. Only the lies remembered now and called 'religion'. But here's the rub all you whiter than white good Christian people; born in Christian Germany he would have ended up in the gas ovens, in Christian America, the land of the free he would have been a nigger and a slave, in South Africa a second class citizen and lived in a ghetto, in the Land of Hope and Glory a dirty wog, Socialist Russia would have seen him incarcerated in a psychiatric ward. Oh no my children it is no good crying to the great white Father in the sky that it

177

was not so. It was so. Daddy left him hanging on a cross and that crucifixion has taken place every day since day one of the year one.. And while he delivers his sermon to a world which will not hear she appears in a divine vision and he holds out his overflowing cup to her in a gesture of sharing. The teaser from across the road appears in pants and bra with an impish smile through only half drawn curtains, glimpses of coquettish delight. But sex has overwhelmed him left him empty. Rena has satiated him with her own Christmas gift of oversex. He swigs again and calls aloud, "Merry Christmas everybody, merry fucking Christmas."

Downstairs in the corner the little tree draped with coloured plastic lights from Buddhist Japan blink on, off, on, off, on off, the rhythm sexual. A little plastic fairy dancing legs akimbo on the treetop, a contented smile and a phallic wand in hand. Everything, everywhere sex. Santa Freudian hetero for the little girls, homo erotic for the boys, neutero for Rena's androgyne. Sex, sex. Sex. The world an egg dropped from some galactic womb. God the phallus. Watch the box tonight little ones, hear the Christian message. Love one another. "Watch the Beeb tonight," he called to the family as he closed the door. "Witness the culmination of your son's genius. But early bed for you little brawd or Santa won't come."

"Gerroutofit, there's no such bloody bloke." Such cynicism from a six year old. Oh the loss of innocence. Nothing left but sex.

On the maroon, double decked, bright lighted bus he exchanged happy yuletide platitudes with cheerful, beerful, hailing faces across the gangway before getting off at the Morlais Hotel. Hotel it might have been on the good old days, now it was a crumbling little pub with a crumbling clientele of pensioners stretching out their halves to last the yuletide eve. God rest ye poor gentlemen let nothing you dismay. Goodnight Dave and Merry Christmas. Dave off to town for further adventures in the skin trade. Himself up, up, and up again through the tumbling streets with the snow starting to wander down on a breeze rising keen and cutting through to the marrow..... 'Me an' the blues, we spent a lot of time together. Me an' the blues travelin' on that gettin' nowhere road.' He could hear the plaintive wailing on the keen wind. Then Lady Day swinging slowly through her sad repertoire. 'Why was I born.' Was it because he was on his way to see Lynda, because in his drugged and alcoholic state of mind he thought he was seeing things clearly for the first time in a long time. Up, up, up he struggled to the little row of houses where she lived with Mamgu – the only constant in his shifting life.

"We thought you were never going to come. Now that you're so famous," Mamgu complained. "Come in and sit by the fire," she invited. "Lynda, here he is, didn't I tell you he would come."

Lynda greeted him with reticence and shyness. "I didn't think you'd come," she said quietly. "All those smart and famous people you mix with these days. Much more interesting than a poor scatterbrain like me."

He looked into her eyes then at Mamgu with a smile. She was fine now, tomorrow there might be a different girl behind them. Her name might well have been Zelda, not Lynda. "I've got a present for you," she said.

"Oh no, my turn first," he insisted, handing her the little jade figurine, an exotic Madrasi dancer which he had picked up in one of the chic Chelsea antique shops.

"Oh look Mamgu isn't it lovely. I bet it cost a fortune," throwing her arms around his neck. "Now my little gift will seem so insignificant in comparison." He entangled himself awkwardly and handed Mamgu a small package too. It contained an old Victorian broach with emeralds and rubies. She kissed his cheek and dashed off predictably to show her next door neighbour.

"And no hanky panky when I'm gone," she teased. "I won't be long."

"And this is mine to you," Lynda presented him with a handbound slim anthology of her own poems. "You see I still write them. Part of my therapy according to Doctor Freud. Those are the best of them I think. You see it doesn't compare......"

"It's so much better than mine to you," he assured her.

"I still love you John. And there are times when, you know, I want you just as much as ever. It doesn't change, even in the bad times."

"I still love you too Lynda," he replied.

"In spite of everything?"

"In spite of, because of, I don't know."

"Then when will we ever...." It was the hardest question of all to answer. "You needn't think of it as taking advantage. I give you my consent now. I'm all right now aren't I. It wouldn't be criminal or anything." He closed his eyes but it didn't stop the tears.

"Not yet love, not yet. It has to be just right," was all he could say and it sounded trite.

"Well then the playing will have to stop – you realise that don't you."

"My play is on the tele tonight," he said. "And I have to go to a party in Cardiff. If I'd known you were so well I'd have...... Why don't you come with me."

"I'm not that well John. Couldn't face up to your beautiful people yet. But perhaps one day quite soon I'll take them all on. No I'll keep Mamgu company tonight. Your Mam and Dad are calling later. We'll watch this latest product of your troubled genius together and Mamgu can show off to the neighbours."

"Perhaps not tonight," he smiled. "It's a bit of a corker, blasphemy and all that."

"Well Mamgu's a bit of a corker herself you know."

"I had noticed."

179

"But blasphemy," she tut tutted. "Mam will have something to say about that. Look out here she comes. She's knitted you a hideous scarf for Christmas, for goodness sake smile and wear it like it's the latest fashion or she'll take umbrage. I'm better for longer and longer periods now John. Freud holds out great hopes for me. Come and see me again soon won't you. Go on bugger off you don't want to be late."

Mamgu gave him his scarf and insisted on walking him to the corner of the street in spite of the wispy snow beginning to drift into the gutters. He draped the scarf around his neck, glad of the protection from the gusty wind. He held her knobbly elbow in the palm of his hand. "I wanted to talk," she said.

"I didn't think you were out for the sleigh ride," he replied.

"John she's a beautiful young woman now," she continued, "with a young woman's needs and desires." There was never any ceremony between these two. In many ways she was closer to him than either of his parents. He was the son she had had to wait another generation for, closer to her than her own daughter who had borne him. She had been a suffragette of the working class kind. An admirable breed less well documented than their aristocratic counterparts.

"I know Mamgu," was all he said.

"Then there's nothing more I need say is there. She's as well as she's ever going to be John but she'll never be completely well, there'll be relapses at times of stress, or so that head shrinker says. You're going to have to make your mind up, all this playing about you're doing, allright it's wild oats I know. But there's love, duty and responsibility too. You can never escape these things, not if you're my grandson you can't. You can run from them for a while that's all. I think it's time to stop running now – don't you?"

"Don't you lecture me Mamgu fach."

"I'll lecture you John Davies," she slapped him playfully. "I'll have your bloody guts for garters if you hurt that girl."

"I love her Mamgu, more than anything in the world. But I'm a coward. I must dash for the bus. See you both soon - promise. We'll talk then OK." He kissed her cheeked, wished her a happy Christmas and before she could argue further he was gone.

It was helter skelter for the Dowlo for a quick one with the boys before the assault on Rena's Pontcanna palace. "Landlord, set up pints and whisky chasers," Dave called as John came into the room. The yuletide spirit was already well established. The room was packed but they made a space for him by the fire. "Well, well, a little tired and withdrawn it is you look boy bach. How was the swinging city then?"

"Sexational."

"Elaborate, please do."

"A surfeit. I suffer a surfeit. Now I know how pop stars and film stars must feel." Though under the influence of Rena's powerful aphrodisiac he wasn't certain where the line between physical and psychological could be drawn.

"Oh my poor heart bleeds for you," Bill said.

John knocked the whisky back in one gulp. "It's enough to freeze the balls off a glycerated yeti ," he complained. "What goes on here anyway, you're all so bloody smug and complacent, been on the booze all day have you. No you're not drunk, something less tangible."

Dave smiled as if about to share a closely guarded secret. "It's all been happening in your absence man. I have been commissioned by none other than the lovely Lady Penelope Pryce Pritchard, or Penny PP as she's known to all her friends in the Welsh aristocracy, to paint her portrait, in the absolutely as the day when she was born of course. Ex model married into nobility, of course you would have known that. Capital chap ex Eton and Guards and all that. More interested in blokes than birds apparently. Remember that case with the boy scouts. Anyway out of the blue I get this missive from his secretary chap, bit limp wrist, asking if I would like to meet his Lordship at his St Fagans country cottage with a view to discussing a possible commission, which I duly did. Never saw the lovely lady in the flesh sadly, but photo's aplenty from her modelling days. He was impressed by what he'd seen on our television broadcast. Very with it In the artistic sense as many of his persuasion are of course. Has his own studio, you should see his collection. Wants me to do it there. Spends most of his time in the big city, property dealing and all that. I start doing preliminary sketches in the new year, commission on completion within three months, one thousand five hundred smackers. How does that get you."

"Fifteen hundred, for three months. I didn't think you could get fifteen hundred mild steel washers for those bloody pornographic daubings you turn out. I don't believe it I know I've been drugged and now I'm also half pissed but Lady Penny PP, no I don't think so."

Dave produced from his inside pocket an envelope containing a typed letter on the very best quality headed paper, complete with coat of arms the contents of which clearly supported his incredible claims. "And to complete the fairytale," Bill added. "Also following our remarkable television success I have had several of my studies accepted for the centrefold of Playfair magazine at a fee not too far removed from Michelangelo there and Geraint's appearing on some dreadful Welsh pop programme singing some inane nonsense about Owain Glyndwr I shouldn't wonder. To cap it all Ted's tendered his resignation from the world of proper work on the basis that he can't get up in the mornings and that we've decided to employ him as our ten percent agent since we're all giving up the day job on the strength of our complete confidence in our dazzling futures. As for you ……."

181

"I came here with my own astonishing news," John blurted. "I'll not be upstaged by a gaggle of upstart crows, all because you did some unspeakably daft things on *my* television programme. *My* lovely play goes out on television tonight, but no, don't applause yet because there's more. My mentor, mentress? Has secured on my behalf a contract to write a film script for the big screen, Hollywood and all that jazz, at a fee too obscene to mention. The world has gone mad, mad. I'm pissed already. Some ethereal juice of the gods has gone to my head. What the fuck, Ted you can have ten percent of me too. Better you than the bloody tax man."

"I'll clean your boots every morning sir, with my tongue. You'll none of you regret it, salaam, salaam. I'll end up with more money than all of you. Then I'll buy my guns and bombs and demolish the fucking lot of you."

"Here you lot you can stop all this 'fucking' in my bar or you'll have to leave.

"Whiskies all round my beautiful buxom Joan," John beamed, " and whatever for yourself ."

"And less of the buxom from you too. I'll have you know I lost five pounds in the last fortnight so I could gorge myself over Christmas.

"You gorge yourself Joan my love, then you'll be more gorgeous than ever." He giggled at his own pun drinking back his shot in one gulp yet again, drunk beyond inebriation now. "Let's sing some carols." So they sat round the fire and did just that. "Balls to Rena's gang and their bloody silly party. Merry bloody Christmas everybody."

It was midnight when they eventually rolled out of the Dowlo. They had watched his play in the bar to the initial consternation of the bar flies, but it was cheered to the echo in the end, excepting the few with religious scruples.

The play opens without title or credits, an authentic view of the interior of a large church or cathedral during a carol service, only the choir boys really singing, the congregation mouthing silently from open books, "adeste fidelis," a scene of cherubic innocence without gusto. Fade out church singing and fade in pub singing the scene still in the church until the volume of the singing is equal, then suddenly cut for a moment to church entrance, then pub entrance as church singing fades out and pub signing takes over.

A young man lingers hesitantly in the door of the pub as if unsure of the propriety of it. Snow starts to fall. He enters and with the opening of the door the volume of the full throated singing within assaults you with its gusto contrasting with the insipidity of the carol service. "A man without a woman is like a wreck upon the sand. There's only one thing worse in the universe and that's a woman, I said a woman, I mean a woman without a ma-a-an." At the edge of the bar a woman sits on a high stool legs crossed boldly advertising her wares. That she is 'on the game' is clear from her extravagant mannerisms and her exaggerated dress. She is rudely made up but in a way which suggests an essentially more homely than erotic attraction.

The young man immediately approaches her and sits beside her. The noisy music which has been coming from a predominantly male group which dominates one half of the bar subsides as someone takes the order for the next round. "Hullo my lovely Liz," he greets. "Business as usual tonight then is it?"

"Jack, believe it or not, tonight being our saviour's eve, and the spirit of love being abroad, tonight I am giving it away gratis, free at the point of service. Just like the NHS"

"You're a one Liz, the only socialist courtesan this side of paradise. Where's the queue?" He tries to attract the attention of the barmaid."

"The line forms on the right Jack, now that Lizzie's back in town. As you can see – no takers. If they can't buy it, it can't be worth having. That's capitalism for you. They know the price of everything and the value of nothing."

"Then what about me? You know me I'm the opposite, anything for nothing has to be a bargain. Come on I'll buy you a drink, we'll join in the communal singing and I'll tell you what a lovely girl you are." He catches the barmaids eye and orders a pint and a gin and orange. Pull back to long angle shot of the interior of the pub as the singing starts up again. Fade out and into the church interior, sound overlay of pub music superimposed the congregation are the same people who were singing in the pub and initially continue to sing a popular song, Bye, Bye Blackbird. Then by televisual trickery morph into churchgoers singing Holy Night. Close, close-ups of pious open mouths with dirty dentures. Sweep to back row where Jack and Liz sit together. She is demure as he shyly reaches out a hand and touches hers as the carol is concluded. She shrinks away with revulsion from his touch. Her eyes light up with joy and passion as the voice from the pulpit proclaims. "Oh Jesus Christ our saviour, who perished on the cross that we might have life eternal, enter into us, (she sighs) on this your birthday and help us realise the true significance of your message of love. Amen."

Cut to the pub where Jack and Liz chat vivaciously together. She has undergone a radical change. Gone the garish overdone makeup and the tart's apparel. She is still sensual but in a less extravagant way.

Down the steps of the church come the 'other' Jack and Liz upon whom a reverse metamorphosis has taken place. She turns to Jack with eyes blazing. "That was a lovely service Jack," she says. The Vicar is standing at the bottom of the steps inviting all and sundry to join the street carollers who are assembling in the vestry. Jack and Liz cross the road to the pub and stand for a moment peering in through the misted window. Jack and Liz inside simultaneously wipe the window and peer out. They gaze at each other as reflections in the glass.

The play develops with scenes alternating between the couples in a way that indicates their differences in attitude to their relationships with each other, not only sexually but in seemingly mundane ways. As the one relationship moves inevitably to its consummation the other deteriorates towards extinction. The most controversial scenes occur when he virtuous Liz is practically raped by a frustrated Jack. After initial resistance however she surrenders and even reciprocates his passion only to demonstrate her absolute revulsion at the climax. This contrasts with their counterparts who reach a tender and mutually compassionate conclusion to their relationship, both physical and emotional. The two episodes are interspersed with the street carollers signing in typically middle class suburbia with port and claret and mince pies in abundance and a block of council flats in one of which sits a lonely pensioner sitting alone in a cold bare room listening to the Christmas Eve service on the radio.

The virtuous Liz takes a shower to wash away her filthy sins while her Jack goes off to the pub and proceeds to get very drunk, where he is picked up by on old dirty tart and led of to a dinghy bedsitter. He is drunk to the point of incapability and the whore demanding pay before pleasure robs him of his wallet as he slumps into a drunken stupor. Meanwhile Liz goes down on her knees and prays for absolution promising never to surrender to her lustful desires ever again.

The 'other' Jack and Liz are seen in a tender but passionate embrace as carollers sing outside their window, "Holy night, silent night," as flurries of snow drift down to give the scene a Christmas card setting. The sexual scenes have been more explicit than anything ever seen on television before, with a realism that leaves nothing to the imagination. For this reason if for no other when the play finally reaches its end with the drunken Jack being picked up in the gutter and spending the night in the local nick, the audience in the Dowlo cheered John to the echo.

"Phwor, that was better than any of those X films in Studio One in Cardiff," was the general consensus.

A few more drinks and the Merthyr Five decided that it wouldn't be such a bad idea to grace Rena's party after all. It took an age and a lot of squabbling over the fare to get one of the few taxis plying their trade on Christmas Eve to agree to take them to Cardiff. But flush with future money cost was no object and the deal was struck.

The crowd was a peculiar mixture of the avante-garde and the garde-derriere, Rena's art bohemians and Marion's leading lights of industry and commerce. Marion seemed to be preoccupied with smoothing over the ruffled feathers of her staid and stuffy flock while Rena basked in the adulation of her lot. Both the women were mad as hell at John though Marion was better at controlling it than Rena. "Where the bloody hell have you been," she snapped bitchily.

184

"Mind your own fucking business," he retorted, at which she smiled and throwing her arms around him kissed him passionately on the lips. Marion smiled icily and Josephine slunk maudlin, drunk and tearful into the corner as he did his best to break away.

A lovely young lady called Saffron, with dewy myopic eyes and a see through dress danced across and drooled all over him. "All hail the conquering hero," she sang, and as John shrugged her off Dave dived opportunistically in so she drooled over him instead. A tubby little minor poet from Merthyr snorted indignantly.

"Here comes the crow beautified with our feathers," he chanted ridiculously to his 'Academi'[9] friends.

"Hullo Harri," John held out a hand for him to shake. "My feathers for what they are worth are but mine own I fear. They certainly owe nothing to you my old friend. Harri reddened and disdained the handshake to be bustled out of the way by a fat moustached walrus of a man held partially in check by Marion.

"Disgusting Sir," he accused. "Disgusting filth and on Christmas Eve." He spoke in that round vowelled nasally strangulated tone which distinguishes those who consider themselves to be the upper echelons of the beastly bourgeoisie.

"Woffle, Woffle, Woffle," John barked back at him in even louder tones. The man stopped speaking in astonishment. "Woffle, Woffle, Woffle," John continued. "When the memsahib and I were out in Rawalpindi," he shouted to the great amusement of Rena's gang, "by God we showed those woggies a thing or two I can tell you. You know nothing about the blightas until you get a whiff of 'em at close range sir. Should be taken into custody soon as they land at Dovah and shipped straight back on the next cargo boat. Coming ovah here and bringing down the property values, I ask you, what right do they have to do that sir? And the way they look at the memsahibs sir, I know that dreadful look, I know what it means madam. Seen them go mad at the sight of white women. Pardon me madam. I could tell you things not fit for ladies' ears. But we know how to deal with the buggers, and all those other foreign Johnnies over the channel you know…" He was suddenly dragged away unceremoniously by a furious Marion.

"You bastard," she said through gritted teeth. "You're not being funny. How much have you had to drink. How dare you. He is a magistrate and chairman of the Watch Committee and here at my invitation."

"I'm not being funny," he retorted suddenly conscious of just how drunk he was. "He's not my friend - he's my enemy. And my enemies friend is my enemy so there you have it." Yes Marion too as a pillar of society would have to be brought tumbling down just like the rest of them. The

---

[9] The Welsh Academy of Literature .

thought absurdly tickled his humour and he burst into laughter. He felt very much like Burton doing his Jimmy Porter bit. "Marion pushed him in the chest and he stumbled backward and finally sat on the floor with his back to Josie who was sobbing silently behind him. "Some people have no principles worth defending," he called after her childishly. Saffron loosened herself from Dave's embrace and came across to him. She knelt and hissed his cheek.

"You're beautiful," she said. "But you could be such an awful bloody boor."

"Bore," he muttered taken aback.

"Boor darling," she repeated. "B-o-o-r boor." She rose and minced her way back to Dave with a wobble of that wonderful mechanism of a beautiful woman in retreat.

He had deep melancholia. He couldn't take direct and blunt criticism especially when he knew that it was true - it triggered off self doubt. A boor, he had to keep repeating it to himself. "Me a boor, no surely not." None of his women would have anything to do with him. Dave had snaffled that lovely Saffron and Bill was making it big with Rena. He had not seen hide nor hair of Josie since he had arrived and caught a glimpse of her in the corner of the room and he doubted that Marion would ever speak to him again. He wished he wasn't here, he should never have come here, he didn't belong here, what the hell was he doing here. He grabbed another drink from the silver tray carried by someone hired specially for this Christmas jamboree.

Eventually, her friends having taken a chilly leave Marion sought him out. She stood for a few seconds her eyes blazing with anger. He knew what was to follow but did nothing to avert it. She raised her arm slowly with exaggerated deliberation then struck him hard across the cheek. "Those," she said, "were my friends." And the tears began to flow.

"I never knew you were such a standard bearer of moral virtue, or should I use the Americanisation, of socio-sexual mores," he said cruelly. "The word hypocrite seems appropriate wouldn't you agree. Anyway you're much too intelligent not to know that whatever power and position you hold in this society has absolutely nothing to do with your membership of the Rotarians, the Industrial Association , or any other silly bloody clique your so called friends belong to. Of course even they bar you from the Freemasons. Whatever your public position is it ultimately boils down to one thing, not you, not Marion Mason, but the Mason millions. And the Mason millions derive from that glass menagerie you operate up there on that windswept hill in Dowlais, and all the other glass menageries you have dotted around the place. Suddenly he was stone cold sober and alert and articulate. You've seen the efficiencies and increased turnover achieved in Dowlais and the massive PR it's generated. We can do the same for all your factories, but you'll have to do it my way."

She stared at him in astonishment like a snake swaying to the melancholy notes of the charmer. She wanted to strike but could only stand there mesmerised. "I love you," she half sobbed gutturally, wretchedly, as if admitting to something despicable that she could not believe herself capable of. "I….love…..you, you bastard."

"*I stand*," he muttered with the tones of an evangelical preacher, his own written words coming to him out of the void

.

> "*I stand above the steep cliffs edge and*
> *peer down the wall of fright*
> *steep to a sea of death.*
> *The wind whistles and eddies*
> *and holds me obliquely*
> *hovering clutching at straws.*
> *It has always been like this,*
> *it's constancy small consolation*
> *in that I attuned myself to it –*
> *but now the horror that I live with*
> *is the certainty that soon it must stop,*
> *and in the awful seconds that preclude it,*
> *as I lean in the direction of the end*
> *I'll reach out for your absent hand.*"

She of course misinterpreted it. Nothing attracts a woman's love and forgiveness more than a vulnerable recalcitrant penitent man. Following so paradoxically his show of strength and masculine superiority it overwhelmed her. Whatever it was he was asking her to do she must do it, even collaborating in her own destruction. He was past the moment of truth, closer to the barely half realised goal of his sub-conscious motivation.

Someone turned the record player up and music indistinguishable from the general cacophony welded itself into the thick smoky atmosphere.. There was a sound of breaking glass and a harsh shriek of forced feminine laughter. A champagne cork popped and Saffron emerged from a bedroom clad only in the briefest of briefs and squirted the frothing nectar over everyone like a racing car driver on the winners rostrum. But it was Josie who provided the star performance which brought this mad night to a close and ruined everybody's Merry Christmas. She only swallowed half the bottle already half conscious from the alcohol she had consumed. She really botched it, puking up immediately over the bedroom carpet. The doctor conveniently present pronounced her fit - the tablets were completely undigested.

CHAPTER 13

It was a dramatic period in which events appeared to have taken on a momentum and volition of their own. The reaction to his film from the establishment was only initially strident. There was the predictable hysteria from Mary Whitehouse and her parliamentary supporters. Of course they were summarily excommunicated from the Beeb, though even that was not to last forever, and the requests for interviews and appearances on the independent channel were like an avalanche. Hardly a night went by when either one or both of them and occasionally also the rest of the Merthyr Five did not put in an appearance. They were definitely flavour of the month, the avante-garde applauding them to the skies and the garde-derriere heaping abusive opprobrium on them.

Josephine got over her drunken death wish and retreated into an introspective self analytical world in which she displayed an outward indifference to him, returning to London to complete her studies. Marion succumbed to his wiles and manipulated the early retirement of one of the more conservative of her board members. His replacement was to be made via an election of the whole of Mason's staff both salaried and workshop floor. John had the local vote swiftly sown up since the trade unions, unable to decide between their own membership, finally compromised on him. Flying visits to the other factories in the Mason's empire produced a similar result. Ultimately only one staff member, the Personnel Officer from the Bristol factory stood against him. The result was a foregone conclusion.

The new director swapped his motorbike for a 3.5 Jag. He embarked on a series of lectures to all Mason's factories, preaching the gospel according to Saint John, Davies that is; he worked both on his novel and on Rena's film script; life was nothing if not hectic. He was still nurturing the cultural revolution but the social and political would have to be postponed until he found more time.

April came in like a lamb and went out like a lion so when May that muddled of months exploded with a golden roar in a heat wave of Mediterranean proportions, the suddenness brought the entire population to its knees. He was exhausted to the point of breakdown. His recurring nightmare was unravelling the sleeve of care and when he looked in the cracked mirror one morning was frightened by what he saw. It was a Friday and he hadn't been to the Dowlo for an age. He supposed they still got together regularly without him, but there had been a change in their lifestyles too. He had to talk for his sanity's sake, for only drunken talk could cure the madness which he now felt. The hot sun beat on his brow bringing to mind those childhood summers, those long double summertime days when it seemed that the evening sky was on fire and the day would go on forever.

Little or nothing had changed in the Dowlo. The fire even still burned brightly in the backroom with all the windows open and everyone in shirtsleeves sweating and soaking up the beer like dehydrated sponges. The boys were all there exactly as they had been six months ago. "Well, well, well the tycoon deigns to join us." Dave welcomed him. "And what does the great man drink these days. Is it something with a stingah?" He accepted the pound note and smiled a sickly smile of thanks turning to address his favourite barmaid.

"Just a beer beautiful," he responded to her querying eyes. "The whisky tends to upset what I fear is the onset of a peptic, duodenal, malignant double ulcer."

"It's old age John boy. It comes sooner and suddener to the likes of you."

"Aye well, *blaze like a meteor and be gay*, as a wise man did say."

"Welcome to le club nouveau riche," Dave said as he took his change and his seat at the stifling table near the fire. He fished in his wallet and removed a folded cheque spreading it on the table surface for John to read. "My first from Lady Bountiful," he grinned. "And more of this and the other to come," he added lasciviously.

"Want my advice take this and leave the other alone," John offered paternally. "They want it all the time the aristocracy, then they tire of it and discard you like a used condom. All that caviar and oysters and horse riding does it. She'll have all your creative energy dribbling down your trouserleg ."

"And what the hell would you know about the aristocracy," Ted countered sardonically. "The only queen you ever had anything to do with was the Queen of Bute and she gave you a nighthood, without a k. Only trouble was it had been used more than once already."

"Oh very droll mister ten percent. You're pissed off because you can't claim your percentage of the other."

"Well it was agreed," Ted shrugged. "I got a barful of witnesses."

"I give up if you're all going to pick on me," John complained. "I suppose it's the price of fame. God it's stifling in here, must be a conspiracy by the breweries to get us all pissed and postpone the revolution. Hullo Bill of the big knob what's this mad rumour about impending nuptials with the zany Rena?"

"Mere innuendo my friend," he grunted. "She gets all her climaxes working on this bloody awful film of yours with no assistance from me whatever. Unlike you she seems devoted to her art exclusively. Life of bloody Christ my arse, what a potty notion, it'll be seen in Cannes then die the death, you mark my word."

"Art," John riposted. "What the fuck is art. I don't know any more."

"You never knew what art was you fucking fake," Dave taunted.

"And I suppose you do," John snorted. "You portrait painter to the upper classes. I told you once – art is truth."

189

Ted couldn't resist his five pennorth. " Plato," he said. They all looked at him without comment. "All art is lies, all artists are liars, invention is their game."

"Plato always was a pratt," John replied. "The first of the fascists. The true artist cannot lie," he insisted, holding up a remonstrative finger. "He may create a fiction to perpetrate a truth, but the fiction as a whole, in its totality must be a truth. Hence the reactionary Balzac tells us more about the nineteenth century French bourgeoisie than the revolutionary Zola. And that's according to Marx."

"In that case what's a lie," Ted insisted.

"A lie is a deliberate misrepresentation of what one knows or believes to be the truth. It has nothing whatever to do with historical fact. It's a moral issue, a matter of artistic integrity. In the end it boils down to a complex dialectic between the artist, what he is, what he perceives and what he feels. It is resolved as much intuitively as intellectually. Beauty is truth and truth is beauty, but Keats forgot to add love. Beauty, truth and love, this is the only holy trinity. Jesus preached it: God is love: Love ye one another, but we still nail our Christs to black crosses and the end is more imminent now. If we don't have social revolution soon one of those brainless pricks who have their fingers on the button will despatch us all to kingdom come."

"Marxist shit," objected Geraint waking from a dream of a Welsh socialist state, buoyant on a capitalist sea. "We don't all feel as threatened as you, you and your Christ. He used the same technique of fiction. He was a bloody revolutionary theorist too. And his adherents have ballsed things up just as much as your lot. They're always going on about the end of the world, Armageddon and all that crap…."

And so it went on talk, talk, talk and more useless talk all leading ultimately nowhere. He went home hoarse and dissatisfied. A cold supper waited for him. His parents seemed happy for his 'success'. He certainly wasn't.

He took her hand and led her gently wordlessly up the stairs. He sat on the bed and carefully undressed her. He sat her down beside him and marvelled again at the almost forgotten beauty of her. He lay her down and kissed her – everywhere. He entered her. He lost himself in her. Childwoman. Earcuff. The figure swinging on the stairs was him. When it was over she smiled at him and he cried.

With her it was qualitatively different than with Josie, Marion or any to her woman. This was his soul mate his other half and she made him whole. Marion, chic and sophisticated, rich and sexy was the ideal mistress. Lynda, warm and affectionate vulnerable and mysterious, earth goddess, was the ideal wife. She also symbolised an intangible rootedness, a continuity with his development, a belonging. In the rapid flux of recent events he clung to her like a drowning man. They were married quietly, almost secretly the following month. Dave was best man. His parents were delirious but Mamgu was apprehensive. They fled to Crete for their honeymoon and marvelled at Minoan culture. They did the grande tour; Athens, Firenza, Roma, Venezia and a host of other fabulous cities in a madcap two months of sailing, flying and railing, until shortage of funds and several pleading telegrams from Rena about missed deadlines forced their return, too soon.

The threads of his frightening new life were not easy to resume. Things had happened which had altered his world forever, not least the marriage but also Josephine had tried again more determinedly. They had got her to the hospital just in time. Marion was numbed by both events and was left with the conclusion that she had sold her soul to the very devil, and all for nothing.

John took out a massive mortgage and moved up into the heights of Cefn Coed, where the crachach lived, with views clear down the valley to Crawshay's Castle and beyond. The novel was completed and sold relatively well for a first, riding on the swell of his new status. He had arrived, the man among men in the avante garde, a soul on fire out of Gwalia. His wife of course was pregnant.

He sat in on a few board meetings, christening them bored meetings, and achieved little. Where was all the power and where his dream of revolution? Even the Dowlo was slowly but surely being taken over by a new pretentious clientele of the Valleys bourgeois, a class which was previously undetectable in this locality, to which the brewery was happy to respond and exploit. The Five were offered sums of money to write intellectual graffiti on the walls of the new 'lounge'. To Ted's utter chagrin the other four refused, it wasn't so much the ten percent, his mad anarchism even encompassed the destruction of the Dowlo.

The prospect of parenthood terrified him. He was convinced that his offspring would be ugly, deformed, two headed, blind, scarred or mentally retarded as a punishment for his own sin and corruption. That was the way God worked wasn't it : visiting the sins of the fathers on the sons and daughters even unto the umpteenth generation. If there was a God, and he was not firm enough in his disbelief to preclude that awful possibility, he would certainly be a vicious one who would use his terrible omnipotent power to get back at him for all his blasphemy. The suffering of the innocent had been the underlying theme of all history, the symbol of his church the dreadful effigy of God's own son hung agonisingly on a black cross.

At the factory Marion was cold and utterly aloof, but she did assent to his redesignation as Cultural Director for the whole Mason's group. A role which kept him on the hoof with less direct contact with the Chairman. He handed the bread and butter job on to a D Litt, an ex Ruskin College boy with links to Littlewood and Wesker. Josephine obtained her degree, a first, came into her inheritance, took a small flat above the post office near the railway station, became interested in social psychology and got a research post graduate scholarship in the psychology of productivity stimulation, or something equally nebulous. It was October's end before he and Marion eventually met face to face again. There was to be a board meeting and he met her in the corridor. She invited him into her office suite, which was really a sumptuous pied a terre with adjoining office facilities.

"Well how is marriage treating you?" she enquired coldly. "I hear your wife is pregnant."

"Very. She's like the side of a house."

"Was that why…. you know…"

"For me marrying in haste – good God no," he smiled.

"Oh," she turned away, lost for words. "A drink?"

"Coffee'd be fine. No, it was impulsive," he shrugged. "I can't offer you an adequate explanation."

"And what about me?"

"You. You never were a consideration in the context of marriage," he said bluntly. "I thought ours was such a good relationship."

"You didn't honestly expect it to continue," she retorted in shocked amazement.

"Why not?"

She sat down with her coffee and tried to analyse it.

"It can't be moral scruple can it? I mean you've had affairs with married men before."

"You're a cruel bastard. What about your wife - your pregnant wife? What do you think I am?"

"Stop being childish. Come here."

"You don't honestly expect me to…" He stopped her protestations with a quick harsh kiss. "….at the drop of a hat." He pulled her roughly to him and kissed her passionately. She struggled briefly then surrendered with a sob. He led her into the adjacent room where there was a divan beside a window open to the sky and the bleak brown hills beyond. He didn't lower the blind, the sun somehow made it seem less sordid.

"For the month of September production increased by two percent for the second month in succession. This in spite of what some of you insisted would follow abolition of time clocking and the piece rate system." John said with a satisfied I told you so smile.

"I have to admit," responded Dewey, "that I was one of those who viewed your proposals with great misgivings, and although it's early days yet I must say that it seems that I might have been wrong. But if the trend continues or even stabilises at current production levels the obvious corollary is that we shall have staff surplus to requirements in our Work Study and Wages sections. I think Chairman that we should therefore give serious consideration to implementing a redundancy programme for these departments. I have taken it upon myself to have the Personnel people draft a provisional voluntary scheme." With a flourish he began distributing copies of the draft around the big oval oak table.

"Chairman," John appealed, his colour rising. "Is this in order. On the basis of two months figures it seems Mr Dewey can't wait to deprive loyal staff of their livelihood. At worst we should be seeking to re - deploy, but more positively these departments should have their terms of reference re-defined to investigate further ways of achieving efficiencies."

"Of course it's in order," one of Dewey's supporters interjected. "One of the results of this report is clearly that there is likely to be redundancy in two departments. I think Mr Dewey should be congratulated on having to foresight to produce his draft."

"And I bet you and one or two others have been instrumental in its production," John retorted angrily. "Why wasn't this document circulated with the minutes and placed on the agenda in the proper manner. Chairman I move that consideration of it is out of order."

"The document was not ready until this morning Madam Chairman," Dewey lied smoothly, "and since it relevant to the item under consideration I think you must allow it."

The *madam* and the *must* were a mistake and John smiled at the anticipated reaction. "What I must or must not do is a matter for my judgement," Marion remonstrated as if dealing with an errant schoolboy. "I have no more idea of what this document contains than the majority of us. It is regrettable Mr Dewey that you saw fit not to consult me on the matter. I might have given you guidance in the matter of procedure."

"But Madam Chairman I......" compounding his earlier error. John smiled again.

"Mr Dewey," she warned sternly with emphasis on the Mr. "We will proceed to discuss the item on the agenda. If the Board should come to the conclusion that there might be an issue concerning redundancy we may instruct you to draw up a preliminary report for which we may set up broad parameters such as consultation with the Trade Unions. Such decisions are the prerogative of this board and not the whim of an individual member. That is my decision and that is final, is that understood?"

Dewey blushed and grumbled and put his documents away.

"May I Chairman," John said with a smirk, "suggest an alternative approach." Marion nodded her assent. "I think Mr Dewey is being typically short sighted. If he hasn't realised by now that personnel relations has a direct bearing on productivity levels then he should no longer be in control of that department. What on earth does he think that the lessons of the past few months have been, and how can he possibly believe that improvements will be maintained if redundancies were to be announced. I think I should warn that if you want to see industrial action send your production figures plunging then follow his advice."

"Now look here you young pup how dare you threaten......."

"I still have the floor," John raised his voice above Dewey's. "Far from threatening I am simply offering you my assessment of the likely consequences of what you propose."

"Our first duty as directors is to this company's shareholders," Dewey shouted back.

"Mine is not," John hammered the table like Kruschev at the United Nations. "I was elected by the workers to represent their point of view. In any case people already sat around this table hold some seventy percent of the shares. He looked pointedly at Marion who he knew always held the 'golden share'. Then "Dewey you're so full of shit."

"Gentlemen, gentlemen. If we can't have a reasonable discussion without resorting to the language of the gutter I'll adjourn until you learn how to behave yourselves. Mr Davies, you have the floor as you put it and we'll do without the interjections."

"I'd just like to say, for the edification of the Neanderthals, that of course we have a moral obligation which should at least consume as much of our attention as the purely commercial considerations. In any case, in the longer term, one is inextricably bound to the other : they are not mutually exclusive. The unemployment figures are as ever much higher here than in the rest of the country. That is how Mason's came to be built here in the first place with considerable government assistance. The chance of a redundant clerical worker finding alternative occupation here is absolutely nil. The workers cannot be held to be responsible for their own redundancies those were caused by our decisions. These are people not just numbers in a filing cabinet, they have families and roots in this company and this community, they have parents, wives, children, homes, rents, mortgages, hire purchase agreements…."

"These considerations are incompatible with our first duty to our shareholders, whoever they may be, and the drive for increased profitability," Dewey insisted again.

"These people have their whole livelihoods invested in this bloody company, not just their pocket money." John was shouting angrily now. "And please don't give me that old shit about poor old widows with their life savings invested in bloody Mason's. Most of this company's stock is neatly distributed round this table as I've already said and the golden share of it resides in the Chair's lovely lap. It took a record dividend to get you to accept a workers' representative on the board. If a little more of it had been ploughed back and more imaginative decisions taken the company would be too busy coping with the expansion to be talking about redundancies. But it's not too late for that if only a few more of you can be dragged screaming and kicking into the twentieth century."

"Why don't we cool things down a bit," insisted smooth slick ambitious young Jim Hawtin. "There's a lot in what Mr Davies has to say of course, though he has his own idiosyncratic way of expressing it at times. We

194

all owe a great deal to the way he has invigorated what was a tired company to a much more dynamic one. I applaud the changes he has persuaded us to make, but after all is said and done socialism and the free enterprise economy are ultimately incompatible.....”

"Surely under Supermac even the Tories talk about the mixed economy rather than that old chestnut. Free enterprise went out with the depression, though I know too many of your backwoodsmen would love a return to that.”

"Of course, of course, a mere slip of the tongue. A mixed economy it is. But although your assertion that the our obligations as members of the Board is not exclusively to our shareholders but must take into account our employees and to a degree even the wider community is essentially correct. Indeed I hardly need to remind anyone here that our founder's principal reasons for setting up shop here in Dowlais was his humane response to the abject poverty of the area and the welcome he received on fleeing from Nazi oppression in the country of his birth. But..... yes there is a but.. Mr Dewey though much of what he said and says is reactionary nonsense, our shareholders have to be the first consideration. That is the way that capitalism works. Everything we have done recently however is ultimately in the best interests of the shareholders and workers alike. We are on the verge of being promoted from the second Division to the First,” how he enjoyed these clichés. John watched him, fascinated. "We must grasp the nettle now,” he almost added 'and strike while the iron is hot', "and seize the moment. Mr Davies, and I disagree with his fundamental political philosophy of course, has nevertheless brought drive and dynamism to this Board, a drive that has previously been conspicuous by its absence, despite the efforts of the Chair and one or two of the more far sighted of us. We have been painfully retarded by the more conservative elements but now that balance is much more even. In the old days perhaps Mr Dewey's way might have been the proper course because our horizons were so limited. Now they are hopelessly out of date. We should be making the very most of the kind of publicity we are currently receiving, we couldn't afford to buy the interest which the media is taking in the efforts of Mr Davies and the Chair. Let us put off any consideration of redundancies for a period of six months. Let us announce our intention to expand and thereby absorb the extra manpower. I think we fully expect Madam Chairman, that before the six months is up we shall have achieved the takeover of the nylon yard production plant that will ensure a regular supply to ourselves while at the same time denying it to our competitors. I so move.”

The clever bugger had John wriggling on the hook. Either he supported this motion, with all its undercurrents of intrigue in the acquisition of the nylon yarn plant the output of which would almost certainly at the very least be reduced in order to create a near monopoly situation, or put up a amendment designed to accommodate the Deweyites. On the other hand support for Hawtin's proposal was far from being a certainty without his approval.

"I second Mr Hawtin's motion," John conceded reluctantly and received a white toothy smile from the proposer

"Is there an amendment?" Dewey moved his amendment for implementation of the redundancy report and strictly according to Citrine, who Marion had studied assiduously, the amendment was considered first. The vote was deadlocked, Marion not having voted initially asserted her position as Chair to break the deadlock and defeat it. The proposal was now put to the vote with the identical outcome. Hawtin was elated but Marion and John less so. Marion had indulged in some uncharacteristic fence sitting in order to keep something of a presence in both camps. She had learned from long experience not to burn her bridges and after all she might yet come to rely on Dewey's support in some future confrontation.

John frowned. He had been forced to trade reduced redundancy here for possible closure of some obscure production facility elsewhere and the magnitude of which was unknown. He felt as if he'd just concluded a Faustian deal. One day the devil would call for his soul. As the meeting drew to a close he felt a hand on his shoulder, taut as a talon. "Care to join me for a quick one. There's a run down pub across the road but it serves a cunning draught." It was oleaginous Hawtin. John tired but intrigued felt bound to accept. Halfway through the second pint underneath a plaque dedicated to the Ancient Order of Buffalos the tone suddenly changed and instead of the quality of the local brew and the rundown state of the premises it was down to the real business of the moment. "You know that you and I and Marion are the only members of this board with any degree of dynamism at all." John shrugged non-commitally and continued to sip appreciatively at his drink. "Now you know I'm no socialist, our motivations are poles apart, but the political reality of the situation we find ourselves in is that unless you and I can reach some kind of understanding neither of us is going to get what he wants." He paused as if it required time for John to get he full import of this. "I think we can be of mutual benefit to one another. To get to the heart of the matter I have Westbury in my pocket and while your power over madam chairman may not be quite so definite you certainly have some degree of influence there."

John took a more protracted gulp of his Pint of Rhymney, wiped his mouth with his sleeve, smiled and asked innocently. "So what have you got on Westbury, apart from his homosexuality." He asked, wishing that he didn't have to hear this. Hawtin's face betrayed just a momentary surprise but recovered it's composure immediately. "That's the general thrust," he conceded, "but the devil of course is in the detail, as they say."

"You're a lousy bastard Hawtin," John muttered matter of factly. Hawtin touched his arm gently with a complicit smile. "We are all guilty of it aren't we," he said smoothly. "The coward does it with a kiss that's all."

"Allright, what is it you're suggesting?"

"O nothing concrete at this stage. Consider this as a sort of general understanding. You scratch my back… Westbury can still be something of a stubborn hindrance and since your appearance he's become somewhat less co-operative . But he's susceptible to bribery as well as blackmail and the time will come when I have to play my trump card with him. But once its played its useless. I'll play it to secure his resignation and your permanent co-option. That will leave place for a new elected member from amongst the brothers…?" Inclining his head as if to say, 'but you'll have that end all tied up.'

"And when you make your bid for the Chair."

"Well that's a long way off. She still holds the golden share but that may not be forever," he hinted. "Then of course it will be a matter for your judgement and conscience. She's a very rich woman in her own right and it may be more of a blessing than a pain, for you I mean. Think about it. As I said in any case that's a long way off. This is the here and now. Who knows, by then you may have designs on the office for yourself, then I would be in difficulty. Let's have one for the road shall we?"

Mephistopheles was calling sooner than he thought.

197

CHAPTER 14

Things began to move at a hectic pace. He felt no longer in control of the speed at which things developed, if indeed he had ever been in control. Josie declared her intention to marry one of her clique of yesteryear with an enthusiasm which saddened John with its suggestion of surrogacy. Hawtin's ambitions for expansion were astutely realised by playing off a small nylon yarn producer against an equally small but significant competitor in the finished lingerie field. The yarn producer with fiscal problems needed Mason's big contract in order to survive and the lingerie producer relied exclusively on the yarn supplier for its raw material. Masons aggressively took both over and tightened its grip on its neo-monopoly position in the industry.

The Financial Times was quick to point out the coincidence of Mason's rapidly improving fortunes with the advent of John's accession to the board. The world of high finance as much as showbiz likes a blazing meteor and young John Davies was surely such a dazzling star: not only an artist and an intellectual genius but a financial wizard to boot, a man of dynamism and acute business acumen. A real poacher turned gamekeeper.

Lynda was swollen beyond the point of satisfactory sexual relations and so the relationship with Marion picked up some of its lost momentum. They conspired a business trip abroad, a conference in the Bahamas. He offered to take Lynda of course, confident in his knowledge of her certain refusal. She was too astute in any case for his shenanigans. "You don't have to start playing those cute little games with me love," she insisted. "Everybody knows about your little sexual adventures. You had them all the time before we married, when I was ill. I didn't asked you to change. You never tried to keep it from me before so don't start now. What's the matter, is it the baby? Do you find my condition so repugnant?"

"No just bloody awkward," he tried to laugh it off but she was always too intuitive for him.

"Well love you just go off on your little business trip if that's what you want to do. Enjoy yourself if you can but remember John love, freedom is a double edged sword. He kissed her cheek lightly and passed a hand over his brow. God she was so perceptive. But now he felt a guilt he had always managed to suppress before. "We'll be allright," he promised. But the promise seemed to lack conviction.

They were whisked away in a silver cigar tube vibrating with piped soothing musac and humming with air conditioner. The world was just a map through cloudy gaps so far below them. Chic stewardesses suave and svelte as film stars responded to their every whim in their segregated first class closeted compartment. They booked into their sumptuous beach complex hotel a million storeys high in the -apex------ suite with its own roof garden and a bottle of the best bubbly on ice. They assiduously decided on only the most cursory acquaintance with the conference and its delegates which was just as well since the whole business appeared to be nothing more than an excuse for a tax free binge for the high flying executives of the world's undergarment industry.

It was morning, the sun high over the shining sea and though drowsy with jetlag they wandered the low white dunes of rough heavy grained sand, she in light white sweater and tights which lent her a balletic quality and radiance in the shimmering morning sun. They splashed their feet in the sea front along the green bay's edge, out of holiday season, out of sight and sound of all humanity. He lay her at the water's edge and kissed her as the tepid tide lapped around them, Lancaster and Kerr in 'From here to Eternity,' and when it was over a barking dog startled them. They rose and retreated deeper into the sea, the morning walker, grizzled, white skinned, colonial gave them an old fashioned disgusted 'harrumph' barked as loudly as his dog then increased his leisurely pace as if to put as much distance as possible in as short as possible a time between him and these nouveau riche desecrators of what he considered to be his shining island.

"Why," she asked simply, finally. "Why her: why not me?"

"I don't know," he said irritably. "Don't spoil it with complex analysis, I'm not capable of that, it's not rational after all. I wanted to, I had to, so I did. Fait accompli. I love her, I love you, I loved Josie, I think. There's nothing terrible in that is there. I don't want to hurt anybody."

"I love, I love, I love, that must be the most overworked cliché in every man's vocabulary," she accused. Your wife, my daughter, me, even Rena. Oh yes I know all about that too. You've hurt me, you've hurt us all you selfish bastard."

"I didn't set out to hurt anybody," he repeated stupidly. "And you women you all demand love as if it's your right. You have responsibility too."

She shook her head, the tears beginning to flow then she too walked away from him, into the sea.

"Perhaps I should just try to stop loving people," he said pathetically.

"Loving people," she reproached. "Loving people. I doubt you understand the meaning of the expression." She looked sad and vulnerable.

"I can't cope with it," he pleaded, his self assurance dissolved in the salt spray. "How could anyone cope with it." He flung his arms up in a theatrical expansive gesture. "All this beauty: all this pain." With a sweep of

199

his arms he took in the broad expanse of the deserted bay and the rocky promontory. The dog barked a distant and fading dream as the man and beast had disappeared from sight among the dunes. He took her hand and they walked, sad lost souls in search of a saviour, but where, as ever, was such a saviour to be found?

That night in bed it was business as usual which preoccupied them. "This new plant was Hawtin's idea wasn't it," he demanded.

"Yes and a good one too. With the envisaged expansion we'll be able to produce our own yarn in sufficient quantity for all our needs, while at the same time denying that of our competitors. You've got to give it to him it is as simple a it is brilliant."

"In fact all our recent acquisitions were his ideas."

"So what, what does all that matter now, I thought you came with me here….."

"For a dirty weekend."

"Is that ALL this is for you, a dirty weekend, and I thought….."

"He's after the chairmanship Marion, you watch out for him."

"Do you think I don't know that, don't teach your….He's got Westbury in his pocket just because he's a fairy. I've got Dewey in mine because he's an old lech'. Aren't we a lovely lot we pillars of society. Now whoever has you has the balance of power. Which of us can find the skeleton in your cupboard. Anyway I have the majority of shares. As long as that's the case I am invulnerable."

"But Josephine will soon hold the balance," he said coldly.

"Hold me," she pleaded like a frightened child. "Hold me close. It's all such a stinking fuck up isn't it."

He rose from the bed and led her to the curtained balcony. The moon flowed like quicksilver over the deep purple sea. "God who wouldn't be a poet here. Look it's written everywhere. I don't want to hurt anybody," he repeated for the third time, and a gull cried out biblically far out over the dark sea. "I abhor pain," he cried. "Why did they torture and crucify Christ, why did they despise him. I'm so small and lost and insignificant: so futile and corrupt. You corrupt me, you know that don't you. But I'm so eager to be corrupted."

Her white chiffon scarf streamed behind her as they strode the white cliffs top, the surf breaking below them white on the black rocks. They stopped and sat awhile listening to the night sounds; the crash of incessant surf on the surf's base; the softer melody of sea on pebbly sand; the call of gulls way out on the black water; a mysterious light far out bobbing on the swell. They removed their shoes and ran through the dew wet blades between their toes. They felt the grass blow free in the soft wind like fingers reaching up towards the moon, close lovely tufts clinging to the mother earth sending tender shoots deep down into her womb. Each blade a lovely gesture of the earth's replenishment and promise of perennial pregnancy. He lay her down on the steep bank's edge and inseminated her while the moon smiled and the sun slept.

"Good morning my love, how's the belly this morning?"

"Fat as ever. How the hell should it be?" She patted it proudly. "It's kicking like Sencyn Powell so it must be a boy," she chuckled. He poured her a mug of coffee from the percolator and handed her the toast in the silver gilt toast rack, both hallmarks of their new lifestyle.

"You know what Lynda, we've turned into a right pair of bourgeois twats. Look at this place, that bloody arsehole of a television director here and it's hardly changed since he swanned off to the Cotwolds. It's so bloody pretentious it's not even funny any more. And the people who live around here are not really our people are they. They may pay lip service to you because your husband writes books and appears on the telly but you're not accepted as one of them are you. I mean it wouldn't be quite so bad if they were the aristocracy or even the haute bourgeoisie, but the petite bourgeois snobs that they are exclude you from their inner circle. Shopkeepers, builders, middle men, salesmen, executives and all the other pieces of shit which adhere to the shoes of the productive masses, they swamp us with the effluvia of their rottenness.

"We've got to get out of here lovely girl. We can't go back to our little terraced house in Dowlais, we can't stay in this God forsaken middle class façade. I think we should join the classless elite and buy the hacienda on the hill. At least it's extravagant and has absolutely no utilitarian virtues, very Clough Ellis. It's a house of outrageous ostentation and worth more than all these bloody four and five bedroom desirable residences all rolled into one and it's going for a song. No we're not discussing it I'm exercising my male chauvinist prerogative. It's a done deal, even a fait accompli. We don't even have to move one stick of this God awful furniture, we can refurnish in a style far out enough to complement the architecture. When we're even more rich and famous we'll probably have it smashed to the ground and replaced with a white marble mausoleum a la the Taj Mahal, or convert it into a municipal cultural centre." He held up his hands in a gesture of supplication. "Whatever happens darling," he entreated, "we simply cannot go on living like this."

She looked at him with bemusement, smiled and said nothing, kissed his cheek and spread her arms wide in resignation. "Easy come easy go."

"Do you think mam and dad might fancy it?"

She grimaced. "You could do that to your own parents."

"You're right as always," he laughed and she smiled wryly.

In two weeks they had moved lock stock and barrel into the grotesque ersatz folly on the hill. Everything in the garden should have been rosy from his selfish perspective. His relationship with Marion continued

201

with increasing ardour. The company was thriving and all the financial pundits had been proved wrong. Money was flowing into his account at an accelerating rate of increase. He should have been happy to the point of oblivion. But he was sick; sick of the sorry deception imposed by himself on his self and others, sick of the corruption and the degradation, sick of illegality, sick of the immorality, sick of the shoddy contradictions of capitalist ethics, sick of sin, sick as Sin.

He even managed to persuade himself in brief moments of euphoria that this was just a temporary condition, that he was only prostituting himself for a little while longer, that as soon as he had manipulated the situation where the little fat commie shop steward was nominated to the Board he could get out and settle down to some real work : another novel or perhaps another film script. 'Jesus Christ' was scheduled for release this summer and in Rena's impeccable judgement it would be the critical success of all time. If they could make a superstar out of Moses then Jesus was a racing cert for Top of the Pops. What a year it had been in retrospect, what a fabulous fantastic year - and yet – it hadn't happened to him had it… at least not to the real him… not the him that must still dwell down deep inside of him somewhere.

CHAPTER 15

The whole world was coming apart with a bang rather than a whisper. Dave had become a 'correspondent' in a very high class divorce petition involving the lesser aristocracy – which was wonderful for his business but catastrophic for his art. He was growing in renown as a portraitist of the elite and the famous. The poor Welshman's Annigoni was how Ted described him.

The first nuptial year of Bill and Rena had turned into a real life re-enactment of 'Who's Afraid of Virginia Woolf' with dire consequences for Bill's dreams of a photojournalistic career. He was rapidly turning into a first class alcoholic while Rena pinned her hopes on 'Jesus Christ'.

Geraint had cashed in on the Welsh monoglot clique at BBC Wales, performing in an abysmally amateurish imitation of an English language folk programme which at least had the talents of Ewan Macgregor and Peggy Seeger at it's disposal. Unfortunately the Welsh version had its hardcore following of Nationalist zealots and a perennial budget. It wasn't the principle of the thing which caused John's hackles to rise so much as the sheer banality and third rate production of it.

The only agent of sanity among the famous five appeared to be Ted who sponged unashamedly on all and sundry remaining as madly anarchist as any Souverein or Kropotkin armed with a bomb with an intermittently sputtering fuse.

In another week it would be Christmas. How life seemed to be punctuated by Christmases – Christmases of disappointment, hope, sadness, joy. "Tomorrow we'll go up to Pant and pick them up in the car," he enthused to Lynda. "They think they're just coming down for Christmas dinner. Afterwards you can present them with their gift. You can give them the keys." She took his head between her hands and shook her own with the futility of it.

"Whatever you think you owe them can't be repaid in hard cash or bricks and mortar," she said. He knew exactly what she meant. How does a man repay his father for all the misunderstandings, all the pain : his mother for all the love and selflessness ? A man is his life's totality not a split second response, a reactionary gesture however well intentioned. But all the same he danced around her like an excited schoolboy with a good report from school.

"Christmas is coming, the goose is getting fat," he sang playfully patting her ripening belly.

The day came crisp and cold and he jauntily parked the newly acquired Jaguar behind the battered old blue Cortina to the accompaniment of twitching curtains from the house across the street. As they went in they met the doctor coming out. Doctors don't come out on Christmas day for something trivial but nonetheless he met him with a little banter. "Hullo Doc, who'd have your job on a day like this eh. Drew the short straw did you. Hasn't fallen down the stairs has he the silly old bugger. Slipped his disc or something."

The response was grave and lacking the bonhomie of Christmas. "It's bad John," was all he said. "The ambulance should be here soon. Sorry I have to dash."

"They never tell you much," his sisters eyes were red from weeping, her face ash grey mascara smudged. The presents were unopened around the foot of the little plastic tree beside the unlit fire. "He had his coughing spell as usual after his morning fag, just making up the fire, and then... and then... she broke into a fresh outpouring of hysterical grief.

Mother came in as calm as a night nurse. "He just lies there," she said, it sounded almost as if she was complaining. "He don't know anybody. It's the dust and the fags, how many times have I told him."

The ambulance seemed an age and the sudden silence interminable. John could hardly bring himself to climb the stairs to the bedroom where he lay. "He's dead," was his first awful thought, but the shallow rise and fall of his belaboured stuttering breaths indicated otherwise. Its allright Dad," he said. "Everything will be allright you'll see."

At the antiseptic hospital the smells were sadly evocative. "I'm scared," John admitted to Lynda. "I don't want him to die. He had an accident in the pit once when I was a kid and I said 'God don't let him die. Don't let him die and I'll promise to be a good boy from now on. I'll go the chapel and pray every night.' And for a while I was and I did, but I haven't been a good little boy have I. I can't make those promises now can I. He doesn't know how much I've always loved him. There's always been that gap which we both found impossible to bridge. I wanted to give them something now for all those wasted years." He wept bitterly.

Why was it that the surgeon approached him when it was all over, not his sister, not his brother, not even his mother but him. Was it because he had become famous, was articulate, rational, of an equal status. But he wanted to feel it had less to do with him than with any of the others. "I'm sorry Mr Davies there's nothing we can do – too advanced for surgery. All we can do is make it easier for him." Was he hinting at a quite massive probably lethal dose of morphine or whatever it was – euthanasia. His expression seemed to full of allusion. He wouldn't live the night. John had been right, he had been dead from the first moment of his coma.

"Thank you doctor," he said stupidly.

"Do you require a priest or ……"

"Good God no. What the hell can a bloody priest do for him now. He's not even a bloody catholic is he." He fought back the rudeness of his anger." I'm sorry he's not anything you see he's an …..he's not quite an atheist I suppose. Thank you ." Thank you, thank you, thank you, they'd been saying thank you all their lives……for nothing – or at most the very little life had given them. He was about to die, as good as dead, had suffered ignominy for the greater part of his life. Thank you very much God, thank you so very bloody much. He shook his head bitterly, the tears rolling down his cheeks. His mother came across silently with arms outstretched. There was no need for words , she clasped him to her boron like a child, for the first time since a child and they both wept.

Mamgu was there now, imperious and serene with the kind of dignity which death deserves. "You should be the last to cry," she said soberly and it was Lynda that she took into her arms as they trooped into the little room, nylon screens the only privacy between them and the public ward. They waited silently and uselessly for signs of that final glimmer of life and recognition. Rage , rage against the dying of the light, do not go gentle into that good night. But gentle he went without sigh, sound or smile.

Out in the corridor Dave had arrived but not been allowed in. He looked him tearfully in the eyes and opened his hands in a gesture of fatalism. Lynda took him by the hand. "Come on love," she said, "let's take your mother home."

Home he thought ironically, the keys were in his pocket, but perhaps in time that at least might still be possible.

> *'Gnarled old inevitable lady*
> *wrinkled as a prune,*
> *does your hard embrace bring peace,*
> *your cracked kiss bring liberation.*
> *What skeletal fiddler calls the tune*
> *in this dark hour of retribution.*
> *The soul deserts the fleece,*
> *leaves cold a chemic body.'*

He muttered the words of his doleful poem silently to himself.

CHAPTER 16

"I know John it's a lovely house, and what it must have cost God only knows, but can you really see us living here Mamgu and me. They'd look down their long snooty noses at us. The new crachach living here now are worse than the old crachach used to be. I was in service here for a time. You didn't know that did you? He was something to do with the colliery that your grampa Tom was working in at the time. Can't remember which colliery now, Manager or Under Manager, something big like that he was. And as for his wife well, perhaps the old crachach were just as bad as the present lot. Well anyway there was a strike and your grampa Tom came marching down like a real revolutionary. No daughter of his was going to skivvy for an old pig like Thomas while all his men were laid off and on relief, and he dragged me off home. I never felt so ashamed in all my life. I cried all night. Now of course when I think of it, how proud it makes me feel to have been my father's girl.

Then there's Mamgu, she was even more political than your grampa in her own way. She wouldn't fit in with that snooty lot down here now would she. At least where we are there's still something left of the old community, though not very much if I'm honest, everybody's way of life seems to have changed. If this is capitalism then by God you can keep it. I could never understand my dad, grampa Tom, even Mamgu , truth to be told, perhaps I do now, now that it's too late. It's down to you, the young to do it now John. They were going to change the world, your dad as much as anybody, working his socks off for the Fed, marching, organising. But in the end it changed him. It's changing you John bach, but it hasn't taken nearly as long as it did with him. He'd be disappointed in you John I've got to tell you that. He was surprised that you were the one that had caught his fire rather than your brother Denzil who was conceived in the heat of it. But you reminded him too much of himself at your age, that's why you clashed so much, but lately reminded him of how he had allowed himself to be changed with your big house and your posh car and your two wives when the one is everything any man could want from a woman. Mrs Dai Bread One and Mrs Dai Bread Two that's what they've become known as round here and they both deserve better than that. But then who am I to try to tell you how to live your life, after all I wasn't much help to him at the end was I. He died slowly John, he did go sadly gently into that good night. He died of hardship and discrimination, dole queues swallowed pride, impotence and disillusionment. He didn't die last Christmas, he died a long time ago." He was moved and disturbed by her simple eloquence which she hard seldom displayed before. It emphasised still further how little he really knew either of them and now it was too late they neither needed nor wanted the material rewards of his new found affluence. By expecting so little of them he felt he had betrayed them, and himself into the process.

"Don't go under," she pleaded. "I heard you arguing with him one night not too long ago. You told him that the struggle now was for minds and not empty bellies, something like that anyway. You were right then but you've been wrong ever since."

"What should I do then," he opened his hands and the tears rolled like a child scolded for a behavioural lapse.

"You have to ask me that," there was a tinge of anger in her reply. She looked him straight in the eye. "Stop being dishonest with yourself," she said. "When you've done that you won't need anybody's advice. You know well enough deep down what needs to be done and you have to do it whatever the cost. I honestly don't know what it is but I know that you do. Have courage," was her final admonition. Of course she was right, courage to face the truth and act upon it that's all it would need. That's all? He kissed her cheek and left more despondent and dejected than ever.

Walking the familiar streets of childhood did nothing to improve his mood. His family had all long since moved from the older parts of Dowlais onto one of the post war council estates. Now he found himself wandering along what was left of the old haunts until finally by accident or subconscious intent he found himself outside the entrance to Susan's flat.

"Good God, what a surprise. Never thought I'd see you here again after you joined the nobs; beautiful wife, rich and sophisticated mistress, hordes of toffee nosed virgins, what can I possibly do for you?" She shrugged and hugged him when she saw his downcast expression. "Sorry to hear about your dad," she added. "Come in and sit down. I'll put the pot on but you've got less than an hour," she warned glancing at her watch smiling coyly. "I'm still a poor working girl you know. Regular client, she shrugged.

"Not so poor these days I think," he smiled sadly looking around the expensively furnished room. "Like something out of House and Home," he commented. "We've all become bloody bourgeois."

"Less of the fancy words John love, there's only one thing I could ever do for you," unfastening her blouse.

But it was no longer what he wanted from her or anyone and he left in an awful mood of despair and misery. He walked the narrow dimlit streets and stopped to watch a pair of ragamuffins rolling in the dirt. It might have been yesterday, but he'd moved away, God how he had moved away from that time of perfect innocence and essence. Perhaps here they still loved, fought and hated with that intensity alien to his newfound bourgeois affluence. Was it still possible to just *be* here. But where was *here* was it just place or was it time, perhaps even time and place. Did it still exist.

An old man sat on his doorstep apparently immune from the cold April breeze. He had been an old man when John had played here as a child.

207

He had always been an old man. "Hullo," he said squinting through failing eyesight. "Don't I know you. You're one of the Davies boys aren't you. Brynseion Street, gone now of course like half of Dowlais. Nothing left at all soon. Now which one are you, the famous one it is isn't it. Little John Davies the writer, on the tele too. Aye well your Grandad had the gift of the gab. Got it from him no doubt. Good to see you again boy. Always had it in you to go places. You was never really one of us."

This last stung John like a sharp blow. 'Never one of us' indeed. Still old man Edwards was genuinely glad to see him and enquire after all the family, most of whom were dead and gone. And his father, yes that was sad, young chap like him, which he was to old man Edwards of course, who must have been well into his nineties. "So many young men dead," he rambled sadly. "The wars, the pits, cancer." And his mother how was she now, such a bonny gel she had been in her day, no disrespect of course but half the town's young men had Maggie Jenkins in their sights, just like her mother before her, a real beauty. "We all get old boy" he bemoaned as if the realisation of some hitherto unconscious truth had suddenly dawned on him.

"Well goodnight now Mr Edwards, nice to talk to you again after all this time."

"Goodnight boy bach, God bless."

Sunday, Sabbath and holy, another day, his head in her lovely lap and his ankles in the deep shaggy pile of the expensive rug which adorned her luxurious lounge. They were listening to a radio broadcast from a Rhondda chapel to the hellfire and brimstone tones of a poetic Iorrie Jenkins, last of the great oratorical Welsh preachers. "The wages of sin is death," he warned, and went on to describe graphically how the great merciful Christian God sent down his angel of death to carry off the innocent firstborn of the enemies of his chosen people.

"Do you really think there could be a God as malevolent as that? She asked sleepily.

"Well if there is a God at all then I suppose he must be. Though he's not such a bad old bastard sometimes," he said sliding his hand up between her thighs.

"Not bad to swine like you maybe. Why should we always have to suffer?"

"Oh, and in what way are you suffering my sweet?"

"How can you ask that knowing the condition I'm in?"

He switched Iorrie Jenkins ranting off. "What do you expect. You're a big girl Marion with a big fat bank account and a personal physician on Harley Street. You didn't have to get pregnant and you certainly don't have to remain pregnant. You can afford your sordid mistakes." He was immediately remorseful for using that word. Why was he exacerbating her

208

wretchedness. It was as if there was another person as spiteful and malevolent as that old testament God lurking inside him.

"Can't you forgive and forget my wealth," she pleaded pathetically.

"Only if you relinquish it," he taunted. "Oh by the way you'll have my resignation on your desk in the morning. I'm sick of it, sick of the lot of you and your bloody Company. Sick of the sycophants and the megalomaniacs, sick with the contagion of your filthy money."

"You want to be rid of me now, now of all times."

"I want you to rid yourself of all that, that.."

"But why?"

"Because it's disgusting." He snapped irrationally.

"And if I do give it up what then?"

"What then. What do you mean 'what then'. Nothing then."

"You won't leave your wife?"

"Of course not, she's having my baby."

She flung herself at him flailing at him with both hands. "And what about me," she sobbed. "I'm having your baby."

"Then you should have known better," he heard himself say as she collapsed in a heap on the sofa. "The trouble with women like you is that you think you can have everything. You think you do have everything. Really you have nothing do you?" And he turned away from her and walked out of the door feeling like the wretched shit that he was.

The ambulance had been sitting there in the drive of their brand new home when he arrived sullen and morose as usual these days from a session at a pub decorated with horse brasses and false beams. "Her waters have burst John," Mamgu said. "I had to call the ambulance."

The corridor was white and antiseptic and smelled as all hospitals did to him of ether and something vaguely more disturbing, a smell of decay and foreboding, if foreboding had a smell. The waiting was interminable as nurses and bleary eyed doctors rushed around urgently. He was not allowed into the delivery room although he had made prior arrangements to do so. There were unfortunately complications was all he had been told. Mamgu and his mother arrived in a taxi and assured him that everything would be allright, she was in the best place and in good hands but in the process betraying the depths of their own anxiety.

The doctor who took him aside and led him into a small room was the very same who had given him the bad news about his father, only yesterday it seemed. This dreadful place was assuming an awful routine in the process of their lives. The doctor's stern visage told him already what he thought he knew. He had been in secret prayer from the moment of their arrival. Prayer to a God who either did not exist or existed most horrifically to punish even the sons of the sons of the sinning fathers.

"I'm afraid I have some very bad news for you Mr Davies. Your wife has lost her baby. Sometimes it happens for no apparent reason," he answered the unasked question.

"Lynda," John croaked, "how is my wife."

The doctor cleared his throat uneasily. "Your wife is allright....physically as far as we can see," he said awkwardly. "But she is going to require more specialised treatment."

"What do you mean, what's wrong with her?"

"Until we can get a specialist diagnosis I can only say that she appears to be catatonic. That is , she seems unable to understand or respond to our questions."

"Oh my God, oh my God."

"From her notes I see that she's been receiving psychiatric treatment over a long period. You can see her for a short time only and you must try to prepare yourself for the condition she's in. She probably won't recognise you and of course she's heavily sedated. I've sent for Mr Swithinbrook who's been supervising her psychiatric treatment and we're expecting him in about an hour. You can wait for him if you have any questions but I doubt he'll make a positive diagnosis In the short term. You may see her now."

When he saw her, her eyes were alive with grief and fear and apology. She did recognise him he was sure, but only with her sad eyes. He too had nothing to say struck dumb by the awful power of this terrible vengeful God, for this was punishment of his own wicked wilfulness wasn't it. He hated himself and loved her. He kissed her brow but she seemed beyond all loving. She said nothing other than with her eyes. Her silence was more total and introspective than he would have thought possible – so remote from him that for a horrible moment he reached out as if to shake her by her shoulders. 'Why don't you cry,' he wanted to shout as his own tears coursed down his cheeks. Could he have helped her, he doubted it. When he turned his back and walked from the room it didn't matter. He walked and left her lying silent, crying inwardly the dry tears of wrenching mental agony."

He walked past Mamgu and his mother out into the chilly drizzle looking up into the deep grey sky and cursing the whole pantheon out there mocking him.

The weeks which followed were the most painful and hellish that John had ever experienced. Of course friends and acquaintances rallied round. There was even a condolence card from Marion though she made no attempt to contact him in person. There was little change in Lynda's condition, she just lay there, fed by intravenous drips, awake but unspeaking, unable it seemed to grasp the reality of what had happened to her. But the ineffable sadness in her eyes told him all he needed to know of her torment.

There was the bleak burial of the child Angharad on a dark Pantyscallog hill, the storm clouds scudding over the western hills and drenching them with their chilling rain, where the preacher a distant cousin of John did his best to make some sense of God's will and purpose.

The psychiatrist eventually provided him with a provisional diagnosis of Catatonic Schizophrenia. "You were aware of course of your wife's prolonged treatment for Schizophrenia to which she was responding very well. You may or may not have been aware that the primary cause of her condition was the severe trauma of her father's death."

"Yes, yes I have been closely involved in her treatment since the outset."

"And you were told of the possibility of relapse."

"Yes but she seemed to be… well normal…"

"Yes, yes," he drummed his fingers irritatingly on the edge of his desk. "She had indeed made quite remarkable progress, but the problem with the condition is that it can be unpredictable… who knows if she hadn't suffered such a terrible trauma… but sadly we cannot predict these things… if the birth had been normal… Well the upshot is that she has become catatonic, but this condition is in almost all cases temporary and responsive … drugs , benzodiazepines and in extreme cases ECT."

"ECT," John reacted in amazement. "I thought that went out with Victorian asylums."

"We only use it as a last resort these days of course." Dr Swithinbrook added . "Though oddly enough it has proved remarkably effective in a number of such cases. I'm sure we won't need to go there. I'm confident that your wife will respond positively to drug treatment. The first thing is to breakdown the catatonia then there will follow prolonged treatment as before utilising drugs and individual psychotherapy.

"It is this aspect of her treatment which will really require your close cooperation Mr Davies and perhaps your grandmother, despite her age, as she has been the principal point of contact in her previous treatment. I don't know how feasible this is because she will require the closest of supervision and care, particularly in the early months of her release from hospital. Of course the Community Psychiatric Nurse and the Social Services will be involved in the care plan which we'll draw up, but one thing is certain, the avoidance of any future trauma will be a first priority, the possibility of a future pregnancy for example. It may well be a very long time, if ever, before, your wife displays what you have referred to as normal behaviour." The doctor sighed and looked John straight in the eyes, Merthyr was a small town and though few of the consultants deigned to live in the area, John knew that this one lived in Crickhowell and was probably a part of Marion's social circuit. "It's not going to be easy Mr Davies," he warned.

"Don't worry," John responded, "I'll arrange for Mamgu, my grandmother that is to move in with us, I'm sure she'll agree to that. My wife will get all the care and attention and …. love," he almost choked on the word, "that she needs."

Easy it certainly was not. Lynda remained for two weeks in a catatonic state coming out of it without recourse to ECT but not to her pre catatonic state. She remained remote and unresponsive and in what appeared to be a deep impenetrable depression. Mamgu was finally persuaded that it would be best if she moved in with John on Lynda's release from hospital. Lynda's bed was brought down into the lounge where she lay silently despite the gentle blandishments of John and Mamgu.

He contacted Rena thinking that he might throw himself into work on the proposed film but hadn't the heart for it or for anything else for that matter. She tried to persuade him down to Manorbier where she had a hideaway in which she was staying with Bill. There were things which need ironing out, she insisted. They were close to casting and the hot favourite for the Jesus role a lean ascetic American who had just starred in a big Sci-fi blockbuster, but had also performed as Brutus in Julius Caesar in the West End, had been invited along. Manorbier, the sea, work, maybe that's what he really needed. Mamgu could take care of Lynda better than he could right now.

"What if I accepted Rena's offer to join her and Bill over in Manorbier," he said to her later.

"Rena, she the one you did that crummy television play with," she asked.

"The very same," he replied. "We're doing a film now," he explained. "The story of Jesus, the real Jesus."

"Well I hope it'll be better than that play. I'm as agnostic as you can get, you know that, but even I was uneasy about it."

"That American actor Michael Reynolds is probably going to play Jesus and he's down there for the weekend. It might be what I need. I know I've been moody and getting under your feet."

She cuffed him mock jovially across the head. "Get out of it you scallywag," she reproached. "So long as it's just work, Lyndi and I'll be just fine. We've been through it before and we'll do it again. Just say hallo to Gerald for me."

"Gerald, who the hell's Gerald?"

"Gerald Cymro, Giraldus Cambrensis - You'll find him in a little garret in Manorbier Castle where he was born. Which is bullshit of course. The garret I mean. He was a wealthy man, a traveller and historian…"

"Allright Mamgu I do know who Gerald was. I'll look him up. That's the sort of stuff our American friend will be interested in I'm sure."

The journey to West Wales would have taxed the patience of old Gerald himself. Somewhat reminiscent of his traipse around Wales signing up recruits for the Third Crusade. Merthyr – Swansea – Llanelli – Carmarthen a little detour to Laugharne for a quick inspirational visit to the boathouse and the little shed overlooking the estuary where Dylan had dreamed up Captain Cat and Polly Garter, who could just as well have been denizens of Dowlais as Llareggub, Merthyr as Under Milk Wood. In the gathering dusk and the incoming tide how romantic it all seemed, who could fail to write enduring verses in such a setting, then down to Brown's with his buddies to put the world to rights. Finally the relatively short leg through Pendine and Saundersfoot to Tenby and ultimately the village of Manorbier with it's small bay and spectacular coastline where Lena's getaway was situated halfway up the hill on the back road to Pembroke. The bungalow was a welcome sight when he finally tracked it down, low roofed and looking out across the black rocks into the choppy channel. Rena threw her arms around him and Bill patted him on the back like an emotional uncle. There was no sign of the famous film star. Rena gave way to tears while Bill shrugged, his own eyes moist. "What can we say," his voice cracking. "How is Lynda?"

"She's not good, but she'll get through it with Mamgu's help. She got through it before and she'll get through it again with love and help."

"And what about you?" It was a double edged question.

John wiped at his own eyes and swallowed hard."She was so beautiful," the memory of the baby Angharad, the colour of white marble in her tiny coffin was almost too much to bear.

"Enough, enough," Bill pronounced. "Come on the Hollywood boy is up at the Castlemead probably regaling the locals who hang on his every word. They want to know all about his friendships with Dylan and Burton of course, not to mention Marilyn and Liz .He's a great raconteur. Come on you'll enjoy it, you need it." And of course he did. It was his selfish reason for being here after all.

Michael (Mike) Reynolds was everything his Hollywood screen image suggested and so much more John was to discover. He'd sought refuge in England during the McCarthy witch-hunt and become a convinced Anglophile. After starring in many screen versions of the classics he had returned to his more traditional 'tough guy' performances which had made him an international star. He was a civil rights activist and the recent sci-fi film he had starred in was an international success with it's stark warning of what dire consequences intergalactic beings might visit upon planet earth if we continued on our merry nuclear expansionist way. Labelled a 'Commie' by the McCarthyists he was still treated with considerable caution by the moguls of Hollywood, hence his interest in another British film with a controversial social message.

As they joined his little entourage before a banked up fire in the small hotel he was entertaining the group with a little homily about Marilyn Monroe and Arthur Miller. "A lovely girl," he concluded. " with an overwhelming desire to be an intellectual. Always a book in her hand and besotted with America's greatest living playwright. A little cookie of course," he chuckled tapping the side of his forehead. "She'd like nothing more than for him to write her a leading part in one of his dramas and of

213

course that's just what he's been doing recently. One of my best buddies from the mad McCarthy days," he reminisced. "A non violent man who broke his own high ethical standards one night when he busted that creepy shit Gary the snitch Cooper on the nose in a Beverly Hills soiree. He rose even higher in my estimation after that. Bogey who was there with Lauren congratulated him on the sweetest left hook he'd seen since Sugar Ray stopped Lamotta. You ever looked at those eyes, you ladies who fall for his charms, little rats eyes, sly and sneaky : High Noon, huh the little turd never realised that Foreman and Zinneman had set him up to play his antithesis. Gary Cooper what a little shit." And so the great Hollywood star continued to entertain them through dinner and after dinner until they wended their drunken way back along the coastal path to Rena's delightful den. Despite his ostentation John liked him and bade him a hearty goodnight before retiring to a room with a view across the channel though it was black now except for a light bobbing about on the swell. The sound of the sea sang him to sleep until the first grey light of dawn.

He was just finishing a telephone conversation with Mamgu, still no change, when Mike came into the room, even after a fairly heavy night it was easy to see why he had become a Hollywood heartthrob with his rugged country boy good looks and an inexplicable 'presence' which was the hallmark of all the stars, male and female. "Mornin' pardner ," he greeted in his famous Western drawl of which there had not been the slightest inflection last night.

"Mornin' " John replied. "We're in Western mode today are we?"

"I guess so," Mike chuckled, back to Boston English, shrugging his broad shoulders impishly. "Now what about this famous Welshman in the castle you were telling me about last night?" So he had been listening.

"After breakfast," John promised. "I'll take you there. Hope there's bacon and eggs."

"Over easy for me."

"Yeah, yeah, you'll be lucky if they're not scrambled pardner." It had been mid morning when they had risen and still no sign of Rena and Bill. John did a good job of the 'over easy' with rashers of bacon and strong hot tea and culfs of brown toast.

"You'll make somebody a good pardner some day," Mike drawled biting his tongue at the faux pas . John smiled ruefully in acknowledgement and no more was said until they had embarked on a tour of the castle and were stood outside the cell where Giraldus sat at his writing.

"So this is the old guy. Doesn't look up to much does he. What was he some sort of warrior king or something."

"Not really. He did a lot of writing and traipsing around Wales trying to drum up support for the Third Crusade. Traipsed around a lot of other countries as well. Spent most of his time in Paris and some time in Rome I seem to remember. Can't blame him with the winters on this coast. The only thing I remember about his writing is something of a truism, that if we, the Welsh, could become 'inseparable' we would be 'insuperable.' Quarrelsome lot we still are, that can't be denied. He had equally unflattering things to say about the Irish to whom that would be equally applicable."

"He coulda' chosen a better place than this turret if he wanted to write. I mean Lena's place is just around the bay. That's a real writer's haven wouldn't you say."

"Yeah, now you come to mention it, it really is. I could write my great novel in a place like this, but on the other hand I like the life around me, that's the great thing about Merthyr I suppose. Very provincial it may be but it has ghosts and characters and blood dripping in the streets, there's no other place like it on earth. It's so bad it's good if you know what I mean. Romance in a rough chemise. That's Idris Davies by the way, via Heine I believe."

"Heine," wasn't he a pal of Marx. Mike said stroking his chin. "Look just because I'm a pal of Miller doesn't mean....."

"That you're a Marxist. Course not. No more than I am because my Jesus is a communist."

"Your script," Mike said. "Could we talk about it. Lets go across to the Castlemead I talk better over a pint. And anyway I don't see this guy as much of a Welsh hero do you? And you're right he did have some unflattering things to say about the Irish," belying his pretence that he had known nothing of Giraldus background.

"You of Irish extraction then you old fraud?" John accused.

"Only on my grandmother's side," he admitted with a chuckle. "Not Bostonian just Philadelphian, Pittsburgan to be more precise. So you see I have something in common with you : my ancestors arrived in Pittsburgh about the same time a gang of your lot from Merthyr came over after the insurrection against the owners there. Steel and coal it's in our blood. Could be my great granddaddy was Merthyr Irish, you had plenty of em I believe. We had our own trouble's with Carnegie's goons you know. So as I said we got a lot in common."

In the lounge of the Castlemead they continued their conversation over a pint.

"I don't think we'll get an Oscar for it," Mike summarised finally. "But with the direction I know its gonna get and a few rough edges addressed in your fine script I think we'll succeed in not making a biblical epic of it. The money guys might have problems not wishing to see it as an attempt by the Zionists to paint Jesus as a commie. That's a problem for other people to resolve. Anyway I understand it's gonna be a mainly British project?"

"You'd best talk to Rena about that I haven't got a clue about the business, I'm just a hewer of wood and a drawer of water. But what about the character? How do you feel about playing the Son of God."

"I couldn't do that. But your character just believes, or comes to believe that he's the Son of God doesn't he? Or have I read it wrong."

"Well he's brought up to believe that. He is of David's line and I think from early in his life he was perceived by Jewish scholars and prophets as the chosen one. That stage managed entry into Jerusalem was clearly the living out of Biblical prophecy. I think however that he was torn between his politics, which was revolutionary and liberationist, and all that religious mysticism. That's the way I try to portray him. But like all these things its a working out not a piece of historical reportage."

"Close enough, close enough," Mike commented. "I need to steep myself in it of course, the script and some other stuff, I know the Bible stuff backwards from my Pittsburgh childhood. Look I don't wanna sit in here boozin' all day you'll get the wrong impression of me, that's just my Hollywood image. Let's take a stroll along this stunning coastline of yours and talk some more."

It was one of those strange magical April days you sometimes get in Wales when the daffodils presage a balmy May and inspires thoughts of a possible summer to come. They dawdled along the beach then up over the black rocks draped with bladder wrack onto the coastal path and up to the megalith where they stopped. Mike stepped close to him and placed a hand lightly on his arm with a knowing look in his blue magnetic eyes. John shrugged him off gently with an equally knowing shake of the head. So it was true then, those rumours in the scandal mags. He hadn't wanted to believe it as he hadn't wanted to believe it of Montgomery Clift, or Burt Lancaster or even Tony Curtis, Rock Hudson didn't seem to matter so much. "Oh well," shrugged Mike, the hero of the Mid West dust bowl, the wild John the Baptist, the baleful Macbeth, the drifter from the plains.

John sought in vain for something to relieve the frisson that for a moment chilled the balmy air. 'Such a waste' was the immediate response that went through his head, thinking of those tempestuous co-stars, Ava Gardner, Kim Novak, Lana Turner, Maureen O'Hara. But wasn't there just a fraction of a millisecond when the thought 'what if' had occurred to him, only to be snuffed out by what could only be described as an intense feeling of moral indignation born seemingly of an atavism which contradicted what he thought he stood for intellectually. "Lana Turner, Maureen O'Hara, Marilyn Monroe even little Doris Day," he muttered aloud with a questioning inflection.

Mike looked at him for a moment as if he didn't understand, then as enlightenment dawned he smiled widely. "The sexual mores of Hollywood," he said, "the gods and goddesses of the great cinema going masses. It's simple really, like all the occupants of the Greek Pantheon we have feet of clay. We want the same things everybody else does : but in that frantic illusion which is Hollywood we can avail ourselves of everything we want. Women, for that's all those sex goddesses are, are for the taking. Not that they ever interested me in that way. I wasn't driven to homoeroticism as a reaction against the perfidy of women, god knows men are even more perfidious. No 'tis but mine own nature."

John took a step forward and made what was for him a brave gesture, he put his arms around Mike and hugged him warmly. "Isn't this a wonderful place," he said stepping back finally and gesturing towards the megalith with its great capstone.

"It sure is," Mike agreed. "What is it?"

"A Dolmen, a burial chamber, The Kings Quoit," John replied.

"The Kings what? Which King was that."

"The name's a puzzle," John replied. "Quoits is an ancient game played with discs, of steel or iron more recently but conceivably with stone in an earlier epoch. I think the Romans brought it over, borrowed from the Greeks. The capstone could be said to resemble such a disk, I don't know. As for which King, well there were plenty of Welsh or British Kings and Princes who knows. Of course there was Henry Tudor who was born in Pembroke Castle just a few miles down the coastline. But this thing has been a monument for the last four thousand years or so- Neolithic I think, when it couldn't have been King anybody's quoit could it?"

"You guys with your history, ours only starts with the Pilgrim Fathers. Conveniently discounting the American Indians of course, who we succeeded in virtually eliminating."

They dawdled along the path for quite a way until their progress was blocked by a high barb wired fence with a notice proclaiming the land to be the property of the MOD which could only be accessed with written authority.

"Well there goes our stroll pardner," John announced. "Let's see if Rena's got anything cooked up for us."

"You know John, I think you and I could become good friends." Mike chuckled. The sun had suffused itself in a grey murk and chilling wind had begun to blow in with the tide.

"That's more like it," John pulled his jacket more lightly around him. "This is the Pembroke I know and love, there'll be rain soon. Come on."

"I heard Bill and Rena talk about your problems," Mike said. "I'm truly sorry. I can only say I hope things turn out well for your wife."

"She'll get through it with help," John said wryly. "It's just that my life has become so fucking complicated, it seems to be happening at a thousand miles an hour and I'm just caught up in it like a whirlwind."

"I know the feeling pardner I've had to put the brakes on mine or I was heading for hell in a handcart."

217

"My father died recently and that caused me to try to take stock. All the things I wanted to say to him to make up for all the silences ands misunderstandings, how I wanted him to share in my success, if only in the material benefits of it."

"Ah the old bitch goddess of success," Mike ruminated. "Don't fall for her charms Pardner, she's a chimera. But I know exactly what you mean. My father died asking why it was I'd never got a real job. All the fame and the big cars and the mansions never impressed him one little bit. But he would have been proud of the stance I took against Macarthy and his stupid Unamerican Activities Committee. That's what you gotta do Pardner if you honour his memory be true to the good things he taught you."

"I think that's what my mother and Mamgu have been trying to say to me, but then this, like the punishment of a wrathful God for all my sins…"

"Don't go there Pardner," Mike took him by the arm. "Such a God is untenable, down that road nihilism lies. There are lots of good things in this life but they have nothing to do with any God. That's at the essence of your script isn't it. Hey Pardner there may not be an Oscar in it for us but it's gonna be a great film, you'll see."

"Here come the returning adventurers ," called Bill his feet up on a stool before the open fire, examining some pages of prints with an eyeglass.

"Could you guys do with a sandwich?" Rena called from the kitchen."I've got a treat for you later, my angler from the Mead has come up with a brace of beautiful sea bass which the clever Rena is going to bake for your delectation. How about that?"

"Bill, don't ever let some suave Lothario steal this gorgeous woman away from you." John teased.

"Hey she only does this for special visitors," Bill complained. "I survive on a diet of beans on toast and quick trips into Tenby to the chippy if I'm lucky."

"You three boys have a sandwich for now, bugger off to the Mead for a couple of pints, only a couple mind I don't want you ruining your appetites. Back here for six o'clock sharp. OK."

"Jah mein liebling your orders will be obeyed at all times without question.?

"I should think so too. John we were so sorry ……. I don't know what to say. We'll talk later if that's allright." John nodded his affirmation. It would have to be broached sometime he supposed.

There still were few customers in the Castlemead this not being the tourist season, so they had the lounge to themselves. Bill had brought along his trusty Leica not being one to lose an opportunity. He took some shots of John and Mike together who had picked up where they left off earlier in the afternoon, discussing the script, which it turned out Bill had read and so was able to make his own contribution.

218

"It would take a bloody atheist like you to write the best Jesus script since, since, well since the beginning of cinematic scripts I suppose. Wouldn't you agree Mike."

Mike sipped slowly not at his pint but at the best malt available, a double of course, nodding his head in agreement. "Oddly enough Jesus has mostly had a supporting role in most of the biblical films, like The Robe with our friend Burton and what was the other one. Cameo roles really."

"Quo Vadis," recited John, "but not all of them, there's B de Mille's King of Kings, I got tips on Mary Magdalene from that, and one recently from Bunuel, Nazerin. Oh I've studied the oeuvre," he smiled."But this will be the best by a centurion mile."

"Of course it will," they slapped each other's backs and toasted their success which Bill was set to share having wormed his way into the publicity department via Rena, hence all the shooting with the Leica.

They were only half an hour late but clever Rena had anticipated that and the bass with herbs and fresh veg and dauphineoise potatoes all swilled down with Niersteiner was a triumph. Crème brulee with percolated coffee to follow and to finish off a cheeseboard with cream crackers and a cigar for the Yank and satisfaction was complete.

With Mike the chivalrous assisting Rena in the kitchen with the washing up Bill and John sipped their brandies before the heaped up log fire. April spring having given way to April showers and now April storm with the wind buffeting the windows. John had rung Mamgu : no change. Bill shifted uncomfortably by the fire. "We got to talk butty," he apologised. "I've had my instructions."

John shrugged. "You mean serious talk like me and Lynda and Marion."

"What happened with Lyn and the baby, well I don't really know what to say. It's just fucking awful but now you've got Marion in the club. She told Rena of course and she's been giving me hell about it as if I'm the prick responsible rather than you, you bloody moron."

"Tell it straight like it is why don't you. You think I don't feel bad enough about it?"

"Not from what Marion says. You've behaved like a first class prick John. As if all this has little or nothing to do with you. She doesn't want an abortion. It's not as easy as that is it?"

"So what am I supposed to do, leave Linda now, you know I can't do that."

"Of course not but you do have an obligation to Marion surely you can see that. It was bad enough what you did to her daughter but this…"

John put his head in his hands and the tears began to flow. "It's just too much," he moaned "I know I'm a bastard, but what can I do?"

"You can start by not feeling so sorry for yourself," Rena had returned with Mike looking sheepish in the background. "You're a green young man John, but with a rare talent. If you don't make the right decision now you're going to fuck up the rest of your life. Look Marion wants a child, Lynda wanted a child, I presume even you wanted a child. Lynda with all her wits about her seemed prepared to share you with Marion, perhaps a ménage a trois could work out, it wouldn't be the first time. Nursing her back to health is understandably your first consideration right now but don't treat Marion like a whore, you know she doesn't deserve that."

John brushed away the tears with his sleeve. "And I came here to hide from it," he said. "That was stupid wasn't it. I was going to talk about my wonderful script. Mine, me, me. What an ego. Well we are going to talk about my script because all this has been about my work and without that there's nothing."

"So let's get on with it," Rena replied arming herself with sheaves of manuscript from her tiny study. Mike's got a few good ideas and the director's got a few more."

And so they talked the night away until the grey dawn revealed a heaving sea. Bill had been the first to retreat wearily to his bed and finally Mike and Rena followed. John sat, his mind a whirl of contradictions and his body alive with an indescribable torment that felt as if he was being torn into tiny fragments. Perhaps there was something in what Rena had said, he would have to make it up with Marion.

It was all very confusing but in John's present state of mind he wasn't at all sure if that's what he wanted and when he left the house he just drove aimlessly, but not aimlessly enough not to end up in Crickhowell, bypassing Merthyr as if he had no business there.

He parked in the street and spent the next couple of hours on a pub crawl. Crickhowell is a small place but still boasts enough bars in which to get considerably drunk. He drank alone, wandering from bar to bar in a semi stupor with glassy staring eyes, but not from the drink. He was consumed with a melancholy loneliness which he felt might never be assuaged because it was a part of him, had always been a part of him integral with all the other traits, inherited and learned, which went to make up the whole complexity of his self. He was still sober as a Methodist Minister when he completed the circle and climbed back into his car and made his way slowly to Carnford Manor. Dusk was rapidly falling and a light beamed onto the driveway. The cars were garaged and smoke trailed from the chimney of the coach house indicating the factotum's presence. What was there to get up to after a hard day's chauffeuring, he wondered.

He rang the bell on the front door of the main house and when she opened it the look he received was simultaneously one of reproach and welcome. "Oh it's you. You might as well come in."

He followed her through the lounge into the kitchen where she had been preparing a healthy fruit drink. The outline beneath her silky nightwear betrayed her budding pregnancy. "I didn't want to hurt anybody," he said

220

stupidly as he came to her side. "But what can you do with an omnipotent God who rains down wrath on the heads of the innocent. God is a bastard," he said quietly. "God is a bastard," he repeated more loudly. "All you hypocritical bastards out there, can you hear me." He walked across to a window and flung it open. "God is a bastard," he shouted to the twinkling lights of the farm houses on the dark hills. "God is a bastard. God is a bastard." He closed the window and returned and said quietly as he sat at the kitchen table. "God is a horrible monstrous bastard." She looked into his red eyes not quite knowing what to do as he began to sob silently. "God is a bastard," he sobbed, "but I won't let the bastard beat me. He can never beat the bad because we have no innocence." She reached out and took his hands in hers. "Just love me," he pleaded. "Lots and lots of love just smother me with it."

"But without innocence it's impossible to love," she said sadly, taking his head in her hands with an almost maternal affection. But like a selfish child he didn't understand.

Was this the face that launched a thousand ships
And burned the topless towers of Ilium.
Sweet Helen make me immortal with a kiss.
Her heart sucks forth my soul, see where it flies.
Come Helen, come give me my soul again.
Here will I dwell for heaven is in those lips,
And all is dross that is not Helen.

He was reading Marlowe's mighty line in his best Dylan Thomas for the cameras when there was competition from the back of the auditorium. The BBC were filming a follow up to the earlier series of the Merthyr Five and the producer was doing his nut at this unrehearsed interruption.

"Allright Dai what the bloody hell are you shouting about now, don't you know its sacrilege to interrupt the magnificent Marlowe's mighty line?"

"Never mind bloody M…Marlowe's m..mighty bloody line," the excitable shop steward stammered. "What about the almighty b..bloody Mason's b..bloody line."

"That's down in Dixie man," he couldn't help retorting for the benefit of his television audience. "What has the mad management done to irritate you now?"

"You, you should b..bloodywell know, you're so thick with the b..bastards."

"Sorry everybody," John announced looks like we've got a minor catastrophe on our hands again. But I'm not on the Board now as you all know : no longer privy to its machinations. But you've got Fred the Red in there to take my place so what can go wrong. Excuse me a minute while I talk to Dai. What is it Dai that's so urgent you've got to ….."

"That's just it F..Fred the Red's resigned. That b..bastard Hawtin's outs..s..smarted him. B..b..big redundancies on the way."

Marion was staying in the Dowlais flat as she more frequently did these days. All the infighting that was taking place on the Mason's Board was energy sapping and pregnancy at her age didn't help. So he was able to visit more easily avoiding the drag over to Crickhowell. Though he never needed to make excuses for that, although little was said between him and Lynda the understanding was still there. She was beginning to come out of her shell a little now but it was much too early for serious discussion about their situation. Talking to Marion had become more difficult however, there was a new steeliness about her, especially in relation to her position at Mason's. If he'd had any thoughts about her easing herself out of that situation he'd had to think again, she was more determined to stay at the helm than ever. She had told him she was taking back control of her life as if he had somehow stolen it from her.

"That bastard Hawtin used that stupid prick Fred (Fred the Red, what a joke) to get rid of that other idiot Dewey," she continued the rant that had begun as soon as he had arrived. "He already had Westbury in his pocket and bought over the other two with promises of bigger salaries and ideas to repeal all the progressive policies that you were persuasive enough to have implemented. I could still have saved the day if it were not for Fred's hot headed 'principled' resignation. But all's not lost yet, none of those bastards is beyond a bribe and my chequebook is still fatter than Hawtin's. He needn't think I wont use it extravagantly if the need arises. What makes the egotistical bastard think he can wrestle control from me."

"Calm down," he counselled all this hypertension is bad for the baby. I'll put the kettle on." The flat was quite small and self contained by Marion's standards, built as it was as an annexe to the Boardroom which He supposed was quite convenient. The lounge had a fine view over the rooftops of Dowlais, if that could be defined as a fine view. The back, where the kitchen was provided an even finer view of the area which had once been the greatest ironworks in the world, of which only the spoil heaps were its monument. "Well the workers won't take it lying down that's for sure," he said handing her a cup of steaming hot tea every bit as good as Dai, the Ammonia plant control room operator, could produce. The thought of it took him back to that moment where it all seemed to have started, when the 'cheeky apprentice' had told his foreman to "fuck off." "Why the hell did Hawtin and his goons have to react like this anyway. The Company has benefitted as much as the workforce. The increase in productivity has been

222

the subject of articles in the industrial press, and Mason's has seen its market share increase in leaps and bounds. Old Lenin was right, the capitalist will sell the rope with which he is about to be hanged and what's more will haggle about the price."

She sipped pensively at her tea for a moment then as if it was too much to ask to keep her anger from bubbling up to the surface she started up again. "Bloody Hawtin," she muttered as much to herself as to John. "The bastard's drunk with the lust for power. What does he care if productivity goes down so long as he's at the helm and able to manipulate things just the way he wants them, with a weak and cringing crew afraid to stand up to him. But don't you worry, he's taken on more than he bargained for. Oh yes he's been clever allright, too damn clever for his own good. Do you know what he did, he's had the Sales group working overtime distributing projected orders two months ahead of schedule and bullying Production into overtime to meet the increased demand. I should never have trusted the bastard, I never used to. I'm either getting soft or going mad and it's all your fault. With the big bulge of school leavers this July he's got a ready made replacement workforce so what does it matter if there should be a few redundancies. There's nothing new in that, that's the way we always worked it. I must have had my head in the sand. Taking on juveniles to replace the more mature staff has been a maxim in this business for as long as I can remember. You used to howl abuse at me for it. But no more of that the iron lady is back in harness."

"That's disgusting," John spat scornfully, "You're just like animals, all of you . No whoremasters, that's what you all are. Last century we had the ironmasters, now we have the whoremasters. Lawrence was right, you are all beetles, dung beetles."

She put down the dregs of her tea and gave him a withering look. "Well now Marx's integrated man has spoken, the great philosopher poet John Davies. You speak with great authority on the question of whoremasters don't you, being such an accomplished one yourself. You used us all like whores; me, my daughter, Rena and worst of all the simple child bride, poor Lynda. Don't you dare to lecture me on morality you... you pimp."

Her words cut him to the quick, was that the way she really felt about him. He sat down and held his head in his hands. What was the matter with him, he could no longer rationalise his relationships. Was he responsible for the baby's death. Had he really incurred the wrath of a vengeful malevolent God. The only way to bring the guilty to repentance being to afflict the innocent. Thus it had been with the firstborn of the poor suffering subjects of the Pharaoh. And when the chosen people had in their turn incurred his jealous wrath He had cursed every unborn innocent Jew down through the ages even to the gates of Dachau.

The fruit of his love with Lynda had been rotten and now Marion's pregnancy was becoming a new cruel affliction which he wished he could avoid. A God as vicious and unjust as this must surely be resisted, His omnipotence challenged if life was to be anything other than a pessimistic fatalism. "I didn't want it this way," he said with a trace of uncertainty. "I didn't, I couldn't create the circumstances responsible for this state of affairs."

"Didn't you," she sneered accusingly. Had he? He had thought of it certainly, talked of it even. Intent there must have been. "Don't worry lover," she said icily. "If it comes to a showdown I can insist on a card vote."

"And you'd win such a vote."

"Oh yes. I've always retained a controlling interest. What he didn't realise was that when Dewey was removed through the machinations of Hawtin and your fat communist friend his stock reverted to me. Hawtin had hoped to buy him off but was unaware that I had Dewey bound under a contractual obligation to offer them to me."

"God if I'd known that I'd have encouraged you to sack the twisting bastard long ago."

"Your days of advice are over John. If that daft disciple of yours had kept his cool we could have smoothed the whole thing over with no fuss. As it is the shit is really going to hit the fan."

"No bloody disciple of mine," John protested. "He's a bloody commie and an orthodox one at that."

She turned away from him impatiently. "All this talk is utterly inconsequential," she insisted. Her confidence growing every minute with the reassertion of her authority. "In future you stick to writing and leave me to the management of my affairs. The flirtation with democracy is over comrade. Democracy is not a holy writ and people are often better off for not having it. I intend to use my power and influence to regain the almost autonomous control I enjoyed before the advent of that imitation Messiah out of Gwalia. A few of the concepts you introduced I shall be happy to retain but workers on the Board is henceforth strictly a no-no. I like my trade unionists on the other side of the table where I can see their eyeballs , that truly symbolises our relationship with them according to the classical Marxist view. Your revisionism is a weakness, an acquiescence to the current managerialism. I prefer polarisation, then we all know exactly where we stand.."

"The tycoon who read Marx," John sniggered."A nice title for my next novel perhaps.

"Oh Marx was right," she continued to taunt him. "He warned against bourgeois social democrats like you. The only real politics is the politics of confrontation and until the dictatorship of the proletariat arrives we have the dictatorship of capital and I know which side my bread is buttered on. We're real opponents now John, you tried to warn me of that from the start in your daft romantic sort of way. You threatened to destroy me and you almost succeeded but like all you wishy washy liberal revolutionaries you completely underestimated the will of capital to survive. I have the real power, it is as always embodied in money. With it I can bribe and buy my fellow mercenaries. Perhaps I can't quite buy your ideology, but I can suppress it, stifle it, smother it, crush it until it is utterly innocuous and emasculated – and I will."

He walked from the room slowly out into the road and up towards Doctor's Pitch and the Guest Keen Memorial Hall where the meeting was being held. She was probably right . He passed a hand over his eyes. He felt slightly faint and dizzy. It was the white heat of repressed anger which seemed to press upward on the inside of his skull producing an emotion which shifted erratically between deep despair and wild euphoria. As he reached the entrance lobby the noise of a crowd simmering just below boiling point drifted out to him. This was not the time or the place, he must pour oil on troubled waters. He composed himself and with a confident smile went in to address them.

Freddy Jones was on the stage with a mike addressing an already angry crowd. John could scarcely suppress his mirth. It was like a comic opera version of Lenin at the Finland Station. He was gesticulating wildly with the crowd growling in response to his simplistic rhetoric. John watched enthralled as the little fat man whipped them up into a frenzy. Fists were waved and voices raised with hackneyed mantras. "What de we want," and "When do we want it. NOW." Suddenly they turned as one and Fred bustled through tem to face the entrance as if they were about to spill into the road and attack the imaginary barricades. They had to be dissuaded for the moment , the time was not yet ripe. He held up his arms palms facing them . Voices called out shrill demands. John gestured again for silence but it took Freddy's presence alongside him eventually to quieten them down.

"We want the Chairman not her messenger boy one of Freddy's lieutenants shouted.

"Now boys," Freddy responded, for it was the boys who were doing most of the shouting, "Give the lad a chance. He's always done allright by us, let him have his say." The crowd's raucous baying subsided enough for him to speak.

"All right ," he called loudly, "I'm not going to beat about the bush. My relationship with the Chairman doesn't alter which side I'm on, it never has. In the end she's just another chiselling bastard from the boss class and I don't forget it. But the point is this - those crooks would welcome an all out strike right now. In fact they're banking on it because they've planned for it as part of their lousy strategy. To strike now would be to play right into their hands."

"Get out of it Davies. Did she send you out to tell us that.?"

There were restless mutterings once again and to John's amazement Ted could be seen with one or two of his anarchist confederates in animated conversation at the back of the crowd.

225

"Wait a minute, wait a minute. What I have to tell you now is the benefit of my inside knowledge. If you don' want to listen then you'll have to suffer the consequences." There were more catcalls at this and once again Fred had to gesticulate to quell their growing impatience. "There's only one way to beat the bastards now," he continued, "and that's to call their bluff; not by going on strike but rather to engage in a work in before their redundancies have been trough the negotiating process, which I have to remind you is only on the books because of the new package on consultation which we recently got through the Board, only we don't have anybody on the Board any more do we," he remonstrated and Fred's face turned a bright red. "Now Listen…no listen," he insisted. "They've had you working overtime to fulfil their overflowing order books. Striking now would be exactly what they want. This would be followed by layoffs as they tear up the recent agreements. July will see a new tranche of potential workers coming out of school - kids anxious to fill the vacancies which your redundancies will have created. It'll be back to the worst of the bad old days. Is that what you want.

"I know it's not what you expected to hear," he continued, in relative silence now that what he was saying was beginning to sink in. "It's a lot for you to take in now but your best plan is not simply to go into work but to push up productivity even higher than the record levels you've been achieving in recent months. Strategically it's the best weapon you have. Hey will have made the fatal mistake of underestimating us. And I can tell you there's a battle going on for control of the Board between the soft and the hard right and we've got an interest in it's outcome and our actions will go some way to determining it. Let them play out their power game at the top. Let them duel to the death if they like but don't allow them to make us the casualties. Let's show them that we still have a trick or two up our sleeves. Continue to work and insist that negotiations take place on the basis of our current agreements. Keep working until the time comes when we can strike on our own terms if those agreements are not kept – when it will hurt them most, when existing orders have been cleared and new one's start to come in as they inevitably will, that's when it will hit them hardest. And if there's a lockout respond with a work in. This way we'll have the media on our side for a change."

The crowd began to mutter again but more mutedly and with less anger. "How do we know you're not just a Boardroom stooge," called the principal heckler.

"Because I don't have to do this for a living any more," John replied, and there must have been something in the finality of what he was saying which convinced them. The sight of Fred nodding his agreement also had it's effect. The crowd broke up slowly and the men and girls went grumbling back to their jobs following a resolution calling for further meetings . John heaved a sigh of relief, the militancy which had just been held in check would be all the easier the re-ignite when the stocks had been exhausted and all and sundry threatened with the dole. That would be the time for action unless madam Chairman could work a miracle.

Sunday afternoon ,roast dinner in the oven, Mamgu and mother in the kitchen John and Lynda listening to the new 'hi-fi' stereo unit MJQ with Milt Jackson tinkling out Skating in Central Park. John tucked behind the Sunday Times, who would become the new leader of the Labour Party, Brown, Wilson, Callaghan? Wilson seemed to be the choice of the Left, Brown was a bit of a drunkard and a loose cannon, while Callaghan was the favourite for some of the Trade Unions, particularly USDAW which sponsored him. As for who was most likely to win an election, well wily Wilson won that one hands down.

Lynda's rehabilitation had been steady and was once again lucid and 'normal' most of the time with occasional lapses to that childhood state of the girl of his nightmares.

"Do you like this music. It's the Modern Jazz Quartet," he explained. "Milt Jackson on the vibes."

"Its very nice, very soothing, I like the sound of that instrument, like a Xylophone but with vibrato."

John chuckled well aren't you the one, that's exactly what it is, and I'm supposed to be the jazz aficionado. Lionel Hampton was the inspiration of course. They're more melodic now, used to be be-bop, played with Dizzie and all." He waved a hand at his enormously expanded record collection on shelves of 'Ladderax' which was all the rage in the houses of the rampantly upward mobile. But you used to love all that Elvis stuff didn't you and those rock and rollers. Why don't you buy a load of those. Remember how we used to jive down the Dowlais School Youth Club and the Catholic Hall. We'll have to go again sometime soon Lynd or the Kirkhouse, you liked it there didn't you?"

Her response to this was to display her melancholia again. "I'll go and help in the kitchen," she said. A few moments later Mamgu came in wagging her finger at him.

"What have you been saying to upset that girl," she accused.

"Upset I didn't know she was upset. We were just talking about music and dancing and how she like to jive in the Kirkhouse. Just making conversation. Why should that upset her?"

"Because she knows that you wont will you, not while you......
while you still...... you're still seeing that bloody woman aren't you?"

"That bloody woman, why do you speak of her as that bloody woman. She's not the devil incarnate you know, in many ways she's an admirable woman. Good Dowlais working class, wasn't born with a silver spoon in her mouth you know."

"No. But she's run that bloody sweat shop long enough hasn't she?" She stood there hands on hips her plump aproned body shaking.

"She gave me my big chance Mamgu, we achieved a lot of good things there. Now Fred the Red has gone and screwed things up, resigning when the inevitable right wing reaction came. Now the shit has really hit the fan."

"And you still stick with her. Do you think Lynda doesn't know that?"

"Of course she bloody knows it. She always knew it. She knew it when we married. Ours is not necessarily the sort of relationship you think it is Mamgu. She knows I'll never desert her as long as she needs me."

"You mean she's prepared to put up with the situation because she really hasn't any choice."

"That's not the way it is at all. Lynda and I …."

"Don't you try to flannel me John Davies. You know what you're doing is wrong."

"Mamgu, just leave it will you. I know you mean well you love Lynda like your own child but despite her illness she's an adult and we can work it out. The situation may be exceptional but its certainly not unique and it can be accommodated."

"Accommodated. They tell me she's pregnant. How can that be accommodated?" How did Mamgu know this, and if she knew did Lynda? Mamgu intuited his concern. "It's only a matter of time before she finds out," she said. "And what do you suppose that will do for her recovery, tell me that my boy. So what do you propose to do about it?"

John shook his head. It would be difficult but he had persuaded himself that it could all be 'accommodated'.

A breathless call from Geraint to meet, not at the Dowlo but the Morlais, popular watering hole for Welsh Nats and say it in undertones, the FWA (Free Wales Army), Captain Hill and his merry band. Well it should prove interesting he supposed and better than sitting here looking out at the dark gray landscape in the bleak gray rain. When he arrived the whole gang were there in the little backroom where all the plots were hatched. In the far corner sat Dai the Bomber and next to him a man who John immediately recognised as Sir Rhys Parry Jones a really grand panjandrum with connections in very high places, alongside him was none other than Guto Ap Griffiths reputed Commander in Chief of the smallest army in the world. Next to him Captain Hill with his right foot in a cast shod with a cutaway rubber tyre, perhaps the consequence of an ill executed manoeuvre on the Twynau Gwynion where such secret activities were rumoured to take place. Well, well, he thought, what brings us all here, something of great moment, perhaps the announcing of a new military strategy to free Wales from the yoke of English Imperialism, no doubt all would be revealed in due course.

Geraint and Ted brought in several pints on a battered tray from the bar in the adjacent room. Then with a surreptitious look into the corridor the door was closed with an air of ritual solemnity as Sir Rhys rose to his feet. He held up his hands for silence before taking two exaggerated strides towards John and standing staring into his eyes, his faced wreathed with a beaming smile and addressed him. "Cymrawd," he said. "It gives me the greatest pleasure to confer upon you the highest civic honour of our organisation." With which he proceeded to hang a small silver dragon on a red ribbon around John's neck. "For your outstanding contribution to Welsh culture," he intoned, then sotto voce "and in recognition of your recent generous donations to our cause." John stood dumbfounded as the little room rang with the cheers of its occupants and John sought explanation in the eyes of Ted and Geraint. Drinks were taken and a solemn oath sworn in Welsh which made the Freemason's consequences for betrayal of confidence sound like a minor admonition.

Ted and Geraint obviously considered this to be a great joke. It transpired that Ted had been making generous donations from his agent's fees via Geraint who had long been a donor to the republican cause, and making them in John's name. "You mean I've been contributing indirectly to these clowns blowing up water pipelines in the Welsh hills," he demanded with an anger which he found hard to sustain given the absurdity of the whole situation.

Ted shrugged with a smile. "Well blowing up pipelines is a more honourable endeavour than blowing cultural farts at the Establishment which is all you lot seem to have been doing recently."

The only sensible response to this nonsense of course was to get drunk.

They had just about succeeded in doing that when there was 'a pounding at the gate' and lo and behold who should be responsible for the hammering but those old stalwarts of the local constabulary who had been responsible for detaining the five following the demonstration in town. They were accompanied on this occasion by two plainclothes men with stony faces, not known to anybody, so clearly not local, looking all the world like those representations of Tweedledum and Tweedledee remembered from an old original print of the Lewis Carol classic, obviously Special Branch John quickly concluded.

In the Station sat with a desk lamp shining in his eyes like something from a film noir starring Fred MacMurray he was put in mind of the old Marxist axiom, first time farce, second time tragedy, for Tweedledum and Tweedledee were deadly serious, scaringly menacing and the outlook inevitably tragic.

"Not the first time you've been in this situation is it," said Tweedledum.

"And what situation is that - being interviewed by two intellectuals from the Special Branch is it - or are you two MI something or other?"

"Oh we've got a clever bugger here," said Tweedledee moving alongside John and digging him in the ribs with the end of a rolled up newspaper, catching him by the scruff of his jacket to prevent him from falling of the chair. "But we know how to respond to clever buggers don't we," digging him again, this time in the solar plexus. This was serious stuff and it hurt like hell. He'd heard about these kinds of interviews and read about them in modern spy novels of course. But this was the real thing and he was scared shitless. "Now," demanded Tweedledee, "let's be having a precise account of your movements today from the time you dragged your tired arse out of bed."

This was not the boys from the local nick – this was serious.

"What if I don't want to answer any of your bloody questions. After all it's not as if I have to. I know my rights."

"Huh," scoffed Tweedledum, "he knows 'is fuckin' rights this one."

"A clever bastard," replied Tweedledee. "A veritable bar-room lawyer."

"Now look sonny," Tweedledum continued. "There's two ways we can do this...."

"The easy way," Tweedledee interpolated.

"....or the hard way," Tweedledum completed. "Now a clever bastard like you surely knows the difference between the easy way and the hard way. All we want to know is how much you know about these lunatics you've been associating with."

"I come into contact with lots of lunatics," John protested, flinching in anticipation. "Which particular lunatics are you referring to?"

"Let's begin with the Captain then shall we. We can state categorically that you've come into contact with him can't we. You were after all the recipient of some sort of decoration conferred on you by the, shall we call it 'the organisation'." He reached across and took the little medallion between forefinger and thumb.

"Wonder what you have to do to receive the 'organisation's' greatest honour," Tweedledee interrupted again. "Must be something very important.."

"Very dangerous even," Tweedledum suggested.

"Like having a section of cast iron pipeline dropped on your big clumsy foot," Tweedledee sniggered upon which they both burst into disdainful laughter. Tweedledum suddenly lurched around he table and stamped his size fourteen on John's toes.

John tried manfully to curb his involuntary yelp of agony but only succeeded in emitting a strangulated scream of pain.

"Oh my I'm so sorry I accidentally stepped on your toes. This time it was Tweedledum who sniggered. "As I was saying there's an easy way and a hard way we can do this. I'm sure you would prefer the easy way, I certainly would. Now tell us, in detail what you and your friends have been up to today. "

"I cant tell you what the people you refer to as my friends have been up to today as I didn't meet them until I came to the pub this evening." John decided it was time to be straightforward. The size fourteen treatment had been the last straw. These idiots meant business.

An hour more of much the same and the Tweedles finally appeared to be satisfied that John was more or less innocent, or at least that there was nothing for the time being with which they could charge him. He was cautioned and released without recourse to one of Marion's legal contacts. Just wait until he got his hands on those other two idiots Ted and Geraint, what the fuck could they possibly be thinking of.

CHAPTER 17

The entrance to Mason's was overwhelmed by the crowd. To add to the hundreds who worked there the local Trade Unions Council had brought out many of it's own members and the other usual fringe groups waved their banners and chanted their slogans. The factory breathed its heavy vapour against a cold sky its windows flashing white as the pale sun occasionally broke through the grey cloud cover. Several speeches had aroused the impatient crowd who had listened with increasing tension and unease to their various representatives, but the one they were still waiting for with growing anticipation was John.

Some of the fringe groups with Geraint and Ted at their core were chanting for radical action and John taking his place at the top of the steps smiled dismissively at them. He started to address the crowd soberly, reminding his audience of the many concessions that had been gained over the past year- concessions that had led corporations across the land to accede to similar demands for what was after all nothing more than a belated recognition of basic workers rights.

"One of the basic rights of anyone in modern British society is the right to a productive life wherever it is possible. But now they seek to violate even that. The management of Mason's want arbitrarily to take away the livelihoods of many of us simply to maximise their profits : there is no other reason given for these layoffs, because there is no other reason. The same people who threw up the slums around the great ironworks of the last century seem still to be running things.

"So what are we going to do about it. Isn't a century of slavery enough. We haven't come very far have we." He paused for effect and great numbers of the crowd shouted their agreement. "No. The power, the money is still in the tight fisted hands of the greedy irresponsible few. Things will never change until we decide to take control of our own destiny; until we own the means of production." This brought great cheers from the far left groups who waved their banners from the fringe. This was the Marxist language they understood and revered.

"There might have been some validity for these redundancies if the company was on its knees but we know the order books are full. The fact is this company is ripe for expansion. These redundancies were deliberately manipulated by ruthless immoral men for whom we are the mere pawns in their political power struggle. Even now they are all up there in the boardroom trying to agree on their next move. And what does our great democratic press have to say about it....nothing, nothing. Can you imagine what the headlines would have been if we had been on strike. They would be screaming about greedy strikers, irresponsible militants, communist agitators. There would be calls for legislation to curb the powers of the unions. But now the shoe is on the on the other foot, nothing. Not a mention that there is a boardroom power struggle and that they are deadlocked, stalemated to the extent that no policy decisions are being made. Well comrades it's about time that some of those decisions were taken for them."

There was a growing restlessness in the crowd now. Voices from the militant fringe were being raised urging all kinds of action. And from the fringes of the throng the first whiff of irrational violence began to emerge. A stone shattered a window in the front of the vestibule. John felt suddenly disturbed by what he took to be the power of his own oratory. 'Work in....takeover....the product of our labour belongs to us...crawl home with your tails between your legs like beaten dogs or stand together now and fight for what is ours by right...' Another stone and another shattered window, then another and another. The whiff of violence now an all pervading stench. The meekest of men were caught up in it and the women too, strange as that seemed. People who knew nothing about Taff Merthyr , Tonypandy and 'The Miners Next Step'. John was suddenly carried forward by the throng which was becoming a mob. Even Fat Freddy that most docile of communists brandished a baton.

"Occupy, occupy, occupy," the call seemed to rise simultaneously from a hundred voices. Those on the fringe were in their element now, dreams of instant revolution, long cherished and called for with a naïve insistence now appeared live and imminent. And the youngsters, of whom there were many in the workforce were all for it. It was a novel situation and weren't they fed up to the teeth with useless words. Words had a place no doubt but it was action that was needed now. John Davies was right he'd done a lot for them during his time on the Board but all that had come to nothing. And now there were other voices being raised making more urgent demands.

The mob was on the move with new leaders now bent it seemed more on some sort of revenge than the advocates of a 'work in'. They waved their arms about like dervishes drunk on dreams of revolution. Those stones had been the first signatures on a deed committing them to action. Shrill yells now escalated above the deeper roar of the mob and some of the girls were close to hysteria. Freddy was turning this way and that surveying the drunken faces of the avante garde his mouth opening and closing inarticulately, this was out of order, too late. The whole mass seemed to move as one in the direction of the gateway chanting oaths and slogans. Behind the gateway a handful of local policemen formed a thin blue line. Nobody had warned them to expect this. They were inevitably and unceremoniously brushed aside with derision. It was almost good fun until one young bloodlust with a score to settle kicked one of the prostrate constables in the face. John caught up in the frenzy went weak at the knees. Brutes like this were not meant to be a part of

233

the cultural revolution that the five had been convinced they were initiating. These same people would just as soon rush to join the fascist brigades to break the heads of the 'new Jews' and the trade unions.

The big glass doors to the vestibule through which access could be gained to the factory were guarded by a small clutch of policemen aided by the factory's own security guard. They were as frightened as rabbits having witnessed what happened to their colleagues at the gate. The mob converged on them angrily to chants of "We want work, we want work," repeated ad infinitum until it became a lamentation, though work did not appear to be uppermost in the minds of their leaders. There followed a hail of bricks and stones and the art nouveau vestibule collapsed in a thousand shards of glass sending the officers retreating to the inner atrium. Ted, now the epitome of the crazed anarchist was swept along with the tide, scared out of his wits now that the theory so glibly preached appeared to be halfway to a frightening reality. One young bloodlust was actually mounted like a cavalry man piggy back on another's broad shoulders, slashing wildly with his stick at policemen's helmets or anything else that moved in his direction. Then his valiant steed stumbled and sent him sprawling across the marble tiled floor where he was immediately pinned down by an overweight policeman bent on his own revenge. He was only the first of many and soon the atrium was filled with scuffling antagonists until the police were overwhelmed a rump of whom retreated to the foot of the stairwell which gave access to the admin offices and the boardroom. Behind them a senior police officer appeared holding a loudhailer, and behind him the figures of Marion, Westbury, Hawtin and the other directors. "The Board will talk to a small delegation," he announced. "This is your last chance to behave responsibly. Reinforcements are on their way and if you do not act appropriately arrests will be made."

"We even have the stupidity of the police working for us," said Freddy to John having sought him out in the chaos. And as if he had heard Fat Fred's remark and obviously taken it as a further endorsement of violence young bloodlust his face now badged with the blood of the scuffle picked up a large stone which had already done duty in the charge on the vestibule and now lay invitingly at his feet, and hurled the answer at the Superintendent who it hit full in the chest and sent him tripping backwards up the stairway. Another missile, for this seemed the signal for a renewed onslaught, missed its intended target and shattered a large plate glass screen which fronted the reception area. The mob now poured into the unprotected atrium and the superintendent and the directors beat a hasty retreat up the stairs and into the administrative area leaving behind only the token resistance offered by three terrified constables.

John fought his way to the back of the atrium where he was joined by others who had now lost all heart for what was taking place. The mob was now clearly hell bent on nothing but destruction. He jumped up on a table in what had been the reception area and tried to address the others, particularly Fred who along with Ted and Geraint seemed to be caught up in a delirium of madness. His futile gesture was met with another hail of missiles until he was dragged down by friendly hands. He covered his face now weeping angrily and found young Joan Samuels trying to placate him. "How pitiful," he muttered to her . "How pitiful it all seems now; a factory in the wilds of Wales soon to be forgotten, like my play, or remembered for all the wrong reasons. Absorbed into a bourgeois culture, a myth never properly understood." She of course made little of his ramblings but intuiting somehow that this , what was happening, signified the end of something, something that had been better than what had been and what was probably to come.

As they approached the entrance to the office suite through which a number of what was now a rabble had already forced its way the sounds of a police siren could be heard wailing in the distance, reinforcements were clearly on the way. Halfway up the stairs he was almost bowled over by a mad stampede pounding back down. He was knocked sideways but managed to keep his feet by hanging onto one of those in retreat. "The mad bastard's set the place alight, call the fire brigade for fucksake they're trapped in the office."John flung him savagely to one side and struggled up against the flow in a mad frenzy. The mad arsonist had done his job well the film library was the centre of the inferno and the records office on the opposite side of the corridor was also a blaze and flames and acrid smoke roared out of the open door cutting it off from the fire escape which led out onto an iron stairway at the end of the corridor. The film library was adjacent to Marion's office and the searing heat completely sealed it off from his end of the corridor. He tried desperately to fight his way through but it was hopeless, the heat singed his hair and burned his cheeks and he was driven back. He dashed back down the stairs and around to the side of the building where the fire escape was. Police were pouring into the compound from several black Mariah's laying to with their truncheons and arresting anyone they could lay their hands on. Everything was chaos and confusion and people were fleeing everywhere. The clang-clang of a fire engine could be heard coming up the hill. A policeman attempted to restrain him but he desperately threw him off. "They're trapped in there," he screamed looking up at the smoke billowing out from under the fire door. The policeman let go and rushed away to direct the fire engine which had just arrived.

How the hell do you open a fire door from the outside. He threw himself at it in desperation again and again. Suddenly bruised numb by his assault and blackened and coughing from the choking smoke he flung himself at it in a final gesture of hopeless futility. To his amazement it burst open outwards almost throwing him over the handrail. A smoke blackened scorched Hawtin hurtled out tumbling onto his knees at the head of the stairs.

"Where is she, where is she you bastard," John screamed, grasping him by his collar and shaking his head like a dog with a rat.

"You cant, its no good," Hawtin choked. "She's, she's.." He began to blubber like a child. John threw him roughly to the floor and dashed insanely regardless of the danger into the inferno, past the blazing records office to her door, which hung ajar on broken hinges. A white haze seared his eyes, there was choking smoke everywhere, his face was scorched red. Inside Marion's room was not ablaze but little flames played all over the carpet in a mad macabre dance. Little orange tongues appeared to be dancing all over her dress. He rushed in and instinctively rolled her up in a rug which was itself scorched but by some miracle not alight. From somewhere within the very core of his being he found the strength to lift her up over his shoulder and crashed through the door at breakneck speed. The rug in which he had wrapped her unconscious frame was now burning, but still he would not let go before collapsing into the merciful arms of two firemen who dragged them outside onto the fire escape landing. He was now immediately aware of his own terrible pain and the blood which was oozing through Marion's skirt. As they laid her down at the head of the steps he looked at her through a yellow veil of fading light. This was the worst agony of all, the beautiful face, the silk smooth breasts horribly mutilated, and the tiny perfectly formed foetus, dead between her legs. Twice cursed, he thought, twice cursed, as the thin red veil turned purple black, the pain drifted away and left him in a semi conscious limbo. A voice boomed in the back of his scull. "For each man kills the thing he loves." He was the coward, the Judas, he was responsible for the crucifixion.

The Mason's empire was expanding. The chairman was nothing if not successful having cleared out the old board and installing enterprising new directors, and a mode employer to boot. Cultural classes with a new enterprising Cultural Executive, sickness benefits, guaranteed minimum wages and a profit sharing scheme for all employees. Dewey's tragic death in the fire and Hawtin's retirement due to his injuries had left her in complete control. Hers was the sole hand on the driving wheel now, and no worker's representative on the board but a consultative Works Council with its own elected chair and representatives. Dewey's death had led to the conviction of a young man from Coventry who had been singularly responsible for the arson. It seems the dispute had attracted many people from 'outside' after all, with their own sinister agendas. John had always pooh poohed the idea of such conspiracy groups of the left, the conspirators of the right of course he was well aware of.

With Mamgu finding it increasingly difficult to cope with Lynda's condition both had moved into a wing at Carnford. Happy families.

The backroom of a newly refurbished Dowlo was packed to capacity, in fact it was not a backroom at all any more having been developed in the open plan style favoured by the national chain which had acquired it from Brenda the buxom landlady. The fame and fortune of the Dowlais Five had established what the cognoscenti and the media referred to 'The Dowlais School' as if it were Newlyn or Glasgow, and the walls were suitably decorated with displays relating to their work. "To the Black Rose of Trecatty," John proclaimed the toast, a glass of claret in his outstretched hand. Next week would celebrate the hundredth performance of his play in the West End. The toast was echoed by Bill, Ted, Geraint, Dave and Rena and a host of hangers on who had been invited to this mutual admiration function.

And what had happened then to their brave new world- what had these radicals achieved. Dave was established as a leading portrait painter of the upper middle classes, celebs and minor aristocracy and even a few aldermen and mayors rich enough to satisfy their egos. His talent in John's view was squandered.

Rena had established herself with the 'failure' of their 'Life of Christ' which was refused a licence for general release but gained an award at the Venice Film Festival and went on to play to minority audiences in art houses of international repute. She was still anxious to engage John in her efforts to establish a cinematic new wave, which he steadfastly avoided.

Bill's magnificent pornography had given way to static poses of skinny models advertising the new London look in haute couture. John suggested a trip to Vietnam.

Geraint was stuck as an ever present groaner of new Welsh folk music on the Welsh language programmes proliferating on television, from which he made a comfortable living forsaking his radical nationalist politics.

Ted, terrified by the experience of the Mason's work in had reverted from anarchistic activism to an abstract ideal.

As for John, he had the Midas touch. The Mason's fiasco had established him as the romantic hero with front page press photographs of his dramatic rescue of Marion. And hadn't he proved to have been right all along to lead the workforce in their revolt against the discredited Machiavellian machinations of the Mason's board. It was hardly his fault that agitators had infiltrated the organisation to pervert their legitimate demands to serve their own 'extremist communistic ends'.

The blast of a car horn extrovertly dual tone audible even above the hubbub interrupted his cosy conversation with Dave who had assumed all the foibles of a latter day Annigoni as he discussed a possible sitting with a member of the Royal circle. "Aha," he paused. "Here comes Mrs Dai Bread Two to drag you away to her Manorial estate. Better drink up."

John upended his glass and smiled his embarrassed apology to his entourage. "Same time next month," he contracted and made his way to the exit. Outside the Jensen Interceptor waited, sleek and ostentatious and he clambered in beside her.

"Enjoy yourself darling," she proffered her cheek and he pecked it.

"Of course darling. It's always good to get together with the gang. You should join us, it would do you good." It was the same old ritual.

When they arrived at Carnford she garaged the latest symbol of her opulence and he kissed her forehead and made as if to retire immediately to his room.

"Now dear you know what night it is," she caught his arm and pulled him back reminding him coyly.

"Oh yes, of course darling, time for conjugationals. But the trudge to her bedroom was increasingly one of trepidation. He told himself that it had nothing to do with the brown wrinkled flesh of her lower abdomen or the lifeless plasticity of her reconstructed face. The truth was that he could no longer bear the awful guilt that accompanied every thrust of the arid coupling, nor the accusative wide open eyes of her own desperate yearning. Her strange lifelessness filled him with a dreadful despair as he did his best to succeed just once in softening that stony glare, to bring her to just one orgasm. He went about it with an excruciating voracity but he never did succeed and never did he gently kiss her rubber lips and week by week, stroke by stroke, he was dying.

———————————————

Lightning Source UK Ltd.
Milton Keynes UK
UKOW051052090713

213459UK00002B/190/P